MURDER UNDER HER SKIN

Also by Stephen Spotswood

Fortune Favours the Dead

MURDER UNDER HER
SKIN

Stephen Spotswood

WILDFIRE

The right of Stephen Spotswood to be identified as the Author of
the Work has been asserted by him in accordance with the
Copyright, Designs and Patents Act 1988.

First published in 2021 by Doubleday

First published in Great Britain in 2021 by
WILDFIRE
an imprint of HEADLINE PUBLISHING GROUP

1

Cataloguing in Publication Data is available from the British Library

Hardback ISBN 978 1 4722 9167 7
Trade paperback ISBN 978 1 4722 9168 4

Offset in 12.99/15.7 pt Dante MT Std by Jouve (UK), Milton Keynes

Printed and bound in Great Britain by Clays Ltd, Elcograf S.p.A.

Headline's policy is to use papers that are natural, renewable and recyclable
products and made from wood grown in well-managed forests and other
controlled sources. The logging and manufacturing processes are expected
to conform to the environmental regulations of the country of origin.

HEADLINE PUBLISHING GROUP
An Hachette UK Company
Carmelite House
50 Victoria Embankment
London EC4Y 0DZ

www.headline.co.uk
www.hachette.co.uk

To found families, yours and mine.

"It hurt something awful.

But it was worth it."

—BETTY BROADBENT, THE TATTOOED VENUS
(1909–1983)

CAST OF CHARACTERS

WILLOWJEAN "WILL" PARKER: Wisecracking leg-woman for Lillian Pentecost. Picking up the detective trade one hard-fought lesson at a time.

LILLIAN PENTECOST: Certified genius and detective for hire. The most dangerous place in the world is between her and justice.

RUBY DONNER: The Amazing Tattooed Woman, her story is etched on her skin. But was it a chapter from her past that put a knife in her back?

BIG BOB HALLOWAY: Owner and ringmaster of Hart & Halloway's Traveling Circus and Sideshow. A big personality who's willing to do whatever it takes to keep his circus alive.

VALENTIN KALISHENKO: Will's knife-throwing circus mentor and now the prime suspect in a brutal murder. He has decades of dark secrets. Would he kill to keep them in the shadows?

SAM LEE BUTCHER: The circus's youngest and most passionate roustabout. Even murder can't keep him from loving the big-top life.

FRIEDA, THE IMPOSSIBLE RUBBER BAND GIRL: Once upon a time, she and Will were more than just friends. But her loyalties have become as elastic as her limbs.

MAEVE BAILEY: The All-Seeing Madame Fortuna. She can read a mark as easy as you can read a menu. How is it she didn't see Ruby's death coming?

RAY NANCE: The proprietor of the House of Venomous Things. Sweet as pie, but can you really trust a guy whose best friends are poisonous?

THE AMAZING ANNABELLE: A magician's assistant with fast fingers and a sharp tongue. She has her eyes set on the top, and you best not get in her way.

PAT "DOC" DONNER: Great War veteran, movie house owner, and hard-drinking absentee uncle to Ruby. His niece's death solves a lot of his problems.

JOE ENGLE: War hero, newly minted policeman, and former flame of Ruby's. He gave his right arm to the war, but who holds his heart?

CARL ENGLE: Father of Joe and hulking pastor of the Blood of the Lamb Church. What weapon is he willing to use to keep his flock on the straight and narrow?

CHIEF THOMAS WHIDDLE: Two hundred pounds of good ol' boy in a ten-gallon hat. There's a sharp, mean mind hiding behind those squinty eyes.

LEROY DECAMBRE: Small-town criminal with a pretty face. He's got his fingers in a lot of pies. Did he also have them wrapped around the knife?

MURDER UNDER HER SKIN

CHAPTER 1

"The prosecution calls Lillian Pentecost to the stand."

A wave of barely hushed whispers washed over the courtroom. Judge Harman, never one to shy away from a good gavel-banging, let it go unscolded for a change. He couldn't really blame folks. They'd been packed shoulder to shoulder on the hard courtroom benches for three long days, watching the calendar flip from July to August 1946 while they slogged through the boring nuts and bolts of the prosecution's case. Waiting for the real drama to start.

The air-conditioning had gone belly-up halfway through day one and the two hundred or so reporters, family members, and assorted lookie-loos were sweating through their stay-pressed as we approached the climax of the city's murder trial of the moment.

My boss was the climax.

Every eye in the room was on Lillian Pentecost as she made her way to the witness stand, cane thumping out an even rhythm on the courtroom's hardwood floor. She cut an impressive figure: tall, slender, on the far side of forty, impeccable posture—the better to show off the lines of her gray herringbone suit, white collared blouse, and favorite blood-red tie. Her long chestnut hair was tied up in a labyrinth of braids, her signature streak of gray weaving through like a vein of quicksilver.

I even got her to slap on some makeup. A little eye shadow to bring out the winter-gray of her eyes, blush to add drama to her hawkish profile, and the palest of pink lipsticks to make her mouth seem a tad less severe. The goal was no-nonsense but approachable. A woman you'd trust to tell you who murdered who.

The defense table was an island of stillness in the midst of the tittering. Forest Whitsun, attorney for the defense, turned in his seat to watch Ms. P's approach, the look on his face steely confidence mixed with a dash of curiosity.

Sure, I'm interested in what she has to say, his expression told the jurors, *but only so I can explain to you good people why she's mistaken.*

As for the defendant, you could have propped him outside a cigar shop, he was so wooden. Over the last few days, Barry Sendak had perfected the look of the unjustly accused, woe-is-me. Now, his eyes were blank, lips pressed in a thin line.

I'll give him this, though—he didn't look like an arsonist.

Which was a problem.

Not that arsonists come ready-to-wear. But you'd expect someone who was responsible for burning seventeen people alive and leaving hundreds more homeless and grieving to show it on his face.

The Old Testament scribblers had it right. Murder should leave a mark.

But that was wishful thinking.

The jury had spent the last three days looking for a tell and coming up empty. All they saw was a soft pudge of a man who barely topped five feet. Who at thirty was sliding to bald and thought a brush mustache would make up the difference. He had the imposed-upon air of a civil servant, which is exactly what he was, having spent the last ten years as a safety inspector for the New York City Fire Department. He had the watery brown eyes of a doe in the forest, and in his one-size-too-big suit he looked more like prey than predator.

I knew different.

I'd been with him when my boss pointed the finger and Lieutenant Nathan Lazenby, one of the city's top homicide cops, slapped on the cuffs. Nobody would have mistaken Sendak for prey then.

When I was little, my father made me help him drag a badger out of its burrow near our garden. It had been making waste of our lettuce and my father decided it was time for the thing to go. He stood behind me with a shotgun while I grabbed it by its legs and pulled. It came out spitting and clawing and if my Dad hadn't been so quick on the trigger, that rodent would have torn my face off.

Sendak had the same look on him when Lazenby led him away. Like he wanted to sink his teeth into Ms. Pentecost's cheek and give a good yank.

The problem was the jury wasn't seeing the beast.

The other problem—and the DA had been clear that this was the larger of the two—was that the three tenement buildings Sendak had torched had been in Harlem. The seventeen dead were all Negroes. And if you could find a more lily-white jury, I'd have given you a medal.

The evidence against Sendak was circumstantial. Sure, there was a truckload of it, but if you were hunting hard for reasonable doubt, you could squint and convince yourself it was there and only have a little trouble sleeping at night.

It took some serious arm-pulling and a few scathing editorials in the papers to convince the DA to move forward with the case. Even then, he only pulled the trigger because of a specific thumb pressing down on the scales.

That thumb, along with its four friends, was at that moment laid out on a Bible, its owner swearing to tell the truth, whole and nothing but.

"Put me on the stand," Ms. Pentecost had told the district attorney. "I promise you I will reveal to the jury just what kind of man Mr. Sendak is."

Lillian Pentecost didn't make promises lightly, and the DA knew it. So here we were. Last day, last witness, and the whole ballgame riding on my boss.

Someone once told me that ladies don't sweat, but I guess I wasn't much of a lady. I was schvitzing along with the rest of the audience.

From the back row of the courtroom, I watched as Howard Clark, the assistant DA who'd drawn the short straw, began to lead Ms. Pentecost through the whys and wherefores. None of it was news to me, so I took the opportunity to pull out the telegram that had been delivered to our door that morning by an out-of-breath Western Union boy and read it again.

RUBY FOUND MURDERED. CIRCUS CURRENTLY IN STOPPARD, VIRGINIA. REQUEST PROFESSIONAL ASSISTANCE. —BH

BH was Big Bob Halloway, owner and operator of Hart & Halloway's Traveling Circus and Sideshow. The telegram included a phone number where he could be reached.

Ms. P had been upstairs putting herself together when it arrived. I hadn't shown it to her yet. I didn't want her mind on anything but the task in front of her.

I, on the other hand, had the luxury of letting my mind wander.

Ruby Donner. The Amazing Tattooed Woman.

An impossible landscape of roses and sailor girls, hearts and mermaids and pirate ships, and an emerald-green serpent spiraling up her left leg from toe to thigh and places beyond. The count had been north of three hundred when I'd last seen her.

Four years since then. I wondered what she would have thought of little Willowjean "Will" Parker, dolled up in her going-to-court jacket and skirt so she'd blend in with the rubes in the cheap seats.

The reporters I was sharing the row with had teased me about my outfit.

"You undercover as someone's secretary?" one wit from the *Times* had asked. "You can sit on my lap and take dictation anytime, Parker."

I showed him my favorite finger and quietly suggested he sit on that.

"Aw, don't be like that, Red. I'm just playing."

That's what passes for flirting from the Fourth Estate.

I self-consciously ran my hand through my frizzy red curls. I'd spent the last eight months growing them out, and they were within spitting distance of shoulder-length for the first time since grade school. My fingers got caught in a tangle and I had to yank them free. I glanced around to see if anyone had noticed, but everyone's eyes were on the witness stand.

Ruby.

I asked her once, "Why do you do it? It's got to hurt like a bastard."

She smiled that smile that always gave me shivers.

"Of course it hurts, honey. But no more than anything else."

There was more to that conversation—one that ended with me making a fool of myself in her bed not long after. But I couldn't afford to think about that now. Clark was wrapping up and it was time for the real show to begin.

Whitsun approached the witness stand, walking with an easy confidence that probably wasn't a put-on. He had a reputation as the best defense lawyer in the city. A profile in *The New Yorker* had dubbed him "the real-life Perry Mason," and people in the know didn't disagree.

It didn't hurt that he could have modeled for the book jackets. Whitsun was six feet of blue eyes, broad shoulders, and a face that was only a few degrees from Gary Cooper. Sure, there were no women on the jury—not that that meant anything—

but he gave off that leader-of-the-posse aura. Basically, where he went people liked to follow. My boss's job was to rip the reins out of his hands.

"Ms. Pentecost. You prefer 'Ms.,' is that right?" he asked.

"I do."

He nodded and smiled, shooting a quick glance at the jury. I wasn't at the angle to catch it, but I imagine the look translated as: "Too good for marriage or 'Miss'? Hard to trust a woman like that."

Out loud he asked, "Who hired you to investigate these fires?"

"No one hired me."

"No one? You devoted two months of your life out of the kindness of your heart?"

"I decided to look into these incidents because people were dying," my boss lobbed back.

"Is this the first time you've assisted the police without a paying client?"

"It is not."

"Actually, you've made something of a reputation for inserting yourself into high-profile cases, haven't you?"

"I don't know if I would say I have a reputation for it."

"I think you're being modest. I don't know if there's anyone in this city who hasn't heard your name," the defense attorney said. "And working on high-profile crimes, that must go a long way toward bringing new clients to your doorstep. Isn't that right?"

"I don't quiz my clients on how they may have heard of me," Ms. P said.

I cringed. Snideness wasn't going to do her any favors.

"No, I don't suppose you would," Whitsun said with just the right amount of good-naturedness and a smile to the jury.

Isn't she a pill, that smile whispered.

"Needless to say, you've made a lot of headlines in this city," he continued. "The bigger the case, the bigger the headlines. And this case? Whoo-wheee. Pretty big."

If Whitsun sounded a little too aw-shucks for a big-city lawyer, he meant to. It was part of his act. It got juries to like him. Witnesses did, too.

Until they didn't.

"How many times did your name appear in print due to your participation in this case?" he asked.

"I can't say. I did not count."

"I did." He ambled over to the defense table and held up a stack of newspapers with a flourish. "Your name appeared in thirty-two articles across fifteen papers and three globally syndicated magazines."

He held up one paper after another, reading the headlines as he did.

"'Pentecost Hunts Harlem Firebug.' 'Lillian Pentecost Combs Scene of Second Blaze.' 'Private Detective Pentecost Leads Police to Arsonist.' 'Pentecost Brings Firestarter to Justice.'"

Whitsun posed there with that last paper, letting the moment stretch out.

"Is there a question?" Ms. P asked with minimal politeness.

"Sure there is." He tossed the newspapers back on the table. "Do you think you'd have gotten a lot of that press if you hadn't handed the police a suspect?"

As he asked the question, my boss reached into her jacket pocket and pulled out a silver lighter. She spun it around in her hand and flipped it open.

Judge Harman leaned over. "Ah . . . Ms. Pentecost? I don't allow smoking in my courtroom."

"I'm sorry, Your Honor. I don't smoke," she said. "As you know, I have multiple sclerosis. Keeping my hands occupied helps with the tremors."

Not exactly a bald-faced lie but pretty damn close.

"I'll put it away if it's distracting," she added with just the right amount of pleading.

"It's quite all right, Your Honor," Whitsun said with a sympathetic smile. "Ms. Pentecost isn't well. Anything that helps settle her nerves."

I called Whitsun an impolite name under my breath and the newshounds on either side of me chuckled. There was no opportunity to give the jury a primer on multiple sclerosis. How her body might give out on occasion, but not her brain.

Still, we'd gotten what we wanted.

Ms. P spun the lighter in her hand, flipped it open, flipped it closed. Did it again.

"Could you repeat your question, Mr. Whitsun?" she asked.

"Is it fair to say that, if you hadn't given the police a suspect, you wouldn't have gotten nearly so many headlines?"

"Yes, that's fair to say." Twist, flip open, flip shut. "And if I hadn't caught Sendak, he'd have continued putting tenements to the torch."

A late, weak jab, and Whitsun barreled through it.

"In your previous testimony, you talked a lot about this so-called evidence against Mr. Sendak, but I noticed that you neglected to mention—or Mr. Clark neglected to ask you about—the first time you met my client. When was that?"

"At the scene of the second fire several days after the crime," Ms. P said. "Ostensibly, he was there to assist the firefighters in making the building safe."

"'Ostensibly'? Ms. Pentecost, what is my client's profession?"

"He's a safety inspector with the New York City Fire Department."

"Yes!" Whitsun exclaimed. "So it's not surprising to find my client there, is it? It was *his* job to be there."

Whitsun was good. He was taking every opportunity to

remind the jury that Ms. Pentecost was a civilian butting in where she didn't belong.

"What did my client say to you when he saw you walking through the wreckage?" Whitsun asked.

"He asked me to leave."

Whitsun chuckled. "Oh, I think he did a little more than ask. What were his exact words? And don't be afraid to use colorful language. We're all adults here." He flashed another aw-shucks grin to the jury. They echoed it. My boss didn't.

"His exact words were 'Listen, you clumsy bitch. Get out or I'll have you thrown out.'"

Twist, flip open, flip shut.

Whitsun threw his hands in the air in mock horror and turned to his client. From the back row I caught a sliver of Sendak's abashed grin. I wondered how many times they'd rehearsed that. Bet you it wasn't as long as I'd rehearsed the lighter trick with Ms. P.

"'Clumsy bitch'? What prompted that?"

"I stumbled over a collapsed doorframe."

Whitsun shook his head.

"My client probably didn't make a very good first impression, did he?"

"To be honest, Sendak left little impression," Ms. Pentecost declared. "At the time, I found him quite forgettable."

Twist, flip open, flip shut.

Sendak shifted uncomfortably in his seat, uncrossing one leg and crossing the other.

"I find that hard to believe, Ms. Pentecost. Considering his language and attitude."

"Oh, it's a rare day when I'm not called a bitch," she said, teasing a couple of chuckles from the jury box.

"Still, you could hardly blame him," Whitsun said. "It was a crime scene. You were a civilian. Not even one with a paying client. Trudging around, kicking up evidence. I probably would have used some blue language as well."

Clark stood up. "Your Honor, Mr. Whitsun is testifying in place of his client."

"I'm sorry, Your Honor. I withdraw that statement," Whitsun said. "Sometimes I just get a little worked up."

I was really starting to hate that how-do-you-do smile.

The trick Ms. Pentecost was looking to pull would have been easier during the prosecution's questioning. That way we could have scripted the thing ourselves. But she'd argued in favor of doing it during cross.

"Mr. Sendak's guard will be down," she'd said to me. "More importantly, his attorney will not be at his side. He will have sat and listened to accounts of his crimes. Crimes that he is proud of, that stem from deep-seated flaws in his character. A need for control. For power. His façade will be worn and fragile. I believe it just needs the right push to crumble."

Theoretically, Sendak had been softened up. The prosecution witnesses had been instructed by the DA to refer to him only by his last name. No "Mr." Like he was a thing, not a person. And they'd sprinkled in words like "cowardly" and "weak" wherever they could.

Chipping away.

The trick with the lighter was part of the package. It was identical to one he'd been carrying when he was arrested. It was meant to focus his attention. Keep his eyes and his mind on Ms. Pentecost, and not on playing to the jury. I'd spent the last two weeks drilling my boss so she didn't fumble it.

These were all techniques we'd picked up working our last big case, which had involved a phony spiritualist who'd used similar tricks to pry secrets out of her clients.

Ms. P explained that this gambit of ours was a lot like a particular maneuver in fencing. She'd taken an interest in the sport after I presented her with a sword cane for Christmas. She labeled the maneuver with a French word I couldn't pronounce then and can't remember now.

"It's where you leave your guard open, inviting an attack, all for the chance of running your opponent through."

For those of you who aren't sword-fighting aficionados, we were basically all in on a draw.

Even if the cards didn't fall in our favor, there was still a chance the jury could find their way to a guilty verdict. A very slim one. I'd called around the night before. None of the number runners were leaning toward a straight-out acquittal. But it was five to two in favor of a hung jury. And it wasn't likely the DA would go for a second bite at the apple.

So here we were. The last, best chance to put Sendak away for good. All Ms. P needed to do was outwit the best defense attorney in the city and get the accused to show just a hint of his true face to the jury, something he'd been rehearsing for the better part of a year not to do.

I'd have said "no sweat," but the back of my blouse was already soaked, so why bother lying?

Whitsun wound up for his next pitch.

"As you testified earlier, the next time you saw Mr. Sendak was two weeks later, at the scene of the next fire. Is that so?"

"That's correct. He was across the street watching the flames."

"As were hundreds of other people, isn't that so?"

"That's correct."

"And yet, you zeroed in on him. You directed your investigation at him. Not a shred of evidence, but you decided he looked like a good candidate. Is that so?"

"That's correct," Ms. P said.

"Was he the only person connected to the fire department there?"

"No."

"No, there were a number of off-duty firefighters who heard

the alarm and came. Because that's their job. Even when they're not on duty. To protect the good people of this city."

I thought maybe Clark would object again, but he smartly kept mum. He was leaving things to my boss.

"Ms. Pentecost, isn't the real reason you directed your ire at Mr. Sendak because your first interaction with him went so poorly? Because he had the temerity to say an amateur didn't belong at a crime scene? Because he called you some nasty names? Weren't you prejudiced against my client from the very beginning?"

Twist, flip open, flip closed.

"Yes."

Every breath in the courtroom hitched, including Whitsun's.

"You admit that you were prejudiced against my client?"

Whitsun could barely keep the joy out of his voice.

"Absolutely, I admit it," Ms. P said matter-of-factly. "But not because he called me names. He simply looked like an arsonist."

That set off a whole new wave of titters, and this time Judge Harman made liberal use of his gavel. Everyone in the room was giving one another looks that ranged from the mildly quizzical to the deeply confused. Everyone except Whitsun, who stood frozen. Like a guy who was walking through a field in France and heard a click under his feet.

The obvious question to ask would have been: "What do you mean he looked like an arsonist?"

But the first rule of trial law is you don't ask a question you don't know the answer to, and Whitsun had no clue what would come out of my boss's mouth if he pressed her.

He basically had two choices. He could drop it, but the jury had heard the comment and would wonder what she meant. Besides, Clark would pick it up on redirect and then it wouldn't be Whitsun's ball anymore.

Or the real-life Perry Mason could craft his next questions carefully and hope he could manage the witness.

Twist, flip open, flip closed. Back at the defense table, Sendak was shifting from side to side like someone had slipped a tack under his seat.

After a second of thought, Whitsun squared up to the witness stand. I couldn't help but smile. He was going to try to manage Lillian Pentecost.

God help him.

"You thought my client—a hardworking, law-abiding man with not a single offense, not even a parking violation, who has devoted his life to making the city safe—*looked* like an arsonist? That's why you used your outsized influence with the police and the district attorney's office to tear his life apart?"

My boss gave the tiniest of shrugs.

"As I understand it, his life was already in shambles," she said. "His wife left him some months earlier, did she not?"

Another wave of murmurs and a full-on spasm from Sendak. I couldn't see his face, but the jury could. Whatever they saw caught their attention.

Judge Harman leaned over again. "Ms. Pentecost? Are you well?"

It was a fair question. Lillian Pentecost wasn't a demonstrative woman and people knew it. She'd sat on the witness stand more times than I had digits, and this is the first time she'd ever seasoned her testimony with attitude.

"Quite well," she answered.

Twist, flip open, flip closed.

Whitsun must have known something was up. But the bait was just too delicious. Here was the prosecution's star witness— the woman who had sized his client up for the electric chair— admitting she had been prejudiced against him from the start.

He must have smelled the trap. But I imagine he figured

that, if all went to hell, he'd at least have grounds to file an appeal. He took the step forward, minefield be damned.

"Ms. Pentecost, what about my client in this first meeting with him made you think he was an arsonist?" he asked, infusing as much incredulity into the question as he could.

My boss took a breath and leaned forward a fraction of an inch. Everyone else in the room, whether they realized it or not, leaned with her.

"Arson is a coward's crime," she began. "One committed at a distance, enjoyed at a remove. The man who committed these crimes would be nervous, on edge, acting in an overly defensive manner. Because he knows himself to be less than those around him, he would take great pleasure in pushing down—or attempting to—those few people he had power over. Exactly as Sendak reacted to me."

As she spoke, she continued to twist the lighter between her long fingers, flipping it open and closed with seeming ease. To the casual observer, she kept her eyes on Whitsun. In reality only her right eye—the glass one—was aimed at the defense attorney. Her good eye was looking over his shoulder right at Sendak.

Her fingers twisted the lighter, flipped it open, and then lit it. A half inch of flame wavered in her hand.

"The man who committed these crimes would be small and physically weak," she said. "Arson is a man's crime, but not a strong, healthy man. He likely wouldn't have served in the war. No service would take him."

"Your Honor, I withdraw the question," Whitsun declared. Ms. P ignored him.

"An arsonist isn't a man. He's a cockroach. Hiding in the crevices, emerging only at night."

"Ms. Pentecost, the question is withdrawn," Judge Harman said.

"I'm almost finished, Your Honor," Ms. P said, barely breaking stride. As she spoke, her thumb passed through the flame, back and forth like a metronome. "That's how I knew it was you. I should have known when I first laid eyes on you. You small, forgettable civil servant, the pale band around your finger where your wedding ring used to be, now gone because you couldn't keep a woman happy, could you?"

"Ms. Pentecost!" The judge gave his gavel a rap, but my boss kept going.

"So you set fire to whole blocks of happy families. You wanted to see them burn. All these women and men who are so much happier than you, so much better than you, so much—"

Sendak came up so quick, his chair went skidding across the floor and into the first row of spectators. For a moment it looked like he was about to leap over the table and make a run at my boss. I think he might have done it, too, if the bailiffs hadn't started moving. It was only when Sendak saw the uniforms closing in that he froze, choking off an obscenity mid-syllable.

Judge Harman gaveled; Whitsun hurried to his client; the journalists beside me were too shocked to even scribble.

And the jury?

All twelve to a man were wearing identical expressions of disgust. They'd been given a glimpse of what we'd seen when Sendak had been arrested. The predator. The rabid animal lurking behind that placid exterior.

He wasn't frothing at the mouth, but it was enough. I saw the scales tip.

I may not speak French, but I can read faces. And I know how to spell *guilty*.

I left to go get the car.

CHAPTER 2

It's a mess, a real mess. Never had anything like this happen and I've been in the business twoscore and some. It's an honest-to-God blowdown."

My boss shot me a look.

I put my hand over the mouthpiece of my phone while Ms. P kept her ear pressed to her own. "A disaster," I explained. "Usually weather-related, but it doesn't have to be."

Ms. P's free hand—the one she'd been using to twirl the lighter—was resting in a bowl of ice water. The effort had left her digits sore and trembling. The ice water wasn't so much a cure as a frigid distraction.

We were sitting at our respective desks talking on our respective phones at the office of Pentecost Investigations, which was nestled on the first floor of the cozy Brooklyn brownstone we both called home. We'd just driven back from the courthouse. I'd shown Ms. P the telegram in the car. She made some grumbling noises about how I should have shown it to her earlier, and I made some grumbling noises about how it wouldn't have done any good and that we had priorities. At the time we left the courthouse, Whitsun had asked for a recess and he and Clark were having a sit-down in Judge Harman's office.

By the time we got home, there was a message waiting. Mrs. Campbell, our housekeeper, relayed it to us in her Scottish brogue. Harman was saying no to a mistrial. Whitsun had asked the question, after all. Ms. Pentecost had just answered truthfully.

The defense attorney must have seen the same thing in the jury that I had because he was asking if a deal was still on the table. Knowing Clark, I doubted he would settle for less than twenty years.

Ms. P turned her attention back to the man on the other end of the line. Big Bob Halloway's voice sounded like it was coming from a million miles away. Like he was calling from the moon, not from the outskirts of some one-horse town in Virginia.

"I'm very sorry for your loss, Mr. Halloway," she said. "Exactly how did Ms. Donner die?"

"Stabbed. In the back." His words might have crackled, but the anger came through crystal clear. "Right after the final all-out on Tuesday."

Another look. "All-out?" she mouthed.

"Just after the last show," I whispered.

"Mysterio's girl found her. Just lying there," Big Bob said. "Saddest goddamn thing I ever saw, and I've seen some sad goddamn things."

The crack in his voice wasn't bad reception. It was bona fide grief—something I'd never heard in the tough circus man before. Something I could have gone without ever hearing.

But I understood.

Ruby had been one of the first circus employees I ran into when I arrived at H&H as a teenage runaway looking for sanctuary. I remembered her peeling off my dirt-caked cap and wrinkling her nose.

"I bet if we scrubbed hard enough we'd find a handsome young woman under all that." The first time anyone had called me a woman, handsome or otherwise.

Everyone loved her. How could you not?

Except somebody had used her for a knife block.

"Is the circus still in Stoppard?" Ms. P asked.

"Still here, all right," Big Bob said. "Tuesday was our first night. First night open, anyway. It's a two-week stint, so we're here through next Sunday. Then we break down and head to Charlotte. Can't stay on longer. Contracts are signed, and signed contracts are scarce these days."

It was Thursday. Which meant we had ten days before the crime scene and everything around it packed up and left town.

"The authorities will let you leave?" Ms. P asked. "I find it surprising that they'd allow so many"—she almost said "suspects" but thought better of it—"people close to the victim to leave before the matter is resolved."

"The police chief made some noise about that when he first showed up. But he swung by this morning. Told me we're free to leave."

"What's changed?" Ms. P asked.

Crackling silence from the other end of the line.

"Mr. Halloway?"

"Yeah, he's got someone on the hook," Big Bob said. "Will? You still on the line?"

"I'm here."

"I hate to break it to you, but . . . they've arrested the Russian. They've had him in lockup since early yesterday. Just charged him official this morning."

It took me a few heartbeats to digest the news.

"Kalishenko? They think he killed Ruby?"

"They do."

"Why the hell do they think that?"

"It was his knife in her back."

Crackling silence.

Valentin Kalishenko was one of H&H's real old-timers: knife-thrower, sword-swallower, fire-eater, and one of my circus mentors. I wouldn't go so far as to say the Mad Russian was like a father to me. More like the perpetually drunk uncle who let me play with sharp things at a tender age.

"That doesn't mean anything," I said, tugging at the knot in my hair. "He had a hundred of the things."

"I know," Big Bob said.

"He was always leaving them everywhere."

"I *know.*"

"What about fingerprints?" I asked. "They find any on the knife?"

"I think just smudges. I heard the cops talking. Something about the wrapping around the hilt not taking prints well."

"So it's his knife and there are no prints. That's nothing. What else do they have?"

"I don't want to get into it over the phone," Bob said. "You know small towns. Can't be sure this isn't a party line."

Ms. Pentecost cleared her throat, took a sip from her glass of honey wine, then asked, "What are your intentions, Mr. Halloway?"

"My intentions?"

"Your telegram said you wanted assistance," Ms. P said. "What kind of assistance?"

"I want you to dig out the truth on who killed Ruby!"

"You don't believe Mr. Kalishenko is responsible?"

Not so much a silence, but a definite pause.

"I . . . uh . . . I don't want to get into it right now, but there's a lot of cold-decking going on down here. The cops are running an alibi store. I don't think truth's on the menu."

A look to me.

"An unbeatable game," I explained. "But not rigged, so technically it's legal."

"I'm not trying to bum a ride," Big Bob said. "I can hire you legitimate."

"Please stay on the line, Mr. Halloway."

She covered the mouthpiece with her hand and instructed me to do the same.

"So."

"So."

"What are your thoughts?" my boss asked, leaning back in her chair.

"To paraphrase you, I don't have nearly enough information to begin answering that question."

"Fair enough," she said. "Then let's narrow it down. Is Mr. Kalishenko capable of murder?"

"Absolutely."

She raised one eyebrow half an inch.

"Everyone's capable of murder," I reminded her. "I'm capable. You're capable. Given the right circumstances, of course."

"And the right circumstances for Mr. Kalishenko would be . . . what?"

I thought about it.

"Self-defense," I offered.

"Obviously. What else?"

"Protecting someone," I added. "Protecting his family."

"His family?"

A memory rose up and tried to swallow me. A roadhouse somewhere on the other side of the Appalachians. Beer breath in my face, rough hands squeezing the breath out of me. Then Kalishenko and his knives and a lot of blood.

"The circus is his family," I said, dragging myself back to the present. "He'd do anything for us. That includes Ruby. So I rescind my paraphrase. My thought is he didn't do it. He'd never do it. Not to one of our own."

Ms. Pentecost sat there for a moment studying me. Typing this out, I realize now what she probably did in the moment. I didn't say "them" and "their." It was "us" and "our."

I included myself on that family tree. Knowing her even

better now than I did then, I imagine that had some influence on her decision.

She removed her hand from the mouthpiece.

"Mr. Halloway, are you still there?"

"I am."

"We will leave for Virginia first thing tomorrow."

I sat back as they worked out the details. My eyes drifted up to the painting above Ms. P's desk. It was a massive thing done in oils, a wide yellow tree in the middle of a prairie somewhere. In the shade of the tree was a woman in a blue dress, her face lost in shadow. I'd had close to four years to study the thing, but I still hadn't decided whether she was lounging or if she had fallen.

Was she waiting for a lover?

Or waiting to die?

With half an ear I listened to Big Bob lay out the best travel route from New York to Stoppard, promising to have a room and a vehicle at our disposal.

I thought about Ruby lying in the dirt of some played-out cornfield in the middle of nowhere. Had she gone quick, or had she lingered? Had she seen it coming? Did she feel the darkness closing in and know what it meant?

I was still picturing her there when my boss told Big Bob we'd see him tomorrow afternoon and hung up the phone.

She took her hand out of the bowl of water and dried it off on the tea towel Mrs. Campbell had left for her. She flexed her fingers. They were raw and red and the pain showed on her face.

"According to Mr. Halloway, there is a train out of Penn Station at six-thirty tomorrow morning," she said. "We can take it as far as Fredericksburg, where there will be a driver waiting."

I didn't say anything, just nodded.

"Though the circus will be departing in a little over a week, we should be prepared for an extended stay. I suggest we pack for three weeks," she said.

Another distracted nod.

"Will?"

"Yeah?" I was surprised at the hoarseness in my voice.

Got to give her credit—she didn't ask any pointless questions like "How are you feeling?" She just gave me the needed seconds to snap out of it.

"Yeah, three weeks is good. Better safe than sorry," I said. "You want me to pack for trouble?"

"I think you should use your best judgment."

"Right," I said. "Trouble it is."

CHAPTER 3

Our trip began at dawn's first crack. Ms. Pentecost and I, along with Mrs. Campbell, pried our luggage out of the back of the Cadillac and onto a porter's trolley outside Penn Station. I have a tendency to overpack, and our massive suitcases nearly toppled the trolley.

"Only one body in there this time," I joked as I tipped the porter. He accepted the dollar with a smile that hadn't quite woken up yet.

Mrs. Campbell gave us both rib-crushing hugs and for the fifth time that morning offered to come with us. For the fifth time we told her we needed someone to hold down the fort in Brooklyn and that we were more likely to have cream pies thrown our way than bullets.

"You best keep an eye on her," she said, though I'm not sure which of us she was speaking to.

We waved goodbye. I cringed as she made a U-turn in the middle of Seventh Avenue, nearly cutting the fender off a midtown bus.

Then the boss and I followed our luggage to a waiting train. The luggage went where luggage goes and we took seats facing each other in a passenger car.

Ms. Pentecost reached into her satchel and pulled out a thick file folder. The typed label on the front read OLIVIA WATERHOUSE. It was a carryover from our last big case, and one that Ms. P picked at whenever she had a spare minute. She was certain we'd come up against that particular character again.

I wasn't so sure. The good professor had disappeared, and hadn't been seen or heard from in months.

Actually, that wasn't entirely true. Not long after Dr. Waterhouse pulled a Houdini, one of the city's least reputable mortgage lenders sent out letters to his hundred poorest clients officially forgiving their loans and signing over the titles to their homes. Three days later he hanged himself from a ceiling fan.

There was no evidence Waterhouse was involved. But I thought it smelled like her, and my boss agreed.

I absentmindedly traced the scar running across my left cheek. Another carryover from that case. It had healed nicely, but my doctors told me I'd grow old seeing that faint crease in the mirror every morning.

While my boss read the same sheaf of pages for the hundredth time, I rummaged through the satchel that I used in place of a handbag for my copy of *The Heart Is a Lonely Hunter*.

Ms. Pentecost had been on me about filling in the canyons in my formal education. I'd run away from home at fifteen and my schooling prior to that hadn't exactly been first-rate. This was followed by five years of circus work and going on four years as Ms. Pentecost's leg-woman. Hardly your standard education.

So my boss suggested I swap out my usual detective novels for some meatier fare. I opted for Carson McCullers's story about a deaf-mute who becomes everybody's confidant in a Georgia backwater. I picked it because McCullers was my age—twenty-three—when it was published. I figured us working girls needed to stick together.

The trip from Penn Station to Fredericksburg, Virginia, was five hours and change, and I intended to make a solid dent in the novel.

Somewhere between Newark and Philly I realized I'd read the same paragraph five times and called it quits. I pulled out the latest copy of *Strange Crime,* but even the article on polygraphs and how to beat them failed to keep my focus.

Not used to being awake when the morning was still in the single digits, Ms. P had fallen asleep and was not-so-softly snoring. I took the file out of her limp hands and tucked it away.

I tried to settle into my own nap, but couldn't get my nerves to agree.

I didn't like trains.

Subways are different. On the subway, if you don't like where you're heading you've got a chance every two minutes to hop off, catch a cab, take it on the heels.

With trains, you've really only got the one option. There's no changing course, no last-second turns. Somebody figured out your route a hundred years ago, and you're on it until the end.

Like an iron coffin.

Ms. Pentecost told me once that it's a product of my claustrophobia. I told her I wasn't claustrophobic. I just didn't like being somewhere I couldn't get out of, and I think that's reasonable enough you don't need to invent a five-syllable word to cover it.

I decided to stretch my legs, so I quietly slipped out and made my way to the dining car. Once there, I bought a cup of coffee and a bagel and found an empty seat at the back of the car.

As I watched the landscape rush by, I let my mind wander over to Ruby and my five years with Hart & Halloway.

I'd arrived at H&H an exhausted, underfed, bruised, and battered girl desperate to escape a life I knew would lead nowhere good. The idea of living in a world full of color and excitement, never staying in one place for more than a couple of weeks—it sounded like heaven.

I learned quick that circus life was far from heaven, but it was a long walk from the hell I'd been living in. I started out on dung duty, mucking stalls and cages and being the go-to girl for picking up whatever the four-legged members of the circus put down.

Eventually I got promoted to the regular crew of roustabouts, did a stint selling sweets under the big top, then stumbled my way into being Kalishenko's lovely assistant. His old one had gotten knocked up courtesy of some lucky lad and I was press-ganged into the role. Squeezed into a glorified bathing suit, I spent twelve hours a day sweating through my spangles as the man everyone in the crew called the Mad Russian flung knives at me.

Things got interesting when I started flinging them back.

Kalishenko thought I showed promise, so he started teaching me the tricks of the trade. That inspired other performers to take me under their wing, training me in the essentials of magic, acrobatics, horse-riding, snake-handling, sharpshooting, fortune-telling, and everything else along the midway, including a handful of burlesque lessons that I only field-tested once and the less said about that, the better.

In short, by the end of my time with the circus, I was a Jill-of-all-trades who could fill in for just about anybody's assistant, as needed.

Then I crossed paths with Ms. Pentecost, saved her life by flinging a knife into the back of a man determined to kill her, and was hired as her assistant because she saw something in me.

But only because Kalishenko had seen it first.

I thought back to the early days of our training. Me missing the target five times out of five and Kalishenko screaming obscenities two feet from my ear.

"What is this bullshit? You are better than this. You know that. I know that. So be better!"

Be better. Like it was that easy.

"You want me to believe that first time was an accident? When you almost took my ear off? That was an accident?"

"I wasn't thinking about it then," I yelled back. "I was just pissed off and I threw."

Kalishenko's beard parted long enough for me to see the grin.

"Good! That is good! That is a place to start. Be angry," he said. "Be angry and throw."

"Keep yelling in my ear and being angry won't be a problem."

He put his hands on my shoulders and squared me up to the target.

"See the target. Feel the knife in your hand. The weight of it. Now think about the person who deserves that knife. The person you want to throw it at. The person who makes your blood boil. The person who has wronged you, hurt you. See them standing there. Do you see them, Willowjean?"

I told him I did.

"Now throw."

I threw. The knife thudded into the wooden target, two inches off the bull's-eye.

Kalishenko clapped his hands together.

"There!" he shouted. "Now that you've stopped thinking, we can start."

Going on nine years later, I was a long way from that gawky teen girl desperate to prove she could hold her own.

Okay, I admitted, maybe not that far removed. But enough.

I owed Kalishenko my life. And in more ways than one.

I was on my third cup of coffee when Ms. P walked into the dining car, carefully using her cane to offset the slow rocking of the train. I waved her over to my table.

"Good morning again. Coffee? Grub?"

"Just coffee," she said, wiping the sleep out of her eyes.

I waved to the porter and motioned for a second cup.

"Where are we?" Ms. P asked.

"Just went through Philly. That's probably what woke you up. Shouldn't be too long until Wilmington."

The porter delivered her coffee and she thanked him. She looked out the window, sipped her cup of joe, and waited for the caffeine to take effect. Once her gears had been properly oiled, she turned back to me.

"Describe Ms. Donner."

One thing about my boss—she doesn't waste time.

"Oh, five foot eight or nine, a hundred and forty pounds, brown eyes, brown hair. As for distinguishing marks, about three hundred of them, from the collarbone down."

"You're very amusing."

Her expression said I wasn't.

"Pretty standard story for a cirky," I said. "Small-town girl dreams of show-biz glamour and packs her bags for New York. She discovers she can't act, can't sing, can't dance. Pretty enough for modeling, but there are ten thousand other pretty-enough girls shouldering for the same spots. One day she's strolling Coney Island and passes a tattoo parlor. Goes in on a whim and gets her first. Something about it gets its teeth in her and won't let go. Over the next year, they ink a hundred more on her. She meets a girl who knows a guy who's on speaking terms with Big Bob Halloway. Next time the circus comes through she gets an introduction. Big Bob sees her potential and snatches her up for the sideshow."

"You learned all this from Ms. Donner?" my boss asked.

"Sure. She told that story all the time. Audiences ate it up," I said. "I mean, yeah, a lot of them probably treated it like a cautionary tale. Girls, stay close to home or you'll end up peddling your flesh in front of a mob of sex-crazed gawkers. Conveniently forgetting that they were part of said mob."

But Ruby was more than skin and ink and a smile. I'd recognized that from the start. Even when she was covered up, she was a standout. And this was among a group of people who were pretty striking in general.

I once caught a glimpse of Susan Hayward cutting her way through Times Square. As starlets went, she was far down my list of stunners. Still, she seemed to be alive in a way that the yokels surrounding her couldn't match. That was Ruby.

A Technicolor girl in a black-and-white world.

"She'd only been there a couple years when I arrived," I said. "Had just been made a full company member. But folks trusted her. She was one of the people you went to if you had something eating you. Not in a den-mother way. She was never an 'Oh, poor dear' kind of woman. She got things done."

"Could you elaborate?"

"Like when Lulu—that's Kalishenko's old assistant—found herself in a family way. Ruby was the one who made the calls, got her an appointment to take care of it, set her up somewhere to recover," I explained. "I'm not saying everyone liked her. She had a mouth on her, especially when she was drinking. But even the ones who weren't asking for autographs respected her."

"How did Mr. Kalishenko feel about her?" Ms. P asked.

I saw that question coming and I wasn't thrilled to answer it.

"He wasn't a fan. The feeling was mutual."

"Any particular reason?

"I don't know if it was one thing in particular," I said. "He was always jabbing her because her act didn't involve any particular skill. She just had to be willing to get poked a few thousand times then strip down and show off the results. She said it took a lot more guts to get tattooed than to get drunk and toss knives at little girls. She called him a lush; he called her a gimmick act; around and around it went. They were two people who just rubbed each other wrong. No getting past it."

The train took that moment to pull into the station in Wilmington. We dog-eared the conversation to allow for a flurry of hurriedly paid checks and a scramble for luggage.

Through the window, I watched as four dozen fedoras were slipped on in unison and the flock of office workers streamed off the platform and in the direction of whoever was writing their paychecks. Probably one of the chemical companies or foundries, all still going strong even with the war over. Half the men on the platform had probably been overseas a year or two before, trying not to get blown up.

Now here they were, working a nine-to-five where the most dangerous part of their day was crossing the street. I figured that would be a relief.

But from the downturned mouths carbon-copied across nearly every man in sight, I might have figured wrong.

We left Wilmington behind, the train weaving through smoking factories and skirting the edge of a river so filthy it made the Gowanus look like a swimming hole.

"What about Mr. Kalishenko?" Ms. P asked.

"With the circus from before Big Bob took it over," I said. "Came over from Russia right after the Revolution. So 1917, 1918. Something like that."

"With family?" she asked.

I shook my head. "He never talked about his family. Unless you count the claim that he's a descendent of Rasputin."

I didn't mention I'd taken that claim at face value for years on account of I didn't know who Rasputin was.

"I think his family died," I said. "Honestly, I know more about your background than his, and you keep your biography locked up tighter than Fort Knox."

If she registered the critique, she didn't let it show.

"Val was never one to get chummy. I was one of a handful that got along with him, and that took having him fail to stab me a few . . . thousand times."

The word *stab* left a bad taste in my mouth. Half a minute ticked by before I got my tongue working again.

"Do you . . . um . . . do you want a tally of the rest of the H and H crew?"

Ms. Pentecost gave it a long think, then shook her head.

"Better to come at things with as few preconceptions as possible. I'll be meeting them all soon enough."

I tried to imagine that—my new life and my old sitting under the same tent together. But my imagination wasn't up to snuff. I sat back and let the iron coffin rumble on.

CHAPTER 4

The rest of the trip was uneventful, except for a memorable incident at Union Station. Our train was exchanging a flock of suits for a herd of southbound weekenders when I looked out the window and caught sight of a group of women waiting to board one of the colored cars.

They looked like they'd run the distance. All were holding placards with messages like PROTECT LIFE AND LIBERTY and LYNCHING SHOWS WEAKNESS. It hit me that they must have arrived in the nation's capital earlier in the week to protest the lynching of two Negro families in Monroe, Georgia.

I was so wrapped up in preparing for the Sendak trial, I hadn't paid much attention to the news. Now I watched as these women, a handful of the thousands who had marched in front of the White House demanding Truman's attention, waited to return home. Before they were allowed to enter the car, a burly porter relieved them of their signs. Once the women were on board, he snapped and folded the placards, shoving the lot into a nearby garbage can.

A lot has happened between then and when I'm typing this, but I still remember the bored, blank look on that porter's face as he shoved their signs into the trash.

A cog in the machine. Grinding away.

After that, the train carved a quick path south through Virginia farms and pastures and a dozen biggish towns, pulling into Fredericksburg around noon. I snagged a luggage cart, retrieved our suitcases, and navigated them and my boss outside.

If I was worried about finding the ride Big Bob had promised, I needn't have been. Parked right in front of the station was an International Harvester pickup—the kind with a flatbed and wooden railings along the sides. Or at least that's what I assumed it was. There wasn't a square inch that wasn't dented, rusting, or threatening to fall off.

The only things that looked new on the truck were the canvas sign strung on the back announcing HART & HALLO-WAY'S TRAVELING CIRCUS AND SIDESHOW, STOPPARD, VA., JULY 30–AUGUST 10 and the driver, who was standing beside the machine, bouncing nervously on the balls of his feet.

When he caught sight of us, he grinned and shouted, "Miss Parker! Miss Parker! Over here, ma'am! I'm your ride!"

"Old friend?" my boss asked as we headed toward the truck.

"Old? It's a coin flip he's even legal to drive."

I pulled the cart over to the truck, but before I could touch our cases, our driver was all over them.

"Hi! Samuel Lee Butcher at your service. You can call me Sam Lee. I'm taking you to the circus. It's a little bit a ways out. Big Bob would have come himself, but doors opened at noon and he gets—well, you know how he gets. Anyway, he tossed me the keys and said, 'Sam Lee, you get Will Parker and Miss Pentecost'—I'm sorry, ma'am, Sam Lee, pleased to meet you. Big Bob said great things about you. Anyways, he tosses me the keys to this heap and said to get you to him as quick and safe as possible and if I had to choose, to err on the side of quick."

He kept up this running monologue while loading our suitcases into the back of the truck, finessing the toss so they came to rest, one beside the other, flush against the cab. Then, never missing a syllable, he helped us into the truck—him behind the wheel, Ms. P on the passenger side, and me sandwiched between them. Once we were packed in, he turned the key, the engine gave a gasping rattle, and we were off.

He turned his mouth off for the few minutes it took to weave his way out of Fredericksburg. That gave me time to assess our escort. I realized that, though I'd never laid eyes on him, I knew him. Denim overalls spotted with a hundred varieties of stains. Barely old enough to drive but given the keys to a two-ton deathtrap. Enthusiasm of a puppy left to run in the backyard.

He was the new kid. Just like me, once upon a time. If I had been half a foot taller, black, and had a set of six-cylinder vocal cords.

Our barely legal driver navigated the truck onto a two-lane highway, then onto a series of winding backroads that took us past forest, factories, and farms of every type. The temperature inside the truck felt like it was approaching triple digits, and we cracked both windows and suffered the smell of manure for want of a little breeze.

It was a good forty minutes until we saw the sign for Stoppard, and if our driver stopped talking for half a minute the entire way, I must have missed it.

Sam Lee, as he proudly told us, was not fresh off the turnip truck. He'd been with the circus a whole six months. He went on to prove it by explaining everything from how to corral the horses to proper tent-raising technique to how to stack your concessions for the main show.

"The butchers—that's a circus word for 'sellers,' I don't know why—they bring the dry, salty stuff out first," he explained to my boss with the passion of a convert. "The popcorn, pretzels, peanuts. Hold off on the drinks until three, four acts in. Until they're nice and parched. Then the kiddy bait, like cotton candy or licorice. You try and get those out right after a clown act. The parents are all laughing and happy and more likely to open their wallets for the little ones. You hold the candy apples until the end. They take too long to eat. Some rube buys one of those right off, they'll be gnawing on it the whole show and never buy anything else."

Talk of food caused my stomach to make an impolite noise, reminding me that it had been several hours since I'd dropped a bagel into it and that Ms. P had only had coffee.

We swung onto the town's main street, which looked like a hundred other main streets I'd passed through during my time with the circus. It had the requisite collection of businesses: one clothing store, one grocery, one bank, one drugstore, one florist, one courthouse situated next to a town square, one adjacent police department.

I wondered if Kalishenko was in there right now, languishing in some tiny cell. I wondered if he even knew we were coming.

Then we were around the square and tallying the other half of the small-town staples: a five-and-dime, a doctor's office, a funeral parlor, et cetera. All you need to get you from birth to death and everywhere in between.

The only thing that stood out was the movie theater. An unlit marquee announced it as THE MAJESTIC. It didn't look like it would live up to the name, but you grade on a curve in small towns.

Beneath the name, spelled out in black plastic letters, read:

CAT PEOPLE

EVENINGS & WKND MATINEES

What a movie theater in a one-horse town was doing showing *Cat People* was a curiosity.

My stomach spoke up again. Ms. P's stomach echoed.

"Is there a diner worth the name in this town?" I asked. Once we got to the H&H grounds all we'd have would be concession food or circus chow. Part of my job was making sure my employer got enough high-grade to keep the mental engine stoked. And while I could subsist on soda and hot dogs, I thought Ms. Pentecost might like some fuel you didn't need to smother in mustard.

Sam Lee squirmed a little at the request. I assumed he was chafing at any detour from Big Bob's instructions. But he guided the truck onto a side street and in front of Henry's Eats, which boasted THE BEST ROAST CHICKEN IN VIRGINIA!

The three of us unfolded out of the cab.

"Let's test out that advertising," I said. "I'm buying."

"I'll stay out here with the truck, Miss Parker," Sam Lee said. "You and Miss Pentecost take your time."

I was about to insist when my boss gave me a nudge and nodded at the window set in the restaurant's front door. It was virtually covered in identical sun-faded yellow flyers.

LEND A HAND TO OUR BOYS! BUY VICTORY BONDS!

I was about to ask what veterans and victory bonds had to do with vittles when I saw the other sign. Eye-level, handwritten, two words:

NO COLOREDS.

This one had been around a while. Long enough that the lettering had been touched up again and again, the letters growing thicker and darker with each pass. They weren't letting that sign fade one bit.

I'm not saying the North was all that much better. The lead-up to the Sendak case had divested me of that illusion. But we advertised it less.

"Wait here," I told the both of them. I returned a few minutes later with three cardboard trays, each holding half a roast chicken, and bottles of Coke to wash them down.

Sam took the wooden railing off the back of the truck and the three of us sat on the bed, legs dangling, and ate under the hot August sun. I don't know if the chicken was the best in the state, but it hit the spot. It was even good enough to coax our driver into silence for the duration of the meal.

And if any of you were holding on to the misconception that my boss is a stuffed shirt, you've never heard the sound she makes while sucking the meat off a chicken leg.

I was wiping the last of the grease off my mouth when a black sedan pulled up. Seeing the flasher on top and the Stoppard Police Department logo stenciled on the side, I deduced we were about to receive a visit from the law.

Beside me, I felt Sam Lee grow tense.

During the few years I'd been working with Ms. Pentecost, I'd gotten to know plenty of cops. Some of them I even liked. A few liked me in return.

But when I was with the circus, an arrival by the local law was never a good thing, and I didn't think that had changed much. I didn't know how much worse it was for Sam Lee. But by the trouble he was having controlling his breathing, I was guessing Stoppard wasn't in the *Green Book,* or at least not in a complimentary way.

I watched as the driver hopped out of the car and cast a wary glance up into the sky, like the sun was making him suspicious. Satisfied nothing up there was going to pull a fast one, he seated a wide brim hat onto a mane of aggressively pomaded silver hair, and ambled the few steps toward us.

I try not to judge books by their cover, but sometimes it's tough. The cover of this particular paperback read: *Small-Town Lawman Looking to Throw His Weight Around.*

The beginnings of a healthy gut peered over the edge of his belt, suggesting that Chief Thomas Whiddle—or so said the brass name tag on his breast pocket—had partaken of more than his fair share of Virginia's best chicken.

That aside, the hands he hitched on his belt were big and strong and he moved with the ease of a man who shouldn't be mistaken for lazy.

"Boy, what did I tell you about parking this eyesore on the street?" he said, drawing out the vowels while being noncommittal about the consonants.

Sam Lee kept his eyes on the lawman's spit-shined boots. "I'm sorry, sir," he said. "We'll be going. Just grabbing a spot of lunch."

Whiddle's eyes, almost squeezed into oblivion by his slab of a forehead, scanned across to take in the out-of-towners. They tallied and tossed me in short order before fixing on my boss. His mouth twitched, but whether it was up or down, I couldn't tell.

"You must be Lillian Pentecost."

My boss nodded, easing herself carefully off the tailgate and wiping her fingers clean on a paper napkin.

"I am," she said.

"I recognize your picture from the newspapers. That firebug case. That was some . . . interesting work."

I hadn't realized the Sendak trial had gotten any play in the Virginia rags. I wasn't sure if that was a good thing or a bad thing.

He held out a paw.

"I'm Thomas Whiddle, chief of police here in Stoppard."

Their hands met in the middle, her slender fingers swallowed by his sweaty paw. The two matched each other in height but Whiddle beat her in girth twice over.

"It's a pleasure to meet you, Chief Whiddle," she said. "This is my associate, Will Parker."

I held out a hand and he gave it a quick shake that was gentler than I'd been expecting.

"I wish I could say it was a pleasure to meet you," he told my boss. "But that doesn't seem quite right, considering."

"No," she said. "I wish I were here under better circumstances. I only hope I can be of assistance in uncovering the truth."

He nodded, slowly and deliberately. Like he really wanted to think the nod out before committing himself.

"I don't think there's all that much to uncover," he announced. "It's a pretty straightforward piece of work."

Matching Whiddle's pace, my boss slowly retrieved her cane from the bed of the truck and casually leaned. Like the topic of conversation was "Boy, howdy, we sure could use some rain," and not murder.

"Straightforward or not," she said, "I do hope you won't mind my presence here."

As I watched this little scene play out, I felt an itch on the back of my neck.

I cocked my head toward the restaurant. Half a dozen faces were pressed to the windows like beagles in a pet store. I looked down the street and saw men and women standing on porches. Some were sweeping away nonexistent dust while others fiddled with rosebushes that didn't need fiddling. A few were just having a smoke and unabashedly watching the show.

I didn't know who was manning the gossip line in Stoppard, but they deserved a raise.

I looked to my right and saw that Sam Lee was just as rapt as the rest of them. He had the tense, ready-to-run look of a guy waiting for a bar fight to kick off. No chance to tell him that my boss wasn't the brawling type.

That's what she kept me around for.

"Mr. Halloway told me you'd be coming," the chief drawled. "I told him he should save his money. But you're more than welcome in town. Long as you obey the law. The letter, and not just the spirit."

Ms. P cocked her head at that last bit.

"The stories I've read—seems you and your assistant get

legally . . . creative in your work," Whiddle said. "We won't put up with any of that foolishness around here."

"Foolishness, Chief Whiddle?" It's not often my boss is called on to do wide-eyed innocence, and she managed it about as well as a cathouse virgin.

"The stunt you pulled on the stand yesterday with that Sendak fellow? The *Times* printed part of the transcript. Pull that in Judge Berry's courtroom and he'll have you spending the night in my jail for contempt."

So our hick lawman read the *Times*, and closely enough that he picked up the legal juggling we'd pulled on the stand. I'd had Whiddle pegged for a checkers player, but I was starting to suspect he knew his rooks from his rutabagas.

"It was merely a way to reveal Mr. Sendak's true character," my boss replied, attempting to defend her queen.

"From what I read, that wasn't too hard a trick to pull," Whiddle said. "His hinges didn't seem screwed on very tight."

"People can be complicated."

"People might be complicated, but murder usually ain't." He took off his hat and wiped a line of sweat off his acre of forehead. "But you feel free to figure that out for yourself."

Check. Though not mate.

This time it was my boss's turn to give a slow, considered nod.

"Would you object to my interviewing Mr. Kalishenko?" she asked.

"No, ma'am. Visiting hours are noon to five, ten to two on Sundays. I'll tell my people that you're to be let through to see . . . Mr. Kalishenko."

He sounded like he wanted to choke on that "Mr."

"We'll have him at our jail until Tuesday."

"What happens Tuesday?" I asked.

"That's when Judge Berry comes back from vacation. He's off fly-fishing the Chattahoochee. On Tuesday we'll get your friend arraigned, then transfer him to the county pen. And before you ask, yes, he'll have a lawyer there. Mr. Halloway has somebody coming up from Richmond."

I made a note to ask Big Bob about this lawyer. Knowing the circus's profit margins, I didn't imagine he was the brightest star in Richmond's firmament.

The police chief tipped his hat. "You ladies take care." Then he pivoted on the heel of a cowboy boot and ambled back to his car.

Having kept my teeth locked through the whole verbal chess match, I couldn't resist picking up a pawn and chucking it.

"It's straightforward, all right. Why break a sweat for some no-name sideshow act," I said just loud enough for Whiddle to hear. "Circus girl, circus killer. Cut-and-dried."

He stopped, turned, and gave me a look. But whatever was happening in those pinprick eyes, I couldn't decipher it.

"You don't know?"

"Know what?" I asked.

"Ruby Donner grew up not half a mile from here. I bounced that girl on my knee," he said. "And if I have anything to say about it, that Russian bastard is gonna fry."

CHAPTER 5

The smell of cotton candy and hot dogs and horseshit; the groan of the Ferris wheel; the squeals of fear and delight from the Roto-Rama; and the cries of a dozen butchers and talkers hawking their games and gimmicks.

Home sweet home.

The circus was set up in a field just south of town. Maybe it had once held corn, but it looked like it hadn't been seeded in years. Instead it had sprouted H&H's games, rides, and booths, all of it centered around the single-ring big top. An eight-foot canvas fence encircled the entire affair.

Sam Lee parked the truck right outside the front entrance, where people were exchanging greenbacks for passage under the giant archway, the circus's name painted on it in letters big enough to be seen from passing airplanes.

After asking one of the parking attendants to keep an eye on the truck and the suitcases in back, he led us inside, where we were allowed to bypass the great unwashed and enter gratis.

Not that there was much of a line worth cutting. It looked like a sparse turnout, even for a Thursday afternoon.

"Big Bob should be getting ready in his trailer," Sam Lee said. "Hopefully we can catch him before he goes on."

He led us on a meandering path that took us past Sideshow Alley, where a sign proclaimed DOORS OPEN AT 1:30. ONLY THE BOLD MAY ENTER!

The sideshow always started a little late, it being a tough sell for early crowds. It was one thing being confronted by the Alligator Boy or the Human Blockhead under the strings of electric lights. It was another to see them under the noonday sun, with all the mystery burned away.

We bypassed the midway and its alley of games and slipped around the much smaller side tent that hosted the acts that worked best in close-up. I caught a strain of Mysterio warming up the crowd—"Nothing up my sleeves. Oh, what's this!"—followed by a lazy smattering of applause.

On the southwestern edge of the grounds we found the crew trailers. Sam Lee walked up to the smallest of the bunch and knocked on the door.

A familiar voice called from inside.

"Come in!"

Sam Lee held the door for us as we stepped up and in. As I passed, he handed me the keys to the truck.

"Big Bob said the jalopy's yours to use as long as you're here," he told me.

"Thanks. I'll try not to scratch the rust."

"It was real good meeting you both," he said. "If you need me for anything, you just yell my name and either I'll hear it or someone will come find me."

Then he ran off to attend to whatever duties the bottom man in the circus dog pile got stuck with.

The trailer had about half the square footage of my tiny bedroom back in Brooklyn. Despite that, Big Bob had managed to squeeze in a sawed-off bed, dresser, desk with typewriter, filing cabinet, and a full-length mirror. The walls were papered with old show posters and handbills: two decades' worth of diving acrobats and prancing clowns, roaring tigers and smiling showgirls.

Their paper eyes stared out at me and made the trailer feel even smaller. It wasn't a pleasant feeling.

However, it was just the right size for Big Bob Halloway. Topping out at about four and a half feet, the owner, operator, and ringmaster of H&H was at that moment standing in front of the mirror and putting the final touches on his ensemble.

He liked to say that, as he was the lone dwarf still employed at the circus, it was only right he take the smallest trailer. That made it a lot harder for anyone else to complain about their own digs.

Bob was decked out in his usual costume: a bright red tux and tails over a black shirt and pants, and a bright red bow tie. His shoulder-length hair was dyed the same color as his patent-leather shoes and was pulled back at the nape of his neck with a silver clasp. I noticed that he'd let the gray start showing in his Vandyke.

He was applying black makeup underneath his eyes—an old showman's trick so his face didn't get washed out by the spotlight. Also, he thought it combined with his beard to give him a Machiavellian air.

He wasn't wrong.

"Sorry, ladies. If I fumble this, it gets in my eyes and I'll be blinking tears by the second clown break. If you can find a clear spot on the bed, feel free to take a load off."

My boss pushed a pile of clothes aside and took a seat, while I stayed standing. Scraping off an errant bit of makeup with his fingernail, Big Bob took a last look in the mirror. Satisfied with what he saw, he turned and took in his guests.

He held out a hand to Ms. Pentecost. This time it was her fingers that did the swallowing.

"A pleasure to see you again, ma'am," he said.

"The pleasure is mine, Mr. Halloway."

"What did I say last time? It's Bob. Or Robert, if you absolutely must."

The two had met back when Ms. P had plucked me for the gig as her assistant. I hadn't been around for the meeting, having been in jail at the time. So I watched this exchange with a certain amount of fascination.

"I'm sorry for your loss, Robert. I hope we can be of assistance."

"I hope so, too."

Big Bob turned to me.

"Parker," he said, making a show of looking me up and down. "You look good. Showering regular these days?"

"Alternate Wednesdays," I replied. "Still buying your briefs in the toddler department?"

"Nope," he said. "Stopped wearing 'em entirely."

We burst into simultaneous grins, and he stepped forward and hugged me, squeezing and bending backward to lift me a good two inches off the floor. Bob might have been small, but he had been a roustabout long before he was a ringmaster and could still sling a sledgehammer with the best of them.

He set me back down and retrieved his bright-red top hat from its perch on the bed frame.

"I got a show to do," he said. "We can have a sit-down later, but I can give you the skinny now if you don't mind walking and listening at the same time."

"I think we can manage," my boss said.

We hopped down out of his trailer and headed in the general direction of the big top, weaving through the hawkers, the scurrying performers still adjusting bits of costume, and the afternoon crowd, who gawked at everything in sight. That included the dwarf in top and tails, the woman in the bespoke suit with the cane, and what they probably thought was somebody's secretary in her third-best slacks, hurrying to keep up.

"Here's the deal," Big Bob was saying. "We were in Pittsburgh through Saturday night, made the jump to Stoppard on Sunday, got in too late to do much, set up Monday, opened Tuesday. Opening day goes off without a hitch. Around eleven that night, last call sounds and the girls go to get Ruby from her booth so they can all go back to their trailers and get prepped for the late show in the side tent. Ruby ain't got a lot of costuming for that show, so she usually lends a hand with everyone else. She tells the girls to count her out of the show that night. Said she—"

A girl of seven or so wandered into his path, her view impeded by a cone of cotton candy as big as her head. Big Bob pirouetted around her, doffed his hat, and executed a simultaneous bow that sent the girl into a fit of giggles, then kept moving without dropping a syllable.

"—had to see me about something. She heads out of Sideshow Alley and that's the last anyone saw of her until she turned up dead. Hang on."

We made a quick zig and zag and slipped around the back of the side tent where we'd heard Mysterio performing on the way in. Big Bob stopped at a rear entrance, its flap tied loosely back. Inside the tent, the crowd was filing out the other side and Mysterio and his assistant were clearing up stage props.

The last few years hadn't been kind to the magician. His face—once all hard planes and dramatic shadows—had started to swell and sag. His tuxedo looked threadbare and it was straining a little around his midsection.

He glanced up and we locked eyes. I tossed him a smile, but he didn't return it. No smile, no surprise, not even a nod. Just a half-second pause and he went back to picking up paper flowers.

I decided not to take it personally.

"This is where they found her," Big Bob said, gesturing at a bare patch of sawdust and dirt just to the side of the flap.

"Who found her?" my boss asked, a little out of breath from the double-time walk.

"Mysterio's assistant. Annabelle." He nodded at the tall brunette in the glorified swimsuit picking up playing cards. "She was on her way to her trailer to get changed for the late show. Nearly tripped over the body on her way out."

"This doesn't seem to be a public path," Ms. Pentecost observed.

"No. This is what we call the Loop. It's basically an alley that circles most of the lot. It runs between the outside fence and the tent and booths, and lets employees move around without having to jostle elbows with the public."

"So it's not strange that Ruby came this way?"

Big Bob cocked his head side to side. "Sorta yes, sorta no. It's a straight shot from the front entrance of Sideshow Alley to the trailers. Even with the crowd filing out, she could have gotten to me a lot quicker going that way."

My boss tossed me a glance and I returned it. We were both thinking the same thing. Maybe she wasn't avoiding the crowd in general, but one ticket buyer in particular.

"Do you know why she wanted to see you?" Ms. P asked.

"No idea," Bob said.

"Had there been any change in her behavior prior to her death?"

"Well . . . she'd been pretty low since Bertha died."

"Bertha? A friend?"

I chimed in. "Her boa constrictor. Well, not hers. It's really Ray's. He's the creepy-crawlies guy. But Ruby used Bertha for her act."

I thought back to the first time I'd seen Ruby pick the snake up and drape it over her shoulders, giggling when it tickled her ear with a flicking tongue. Ruby was something to see. But Ruby with a six-foot boa wrapped around her could stop your heart.

"Ruby found Bertha dead in her cage Saturday morning. She was all kinds of upset," Bob said.

"How did the snake die?" my boss asked.

"Natural causes, as far as I know. She was getting up in years."

"If Ruby was upset, I bet Ray's a mess," I said. "Assuming he's still on the payroll."

"Oh, yeah," Bob said. "Ray's not going anywhere. This place ever folds, they'll have to roll the two of us up with the tents."

My boss pulled us out of the conversational cul-de-sac. "How many visitors did you have Tuesday evening?"

Bob shook his head. "Can't say exactly. I can check the books tonight."

"We can ask Dee," I said. "Does she still keep a table set up at the chow tent?" Dee was the retired showgirl who did the circus's books and injected a regular dose of common sense into Big Bob.

Another headshake, sadder this time. "Sorry, kiddo. Dee jumped ship not long after you left. Lives in Florida now. Setting up some kind of sideshow museum in the Keys."

That threw me. Dee was as much a part of Hart & Halloway as the creak of the Ferris wheel or the smell of cotton candy. I couldn't imagine the circus operating without her.

As if reading my mind, Big Bob added, "I had twenty years looking over Dee's shoulder, so the books are in good hands. Besides, it's mostly simple subtraction these days."

Ms. Pentecost traded leaning on one leg for the other—a sign that she was tired or impatient or both. I hurried things along.

"Bertha dying probably wasn't what she was running to see you about. Anything else eating at her?"

He shrugged. "If there was, I don't know about it."

Big Bob pulled out a battered pocket watch on a silver chain and took a quick peek at where the hands lay.

"You mind if we keep moving? It doesn't look good for the owner to hold up the show."

We set off again, this time taking the Loop and avoiding the crowd.

"So, Bob," I said, "any reason you didn't mention Ruby was from Stoppard?"

He shot me a look. "Other than I got a hundred other things running through my head? Not particularly. Sorry about that."

"It's just we had a meet and greet with Chief Whiddle and he dropped that surprise nugget on us."

His face twisted and he let out a snort.

"That bull? He's already measuring out rope for the noose," Bob said.

We stepped to the side to let a trio of clowns squeeze through. They were laden down with armfuls of giant inflatable balls and an equally giant inflatable bat. The clown bringing up the rear tossed me a grin through his face paint. I lobbed it back and made a note to track him down later.

Paulie Pagliano was another H&H old-timer. Even if he didn't have anything to add to the case, he was one of my favorite folk and I wouldn't mind swapping war stories.

"Anyway, yeah. Ruby grew up around here," Bob continued. "That's how we got this spot for so cheap after Richmond fell through. This is her family's land. Her uncle's place is one field over. Just past that line of trees."

Half a circus and the eight-foot-tall canvas fence were in the way, so I took his word for it.

"That's where I got the two of you bunking, by the way. They don't have a hotel around here worth the name and I don't have a trailer to spare. Used to belong to Ruby's folks, but they died a while back. Car crash. The uncle's a good guy. Bit of a lush, but all right."

Ms. P was lagging behind, and I put a hand on Big Bob's shoulder to slow him up.

"Sorry," he said. "Half a lifetime at this and I still get antsy before a show."

"So, Ms. Donner is the reason the circus is in Stoppard at all," my boss said when she caught up.

"Guess you could say that. She bucked and kicked when I brought up the idea. She'd never been back, not even for her folks' funeral. She wasn't in the market for a homecoming. But, you know, needs must when the devil loses you Richmond."

We had arrived at the back entrance to the big top. A collection of acrobats, clowns, and assorted fauna were getting into place for the start of the show. A few recognized me and nodded or waved.

"The funeral is tomorrow morning," Big Bob said. "They got a family plot over by the house. I'm doing most of the arranging. Her uncle didn't seem up for it."

A stone settled in my stomach.

I thought of funerals in the same way I did pencil skirts: an occasional and uncomfortable necessity of the job. Except with most murder investigations, I didn't know the deceased and could keep my mind on sorting through suspects. Not so this time.

"Look, I gotta go do my thing," Big Bob told us. "You're welcome to watch."

He reached into his jacket and pulled out two red chips with H&H's logo emblazoned on either side.

"Show these to any ticket taker and they'll let you in gratis," he said. "Same with concessions. It's all on the house. I'll be wrapped up until closing. You need anything in the meantime, find Sam Lee. I've got him filling in on some of the games, so you can track him down there. Now, if there isn't anything else, I got a crowd to mesmerize."

He took a step toward the open flap, but Ms. Pentecost raised her cane to bar his way.

"There is one thing, Robert," she said. "Why is Chief Whiddle so positive that Mr. Kalishenko committed this crime? You were rather vague on the phone. And the chief seemed quite sure of himself."

Big Bob looked down at his patent leathers, kicking at a

clump of sod. When he picked his head back up, he kept his eyes fixed on Ms. Pentecost and not at me.

"He . . . um . . . Well, Val and Ruby had a shouting match that morning. Kind of a nasty one from what I hear. Afterward, he started on the bottle. Was pretty drunk by that night. Blackout, he says. Doesn't remember anything."

Blackout was never good. Not when it came to a murder investigation and people started asking you where you were when.

"Could that be what Ruby wanted to see you about?" Ms. P asked. "A complaint against Mr. Kalishenko?"

"I don't see that," he said. "She'd have known my answer. I'd have told her they needed to work it out themselves."

Big Bob was doing this shuffling, back-and-forth half step in the direction of the tent, like a schoolboy waiting for the end-of-day bell and hoping his teacher didn't lob one last question at him.

"There's more, isn't there?" I said.

He took off his top hat and examined the lining. Maybe hoping there was a better answer written there than the one he had.

"Yeah, there's more," he said. "A witness puts him in Ruby's vicinity right before she was killed. And when they put the question to him—'Did you kill her?'—he said, and I quote, 'Maybe I did.'"

He shifted his eyes to mine.

"Sorry, Will," he said.

"Nothing to be sorry for," I said. "I'm not the one on the hook for murder."

"I know. But . . ."

He didn't need to finish the sentence. But it wasn't good news. As collections of circumstantial evidence went, it was a robust lot. Basically, if my boss wasn't able to work her magic, Val's circus career was going to come to a very abrupt, and permanent, end.

CHAPTER **6**

We left Big Bob to get ready and made our way out to the front of the tent, where people were still filing in. I glanced at my watch and saw the hour hand sneaking up on two o'clock.

"Time's getting short," I said, thinking of the five o'clock visiting-hour deadline at the jail. "We can check out the show later."

Ms. Pentecost scanned her eyes across the circus grounds, tracking the crowd as it split up into clumps and couples on their way to try their hand at the games, lining up for the Ferris wheel, or making a beeline for the big top.

"Will Sideshow Alley be open by now?" she finally asked.

"It should be," I said. "But we can pay a visit later. We need to go talk to Val. Whiddle seems like the kind of man to cut things at the minute mark."

"I'd like to see Sideshow Alley," she said placidly, joining the stream of people headed that way. I tucked the ticking clock out of my mind and followed.

Sideshow Alley was cut off from the midway proper by a high wooden fence adorned with tall canvas banners. They let the audience know what they could expect to find inside: THE ALLIGATOR BOY; SERPENTS FROM THE EAST; THE ALL-SEEING MADAME FORTUNA.

Their duplicates could be found hanging from the circus's

outer fence, so as to let the folks driving by know what they were missing.

The sign announcing the Amazing Tattooed Woman was still hanging.

DISCOVER THE SECRETS ETCHED ONTO HER SKIN.

A black ribbon bisected the painted canvas, and bouquets of flowers were scattered on the ground.

At the center of the banner display was a wooden archway—a miniature of the one over the main entrance. This one was painted with images of tarot cards, slithering snakes, and bare human bodies arranged in such a way that raised eyebrows. At the top of the arch was a message spelled out in glowing electric light: WHO DARES ENTER THE WORLD BEYOND?

There was no way to see what the Alley held without dropping your twenty-five cents to the talker at the front—a skeleton-thin man about my age in a battered bowler hat and the wispy suggestion of a goatee who was keeping up a steady stream of patter.

"Step right up, step right up!" he cried. "For twenty-five cents, a quarter of a dollar, two bits! For the price of a handful of candy you can change your life! That's right! What you see beyond this entrance will make you believe in miracles, in curses, in angels and devils and everything in between. Fellas, find your guts. Ladies, cling tight to your fellas."

It was usual operating procedure for one of the Alley's performers to stand beside the talker and act as the bally—the tease for what the audience could expect inside. During my time that bally was usually Ruby. There was nothing gruesome about her act to put off the squeamish, and the men in the crowd figured that if she was the tease, the payoff must be spectacular.

This afternoon the talker was joined by the Impossible

Rubber Band Girl. Known as Frieda behind closed doors, she was dressed in a skintight electric-blue singlet. The butter-blond ringlets that used to reach her shoulders had been shorn to a feathered few inches, giving her an exotic, almost androgynous look.

She was giving the passersby a demonstration of her double-jointed talents. Actually, she explained to me once that there was no such thing as having extra joints. She was just very, very flexible, she said, and that with enough practice I could pull a lot of the same moves.

To this day, I don't know if she was playing it straight or flirting.

As we walked up, Frieda smiled and gave me a behind-the-back wave. "Hiya, Will. I heard you were in town."

"Hey, Frieda. I love your hair."

"Yeah. I've been doing more human pretzel bits and it got in the way," she said, running a hand through her factory cut. She twisted her other arm back and around her head so it draped over her shoulders like a scarf. This drew a chorus of exclamations from the crowd, and a few groans from the weak-stomached.

"Is Ruby's booth still set up?" I asked.

Frieda lost her smile and nodded. "Yeah. Usual place near the back."

I didn't want to use the freebie tokens in front of the crowd. No good giving the rubes the idea they could get in for free. I slipped the talker a pair of quarters. He doffed his bowler and fed the coins to a lockbox that was fastened to a post in the ground.

Occasionally some genius would get the notion to grab the post and try to pull it up and run. They'd quickly and violently discover that the thing had been driven six feet deep by the same roustabouts who raised the tent. It was fun to watch. Even more fun when those same roustabouts went for a new distance record throwing the moron out the front gate.

"Behold!" the talker announced to the passersby. "A pair of brave ladies who want to expand their horizons. Go forth, my beauties. Discover the world that lies just next door to this one!"

He had a good line for a newbie. He'd eventually learn to drop the purple prose and keep things simple: Pay your money and be scared, disgusted, or aroused. With the best acts, all three at once.

"Maybe see you at the late show?" Frieda asked in a side-mouth whisper as we passed.

"Probably not," I whispered back.

"You should come," she said, reaching behind her back and giving my shoulder a squeeze. "I've got a new act I think you'll like."

"Then I'll definitely consider it."

Ms. Pentecost and I walked under the archway and found ourselves in a narrow alley formed by wooden fencing and booths of various sizes.

"A friend?" Ms. P asked, throwing a backward glance.

"Frieda? Oh, sure. We were real good pals."

She raised an eyebrow.

"Okay, maybe occasionally we were more," I admitted. "Nothing serious, though."

"You'd mentioned a relationship with a contortionist, but I was under the impression it was a man."

"Different contortionist."

Both eyebrows this time.

"Don't give me that look," I said. "I was very young and . . . young. Now you wanted to see the sideshow. Here's the sideshow."

I quick-stepped away from my boss and any further awkward examination of my youthful indiscretions.

The booths on either side of Sideshow Alley were staggered so you never pitted one act against another and each performer was given a chance to grab the audience's attention.

I waved hello to the Alligator Boy (real name Manuel) whose naturally occurring skin condition was given daily cosmetic assistance, nodded to the Human Blockhead (real name Eddie) who was making a couple coeds gag by shoving a three-inch nail up his nostril, and peeked in on the World's Smallest Horse (a miniature Appaloosa named Jingles) who came up and nuzzled my hand.

About halfway down the Alley, right where the path took a ninety-degree turn, the booths were replaced by a trailer. It was a converted train car that had about ten times the square footage of Big Bob's living quarters. That didn't include the new addition—a makeshift shack attached to the top of the car. A tiny window built into one side suggested it was being used for more than storage.

The sign above the doorway announced the HOUSE OF VENOMOUS THINGS, each letter formed by a twisting snake or curling spider.

I waited for Ms. Pentecost to catch up. "Come on," I said. "You gotta meet Ray."

The inside was dim and a good ten degrees warmer than the August afternoon outside. Squeezed into the room were three rows of glass cases—two on either side and one down the middle—creating a U-shaped path so visitors could loop through the display and exit the way they came. The cases were all sitting on long, bunting-covered crates that raised them to perfect peering height. Atop every case was a sign warning visitors, DO NOT REMOVE LID: FOR YOUR OWN SAFETY in fire-engine red.

Really, the lids were there to protect the inhabitants of the cases, who were much more likely to be damaged by fumbling visitors than vice versa.

The room was empty except for a tall, thin gentleman at the far end and a hand-holding couple halfway down the row. The woman was making muffled squeals every three steps and clutching at her date. That both had on wedding bands with a little wear to them said they were married, but the way the woman was taking every opportunity to put her hands on her companion made me suspect not to each other.

Wouldn't be the first time the circus had served as a rendez-vous for secret lovers. Lots of cozy corners, easy to get lost in a crowd. Or maybe I was seeing philandering where there was none. One of the perils of the detective business.

We peered in at the hissing cockroaches and the scorpions. A king cobra reared up to say hello, its head almost hitting the top of the case. There was a rattlesnake that looked impressive, but was too tired to shake its maraca. At the end of the trailer, the lid was off one of the cases and the spindly guy was bent over it, his arms deep inside.

He resembled a misplaced librarian: around fifty years old with knobbly arms and legs that looked like they might fall off if you shook him hard enough. He sported bifocals over a pair of watery blue eyes that were set in a narrow, nearly bald head. He was wearing a white button-up, and matching black vest and string tie.

I peeked over his shoulder. His sleeves were rolled up to the elbows and a half-dozen tarantulas were making their way up his wrists and arms.

"Hey, buddy," I said. "Didn't you read the sign? Those things are dangerous."

He gave a start and one of the tarantulas toppled off his arm and back into the case. It took him a full two seconds to recognize who I was.

"Will!" Ray exclaimed. "Bob told me you were coming. I almost didn't recognize you. My gosh. You look um . . . uh . . ."

He fumbled for a word that wouldn't get him in trouble.

"I clean up good, I know," I said, letting him off the hook. "Ms. Lillian Pentecost, meet Ray Nance—snake wrangler, spider handler, and one of the longest-serving company members of H and H."

"I'd shake your hand but . . ." He looked down at the arachnids marking time on his forearms.

"I understand," she said. "Don't let us keep you from attending to your charges."

He smiled. "My charges—what a wonderful word. That's exactly how I think of them. Will, dear, could you reach into my left vest pocket and feed the one crawling up my forearm. I'd do it, but I don't want to dislodge the others."

I reached into his pocket and plucked out a cricket, still live and squirming. Then I held it out to the hairy arachnid making its way up Ray's arm. It stopped in front of the cricket, tensed, then plunged its fangs into the insect. The cricket went immediately still and the spider carried it down Ray's arm.

"I was under the impression that tarantulas could not be kept in groups," my boss said. "Being cannibalistic."

"Ah, you know your arachnids!" Ray almost squealed. "In most cases that's true. But if you look closely at this one rounding my elbow . . . see the faint reddish hue around its legs?"

"I do."

"That coloring is where the pinktoe gets its name," he explained. "They're a much more docile species. Provided you keep them well fed."

"Do you hand-feed all your spiders?" Ms. Pentecost asked.

"Oh, no. No time for that, sadly," Ray said, as he gently plucked the furry creatures off his hands and placed them back in the terrarium with their fellows. "But I do like to give them a little extra attention every now and then."

He bent down and picked up a jar filled with live crickets, unthreaded the lid, and dumped a handful in. The crickets began jumping in all directions. I knew from my stint helping Ray that they wouldn't survive long.

The spiders began moving toward their prey. Individually they were silent, but when they moved as a group they made a *shhh*-ing sound, like dry leaves skittering across the sidewalk.

"Spiders are really very intelligent creatures," he said, putting the lid back onto the tank and fastening the latches on the two short ends. "If you treat them well and feed them regularly, they'll remain quite friendly."

In other words, cross them or make them miss a meal and they'll start biting each other's heads off. Not too different from people, when you think about it.

"Friendly or not, I get the shakes just looking at them crawling on you," I said, giving a shiver that was only half-exaggerated.

"She's being silly," Ray told Ms. P. "Will here was one of my best assistants. All my creatures got along with her very well."

"Not that I needed to assist very often. Ray practically sleeps with the snakes."

"I *do* sleep with them now," he said, grinning and pointing to a trapdoor in the ceiling. "I got Bob to build me a little loft on top of the trailer. Now I don't have to leave my—what was the word—my *charges* alone all night."

"That reminds me," I said. "I'm sorry to hear about Bertha."

His eyes clouded over. "Oh, yes. Bertha."

He shuffled down the other aisle, past the colorful tree vipers and the double-headed corn snake, its tongues flicking in unison, to the largest glass case of the lot. It held nothing but rocks and moss and dirt atop a layer of old newspaper. I was amused to see a page from the *Chicago Tribune* from a week back. Ms. Pentecost's face stared up at me from the bottom of the cage, the caption underneath reading HARLEM FIREBUG TRIAL STARTS NEXT WEEK, LILLIAN PENTECOST SET TO . . . The rest was obscured by grass and sawdust.

"Fifteen years she'd been with me. Longer than any of the others."

A tear got caught on the bottom of his bifocals. He pulled them off and wiped them on his shirt.

"Is fifteen particularly old for a boa constrictor?" Ms. P asked.

"Oh, I don't know," he said, giving a sniff. "Pretty good age. Figure she was two or three when I got her. And all the traveling. That shaves years off any animal. But still . . . I could have been easier on her. It's my fault, really."

"When you say you'd have been easier on her, do you mean you wouldn't have let Ms. Donner use her in her act?"

The mention of Ruby snapped Ray out of whatever spiral he was slipping down.

"Oh, no!" he said. "I would never . . . I mean, Bertha really got along with Ruby. And Ruby loved her. Treated her real nice. It was good for her. Bertha, I mean. Nothing should spend its whole life in a cage."

"Was Ms. Donner very upset?"

"Oh, yes," Ray said. "Terribly, terribly upset."

"Was it just the snake's death, or was she upset about anything else?"

"I don't understand. Like what?"

My boss shrugged. "Anything at all," she said. "Something she thought worth informing Mr. Halloway about."

Ray gave it a second of thought, then shook his head. "Not that I know of. Just Bertha. And I don't know why she'd go to Bob about that."

"You gonna replace her?" I asked.

"Well, I'll never *really* replace her. Snakes are as individual as humans, you know? Once you get to know them," Ray said. "However, I've been corresponding with a gentleman in Kansas City who says he's got a nine-foot python that he's willing to part with. I'm trying to get his price down."

Ray walked with us out of the trailer and down the steps.

"You look good, Will. I think your new career agrees with you."

"Sometimes yes, sometimes maybe," I said. "Still miss it here, though."

He gave a look I couldn't quite decipher. "As long as you're living a life where you don't have to dicker over the price of pythons, you've probably made the right choice."

He nodded to my boss. "It was a pleasure, Ms. Pentecost."

With that, Ray disappeared back into his hot, dim cave filled with darting tongues and the sound of dry leaves.

CHAPTER 7

We made our way down the Alley, past a lot of performers who had arrived at the circus after my time. There was the Hindu fakir who pierced his skin with foot-long needles. I was pretty sure the Hindu part was fake, but the needles were real enough. And there was Lightning Lucy, who could light up unsocketed bulbs just by touching them. Probably a better act after sundown.

There were signs noting that this or that performer was elsewhere and would return in an hour. My boss asked me about those, if it was common for Alley performers to go wandering.

"A lot of sideshow acts pull double-duty in the big spec or have solo shows in the side tent," I explained. "Or they could just be grabbing a bite. Either way, if a customer has a hankering to check them out, they'll have to come back later and drop some more dough."

We took a quick lap through the House of Oddities, which was also a converted train car. Ms. Pentecost spent a good five minutes peering at the two-headed baby, figuring out which head on the skeleton was real and which was the fake.

"I don't think either is original," she said, whispering so she didn't spoil the gimmick for the handful of other rubes nearby. "Both skulls belong to an older child. A calculated choice, since it gives the skeleton an added grotesquerie."

"Yeah, most of this is Paulie's work. He's on the clown crew.

We passed him when we were grilling Bob. He's the dour-looking one. He does double duty keeping this place up. Give him time, he can make anything."

She pressed her face right up against the glass case. "Yes, I see. This top vertebra—the bifurcated one—is made of plaster. The texture is very good, though."

I looked at my watch and saw the hour hand was now closer to the three than the two.

"Good eye. You win a kewpie doll," I said, not-so-subtly herding her out the door.

Near the end of the Alley's loop, we came to Ruby's booth. A stand held a framed photo draped in flowers. The snap showed a smiling Ruby in a skimpy two-piece, nine-tenths of her tattoos on display. Her face was set between a smile and a smirk—a forever come-on letting the audience know they could try their luck, but their chances were slim.

The photo tugged on something in my chest, and I turned away.

Across from Ruby's booth was the last stop before the Alley vomited its passengers back out into the circus proper. It was a tiny tent painted in rainbow colors, its entrance shielded by a beaded curtain. The sign above the entrance read MADAME FORTUNA KNOWS YOUR FUTURE! A smaller sign hung on a nail next to the beads read THE MADAME IS IN, signifying that the fortune-teller was at that moment sans client.

We were pressed for time, but I couldn't leave the Alley without stopping by.

"Come on," I said to my boss. "Someone else you should meet while we're in the neighborhood. It'll just take a second, then we can get to the jail."

I parted the beads and entered Madame Fortuna's parlor. The last time the boss and I had visited a fortune-teller, things hadn't gone so well. I didn't think Ms. P would hold that against Madame Fortuna, though.

The floor was made of thick pseudo-Persian rugs layered over bare dirt. The walls of the tent were sufficiently translucent to let the sunlight filter through in rainbow streaks. The inside was just big enough for the round table in the center, draped in midnight-blue velvet, and three chairs. The one opposite the door was occupied.

I took in the bouffant hairdo kept copper from a bottle and woven through with tiny bells, the red silk robe, the slender hands spread out over the velvet. I saw how arthritis was starting to bend those long, ring-covered fingers out of true.

"Come in, come in. All are welcome here," the woman said, rounding her vowels off with the kind of semi-European accent you only hear in movies. She peered up at us through glasses so thick they could act as crystal balls. I knew for a fact they were plain glass, their only purpose to make the Madame's hazel eyes appear more all-seeing.

"Come, ladies. Leave your present at the door and have a seat, so we can talk of your future. Will you find true love? True fortune? True happiness? Come. Sit."

I plopped down in the chair opposite her, which was flimsy enough to almost topple me sideways.

"I don't know about happiness or fortune," I said. "But I'd love to find a good New York bagel. What do you say, Maeve? They got those down here in farm country?"

No surprised look of recognition from Madame Fortuna. She knew how to keep her face flat. But when she spoke again, she'd tossed the accent, unveiling her inner Staten Islander.

"Goddamn it, Will. What did I tell you about dropping that name during business hours. That curtain ain't soundproof, ya know. Jesus Christ—gone half a minute and you forget every single thing I taught you."

She gestured for Ms. Pentecost to take the other chair, which she did, perching gracefully so as not to half topple like I had and laying her cane across her lap.

"Lillian Pentecost, meet Maeve Bailey, better known as Madame Fortuna."

"A pleasure to meet you," Maeve said, slipping her faux accent back on like a favorite coat.

"The pleasure is all mine," my boss replied. "I've heard quite a bit about you."

"All good, I hope."

"Quite good," Ms. P said. "Will has especially praised your powers of observation."

Maeve nodded. She was never one to be slow on the uptake.

"If you have questions about what happened to Ruby, ask them. Though I don't know how much use I'll be."

"Were you here the night of Ms. Donner's death?" my boss asked.

"I was. Right here, exactly."

Ms. Pentecost turned around in her chair and looked out the beaded curtain.

"You don't have a direct view of her booth, but you can see some of it."

Maeve nodded. "If she leaned over she could wave to me."

"Was there anything out of the ordinary that evening? Out of the ordinary for this environment, I mean?"

Maeve thought about it for a second, then shook her head.

"It was a pretty standard night," she said. "It was opening, which is always a little rough, though the crew does their best to make sure everything's hammered down tight and all the machinery is greased."

"Nothing happened of note?" my boss asked again. "Nothing that could account for Ms. Donner's actions that evening?"

"Her actions?"

"Neglecting her duties with the evening performance in order to discuss something with Mr. Halloway? Choosing the Loop rather than the most direct route."

"If something happened, she didn't say anything to me,"

Maeve said. "But we don't chat during hours. Seeing the side-show folks socializing ruins the mystique."

My boss was crafting her next question when Maeve held up a ring-covered hand.

"Hang on," she said. "There *was* something. Or maybe nothing. It's a coin flip."

"Tell me," Ms. Pentecost said.

Maeve closed her eyes and tilted her head back—the same pose she struck when she was "peering into the dark depths of the spirit world." As she spoke, she let the accent slip some.

"I had a client in the chair. Thirty-ish housewife. Straitlaced but she'd had a nip of something, so her purse strings were loose. Her husband died overseas. She came in asking about contacting him, making sure he didn't suffer. But really she was looking for permission to start relations with a neighbor fella. Or continue relations. The way she tiptoed around some things, I'm pretty sure they'd spent time on top of the sheets if not under them."

She brought her head back to level and opened her eyes.

"When the widow sat down, Ruby was passing words with someone at her booth. Spent a few minutes doing it, too, because I remember looking up a second time and she was still at it."

"Was this unusual?" Ms. P asked.

"Not particularly," Maeve said. "Men like to hang out there. More so if they don't have a girl to drag them away."

"So why note this time?"

Maeve thought about it.

"The way she was passing words. It was a little urgent," she said. "I didn't think about it at the time. I was busy with the merry widow. But I got the sense she was trying to hurry him off."

"A customer giving her trouble?" I suggested.

"If that was all it was, she could have rung the bell."

"The bell?" my boss asked.

"Every booth has a bell—one of those big hand-ringers," I explained. "Something goes wrong, the performer rings the bell. One ring brings the talker to help shoo away whoever's being an annoyance. Keep ringing the bell and everybody comes running. That's usually reserved for when things get physical."

"What time was this?" Ms. P asked.

"Near last call," Maeve said. "So ten-thirty or so."

"What did this person look like?"

"That's just it. I didn't see him. Not a scrap," she said. "I didn't even really see Ruby. Only a sliver of her. Mostly I just heard her voice."

"Did you hear the other person's voice?"

Maeve shook her head, causing the chimes woven into her dyed-black bouffant to tinkle. "I'm sorry. There was someone there. He stayed longer than usual. I don't think Ruby wanted him there."

Ms. P cocked her head.

"You believe it was a man?"

Maeve gave it a think.

"Yeah," she said. "I guess I do."

"Why?"

"I only saw a corner of her body, you know. But her head was cocked up. Like the person she was talking to was on the tall side," she explained. "Also, I suppose I think it's a man because I didn't hear the person's voice. A woman's voice is higher. It cuts through the din better. But it could have been a soft-spoken woman in heels, for all I know."

I figured I'd save my boss the trouble of asking the obvious.

"Could it have been Val?"

When she shook her head this time, even the bells sounded sad.

"Sorry, honey. I don't know."

"Did you tell police about this mystery man?" I asked.

"Shoot, kid, they never talked to me. And I didn't remember it until just now."

So Chief Whiddle had neglected to talk to the one person who was within earshot of Ruby nearly all Tuesday. If I hadn't already thought the game was rigged, this confirmed it.

There was a mystery man who'd had a long chat with Ruby less than half an hour before she was killed. Maybe somebody with a grudge from Ruby's younger days. Maybe a stranger who made a pass and couldn't accept "Get lost" for an answer.

"Do you know what Ms. Donner and Mr. Kalishenko were arguing about earlier that day?" Ms. P asked.

I thought it was a time-waster of a question. Ruby and Val were always arguing, and if we wanted specifics we could just ask Val. I glanced anxiously at my watch. I was about to remind my boss that we needed to get to the jail before all the sand ran out of the hourglass when Maeve lied.

"Sorry," she said. "No idea. They had spats more or less regularly. I stopped paying attention to the specifics years ago. It was probably the old made-freak versus skilled-performer argument. They gnawed on that old bone every month or so."

Maeve basically lies for a living, so the fact that I caught this one was a minor miracle. Her only tell—and it was so slight it barely counted—was that she had a tendency to peer over her glasses rather than through them when she was really winding up a pitch.

Which means not only did Maeve know what the fight was about, but it was something she didn't want to spill. I made a note to corner her later and see if she had looser lips when my boss wasn't around.

Speaking of, I glanced over at Ms. P to see if she'd picked up on the lie. If she had, she wasn't letting it show.

She pushed her cane into the layered carpet and stood up.

"It was a pleasure, Madame," she said.

Maeve stood and walked around the table to shake her hand.

"A pleasure for me, too," she said. She reached out a hand and squeezed my upper arm, like a witch testing how meaty a stew I'd make.

"It's good to see you, girl. I hope the two of you figure this mess out."

As we parted the beaded curtain and walked outside, I was left wondering if her last words were a lie, too.

CHAPTER 8

After our time inside Maeve's rainbow-filtered world, the plain August sunshine felt disappointingly flat.

As soon as we were out of earshot, I let Ms. Pentecost know my suspicions that the fortune-teller was holding something back.

"We will need to approach her again. Perhaps when we have a better idea what she is withholding," my boss said.

I agreed. Maeve was sharp. I didn't want to call her a liar without better cards in my hand.

We continued down the last ten feet of Sideshow Alley, which was little more than a chute covered in banners advertising the big-top acts. I pulled aside the banner advertising the Flying Sabatinis to show my boss the opening that would let someone into the Loop.

"Does this pathway run the entire circumference of the circus?" she asked.

"Not the entire," I said. "It starts here and loops around the big top and then the side tent and comes out between the chow tent and the crew trailers. Say Manuel has a solo show in the side tent or wants to grab lunch, but he doesn't want to be stopped twenty times by people clamoring to see the Alligator Boy. He can take the Loop."

"How likely would it be for someone who is not employed by the circus to know of this path's existence?" she asked.

"In a perfect world, not very likely," I said. "In the real world, performers come and go through here all the time. It wouldn't take much to catch them at it. And most of the entrances into the Loop are like this. Anyone can go through. If someone had eyes on Ruby, was following her . . ."

I left the rest unsaid.

At the end of Sideshow Alley, a one-way door dumped us back into the circus proper. The crowd had picked up, so I pulled Ms. Pentecost to a semi-secluded corner near a popcorn cart.

"How about I run ahead to the truck and get it warmed up. Make sure the engine hasn't fallen out," I said. "If we don't hit any roadblocks, we should still have half an hour to spare with Val."

Ms. P took a frustratingly long scan of that corner of the circus grounds.

"Where would Ms. Donner's trailer be located?" she asked.

"Boss, we're not gonna have time for a decent search and still get to the jail for visiting hours."

She gave me a look and the penny dropped.

"You're not talking to Kalishenko today," I said, the words coming out more like an accusation than a question.

"We'll see Mr. Kalishenko at start of visiting hours tomorrow," she said.

"If you're trying to piece together what happened the night of the murder, he should be top of your list." I was trying to keep my voice down and failing.

"He's certainly not at the bottom," my boss parried. "But reportedly Mr. Kalishenko remembers nothing of the events leading up to Ms. Donner's death. Which makes him a particularly limited witness. In the meantime, I would like to see where our victim lived."

"We're three days past the murder. If there's something in her trailer, it'll still be there tonight or tomorrow."

She stared me down, her glass eye and the one she was

born with competing for coldness. I tried to return the glare but eventually gave up. I let a four-letter word slip out. A woman passing by with two small children in tow shot me a look and hurried away.

Ms. Pentecost took a deep breath, her face arranging itself into an expression she usually reserved for our mutual friend Lieutenant Lazenby when he was being particularly obtuse.

"The more I know about our victim, the more useful my time with Mr. Kalishenko will be," she said. "Right now, I do not know Ms. Donner well enough to know what to ask."

"But *I* know her," I said, hearing the whine creeping into my voice and hating it. "Knew her. And I know him and . . ."

I hamstrung that sentence before it could run any further.

Of course we needed more on Ruby. Shoot—we needed more on everything and everybody. If you wanted to pin a modus operandi on Lillian Pentecost, that would be it. Understand the victim and maybe you can understand their actions. If you can do that, maybe you can figure out how they rubbed up against a killer.

Seems obvious, but during the course of a normal murder investigation—if you can ever call such a thing normal—the victim had a tendency to get lost in the shuffle. It all becomes about the killer: shoe prints and angles of entry and methods and motives. By the time you pin a name to whoever did the deed, the victim becomes a prop in the killer's story.

And if the victim's a woman, half the time she gets slapped with the label of tragic bystander. The other half of the time, she was asking for it. Three guesses which side Ruby would have landed on.

"If you would like to visit Mr. Kalishenko yourself, you're free to," my boss said. "You can take the truck and I'll find Sam Lee to escort me to Ruby's trailer."

I was about to take her up on the offer when I actually looked at her. She was leaning heavily on her cane. Finger-width loops of auburn hair had escaped her braids. Her suit hung limp and wrinkled—a semaphore flashing me the signal that its wearer was exhausted.

Of course she was. We'd been up and moving since dawn, had crossed four states and the nation's capital, spent a day at the circus, and all this on top of a long week of trial prep.

To make matters more fraught, Ms. P's multiple sclerosis and the August heat did not get along well together. While the woman herself much preferred summer to winter, too much time under the sun and her symptoms had a tendency to ratchet up a notch.

I didn't think it had happened yet, but she couldn't have been far from the edge.

Now that I saw the exhaustion, I couldn't unsee it. I didn't want to leave Val stranded in a cell for another day, but I wasn't about to abandon Ms. P in the middle of an investigation. Not when her tank was almost empty.

I realized my hands were clenched into fists. With conscious effort, I unfolded my fingers. My nails had carved half-moon grooves into my palm.

"Come on," I said. "Let's go take a look at Ruby's digs. Maybe we'll get lucky and there's a diary with an entry labeled 'Who I Expect to Be Murdered By.'"

After asking for directions from some of the circus crew, we found our way to Ruby's trailer. It wasn't far from Big Bob's and a short walk from a field shower tent that screamed U.S. Army surplus. I wondered idly if the new showers had hot water, which they certainly hadn't when I was there.

The trailer was sporting a shiny new padlock on the door, likely courtesy of the Stoppard Police Department. While I was never a Boy Scout, I still like to be prepared. I slipped out a pair of lockpicks and made short work of the Stanley. We stepped inside and shut the door behind us.

Ruby's trailer was half again as large as Big Bob's. And since

she was a full-time company member, she had it all to herself.
There was the regulation fold-down bed, fold-down table, footlocker with pop-up drawers, and a hanging rack for costume
pieces that Ruby hadn't wanted creased.

It was clear the place had been pawed through. Clothes
were scattered. Bedding was piled in a corner. Everything that
wasn't nailed down had been put back just a little off-center.

We spent half an hour going through the tiny space. Now
that I wasn't rushing, I could do the job right. But we didn't
catch a whiff of anything that could be called a clue. In fact,
there wasn't much that pointed to Ruby's personality other than
a few paperback mysteries and a couple of movie magazines.

There should have been more.

I knew that for a fact because I'd been in Ruby's trailer on a
number of occasions. The first time was the most memorable,
though I didn't like to dwell on it, since it was an incident where
I'd shown my ass in more ways than one.

I was young and not all that sharp when it came to romance.
I'd only been with the circus a few months and was still getting
my sea legs. I was also still getting used to being with a group of
people who actually cared about me. Who I didn't have to walk
on eggshells around for fear of getting a smack upside the head.

Ruby paid attention to me, asked me questions, smiled at
me, gave me looks that I read more into than she'd intended.
She was also beautiful, sophisticated—at least by my standards
at the time—and mature in a way that was alluring rather than
intimidating.

This was well before my time with the his-and-her contor-
tionists, so the majority of my hands-on sexual experience was
letting Bobby Newberry get a hand under my shirt while we
necked behind his father's cowshed. Most of what I knew about
women I'd learned from a stash of pulps I'd found while visiting
my aunt, who ran a roadhouse. Even as a teenager I found the
veracity of the stories in those magazines deeply suspect.

All that's to say that I was flying blind on hormones when I snuck into Ruby's trailer one night after last bell, folded down her bed, and slipped under the sheets to surprise her.

She was surprised, all right.

After I fumbled my way through my pitch, Ruby calmly and compassionately explained that while she was very flattered at my attention, she didn't go in for girls. And even if she did, she'd learned not to dip her wick in the company ink.

She helped me get myself together and didn't let me leave until I'd stopped crying. Then she walked me back to the trailer I was sharing with one of the spec girls.

Not a moment I'm very proud of. But I do remember that while I was lying in Ruby's bed, shivering with nerves, I'd seen a lot more personal items scattered about than were here now.

It was possible the cops had emptied the place, but I doubted it. If they thought they had Val nailed, there was no reason to scoop up Ruby's belongings. And if someone were packing things to give to next of kin, they would have taken everything, clothes included.

Somebody had done a sweep, and I had a feeling I knew who.

CHAPTER 9

Having struck out at Ruby's trailer, we weaved our way to the front entrance. It was pushing four o'clock and the after-work crowd was starting to show.

I walked in the direction of the truck, fingers crossed that the parking attendant had done his job and our bags had remained unmolested. I was so preoccupied that I almost walked right through the woman with the pamphlet.

"Have you let God into your heart?" she asked, shoving the folded paper right under my nose, like I was supposed to snort it instead of read it.

"Sorry," I said. "It's plenty crowded in there already."

She gave a few quick blinks, her smile quivering but not cracking. She was somewhere under forty with long, grayish hair framing a sunburned face that still managed to look wan. Someone had vandalized her visage with frown lines, and stolen her lips while they were at it. She was wearing a wash-faded, flower-print dress whose hem flirted with dragging in the dust.

If Ruby was a Technicolor girl, this woman was rooted firmly in black and white.

The hand holding the pamphlet advanced.

"Here," she said. "It has the times of our services. All are welcome. God has room for you even if you don't have room for him."

I relented and took the pamphlet out of her hand. The

front had a picture of Jesus as a shepherd surrounded by a flock of lambs. Above the image it read THE BLOOD OF THE LAMB CHURCH.

I recognized Sister Pamphlet as a certain breed of Bible-pounder I knew from my childhood. The kind that liked their women like they liked their cocktails: weak, if not entirely virginal.

"Have you been handing out pamphlets here since the circus opened?" Ms. P asked, managing to loom over the woman even though she only had her by a couple inches.

"Oh, um . . . well, yes," Sister Pamphlet stammered. "I mean, not me personally, but we've had someone here from opening until close."

"Did you have someone here Tuesday evening?"

Now I saw what my boss was getting at.

"I think Brother Carl was here that night."

"Was he here through closing?" I asked.

"I believe so."

The woman stood on her tiptoes and called out across the lot.

"Brother Carl!"

Near the far end of the line to get in, a head turned. She waved him over, and the man, Brother Carl, I presumed, headed our way.

He walked toward us with the assurance of Christ strolling across his apostles' fishing hole to deliver the good news. But Brother Carl looked less like Christ and more like John the Baptist, not long out of the wilderness and squeezed into a powder-blue suit. Pushing six feet, he had a brawler's chest and shoulders. His crew cut was more gray than black and he had a five-o'clock shadow that had arrived an hour early. The sun winked off his cross-shaped tiepin.

"Yes, Sister Evelyn?" he said in a voice that was surprisingly more sotto voce than forte.

"This lady was asking whether we had someone here Tuesday night. You were here, weren't you?"

Instead of turning his head, he swiveled his entire body to face my boss, like he only had one pivot point and it operated from the waist.

"I was here, Mrs. . . ."

"Pentecost. Ms. Lillian Pentecost."

No glimmer of recognition from the name. I wondered if the Blood of the Lamb Church had something against newspapers.

"Carl Engle," he said, sticking out his paw to shake. "I'm the pastor at Blood of the Lamb."

We did a round of handshakes. It was only when Ms. P told him we'd been "employed by Mr. Halloway to look into the unfortunate death of Ruby Donner" that anything passing for recognition crossed his face.

"Bert said something about the circus bringing in a detective. I didn't think . . ."

I didn't know who Bert was, but I knew that sentence ended with "the detective would be a woman."

My boss jumped into the pause. She never passed up the opportunity to fling questions.

"Have you been the pastor at Blood of the Lamb for very long?"

"Built the meetinghouse with my own hands in 1921," Brother Carl said with a proud smile.

"It's quite a step from felling trees to preaching sermons," Ms. P said. "Why found your church here and not closer to the Great North Woods?"

Carl looked at Evelyn, who shrugged and shook her head. No, she hadn't been telling tales out of school.

"The accent, Mr. Engle," my boss explained. "Twenty-five years, but it still has echoes of Maine. The style and arrangement of scars on your hands speak to your history with handsaws. And your back—it's a common injury in the logging industry. From the repetitive movements of sawing and lifting logs."

Brother Carl clapped and beamed. "That's remarkable!"

Ms. Pentecost didn't pull these kinds of Sherlock Holmes shenanigans often, but when she did, she went all out. According to her if witnesses thought you saw everything, they were less likely to try to pass you the casual lie.

Now that Carl and Evelyn were dutifully impressed, she started in on the real questions.

"Did you know Ruby Donner?" she asked.

"Oh, yes," the pastor said. "Her parents were members of our congregation."

"Ruby as well?"

He and Sister Evelyn passed each other a look.

"She was . . . a bit lost," Evelyn said. "Even before she left."

"Lost?"

"To the Devil," Evelyn said, as if that should be perfectly obvious.

Something flared up in my boss's "very good eye." Her lips twisted into a grim smile. She quickly clamped it down.

"She must have been quite the sinner," she said, "to have been considered lost so young."

To give the pastor credit, he saw the pit Evelyn had led him toward and executed a graceful leap.

"There is no one lost who cannot be saved," he declared. "Neither death, nor life, nor angels, nor principalities, nor the present, nor the future, nor anything else in all creation will be able to separate us from the love of God."

The verse rolled out of him like a wave, and everyone it washed over turned a head his way. Say what you will about preachers, they perform for a living and the best of them know it.

"Romans 8:38," Ms. P said. I didn't have a King James on me, but from Brother Carl's face, I knew she'd hit the mark.

"Well, that's why we're here," he said. "To reach out to the lost. Or to trip up those who are walking the path away from God."

Ms. P looked back at the stream of people heading in: happy families, smiling couples holding hands, children surging ahead, drawn by the music and the smell of spun sugar.

"Is the circus so very evil?"

"Oh, not truly evil," he said. "It's more a metaphor. A microcosm of the world, which is designed to seduce through the senses. To distract you. To wrap you up in lights and sounds and tastes. A world dedicated to the pleasures of the flesh—flesh that will go the way of all earthly things. To ashes and dust."

Metaphor? Microcosm? I did a quick reevaluation of the preacher. He might have spent some time in the wilderness, but he had clearly stumbled on a dictionary while he was out there.

I also managed to catch a look on Sister Evelyn's face—one that suggested she had a very different answer to the "Is the circus evil" question and it included words like "Yes" and "Very."

"Did you see Ms. Donner before her death?" Ms. P asked.

He shook his head. "I'm afraid I did not."

"Were you here until closing Tuesday evening?"

"Half an hour or more past it," he said. "I realize few people leaving a circus are receptive to the word of God. But if I can reach just one person, it's worth my time."

"And did you see anything out of the ordinary? Anyone of note going in or coming out?"

Any blood-covered so-and-sos running away from the scene, she meant.

Brother Carl shook his head. "I'm afraid not. It was dark by then. And when I'm spreading the gospel I try to focus on the person I'm speaking with."

"Is there anyone in town that Ms. Donner might have—"

A car horn cut her off. An egg-shaped head with a forgettable face popped out of the window of a battered sedan. It was holding up the line of cars and the attendant was giving it the stink eye.

"Carl! It's getting past four. We need to shake a leg if we want to make all our stops before dark."

Carl waved at him.

"I'll be right there, Bert!"

He turned back to us.

"I'm sorry, but I have to take my leave," he said in a tone that suggested his sorrow at departing was limited. "On Fridays I minister to our sick and elderly parishioners in their homes."

"We also deliver food and clothing around the county," Sister Evelyn chimed in. "Rationing was tough on a lot of people. They're still struggling."

I looked at the sedan again and saw that its backseat was packed to the roof with cardboard boxes. A chorus of car horns was beginning to sound from the line of impatient circus-goers.

"I'll leave you to your work," Ms. Pentecost told the pastor. "But I would like to find time to talk further about Ms. Donner. I would dearly like to know more about her life before she left Stoppard."

"I'm at the meetinghouse from dawn to dusk on Sundays. And we have two sermons," Brother Carl said, nodding at the pamphlet in my hand. "Ten a.m. and six p.m. You're welcome at either."

"Thank you, Mr. Engle," Ms. P said. "Though I feel our work in Stoppard may keep us busy."

"There's always time for God, Ms. Pentecost."

With that, he did a full-body swivel and strolled to the waiting sedan. Sister Evelyn gave a curt goodbye and hurried off, pamphlet leading the way.

As we walked back to the truck, I turned to my boss.

"That was a nice trick with the preacher. Pegging him for a lumberjack," I said. "And knowing the Bible verse. Good thing the Devil can cite scripture, too."

"My father read out loud from the Bible every evening after supper. That was one of his favorite verses."

"Dad was a fan of the Good Book?"

"I should think so," she said, making her way carefully across the uneven ruts of the field turned parking lot. "He was a minister."

It took ten minutes to get the truck out of the quickly filling lot and half a minute to swing onto the highway and then in to the gravel drive that led to the Donner house. I spent all ten and a half minutes peppering Ms. Pentecost with questions, but to no avail. I couldn't even pry loose what denomination her pops had been.

Biographical details of Ms. Pentecost's life before she got so famous *The New York Times* took notice were thin on the ground. Nearly four years working together and I knew next to nothing.

As we were heading down the gravel drive, an ambulance was heading up. We came close to scraping doors as we edged by it on the narrow lane. It didn't seem to be in a hurry, so I assumed nobody was bleeding out in the back.

The Donner place looked like a hundred others that we'd passed on the drive down from Fredericksburg: a two-story farmhouse in fading whitewash, with a screened-in porch and a sizable barn off to one side. From the weeds growing up around the barn's padlocked doors, I was guessing it was long out of use.

I parked the circus truck beside an equally junky pickup of indeterminate color. Getting out, I slammed the door so I could give this uncle of Ruby's some warning. A few moments later the front door opened and a scarecrow tottered out onto the porch: tall, thin, overalls over a checkered shirt, a bushel of hair that could have been straw if it came in that shade of gray, and a beard that could have provided a second home to passing spar-rows. His wire-rimmed cheaters were set crooked on a round face with lines so deep you could get lost in them.

"Oh, I'm sorry," the scarecrow said, swinging open the screen door. "Heard a car and thought you were the men com-ing back. The orderlies? . . . Attendants? . . . Sorry, I don't know what to call them. Don't know why I'm apologizing, either."

He teetered down the porch steps on stiff, stiltish legs.

"I'm a little . . . well . . . drunk, to be honest. I'm sorry. There I go apologizing again. Can I help you?"

"I believe arrangements have been made for us to board here," my boss said.

"Right, right—the detectives. Sorry. I'm Pat Donner. But you can call me 'Doc.' Everyone else does."

"Lillian Pentecost. This is my associate, Will Parker."

He smiled when she said my name, and any resemblance to a scarecrow was lost. Nobody who had a smile that bright was going to frighten anyone. Not even crows.

"You knew my niece, didn't you?"

"I did know her. Once upon a time."

"Me, too," he said, his smile dying a quick death. "Once upon a time . . ."

He gave his head a brisk shake and turned back to the house.

"Might as well come on in and see her," he said. "They just dropped her off."

CHAPTER *10*

He led us inside, through a small kitchen and down a dim, narrow hallway toward the back of the house. Just dropped her off? I thought Doc's senses might have been past their expiration date.

Then he opened a door at the end of the hall.

As promised, there was Ruby. Lying on a bed barely big enough to fit her, in a room barely big enough to fit the bed and a nightstand barely big enough to hold a paperback. A single, unshaded electric bulb burned bright in the center of the ceiling, illuminating the pale rose-print wallpaper, the crisp white sheets, and the corpse at their center. She was dressed in a long-sleeved blue gingham dress that went down to her ankles so only her hands and feet and face showed. A small window to the left of the bed had been cracked open. The lace curtains, yellowed with age, fluttered in the breeze.

The three of us squeezed into a semicircle at the foot of the bed and looked down.

There were spots of red peeking out from underneath her, and at first I thought she might somehow still be bleeding. Then I peered close and saw that the red came from the two dozen rubber water bottles that had been placed between the body and the sheets.

"Those are filled with ice," Doc stammered. "She hasn't

been . . . um . . . embalmed. So with the heat . . . Anyway, they figure with the ice she should . . . um . . ."

The word he was stretching for was "keep." I couldn't bring myself to hand it to him.

I looked away. There was a thigh-high bookshelf in the corner to the left of the door. Glancing at the spines, I saw *The Velveteen Rabbit, Mary Poppins, Murder on the Orient Express, Gentlemen Prefer Blondes,* and a massive tome called *The Language of Flowers* that I pegged for poetry.

I realized we were standing in what used to be Ruby's bedroom. Her shelves still held what you'd expect from a girl-turned-young-woman wishing for a wider, lusher world.

My mind must have drifted along with my gaze, because when I came back Doc was mid-monologue.

"—wanted the viewing at Demblin's. That's the funeral home," he was saying. "Dan Demblin himself stopped by. Said they'd treat her right. That I shouldn't have to be bothered with the details. I told him no thank you. I just . . . She's the only family I have left. I wanted to help put her in the ground myself. And I didn't want her carved up any more than she already had been."

"Mr. Halloway said the funeral is tomorrow?" Ms. P said, making it half statement, half question.

"Mr. . . . ? Oh, right. The little fella. Yeah, he said he'd spring for a coffin. Get the pallbearers together and all. We have a family plot out back. Her parents are there. And our folks and um . . ."

He trailed off. In the quiet, we could make out the music and shouts and laughter of the circus drifting from the adjacent field.

Unable to stand the silence, I shattered it.

"No way in hell that's her own dress."

Doc chuckled. "No. The hospital got it from a donation pile. Said that what she was wearing was evidence."

"She'd have hated it," I said.

"Mr. Halloway. Bob. He said he'd stop by tonight with some of her clothes. Something she can be buried in. When he does, it might be more proper if . . . um . . . being her friend. And a woman . . . If you wouldn't mind . . ."

"Sure," I said, connecting the dots on his line of thought. "I'll dress her."

I said it with a smile, but something inside me lurched. Stomach or heart, I couldn't tell. Everything seemed a little unreal. Disconnected.

Ms. P turned to Doc.

"Mr. Donner? Would you mind giving us some time alone?"

"Sure," he said, looking puzzled.

"I'd like to examine the body," she explained.

And just like that, the clockwork of the world started up again. This was a murder. We had a job to do.

Thankfully, Doc seemed to get it, too.

"Right," he said. "I'll get your bags upstairs and change the sheets on your beds. Take your time."

Then he left us to our business.

We tried to shimmy the dress off her, but Ruby wasn't a slight woman and they call it dead weight for a reason. Eventually I gave up and went at the ugly blue thing with my switch-blade. I dropped the remains on the floor.

If you've never seen a body post-autopsy, try and keep it that way. A Y-incision is an awful thing. They aren't neat when they stitch them back up, either, figuring nobody will see it but the mortician. And unlucky detectives.

This one was made even worse because it cut through two dozen of Ruby's tattoos. A mermaid was separated from her tail, an eagle from a wing, a sailing ship from its mast. All sewn back a little off-center. Some of the smaller tattoos had been obliterated entirely.

I'd seen dead bodies with tattoos before, but most of those had been one-offs on chests or arms, and most on men who had a layer of body hair. With no blood pumping through it, Ruby's flesh had gone the sickly pale of the dead. Without that rosy background glow, the ink of her tattoos stood out brilliantly, floating on top of her skin like leaves on a pond.

At least they hadn't bothered opening her skull. For once I was grateful for a medical examiner's laziness.

We rolled her over, scattering red rubber bags of ice onto the floor.

There was the stab wound—center left and high on her back. A dainty cut compared to the Y-incision. Ms. P bent over the body, her nose practically brushing against a leaping tiger that stretched the length of Ruby's shoulder blade.

"Knife," she said. I passed her the switchblade.

I cringed as she carefully slid the knife into the wound, following the track of the blade that killed Ruby.

"What do you see?" she said.

"Definitely not thrown. That marking there is from the hilt. A thrown blade isn't going that deep, no matter how good an arm you have."

I looked at the angle of the switchblade.

"Down and from the right," I added. "So our killer was probably right-handed. And while he didn't have to be tall, he definitely wasn't short."

I reached out and brushed my fingers across the edge of the wound.

"Not a weakling, either," I added. "Through the back ribs, all the way to the hilt. That takes force. I miss anything?"

Ms. Pentecost shook her head.

"Nothing I can see," she said, plucking out the switchblade and handing it back. I thought about throwing it on the nearest junk pile, then thought better. I retrieved a scrap of dress and wiped the blade down.

We spent another half hour searching the body for other marks, which was a difficult proposition considering the amount of ink needled into her skin. Other than the razor nicks you'd expect to find on a woman who spent her working hours in a bathing suit, we discovered nothing of note.

Ms. P took the opportunity to examine Ruby's tattoos.

"Many seem to have faded to a consistent degree," she said, more to herself than to me. "I assume those were the ones she accumulated during that first year. The others are newer, brighter. They also exhibit better craftsmanship."

"Yeah, once she started running out of canvas, Ruby got pickier. She wanted pieces you couldn't find on just any old sailor strolling the waterfront."

The pièce de résistance was the serpent wrapped around the full length of her left leg. It continued up her hip, then curled onto her pelvis, traveling so far that her belly button became the snake's eye.

That one, I knew, had taken multiple sessions with a tattooer in Brooklyn. It was so big that the artist had managed to get in individual scales, using different shades of green to give the impression the snake's skin was shimmering.

She'd had her belly button pierced and wore a tiny faux-diamond stud. In the right light—and she was a master of finding the right light—the snake seemed to wink at you.

Someone had taken the stud out, and the snake looked as dead and lifeless as its mistress.

But the one that really caught Ms. Pentecost's attention was over Ruby's left breast—a rose about the size of my palm. It was striking because it wasn't. The line work was shaky, the colors dark and muddy. If we weren't up close and personal, I don't even know I'd have recognized it as a rose.

"There's nothing else on her body like it," my boss noted. "I wonder what she had covered up."

"You're sure it's a cover-up?" I asked. "Could be just a bad job on the artist's part."

She shook her head.

"Look how it overlaps its neighbors slightly here and here. It was done later. Also, this rose is so . . . prosaic."

I had to agree. That space over her heart was prime real estate—why waste it?

So what had the rose replaced?

Ms. P ran her fingers over the bloom, like she could rub it away to see what was underneath.

"She had that when I met her," I said. "I remember clocking it when we were first introduced. But this was a woman with a snake wrapping up her leg. A shoddy rose wasn't high on the list of curiosities. You think it could be relevant?"

"Everything is relevant," Ms. P reminded me, and not for the first time. "If it was important to our victim, it's important to us."

She propped herself on the windowsill and pondered.

"Some of the older members of the circus might know," she said. "However, they might not. And she is scheduled to be buried tomorrow. . . ."

She frowned down at the body.

"During the Sendak case, I read about a way to recover tattoos obliterated by fire. It's possible this technique could be used here. I would need to put in a call to Hiram," she said, referring to our longtime friend at the coroner's office in New York City. "He might have to talk me through some steps. However, I'm afraid it would certainly involve excising that area of her skin."

She turned and gave me her best sympathetic look.

"I know this might seem distasteful, since she was your friend, so I understand if you want to absent yourself from the task. I believe, with some guidance from Hiram, I could do the excision myself. As for the chemicals we'd need, they might not be readily available locally. Perhaps in Richmond. We'd have to send someone to—"

She noticed my flapping hand and put the brakes on.

"Yes?"

"I realize you're excited to try out a new science project," I said. "But maybe we should go an easier route first. One that doesn't involve carving up our victim's body."

"Do you have a suggestion?"

I did.

CHAPTER 11

I joined the line of people heading into the side tent. It was a hair past midnight and the lights of the circus had been snuffed. All except for the golden glow that escaped through the tent flap each time a person handed over their buck to the doorman.

A Morse code come-on.

No talker for this show. No need for it. People who were interested had learned about it in careful whispers or from fly-ers posted in the right bars and gentlemen's clubs. There were a few women in the line but the vast majority were men. All of them were white. But that was true of most stops below the Mason-Dixon, and half the ones above it.

I was surprised the late show was still on, what with the murder and all. Not to mention the Blood of the Lamb folks looking to put the kibosh on sin.

While the circus proper could be brushed off as good clean fun, there wasn't much clean about the Midnight Circus. Which is why, despite it being a hush-hush performance, the line to get in was so long.

The doorman didn't see me until I was right on top of him. Pushing fifty, Paulie still had the energy of a twelve-year old—the sense of humor as well—all packaged in the body of an Irish boxer. He was dressed down in a white undershirt, suspenders, and a battered porkpie, his face still obscured by greasepaint.

Paulie had explained the philosophy of clown makeup to me once. How the goal was to keep the makeup neutral and let your own expression drive how the audience sees you. In repose, Paulie's face was naturally dour. That was why the audience always referred to him as "the sad one."

It also meant that when he smiled, it wasn't just an expression. It was an event.

"Well, well, well! If it isn't Will 'Sparkleshorts' Parker," he said, beaming.

"You're never gonna let me live that down, are you, Paulie?"

"Hey—you're the one who wore the shorts."

"Once," I hissed. "One goddamn show and only because Frieda spent two weeks teaching me to shimmy and I didn't want to let her down."

"You definitely didn't let Frieda down," he said. "Your skirt, your suspenders, and at least one tassel—but not Frieda."

"Here." I passed him a dollar. "Will this shut you up?"

"No," he said, grinning beneath his makeup. "But it buys you a temporary reprieve."

He opened the tent flap and I slipped through. The air inside was thick, but the worst of the heat was escaping out the open vents at the tent's apex. The usual three-quarters seating had been rearranged into a tight in-the-round. Multicolored lights were strung around the full circumference of the tent, and a single spot illuminated the center of the circle. The floor had been covered with layers of Egyptian rugs that were probably stitched in Dayton.

The intended effect was exotic, and it hit the mark if you considered West Virginia to be world travel.

I claimed an aisle seat on the opposite side of the tent, right by the performers' entrance. One of the spec girls—she was maybe eighteen, so after my time—came in and played candy butcher. I traded another buck for one of the hand-wrapped candy bars.

"Frieda on tonight?" I asked.

"Yeah. She's got a couple numbers tonight," the girl replied in an accent imported from Jersey. She was dressed in a version of the costume she'd wear for the big-top spectacles. Except this version started lower and ended higher.

"Could you tell her Will wants a word when she's got a second?"

The girl frowned, probably making me for an admirer.

"I'm a friend," I said, giving up a third dollar, which she made disappear down her barely contained cleavage.

"Whatever you say."

She did another round of the crowd and then went back through the flap beside me. I carefully unwrapped the candy bar to reveal the reason it was so pricey—the photo pressed between the chocolate and the foil.

It was a wallet-size snap of Lightning Lucy, who I almost didn't recognize sans light bulbs. Actually, she was sans everything but a smile.

I tucked the photo in a pocket and devoured the chocolate. I hadn't eaten since lunch and wondered if there was still any grub at the cookhouse. I could subsist on candy, but I didn't think Ms. Pentecost could.

After we had finished with Ruby's body, we had replaced the bags of ice and covered her with a sheet. Then we went to find Doc, who was making up our rooms upstairs. Ms. Pentecost's was a sunlit bedroom near the front of the house. It had a queen-size bed, a dresser, and a writing desk, and smelled of mothballs. Ruby's parents' room.

Our luggage was stacked in a corner. I helped Ms. P get her bag on the bed, then took my pair of overstuffed suitcases and followed Doc to a bedroom in the back. This one wasn't quite as small as Ruby's, but it wasn't much bigger. It had a narrow slat of a bed, a battered footlocker that served as a dresser, and a nightstand with a hurricane lamp. It smelled like whiskey sweat and wood cleaner.

"I never got around to getting electric in this room," Doc explained. "It's mine, by the way. I'll be bunking on the settee in the drawing room."

"I hate to put you out," I said. "I can take the settee."

"Oh, no, no. You should have your own room. Besides, I get home late from work and I don't want to wake you."

I thought about arguing, but decided against it. I'd bedded down in worse.

"Where do you work?" I asked.

"The Majestic movie theater," he said, managing a smile. "Owner, operator, and sole employee."

I don't know what I was expecting, but it wasn't that.

"I saw it on the way in. You've got *Cat People* showing?"

His smile soured. "Ruby sent me a postcard saying she'd seen it and liked it. She was always doing that. Sending me postcards and telling me what movies I should get. I got 'em all bundled up somewhere. The postcards."

He laughed. Or I assumed that brittle sound was a laugh.

"It's kind of funny. I used to be the one mailing her postcards. From when I was traveling. Wanted to give her an idea of what the world was like outside Stoppard. Abigail—that's Ruby's mom—she wrote me and told me to stop. Said it would give Ruby ideas."

He sniffed and shuffled his feet.

"Anyway, I . . . um . . . I got *Cat People* in just for her. Thought it would be fun to watch it together."

I couldn't think of anything to say to that, which was just as well. A minute later, he excused himself. He had to go into town to open up the Majestic.

"I'll be back around midnight or so," he said. "Providing anyone comes to the evening show."

I spent fifteen minutes unpacking, hanging what I could in the narrow closet and draping the rest over the footlocker. A few specialty items I tucked under the mattress.

When I was done, I went to check on Ms. Pentecost and found her sprawled out on the bed, fast asleep. She'd managed to get her jacket and shoes off, but that was all. She'd been running hot and hard for days, and I wasn't about to wake her.

I eased her door shut and proceeded to give myself a thorough tour of the house. I figured Doc wouldn't mind. You don't invite a pair of detectives to bunk with you unless you're ready to put up with a little snooping.

Everything was neater than I expected. Upholstery was worn thin and all the carpets were sun-faded, but the surfaces were dust-free and all the loose sundries were tucked away. Even the basement—packed with shelves of canned goods and preserves where it wasn't taken up with old farm equipment—was neatly sorted.

I found a photo album lying out on the kitchen table and sat down and began flipping through.

In the early pages, I discovered crumbling daguerreotypes depicting generations of farmers. Following those were a dozen pages dedicated to a pair of boys, one a couple years older than the other. Both kept their baby faces well into their teens. The older of the two eventually appeared in a cap and gown.

The younger one disappeared for a bit then turned up leaning against the side of an ambulance. Behind him was a desolate landscape of churned-up mud and blighted forest. Somewhere along the line, he'd traded in the baby face for a thousand-yard stare.

I peered at the faded script at the bottom.

PATRICK DONNER.
VERDUN, 1916.

My history of the Great War was rusty, but I knew Verdun was the site of a long, bloody slog. So Doc had been a military man, maybe an ambulance driver. And if he was overseas that early it meant he'd probably volunteered for it.

After that came more pictures of the older brother, Charlie, in the arms of his wife, Abigail. The album documented courtship through marriage and beyond. I could see Ruby in the man's eyes and the woman's chin.

Eventually a little girl appeared with the couple: long, dark hair, darker eyes, and a toothy grin. In every picture she was in motion—running, jumping, straining against her mother's clutching hand. In one she and a cluster of other little girls were sprinting through a field, flowers woven into their hair. Ruby was little more than a blur.

Then puberty hit and the blur settled. She grew, rounded, started to resemble the woman I'd known. Her smile dimmed. Her eyes never quite met the camera. They were always looking off to the side. Searching for an exit.

Or maybe I was imagining things.

I went back up to my room and laid down to think. I was beat, but I figured I had exactly zero chance of nodding off. How could I sleep in this dark, musty room with only old floorboards and empty air separating me from Ruby's body?

When I woke, it was dark. So much for my oddsmaking.

I opened the curtains and saw the lights of the circus across the field and beyond the line of trees. The moonlight and my watch told me it was going on eleven o'clock.

I checked in on Ms. Pentecost and found her still snoring. At some point she'd regained consciousness long enough to strip off the rest of her suit. Assured that she was safe and sound, I went to the bathroom, splashed water on my face, then went downstairs and checked the fridge, hoping for sandwich fixings.

Nothing but stale cheese, moldy bread, and enough beer bottles to qualify as concerning. Out the kitchen window, I saw the electric eye of the Ferris wheel blink once, then go dark.

If I couldn't find grub, at least I could dig up some answers.

And that brings me to the side tent waiting for things to kick off and wishing I'd picked a different outfit. I'd settled on a pair of snug, high-waisted pants and a short-sleeved cotton blouse, both of which I'd chosen for their color, mint green and cream respectively. I had on eye shadow in the same shade as the pants and I'd applied it liberally.

Frieda always said I looked good in green.

I wasn't looking to rekindle anything with my contortionist more-than-friend. I'd given Ms. P the straight truth. We were never an official item. But it never hurt to show a girl what she was missing.

However, the cotton blouse was sprouting wrinkles, the pants were apparently designed to emphasize sweat stains as well as my hips, and the humidity had gone to work on my hair.

I was trying to pat and smooth when the lights hanging around the walls of the tent blinked out and Paulie tumbled into the spotlight.

"Good evening, gentlemen and ladies, ladies and gentlemen, ladies and ladies and ladies . . . Really, just the ladies. You fellas can fend for yourselves."

He spoke in a hyped-up vaudeville patois. Or at least vaudeville as imagined by Hollywood, with a heavy dose of Groucho Marx. The audience gobbled it up like peanut pie.

"My lovelies! Welcome to the late show. The under-the-covers, whisper-it-to-your-friends show. The don't-tell-the-missus show. Welcome to the mildly dark, slightly sweaty underbelly that is the Midnight Circus!"

The crowd cheered.

"We're a little sexy, a little silly, a little sinful."

A shrill voice cried out from one of the front-row seats. "Sinful!?"

All eyes turned as Frieda strode into the ring. She was done up as a Puritan housewife—long sleeves, long skirt, and her hair hidden under an oversize bonnet.

"Did you say sin?" she asked in a clutch-my-pearls quiver.

"Just a little sin," Paulie assured her.

"A little?"

The clown held his fingers an inch or so apart, squinted, then widened the gap.

"That's far too much sin!" Puritan Frieda gasped.

"I've never had that complaint before, but I'll take it," Paulie said. The crowd hooted. Apparently there were no Blood of the Lamb members present, or if there were, they weren't advertising.

"Madam, this is a public performance," the clown said. "Would you please take your seat and be quiet?"

"Matthew 5:15 says you should not hide your light under a bushel."

"A light under your bush, you say?"

With that, Paulie dove under her long skirts, sending the audience into roars of laughter.

"Why I never!" Frieda shrieked.

Popping his head out between her legs, Paulie served up the punch line: "Madam, I think that might be your problem."

From there, the bit devolved into straight-up burlesque, with Puritan Frieda accidentally losing parts of her outfit until she was stripped down to a skimpy two-piece. With a snap and a flick, two pieces became one and a pair of tassels. She gave them a quick twirl. The audience applauded vigorously—me along with them—as she skipped offstage.

That must have been the new act she'd been referring to. Not bad, I thought, though nothing I hadn't seen in a dozen other variations.

After that, the girl I'd bought the candy bar from came out accompanied by the Sideshow Alley talker, who was armed with a violin. He played a hectic jig while she executed a tumbling routine, complete with backflips and handstands designed to showcase more than her acrobatics.

They were followed by a slender number with long, dark hair in a get-up that paired a violently blue tuxedo top with black fishnets and thigh-high boots. Her face paired seawater-green eyes that said "come hither" with a mean, gap-toothed grin that said "but not too close."

It was only when she introduced herself as the Amazing Annabelle that I recognized her as the assistant I'd seen cleaning up with Mysterio.

She did a series of increasingly risqué magic tricks. For example, reaching into the collar of a delightfully embarrassed man in the front and pulling out a string of colorful handkerchiefs, to the last of which was tied a pair of equally colorful silk underwear.

"Most men go for basic white, but I say they're cowards," she said while perched on his knee. "I applaud you, sir!"

Hidden in the silliness was some solid sleight of hand. I wondered how much of it she'd learned from Mysterio. He was famously stingy with his act, rarely giving assistants a peek at the technique behind the tricks.

She was followed by Eddie, who performed a modified version of his blockhead routine. He had the audience grimacing as he hefted ten-pound weights that he hung from progressively more sensitive places.

After that, Frieda returned. She'd changed into her electric-blue singlet and was accompanied by Carlotta, the Mistress of Cats.

Carlotta was squeezed into a leopard-print leotard that showed off the kind of physique you get from spending your days wrestling three-hundred-pound tigers. Her kittens weren't in attendance, but she'd brought her whip. Each time she cracked it, Frieda twisted her body into another impossible position.

Carlotta pretended to be displeased with Frieda's performance, picked her up, and began swinging, spinning, and draping Frieda around her body like she weighed nothing. All while the violinist played a breathless version of a Kay Kyser number.

I kept one eye on them and one on the audience, wondering how this act would fly, especially in a rural Virginia crowd. Carlotta was from somewhere in South America—I want to say Brazil—but anyone who didn't know better would mistake her for Negro.

Her cracking a whip on blond-haired, blue-eyed Frieda contained some real specific undertones. But the audience either didn't notice or didn't care, because the act ended in applause instead of a riot.

As the pair exited, Frieda paused by my seat.

"You needed to chat?"

"Did you clean out Ruby's trailer?"

Her eyes slid away.

"Come on," I said. "If my boss and I are going to spring Val, we need the lot."

I could see her thinking about it.

"Frieda—it's me. I'm not gonna air any dirty laundry if I don't need to."

Just then Paulie came back out with Lightning Lucy in tow and Frieda used the applause to slip off.

I thought about what I would do if she didn't come through. I could go to Big Bob and use him to pry the goods out of her. I hated to do that, though. First of all, tattling to the boss was bad form. Second, it meant admitting that Frieda didn't trust me.

In the ring, Paulie and Lucy were playing at being duelists, the goal being not to run the other person through but to swallow increasingly lengthy, nasty-looking swords.

During Lucy's turn, some wit in the back row volunteered an alternative to her blade.

"If she's ever looking for a soggy butter knife, you'll be the first person she calls," Paulie cracked back.

There was a tap on my shoulder—Frieda. While the heckler blushed and the audience roared, she led me out of my seat and through the flap. Outside, the other performers were changing into new outfits for the showstopper. The Amazing Annabelle gave me a decidedly unfriendly look. I wondered what I'd done to piss her off.

Once we were out of earshot, Frieda handed me a canvas laundry bag. I peeked inside.

"This is everything?" I asked.

Frieda nodded. "Everything we took."

"We?"

"Maeve helped."

The old fortune-teller had sat two feet from me without tipping me the wink. That was in addition to dropping another lie, though I had yet to discover its particulars.

I was starting to feel insulted.

"You meant what you said?" Frieda asked. "That you won't let any of this out if . . . if you don't have to?"

"Of course," I told her. "Ruby was my friend, too."

She didn't look entirely convinced. I was thinking up something to reassure her when the sound of applause rolled out of the tent. Without even saying goodbye, Frieda darted inside along with the rest of the performers.

My desire to see the final number was trumped by my curiosity about what was in the bag. I reached in and rummaged. I was wondering what Frieda had been so anxious about when my fingers closed on something small tucked at the bottom.

I pulled it out, peered close, and everything I thought I knew about Ruby went out the window.

CHAPTER 12

The cars in the driveway of the Donner farmhouse had bred while I was gone. Along with the circus junker and the other pickup I took to be Doc's, a Stoppard police car had been added to the mix.

Not a welcome sight, considering what was inside the laundry bag I had slung over my shoulder. Not to mention the surprise I'd found hiding in the bottom, which was now tucked in my pocket.

I was looking for a place to stash it when I noticed a splash of light from the barn. The padlock had been undone and the big double doors were cracked open. As I got closer I heard a litany of muttered curses and clanging.

I slipped through the doors to find a circle of hurricane lamps illuminating a motorcycle and a man. The two were in a wrestling match and the bike appeared to be winning.

I knew a little about motorcycles and was pretty sure it was a Harley-Davidson WLA. Army-issue, if the paint job was any indication. Other than a few parts scattered about, it looked in good shape.

Beyond the pool of light, I could make out piles of farm equipment—tillers and plows and less identifiable machinery—all in various stages of rust. A ladder led up to a hayloft, whose neatness I couldn't judge, as it was lost in darkness.

I couldn't judge much about the man, either.

He was on his back, head and arms hidden beneath the belly of the bike. Barefoot and bare-chested, he wore only a pair of grease-stained khaki trousers that also looked Army-issue. The inside of the barn was a sauna. The fire from the lamps flickered off the rivulets of sweat crisscrossing their way down a torso Charles Atlas would have signed off on.

A particularly creative string of profanity was punctuated by a wrench skittering across the wooden planks of the floor. The mechanic stretched out his left arm, searching blindly for the escaped tool.

"Hey, you need a hand?" I asked, nudging the wrench toward his grasping fingers with the toe of my shoe.

Beneath the bike, the mechanic suggested I do something physically uncomfortable.

"I saw a guy do that trick once, but he was double-jointed and pretty drunk," I said, not sure what I'd done to warrant such ire. "If you don't need a hand, just say so."

He slid out from beneath the motorcycle, and I caught up quick. Like the motorcycle, he was missing some parts. Specifically, his right arm from just above the elbow.

Need a hand? Jesus Christ, Will.

He was winding up another string of curses, but bit it off when he saw me. I'd like to think he was struck dumb by my beauty. But after an hour in a crowded tent, my blouse was a dishrag, my hair a mop, and the little makeup I had on a smeary memory.

I felt like an asshole and didn't look much better.

He, on the other hand, had a square jaw and smooth brow that paired nicely with the torso. The look was rounded off by a shock of sandy-brown hair, matching eyes, and the kind of lips you'd call bee-stung if you found them on a woman.

"I'm sorry," I said. "I didn't mean . . . um . . . About the arm . . . I didn't know you . . ." Eventually I had the good sense to put that sentence out of its misery.

"No, it's . . . um . . . it's okay," he said. "Sorry for the language."

"That's all right," I replied. "I've heard worse on a two-stop subway ride in New York."

That sparked some look of recognition.

"Right. The detectives."

"Will Parker." I stepped forward and held out my hand. I quickly realized I was holding out my right hand, tried to swap mid-stride, forgot I was holding the laundry bag, and dropped it on the floor. A half-dozen wallet-size snaps spilled out. All of them were of Ruby wearing nothing but a snake and a smile.

The mechanic stared down at them, something close to horror flickering over his face. Nudity, it seemed, offended his sensibilities.

I bent down and scooped them back in as quickly as I could. Then in traditional show-must-go-on fashion, I held out my left.

"Will Parker," I repeated, now blushing wildly.

He held up his hand, palm out, to show it was covered in grease.

"Joe Engle."

"Any relation to Carl?" I asked.

That drew another look—surprise with a dash of something more complicated.

"My father," he said.

I couldn't conjure a follow-up and neither could he, apparently, so we counted out five seconds of awkward silence.

I took the time to better categorize his features: six feet, 170 pounds, nose broken at least once, a spattering of pockmarks scattered across the right side of his face and neck. The place where his right arm stopped was a web of nasty-looking scars.

Whatever had taken his limb, it hadn't been a clean cut.

I realized I was staring and moved my eyes, but they landed on his chest, which hadn't gotten any less appealing. And while you may judge my inner monologue for playing in the shallow end of the pool, you hadn't gone through my recent drought and he really was very pretty.

He finally took the leap and broke the silence.

"I don't want to be rude, but I pay Doc five bucks a month to use his barn so I can have the room and the privacy. So . . . uh . . . do you mind?"

That *was* a little rude whether he wanted it to be or not, but I didn't call him on it.

Instead, I slapped on a smile.

"Sorry," I said. "I'll leave you to your surgery. Nice bike, by the way."

He grunted and nodded, but nothing that could get mistaken for a grin. Then he picked up the wrench and slid back under the bike, trusting I could find my way out.

Slinging the laundry bag and my bruised ego over my shoulder, I did just that.

I was stepping up onto the porch when I realized there was still a Stoppard police car in the drive and I'd never stashed the laundry bag. I was looking around for a place to hide it when I heard a sound so surprising I almost dropped it again.

It was Lillian Pentecost laughing.

I shoved the bag behind one of the porch rocking chairs and went inside. There I found my boss sitting at the kitchen table with Doc and Big Bob. All three were wearing matching uniforms of white shirts and suspenders, but Doc's and Bob's were strapped undershirts and Ms. P's was French silk. All three were nursing Mason jars filled with whiskey. At least that's what I gathered from the half-empty bottle of Four Roses center-table. There was a pot simmering on the stove and what looked like a shred of beef in Doc's beard. Being a detective, I figured stew.

Doc and Ms. P were both in post-laughter convulsions. Big Bob was mid-story.

"The crowd's eating it up. This guy's face is tomato-red.

I'm thinking he's gonna take a swing at her and I'm wondering where our bouncer is. Then he just gets up and scurries out with his tail between his legs. And Ruby—she gives the nod to the musician and she starts right back into her bump-and-grind. This woman slips her a C-note after the show. Said it was the best comedy she'd seen all year."

That set off another wave of laughter. I made my entrance.

"Can anyone join this party, or is it invitation only?"

"Will! Pull up a seat!" Big Bob said a little too loudly. "I was just telling them about the time Ruby cut the knees off that heckler. The one in St. Louis who said she should—well, you remember what he said, I don't need to repeat it."

"Must have been before or after my time," I told him.

"Right. Right. Anyway, it was a hell of a good story." He picked up his jar and downed what was left. Doc immediately poured him another one.

"Robert delivered a dress more appropriate for Ms. Donner to be buried in," my boss said. "He and Mr. Donner have been kind enough to answer some questions about her life."

Which meant my boss probably knew more about my dead friend than I did. Par for the course with Lillian Pentecost.

"How was the show?" she asked. Translation: *Did you get what you went for?*

"Everything was as advertised." Translation: *I did.*

Bob pulled out his pocket watch and frowned at the verdict.

"The late show's done? Shoot. Where'd the time go?" he said, sliding off the kitchen chair. "Here, Will, take my seat. I should get back. Early morning tomorrow."

"The funeral's not until ten—is that right?" Doc asked.

"That's the plan. Funeral at ten, wake tomorrow night after last bell," Big Bob replied. "But I gotta get up early and do receipts from tonight. Figure out what bills are getting paid now, which are getting paid later, and which are getting tragically misplaced."

"Things are that tight?" I asked.

"Things are that tight," the circus man answered. "Thank Barnum for our golden goose."

My cocked head asked the obvious question.

"Some anonymous philanthropist included us in his will," he said. "Turns out this guy had been a big fan of the circus. Took his kids to see us every time we were in town. So he set up a trust and we get checks four times a year."

"Did you know this moneybags?" I asked.

"Not sure. It's all anonymous. We get the checks through a law firm."

"Is this kind of largess common in your world?" my boss asked.

"Usually the only surprise cash we get is whatever rattles out of people's pockets in the Roto-Rama," Big Bob admitted. "But Mama Halloway taught me never to look a gift horse in the mouth."

"Though anonymous gift horses might deserve more scrutiny," Ms. P suggested. "Whatever its provenance, this trust proved very fortunate."

"Fortunate, but not a fortune," Big Bob said. "Mid–four figures—sometimes more, sometimes less. Guess that's due to whatchamajiggers in the market. Anyway, without it I'd have had to sell. Got an open offer from Baxter and Brass, but I don't want to take it."

"A lot of overlap?" I asked. During my years with the circus I'd heard stories of smaller outfits getting swallowed by the bigger ones. The latter stripped the former for parts and tossed the rest.

"Yeah, a bunch of doubling," Big Bob confirmed. "They'd keep most of the performers, at least on a seasonal basis. Most of the crew would get cut, though. And you have to figure some of those seasonals wouldn't last long."

Whatever good cheer left in the room escaped like air out

of a dying balloon. Then the circus owner gave his head a shake and ginned up a grin.

"Not to mention, if I sold, then I wouldn't get to see my name all big and lit up. Can't give up that perk without a fight."

He stumbled to the door.

"Doc, I'll have a pair of men with shovels over tomorrow," he said. "See you folks graveside."

He walked out and I took his empty seat at the table. Doc went to pour me a glass, but I held up a hand.

"I'm a water girl."

I could feel him judging, but he went to the sink and accommodated.

"I think . . . um . . . I think I'm going to call it a night. I want to help with the grave tomorrow," the kindly scarecrow said. "There's stew left on the stove. Neighbor down the way dropped it off, so it's better than anything I usually whip up. I'll get to the A&P tomorrow. Promise."

He started to totter toward the drawing room, but I stopped him.

"Hey, Doc, what's with the club car in the drive?"

"The what?"

"The police car," I explained, taking the opportunity to pick the bit of stew out of his beard.

"Ah—oh, thank you. Sorry. Um . . . that's Joe's car. I let out the barn to him."

"Joe's a cop?"

"Tom Whiddle hired him on when he got back from . . . um . . . from overseas," Doc said. "He lives with his father. He's a preacher at . . . um . . . what is it? Blood of God? Blood of the Lamb? Blood of something. But it's a small place, his father's, so I let Joe use the barn to work on his bike. Think he sleeps there sometimes. Up in the hayloft. I don't mind that, though. I know what it's like after you get back."

"That was nice of you," I said.

"Well, I charge him, so it ain't charity. And he and Carl, that's his dad—they were friends of the family. Of Charlie and Abigail, anyway. Joe and Ruby even dated for a bit in high school. I wasn't around then, though."

So the Charles Atlas stand-in was the law. And had a thing with Ruby to boot. People should come with their résumés attached.

Though that did explain his reaction to the photos. Minding his own business and suddenly there's his dead ex-girlfriend, wallet-size and naked, scattered at his feet.

Doc said good night and a moment later we heard him settling into his makeshift bed on the settee. I retrieved the laundry bag from the porch, then fixed myself a bowl of stew and returned to my seat at the kitchen table. I ate as the two of us sat in silence, listening. Soon, we heard snores coming from the drawing room.

"You gonna fill me in on whatever gossip you pried out of Bob and Doc?" I asked.

"Of course. But first . . ."

"Right," I said. "Show, then tell."

I started pulling out the bag's contents. Some racy paperbacks; a few magazines you'd have to order special (probably used for costume ideas); a Ramses tin (the tin was at least a decade old, but the condoms inside were fresh); a bundle of letters and postcards—a lot of them old ones from Doc—that we put aside to peruse later. Then I pulled out the stack of wallet-size nudes, along with some larger prints, and Ms. P's eyes lit up.

"Looks like she had new ones taken every few years," I said. "Here's the oldest."

I handed her a six-by-four. In it, a young Ruby stretched out on a chaise lounge. A feathered boa was in place of Bertha, draping off her shoulders in a way that let her admirers get their dollar's worth.

Ms. Pentecost pulled a miniature magnifying glass out of a trouser pocket and settled it over the print. I got up and peered over her shoulder. The photo was from before the rose cover-up. Ruby's collection of tattoos was a few dozen short of complete, and the snake on her leg was only partially filled in.

"Those are daisies, I believe," Ms. P said.

I squinted and, indeed, that was what was inked just above Ruby's left breast. A bouquet of daisies. The snap was black and white, but I imagined the flowers were done in a bright yellow, the ribbon tying them together in an equally cheery shade.

"It seems like a well-crafted tattoo," my boss said.

"I agree. Certainly better than what she replaced it with."

So why cover it? The obvious answer: She didn't like it anymore. Why? Because it meant something beyond a simple bouquet.

I went for the low-hanging fruit first.

"We should ask around. See if there was a Daisy in her life. Maybe here in town or in her early years at the circus."

"A lover?" my boss suggested.

"Ruby didn't swing that way," I said, thinking about my embarrassing adventure in her bed. Then I wondered if maybe she'd lied to protect my feelings. I hadn't done a survey of tattoo parlors but I would guess the most requested cover-up was an old flame's name.

Maybe Ruby was into women. She just wasn't into me.

"We'll inquire at the wake tomorrow," Ms. P said. "Discreetly, of course."

"Yeah, yeah—that's me. Discretion coming out both ends."

Ms. P wasn't in the mood for levity, and really neither was I.

"Look, it's a long shot that an old tattoo has anything to do with Ruby getting killed," I said. Then I reached into my pocket and pulled out the item I'd found hiding at the bottom of the bag. I tossed it on the kitchen table. "Odds are a lot better that this plays into it."

My boss picked up the small, folded square of stiff white paper—about the thickness of the cardboard they package men's dress shirts with. She gave it a sniff, then carefully unfolded it. It was beginner's origami, but it did the trick, which was to keep its contents safe and snug. We both peered at the clump of brownish powder. Even from across the table, I caught a whiff of its acrid, vinegary smell.

"I was kind of hoping it was a sachet gone sour."

"I'm afraid not," Ms. P said. "It's heroin."

CHAPTER 13

That Saturday broke clean and cool, with only a few tattered wisps of clouds spoiling the blue. A perfect morning for a funeral.

Doc and I were both up with the dawn, him a little more bloodshot than me. Good to his word, Big Bob sent us some gravediggers—Sam Lee and a quiet, shaggy giant who spent his daily quota of words introducing himself as Clover.

Halfway between the house and the line of trees separating the circus grounds from the rest of the property was a cluster of scraggly trees that provided shade for a tiny row of tombstones. The oldest was worn nearly smooth with only the rumor of a name left; the newest belonged to Ruby's parents, who shared a single tombstone and a single date of death.

Sam Lee and Clover began carving out a hole two paces down the row. The two were polite enough to let Doc take a spell, but they made sure it was a short one. I stuck to the role of lemonade fetcher. Gravedigger was on the short list of jobs I never want to add to my résumé.

Ms. Pentecost was still in bed. We'd chalked up another late night. While Doc sawed logs on the settee, we had gone to Ruby's room to do a twice-over of the body. The ice in the rubber water bottles had melted. While Ms. P began the examination, I took the time to replace what I could, using the ice trays in the refrigerator. I only managed to fill two of the two dozen and I hoped it was enough.

Then I joined Ms. P in her exam.

We took more time with this pass, since there are a lot of places you can slide a needle. Ruby having so much ink on her skin made the job particularly difficult.

We might have missed a puncture or two and not have known it, but when we were done, we both agreed that if she'd been a user, she wasn't a regular one.

I had a growing list of questions for Frieda. Had she ever seen Ruby shooting dope? Had she found a needle along with the rest and tossed it? Anyone else in the circus using?

After we finished our puncture hunt, we got Ruby into the dress Big Bob had brought—a shimmering emerald sleeveless number with a slit high up the leg to show off her snake. Bob hadn't said anything about sending someone to do her hair and makeup. We chalked it up to things men don't think about, and took up the slack.

While Ms. P brushed out and bobby-pinned Ruby's hair, I used my limited supply of Max Factor to fix her face. There was no helping the paleness, but the least I could do was give her some eye shadow and lipstick that matched the dress she'd be sporting for eternity.

As we worked, my boss filled me in on what she'd learned from Doc and Big Bob.

Here are the standouts, in no particular order.

Because the circus had arrived so late Sunday, Doc didn't see his niece until Monday evening when she came over to the farmhouse for dinner. They played catch-up for an hour, then she walked back to the circus. Doc had no hint that anything was eating her.

If someone in town had been nursing an old grudge against his niece, Doc didn't know about it.

He confirmed Ruby's tale of why she'd left Stoppard in the first place.

"She'd always been a restless girl," he told my boss. "Stoppard didn't have much in the way of room to grow."

To exacerbate matters, her parents had found religion but hadn't figured out how to share it with their daughter.

"Honestly, I'm surprised she didn't leave sooner," Doc had said.

According to Bob, Ruby had turned down three offers over the last couple of years from other circuses looking to shoplift her. One of them had sent a representative who had gotten a little too persistent and had to be removed from the premises. That was two months and eight cities ago.

Speaking of unwanted persistence, there had been a guy at the late show in Pittsburgh who tried to look with his hands. He also got escorted out, though less politely. Somewhere along the way he tripped and fell and came back up with a bloody nose and two broken fingers.

It wasn't likely that the charmer had followed her to Virginia, but to be thorough we kept him in the frame.

Speaking of the frame, the person who had seen Val in the Loop right before Ruby had been killed was Nedley Johnson, a.k.a. the Great Mysterio. He had sworn up and down to both Big Bob and Chief Whiddle that he'd seen the knife-thrower through the open tent flap not five minutes before his assistant stumbled over Ruby's body.

"Would he lie?" Ms. P asked me.

"He's a magician, so sure. He'd do it real well, too."

"Would he lie to frame Mr. Kalishenko? Or does he have reason to harm Ms. Donner himself?"

"No to both," I said. "But I haven't seen any of these folks in nearly four years. A lot can change."

Ms. P had asked the circus owner who in the troupe had

a criminal record. A standard question during a case. Big Bob came back with a nonstandard answer.

"Oh, just about everybody," he said.

Half the troupe had gotten pegged for vagrancy, lewd conduct, and a grab bag of misdemeanors. Maeve had done six months for check fraud in her youth. Bob himself had spent a year on a road gang for assault.

Even mild-mannered Ray had a record. I couldn't believe it.

"Apparently he spent five years in Stateville Penitentiary in Illinois for assaulting a police officer," Ms. P informed me. "They were foreclosing on his pet store and he struck the officer with a birdcage."

Okay, that I could believe.

All of this I sorted while watching Sam Lee and Clover carve a hole in the earth one shovelful at a time. I appreciated Ms. P's axiom that when it comes to understanding people everything is relevant. But this was an especially anemic collection of trivia, more questions than answers, and not a single thing we could use to pry Val out of jail, which is where we were headed after the funeral. I knew we hadn't even been in town a day, but it already felt too long to have left my old mentor languishing in lockup.

I was thinking about what I'd say when I saw him when one of the circus's smaller flatbeds pulled into the driveway. I walked over to meet it.

Paulie was in the driver's seat, Big Bob riding along in the rear, his back pressed against something large that was covered in a tarp. Both men were in undershirts and dirty jeans.

"You fellas need to borrow a tie? I think my boss has a couple to spare."

"We're gonna go back to change," Paulie said as he hopped out. "Besides, my neck's too thick. Gotta have all my ties special-ordered."

In the back, Big Bob pulled off the tarp.

Calling it a coffin doesn't do it justice. Sure, it was the standard-size pine box. But every inch of it had been painted in brilliant colors: flowers and snakes and stars and mermaids. Everything Ruby had etched onto her skin and then some.

I looked at Paulie, who I knew doubled as a scenic painter, while keeping up the House of Oddities. He was the one who had created the painted arch at the mouth of Sideshow Alley.

"Did you do this?"

"I painted it," he said. "Building it was a joint effort."

I threw my arms around the pugnacious clown and squeezed.

"It's perfect."

"Oh, stop pawing at me, Parker. You're young enough to be my sister."

I let him go and helped them maneuver the box onto the screened-in porch. Then I showed them to Ruby's bedroom and supervised while they carried the body through the house with as much dignity as they could manage and lowered her into her painted bed.

Paulie went to put the lid on, but the ringmaster stopped him.

"Not yet," Big Bob said. "It's bad luck."

Paulie didn't argue and the two took the truck back to the circus to change. Ruby was left on the porch, lying in her open coffin like a dolled-up Snow White. Waiting for a fairy-tale ending that wasn't coming.

I went upstairs to change. Ms. Pentecost was awake and getting herself into a two-piece black fitted suit accented by a white four-in-hand tie. I helped skewer a long silver hairpin through her braids.

She cut an impressive figure. As if Death herself had come calling, having traded in a scythe for a silver-headed cane.

I kept it simple. I owned exactly one black dress and that's what I went with: a basic, sleeveless A-line that ended below the knee. Modest but not morose. When I was finished, I went downstairs and helped Doc get his tie on. His suit used to be black, but had faded in patches and bunched angrily around the joints.

"Ain't worn it since Charlie and Abigail's funeral," he said as he brushed the knots out of his hair. "Didn't fit then, either."

A little before nine, the three of us walked out to the waiting grave. Sam Lee and Clover stood a respectful distance away, leaning on their shovels and sharing a cigarette, as if someone had told them that's how gravediggers were supposed to pose.

We only had to wait a few minutes before we heard the first strains of music coming from the other side of the trees. I cocked my head. The tune was both familiar and strange.

Then I realized it was almost identical to the music that played when the performers filed into the big top for the opening number. But this version had been slowed down and tweaked just a little, major chords swapped for minor ones.

It was a carnival dirge.

They strode out of the trees like a dream, Big Bob leading the way, a starburst of color in his red ringmaster's uniform. He was followed by Maeve in rainbow taffeta, bells jingling in her hair, her skirts trailing after her on the ground, and Frieda in skintight silver, a crown of woven daisies circling her cropped locks. On her heels was Carlotta, more traditionally attired in lacy black, but with her face painted in a candy-colored death's mask.

Ray came dressed in a tuxedo so white it hurt to look at. He carried a canvas bundle in both arms. It looked heavy. Mysterio was in his top hat, tails, and a brilliant azure cape, arm in arm with the Amazing Annabelle, who was in a matching blue satin number that kept her upper parts contained but had thigh-high slits up both sides. Her legs cut through the dress like whitecaps on rough water.

The Flying Sabatinis appeared as one, each in skintight yellow satin with a short cape, like the superheroes from the comics I had tucked under my bed. Paulie and the rest of the clowns trailed after, all of them wearing their usual makeup and identical black suits, like a flock of greasepaint blackbirds.

The rest of the circus followed. Even the crew—roustabouts who maybe owned two pairs of overalls apiece—were dressed for the occasion in patchwork suits stitched together from old tent fabric.

Bringing up the rear was the band, a brass quartet accompanied by Lightning Lucy on accordion and the talker-violinist from the late show.

Big Bob, Paulie, and a trio of Sabatini brothers disappeared around the front of the house while the rest of the circus gathered in a ragged half circle around the grave. The men returned a moment later, walking in lockstep to the band's calliope dirge, the coffin balanced on their shoulders, Big Bob leading the way.

When they were a few steps from the open pit, they stopped and gently lowered their grim burden to the ground. Someone produced a crate and Big Bob climbed atop it.

The band fell silent.

"There are no words," he began. "But that's never stopped me."

He cleared his throat, stuffing down the tears.

"Ruby Donner was a circus woman. She was gracious and kind and sometimes mean and always a little sad. She was as fearless as a daredevil, and stronger than any man here who swung a sledge. She was as stubborn as me on my worst days, and as cunning as me on my best. She knew who she was, and she never apologized for it. She was the best of us. She was a circus woman through and through. And I'll miss her something fierce."

I was in tears. I'll admit it. So was most everybody else.

When he was finished, the ringmaster hopped down, leaned over the coffin, and kissed Ruby on her cool cheek.

"See you down the road, darling."

The band started again—something slower and softer. One by one, each person walked to the coffin and said goodbye. A ticking clock of colorful figures, pacing counterclockwise, as if together we could turn back time and bring the body in that pine box back to life.

Some dropped flowers in the coffin, others folded notes. Ray placed in what I realized was the canvas-wrapped body of Bertha the boa.

There were more whispers of "See you down the road." Circus superstition dictates that when you know you're not going to see someone for a while, you never say, "Goodbye." "Goodbye" means forever. "See you down the road" means . . . hope.

When it came my turn, I found myself at a loss. I looked down at Ruby's face. The makeup I'd done the night before looked shoddy and ghoulish in the late-morning light.

I couldn't think of a damn thing to say.

I saw that her dress had ridden up, so I reached down and adjusted it. As I did, the slit gaped open, revealing a soaring bluebird on her inner thigh tucked just above the last of the snake's spirals.

I was suddenly struck by a vivid memory—cigarette smoke undercut with sweat and ink. And the sound. That clattering buzz of the tattoo needle stitching bright blue ink into tender flesh.

It had been St. Louis, a hole-in-the-wall parlor, and the tattooist had been a woman, the wife of the owner, who had enough tattoos to join the sideshow herself. Ruby had sought her out special.

I'd tagged along and had gotten queasy right from the start: from the smoke and the sound and the sight of the blood trickling down Ruby's thigh. Which is my only excuse for saying something rube-stupid like "What do you think they're all gonna look like when you get old?"

The two women traded looks and Ruby let loose with that laugh of hers, the one that started simmering deep in her diaphragm before it bubbled out between her lips. It cut through the buzz of the needle like a bright blade, and hearing it made whatever was clenching my innards release its grip.

"Oh, honey," Ruby had said. "I can't wait to find out."

I snapped back to the present.

I was suddenly aware I'd been standing at the coffin for I don't know long and everyone was eyeing me. I walked away without saying a word. The circle continued.

Once everyone had gotten a turn, Paulie and a pair of roustabouts appeared with the coffin lid and hammered it shut. Some tent-grade ropes were produced and a sling was created for the coffin.

Big Bob hopped back on his apple-crate stage.

"Ruby's uncle . . ." He nodded at Doc, who had his glasses in one hand and was wiping away tears with the other. "He's asked if we'd sing a hymn. Just the one, because we've got a circus to open and I know you're all heathens."

He nodded at the band and they started in on "Amazing Grace."

Big Bob led the singing, and maybe half the crowd joined in, most halfheartedly, and many stumbling over the verses. Then from behind me a new voice joined the chorus—a crystal-clear alto that I'd never heard before. Not like this.

Lillian Pentecost was singing.

> 'Twas grace that taught my heart to fear
> And grace my fears relieved
> How precious did that grace appear
> The hour I first believed

Her voice acted like a center pole, grounding the song and lifting everyone's voices up until all the mourners were joining in, full-throated and fearless.

Through many dangers, toils, and snares
I have already come
'Twas grace that brought me safe thus far
And grace will lead me home

We moved through the verses while the men who'd carried the coffin to the grave took the ropes and gently lowered it into the ground.

As the rainbow-painted pine sank out of sight, I imagined taking all of my sadness, the grief and the could-have-said, should-have-dones, and throwing them down into the dark with her. Until all that was left was anger. That cold rage like a knife through my own heart.

I made a silent promise. That we'd find who had done this. And we'd put him in a hole, too.

CHAPTER 14

The performers double-timed it back to the circus so they could be ready to open the gates at noon. Meanwhile, Ms. Pentecost and I went straight to the jail.

We didn't bother to change out of our funeral weeds. If Chief Whiddle decided to backslide on visiting hours, we were ready to play the "We just put our friend in the ground" card.

The Stoppard Police Department was housed just off the town square—ten paces from the courthouse and a hundred from the Majestic, where a sign hung on the door announcing the movie house was closed on account of grieving.

Our fears about Whiddle were groundless. He wasn't even there when we arrived. Instead, we found the office manned by a secretary in her seventies wearing a dun-colored pantsuit, her cat-eye glasses framing a baked-in scowl.

It was only ten minutes to noon, but she directed us to a bench by the wall to wait out the clock. She kept a close eye on us from the gunner's turret of her desk.

A few minutes before twelve, the sound of echoing footsteps came from an open doorway on the other side of the room.

A man emerged, blinking at the sunlight shining through the office windows. He might have been handsome if you subtracted the matted hair and clothes that looked like they'd been slept in. I caught the stench of cigarettes and whiskey from ten paces, and deduced he'd done an overnight swim in the drunk tank.

On his heels was the one-armed mechanic from the night before. He'd traded army trousers for something less grease-stained, which was a plus. But he'd also put on a shirt, so I docked him a few points.

"You think you can keep out of trouble, Leroy?" he asked the drunk.

Leroy either didn't hear or didn't care, and hurried to the exit, looking warily at us as he passed. Probably worried we were members of the Women's Christian Temperance Union. Then he was out the front door and headed to wherever would serve him a drink at 11:58 in the morning.

"The Russian's got visitors," the secretary announced.

"Thank you, Mrs. Gibson," he said, looking our way.

I waved from our seat on the bench.

"Officer Engle, we meet again."

"Good morning, Miss . . . Parker? And you must be Lillian Pentecost."

"I am," my boss said, extending her left hand without having to triple-think it. I noticed someone had tailored his right sleeve so it was half the length of the left. He had a gun belt on, the revolver situated backward on the right side for a cross-body draw. "Chief Whiddle said that we would be able to speak with Mr. Kalishenko."

He looked at Ms. P's cane.

"Are you comfortable with stairs?"

"If they're reasonable."

He led us through the open doorway and down a flight of narrow, concrete steps. Just before I stepped through, I caught Mrs. Gibson picking up the phone and dialing with Olympian speed.

Stoppard's grapevine going strong.

The stairs let us out into a low-ceilinged hallway with three cells along one side, bare concrete on the other. Each cell was outfitted with a cot bolted to the wall, a toilet, and the smallest of barred windows situated just above head height. The first two had their doors open. Only the third was closed and locked. Two wooden folding chairs were set up in front of it.

"No passing the prisoner anything through the bars," Officer Joe told us before heading back up the stairs. "And if you need anything, just give a yell."

When we got to the third cell and looked inside, I thought someone had made a mistake. The only person in the cell was an old, bare-faced, mostly bald man sitting on the cot and shoveling a limp sandwich into his mouth. He looked nothing like Valentin Kalishenko, who had a Russian bear of a beard and a demeanor to match.

The man in the cell looked sad and weak.

Broken.

Then he glanced up and I saw his eyes. They were the same ones that had squinted across forty feet of circus ground before putting a knife a hair's breadth from my cheek.

"Val?"

He smiled.

"Hello, Willowjean," he said, voice still soaked with the steppes even after nearly three decades in the U.S. "You look very good."

"You look . . ."

He waved me off.

"I was going to say clean-shaven."

"Ah, yes," he said. "A few weeks ago, I get lice. The medicine—it smells very bad. I decide to shave it off."

He stood and walked over to the bars. Just that little bit of movement brought some of the old Kalishenko back. Even in his fifties, the man could compete with tigers for grace. He wrapped his hands around the bars, muscles popping out of his forearms like rebar in concrete.

"Ms. Pentecost."

"Mr. Kalishenko."

The two had met briefly right before I was hired. Val had passed on a goodbye note along with a set of his best throwing knives.

"I'm sorry we didn't come yesterday," I said. "It got late and—"

He waved me off again.

"It is all right. You are here now. It's good to see you, padcheritsa," he said, forcing a smile. "But as I told Robert, I do not know if you can do much to help me."

Ms. Pentecost eased herself into one of the chairs.

"Let us be the judge of that."

She looked at me, and I took the seat next to her. I removed a fresh notebook and a newly sharpened Blackwing out of my bag.

"You should have a seat, Val," I said. "These things can take a while."

A while lasted an hour and change. We learned a lot. Nothing that broke the case. Not even anything that could rightfully be considered a clue. But my detective mentor pulled more personal information out of my knife-throwing mentor in seventy-some minutes than I had in five years.

I filled up the better part of a notebook with shorthand. Here's some of what Ms. P and I eventually extracted from the dross.

LILLIAN PENTECOST: What is your full name?

    VALENTIN KALISHENKO: Valentin Kalishenko, Dancer of Blades, Master of Fire, Last and Final Heir of Rasputin

LP: Rasputin?

    VK: A flourish.

LP: Where were you born?

VK: A small village half an hour's hard ride from St. Petersburg.

LP: And what brought you to the United States?

VK: I was on the wrong side of the revolution. I made enemies. I traveled to America to . . . to lose the person I had been. To reinvent myself.

I arrived in San Francisco in September of 1919. I worked as a bodyguard for an . . . um . . . a pakhan. A wealthy criminal. A businessman. I work for him for two years and then we part ways.

LP: Was it amicable?

VK: Not so much, no. He was killed by a rival. I was not present. Otherwise, he would not have been killed. Or not killed so easily. I did not wish to work for this new pakhan, so I left.

I had met Mr. Hart at a bar. His circus was in town. I was showing off with my knives. He said that if I wanted to have a new career I should see him.

I caught up with the circus in Los Angeles and my dream came true. I reinvented myself. The Master of Knives, Heir to Rasputin.

Robert was there. He was merely a clown then. But you could tell that he would be more someday.

Like when I met you, Will. I knew you would be more.

LP: And you have been with Hart and Halloway since then?

VK: Yes! Twenty-five years. No vacations. Every show. When Robert became a partner, he asked me to be a full member of the company. Easy decision. It was my home. It is my home. My family.

LP: Was Ruby Donner included in this family?

VK: Of course Ruby was part of my family! She was part of the circus, she was part of my family.

LP: But there was friction between you?

VK: It is family. There is always . . . friction.

LP: But even the conflict that happens within a family happens for a reason. It has an origin. What was the origin between you and Ms. Donner?

VK: It is not something . . . I do not wish to speak of this in front of Will.

LP: Mr. Kalishenko—while Miss Parker might once have been your apprentice, she is now mine. Anything you confide to me, I will reveal to her in short order. She is, I assure you, a detective in her own right. What you say here will be used to discover the circumstances of Ms. Donner's death, and that alone.

VK: Ruby and I had a . . . a relationship. When she first joined the circus.

LP: This was a romantic relationship?

VK: We were lovers, yes.

LP: How long did this relationship last?

VK: A few months only. We were very discreet. She was new. She did not want a reputation.

LP: Why did it end?

VK: She discovered that I have a wife. There were letters in my trailer. Ruby found them. They were in Russian, but I had taught her a few words. She knew enough to understand the letters to be . . . intimate.

LP: You had this wife when you left Russia?

VK: Yes. My wife, she came from a large family. She would not leave them. Also, she was pregnant with our first child. She did not think she could stand the long voyage.

She went south. She had much family there. They never approved of our marriage. Her father—I think he was happy to see me leave.

I told them I would send for them. After I established myself.

But my job in San Francisco. It was not good for a family. I wrote to my wife this. She understood.

LP: And when you joined the circus?

VK: We had been apart for so long. Longer than we had been together. I wrote to her that the circus life was also not for a family. That I would send money. It was . . . I thought it was easier this way.

LP: Did you ever divorce?

   VK: My wife is very religious. She would not agree to one. I told Ruby this. That we were no longer truly husband and wife. That we had not been for many years. But she was angry. Angry that I did not tell her I was married. I told her it did not matter, but . . . she was stubborn and foolish and . . .

LP: And the remains of this relationship festered?

   VK: Yes! Festered. But when we fought, it was never about this. It was about stupid things. She had many tattoos. Enough. More than enough to be the Amazing Tattooed Woman. But she kept getting more. Like she was . . . hiding herself.

LP: Do you know the significance of the daisies over Ms. Donner's left breast?

   VK: Daisies?

LP: She had them when she first arrived at the circus, but would later cover them up.

   VK: Yes, the rose! I remember teasing her. It did not look like a rose. It looked like . . . dung. But I did not say dung. The daisies were pretty. I tease her and ask why cover a pretty tattoo with an ugly one.

LP: Did she answer?

   VK: Yes. She told me to . . . do something that was not polite.

LP: Moving on to the events leading to her murder: It's been reported that you and Ms. Donner had a particularly loud argument the day she died. What precipitated that, Mr. Kalishenko?

   VK: My daughter. She has written many times saying she wishes to come to America. She wishes to meet me. I write back that she cannot. It is not a good time. The war—it made such things easy to say. Ruby knew this. She knew that my daughter wanted to come here and she knew I forbid it.

   On Monday, I received a letter from my wife. She wrote to tell me that my daughter was on her way to America. That they had received a letter from my friend in the circus. Ruby had . . .

she had written. She said where the circus would be. She sent money for a ticket on a ship. A boat. This boat will arrive next week. My daughter will be in Charlotte. Waiting for the circus. Waiting for me.

LP: *You confronted Ms. Donner?*

VK: I looked for her Monday night, but I could not find her. Eventually I . . . I drank and slept.

But I found her Tuesday morning. Setting up her booth. I told her she should not have interfered. That I did not want to see my daughter. That she did not want to see me. Not really.

I said many things that I regret.

LP: *Did this conversation upset Ms. Donner?*

VK: Yes?

LP: *You're unsure?*

VK: She was . . . distracted? Like she did not have the time to speak with me. This made me even more angry. That I was not important to her. I was . . . I am not proud.

LP: *Did you see Ms. Donner again that day?*

VK: I do not know.

I did my first performance at noon. And the two o'clock. The four o'clock was . . . My aim was not true. I grazed Miranda's cheek. She said I was too drunk to perform. That she did not feel safe. I . . . said more things that I regret.

After that I remember little.

LP: *What do you recall?*

VK: Wandering the circus grounds. Sitting in my trailer. Rereading my wife's letter.

I would put the bottle away. Then I would think about Masha, my daughter. About seeing her for the first time.

All she has are letters. Postcards. Stories. To her I am a story. A performance.

In real life I am an old drunk who ran away and left his family behind. I would think about this and pick up the bottle again.

LP: Do you remember being in the Loop that evening just after closing?

VK: I do not. By then I remember little. Just the vodka.

LP: When you were questioned by the police, you said that though you remembered nothing, you might have killed Ms. Donner. Do you believe that's possible?

VK: I do not want to believe. But I cannot say no. I was very angry.

This is where I couldn't hold my tongue any longer.

"Bullshit!" I yelled. "You did not kill her."

"Padcheritsa . . ."

"Don't Paddy Rita me," I said, slapping my notebook against the bars. "I don't care how angry you were, you'd never hurt Ruby. You'd never hurt anybody at the circus."

He reached a hand through the bars, but I refused to take it.

"Willowjean," he said. "I was very drunk. Liquor makes people not themselves. You know this."

Yeah, sure I knew this. My father came from a long line of drunks. There were plenty of times he'd taken his belt to my mother. And after she died, he took it to me. Though I would argue that in his case the liquor made him *more* himself, not less.

Still, I wasn't having it.

"She was stabbed in the back," I growled. "In the back."

Ms. Pentecost put a steadying hand on my shoulder. I shrugged it off. I wasn't in the mood to be steadied.

"I don't care if you were flying higher than the *Enola Gay*. You wouldn't do that."

He didn't reply. Just gave his bald pate a sad little shake.

"Have you ever been arrested before, Mr. Kalishenko?" my boss asked.

He nodded. "Yes. Several times in San Francisco."

"This was in relation to your work as a bodyguard?"

Another nod.

"Were the crimes you were arrested for violent in nature?"

"Yes," he said. "They were little things. People who would not pay their debts. Thanks to the influence of my employer, I was never convicted."

"Did you ever kill anyone as part of your job in San Francisco?"

His eyes darted my way.

"No," he said.

I held my breath, hoping she'd drop the thread. No such luck.

"Have you *ever* killed anyone, Mr. Kalishenko?"

Val looked to me again, a question on his face.

"You have not told her?"

I shook my head.

"Told me what?" Ms. Pentecost asked.

Damn it.

"Do you want the long version or the short version?" I asked.

"Any version will do," she said through a stiff jaw. I wasn't going to wriggle loose.

"It was near the end of my first year with the circus. I was working regular as Val's assistant by then. We were somewhere in eastern Ohio. I can't remember the place. Bigger than Stoppard, smaller than Cincinnati—that's all I know."

I kept my voice to a near whisper. I was pretty sure we couldn't be heard by any interested parties upstairs, but I didn't want to chance it.

"Val and I finished the last show of the night and discovered we were low on . . . provisions."

"Vodka," Val clarified. "I was out of vodka. There was a bar nearby. I thought to buy a bottle. Will—she came with me. She thought I would get in trouble if . . ."

"If left to his own devices," I finished. "So we took one of the trucks out to this roadhouse in the middle of nowhere. I went in with him, but the bartender yelled at me to scram. I was sixteen and looked thirteen, so I went outside and waited. Too hot to sit in the truck, so I hop on the tailgate. After a minute, a couple of roughnecks who'd been in the bar come out. They pull out cigarettes and do the ol' where's-my-lighter pocket pat-down. One of them yells to me and asks if I have any matches. I say I do, so they stroll over."

I feel as stupid typing this as I did telling it to Ms. Pente-cost. What are the chances both had cigarettes but neither had a light? Why not just hop back in the bar, where there were matchbooks scattered on every table?

I was sixteen and still learning, so I didn't ask any of those questions. Which was why I was so shocked when one of the men grabbed my arm and twisted it behind my back while the other began turning my pockets inside out.

I didn't know much, but I knew enough to defend myself. I lifted my legs, put both heels against the side of the truck, and pushed. The man twisting my arm fell back and we both ended up scrambling in the dusty gravel. I was on my feet before he was, but his friend was waiting.

He sent a vicious hook right into my liver. While I was bent over vomiting up my dinner, he wrapped an arm around my neck and began to squeeze.

I was halfway to unconscious when the man grunted and let go. I fell on my ass and looked up to find Val there, bottle in one hand, knife in the other. The man who had been holding me was lying facedown in the dirt.

The knife-thrower leaped over me and dove into the second man. Blood sprayed across my face.

Val grabbed me and dragged me into the truck and we sped off. We didn't speak of the incident to anyone, not even friends at the circus.

"Did you kill those men?" Ms. P quietly asked Val.

He shrugged. "I do not know. I hurt them. Badly. The circus jumped town the next day."

Ms. P looked to me.

"It's fifty-fifty," I told her. "I didn't check for a pulse before we left. All I know is the cops never came calling."

My boss put on her pondering face.

"It doesn't matter one way or another," I argued. "The cops here don't know about it. And as far as Ruby's murder goes, it's neither here nor there. It's not relevant."

I could hear myself protesting too much. To Ms. Pentecost's mind it was relevant, and I knew why. Once a person solves a problem with murder—even if it's self-defense—it becomes easier to do it the second time. Especially if they got away with it the first.

The point of my boss prying out that story was this: Kalishenko was willing to kill.

If he felt threatened or saw someone he loved threatened, he wouldn't hesitate to put a blade in them. The question became: Did Ruby meddling in his family life qualify as a threat?

What about when he was blackout drunk? Did it qualify then?

Was my old mentor capable of killing Ruby Donner?

By the time the interview was over, I couldn't give an honest answer.

CHAPTER 15

We said our goodbyes to Val and I told him we'd come back soon with word on our progress. We were on our way out of the station when Officer Joe motioned me aside, away from the prying ears of the secretary.

"I'm sorry about last night," he said. "You startled me and I was a little . . . um . . ."

"Bit of an asshole?" I offered. After the interview downstairs, I was not in the mood to mince words.

"I was going to say rude, but I guess that'll do," he said. "Anyway, I . . . um . . . I work on my bike to take my mind off things. I wasn't having the best day, and there was a stripped bolt on the carburetor. I've got seven wrenches and none of the damn things were working and—"

I held up a hand. "Is there an apology at the end of this sentence?"

"Yeah," he said, blushing. "I'm sorry. I didn't mean to be . . ."

"An asshole."

"An asshole."

"Well," I began, admiring the gloss on my nails, "you really weren't too much of one. No reason to fret, Officer."

"Call me Joe. Please."

"No reason to fret, Joe."

"Regardless, I'd like to make it up to you," he said. "Can I buy you lunch?"

I wasn't expecting a preacher's boy to move so quick.

"Sure," I said. "I've been known to eat. When were you thinking?"

He glanced at the battered steel watch on his wrist.

"How about now?"

I looked back at the door, where my boss was waiting.

"I have to run Ms. Pentecost back. How does now plus thirty minutes sound?"

"Thirty? It's only a five-minute drive back to Doc's place," he said.

He thought I was going out to lunch wearing my funeral duds. Men are adorable.

"Plus thirty or another day," I insisted.

"Thirty minutes it is," he said.

Out of the corner of my eye, I saw Mrs. Gibson lean her ear so far our way she threatened to fall out of her chair.

"Anyplace around here to get a bite that's not the state's best chicken?"

"Lion's Pharmacy has a lunch counter," Joe said. "They have some booths that are relatively private."

"I'll see you in half an hour," I said, though I didn't think privacy was in the cards in Stoppard regardless of where we dined.

"See you then." He flashed a smile that I imagine scored direct hits with the country girls. It only dealt this city girl a glancing blow.

Outside in the truck, I told Ms. P about my unexpected date.

"Are you sure this is wise?" she asked. The subtext being that the last time I got asked on a date by someone involved in a case, it hadn't turned out so hot.

"He and Ruby used to be an item, or so says Doc," I told

her, looping the truck around the town square and heading circus-ward. "You wanted to know about her life in Stoppard. Joe might be able to fill us in."

She arched an eyebrow.

"He asked that I call him Joe. It would be impolite to do otherwise."

Ms. P cranked her window down a couple of inches. Hot air whipped loose strands of her hair into a frenzy.

"It's more likely that he expects to get information from you," she said. "Either for his own purposes or at the request of Chief Whiddle."

"Right," I said. "An attractive so-and-so asks me out—obviously he's looking to pickpocket clues."

No response from the great detective. Because, again, there was precedent. "Luckily, we have no information for him to pick," I said around grinding molars.

"We have *some*."

"I'm not about to tell him about Val's history of stabbing."

"I wouldn't expect you to," she said. "Though I am disappointed you did not tell me about it before now."

I didn't have a response to that other than to press down on the accelerator in the hopes of cutting as many uncomfortable seconds off the drive as possible.

Ms. Pentecost filled in the blank for me. "You wanted to protect Mr. Kalishenko."

"Yes," I said. "Obviously."

"But your job is not to protect Mr. Kalishenko. It's to discover who killed Ruby Donner. Holding information back does not help us accomplish that."

"Spilling that story doesn't help, either."

"Perhaps. Perhaps not," she said, trying to tuck the loose strands back into her braids and failing. "But now I'm forced to wonder what else you might hold back."

She might as well have reached across the cab and smacked

me in the face. I looked at her, my jaw a little loose on its hinges. Did she really think I'd lie to her?

I didn't know. She kept her gaze fixed out the passenger window.

"I'm not holding anything else back," I assured her. "Swear on my mother."

She nodded—once, short and quick. She still didn't meet my eyes.

We rode the rest of the way to Doc's in silence.

When we arrived, I went straight to my borrowed bedroom to brush out the tangles, retouch my lipstick, and spend a fruitless few minutes trying to do something about the clumps of freckles the summer sun had brought out on my cheeks. This was followed by an embarrassingly long time deciding between a shirtwaist dress in blue and white checks and a slack suit in canary yellow.

The former paired well with small-town life, being just on this side of inoffensive. The latter paired well with my eyes and hair and the rising mercury, the sleeves ending above my elbows and the slacks having been hemmed into long shorts.

I was trying out the checked dress for the mirror when there was a rap at the door.

"Come in."

Ms. P entered and closed the door firmly behind her. She came over and sat on the narrow bed. I was half expecting some kind of heartfelt apology, but that was from the half of me that didn't know my boss.

"I was talking about the heroin."

"When? To who?" I asked, shucking off the dress.

"To you. When I said that we did have details that Officer Engle might be interested in, that was what I was thinking of, not Mr. Kalishenko's criminal past."

I held both outfits.

"Which do you think?" I asked. "I'm torn between girl next door and Kate Hepburn."

"Do you have time to iron?" she asked.

"I barely have time to button it."

"Then the yellow suit."

I tossed the checked dress to the floor and slipped into the slack suit.

"So . . . the heroin," my boss prodded. "We should do our best to keep that to ourselves for the moment."

"I was going to bring it along with me," I said, buttoning the suit. "Give Joe a taste. Ask his opinion about the recipe. Maybe bring Chief Whiddle over and let him have a—"

"I receive your point," she said with a sigh.

"Pretty sure I can manage not to spill that one," I said, rummaging in my suitcase for a pair of shoes that complimented canary.

"Though," Ms. P continued, "if the opportunity presents itself to inquire about any rebellious habits Ms. Donner might have possessed prior to her joining the circus, that would be appreciated."

I pulled out a pair of white stacked-heel oxfords. Not the most practical, but nothing else I had paired with canary.

"So what you're saying is I should get more than I give," I said, squeezing my size-eights into the shoes. "Preferably something that would be useful in solving a murder."

She gave me a familiar, long-suffering look, then reached out and picked a piece of microscopic lint off my shoulder.

"However you proceed, please be careful," she said.

"I think I can handle it," I told her, giving my hair another quick brush. "Besides, one of the few pieces of information we have is that Ruby's murderer went at it right-handed. That makes my lunch date the only person in town who's definitely out of the frame."

CHAPTER **16**

The lunch counter at Lion's Pharmacy was basically identical to the one three blocks away from our brownstone in New York. Save for the narrowness of the menu (not a single instance of the word "kosher"), the accent of the counterman (more backwoods than Brooklyn), the view out the windows (nothing above two stories), and the fact that I was the entertainment. That's what I was assuming, considering the not-so-subtle looks from folks sitting in the other booths.

Joe took notice, as well.

"Sorry about the stares," he said around a forkful of coleslaw. "I think word's out who you are and why you're in town."

"With a little assistance from your secretary, I bet." I peeled back the top slice of bread on my "Reuben" and wrinkled my nose. I'd had worse, but not blander.

"Well, she's Marty Gibson's widow," he said, as if that explained everything.

While I had burned brain cells choosing a new outfit, he was still in uniform. He filled it out nicely, though, and had been polite enough to take off the gun belt and set it on the seat beside him.

Eventually, I was forced to ask the obvious. "Who's Marty Gibson?"

"He was the chief before Tom Whiddle," Joe said. "He died on the job. Heart attack. Tom was the deputy chief, so he became acting. Then the town council gave him the job permanent and he's had it ever since. That was twenty-some years ago. Ruth—that's Mrs. Gibson—she had two boys in high school and couldn't live on the pension. He basically created the front-desk job just for her."

"And her being Stoppard's answer to Hedda Hopper comes into it how?" I asked.

"She doesn't gossip that much," he said unconvincingly. "But she's loyal to the chief. Sees herself as sort of a watchdog. She takes any kind of troublemaking around here personal."

"I'm a troublemaker?"

"You're . . . unusual," he said, ducking the question nicely.

"Ah, *unusual.*" I chewed on the word along with the Reuben. "Who cares about smart or pretty? Unusual is where it's at."

I could see him scraping together an apology when he stopped and narrowed his eyes.

"You're teasing me, aren't you?"

"Keep it up, you could be a detective."

"Speaking of being a detective, how's a smart, pretty girl like you fall into a job like that?"

"A little bit of happenstance, and a lot of being unusual."

I proceeded to give him the back-of-the-book version of how Ms. Pentecost and I had come to be. I skated over a few details, not least of which was that I had put a knife in a man's back in the process of saving Ms. P's life.

"That's pretty incredible," he said when I finished.

"It's an interesting life," I said, eyeing the milkshake options. "How about you? Interesting life so far?"

That pried a grin out of him. "That's the best way I've heard yet of asking how I lost my arm."

"I was leaning toward alligator wrestling," I said. "Then I remembered seeing those."

I nodded at the window where there was taped a faded yellow flyer:

LEND A HAND TO OUR BOYS! BUY VICTORY BONDS!

He glanced at it, then turned away in disgust.

"Somebody at the bank came up with that," he said between sips of root beer. "They gave me a little parade. Me and a couple other guys who came back at the same time. Put us in the back of the mayor's Chevy convertible and drove us down Main Street."

"Did you get to wear a pretty gown?"

Joe snorted and began coughing up soda. If everyone wasn't looking at us already, they were now.

"God damn," he said, blowing root beer out his nose. "You snuck up on me with that one."

"I'll ask the straight-ahead question, then. How did you lose it?"

"The Ardennes," he said, grabbing a fistful of napkins and wiping the soda off his face. "Second week of the counteroffensive. German artillery shell went off right by me. Didn't even know what happened until I woke up in a surgical tent two days later."

It had the practiced pacing of a canned response. I wondered how many times—how many hundreds of times—he'd been asked the question.

"Don't suppose you were a lefty."

He shook his head. "I'm having to relearn everything. I was always pretty good with my off hand. My shooting's not too bad. Handwriting is pretty awful, though. And I've got to hunt and peck when I'm typing up reports."

I burned a minute praising the merits of shorthand for those of us whose handwriting looks like monkey scribble. Long enough to put him at ease so my next question caught him sleeping.

"So I hear you and Ruby were an item?"

Apparently he wasn't napping. More likely he saw the question coming a mile away.

"We were," he said, his expression as bland as my Reuben. "For most of a year in high school."

"Not a big secret, I take it?"

He shook his head. "Not at all. I mean—shoot—you've been in town a day and you already know about it."

"Sure, but I'm a professional detective. It's my job to take a shovel to people's lives."

"No digging needed here," he said, picking at the last of his fries. "I was captain of the football team. She was runner-up for homecoming queen. Our picture's in the yearbook, for shuck's sake."

I resisted the urge to rib him about "shucks."

Instead I said, "Sounds like a storybook romance."

Those bee-stung lips compressed into a line so thin you could shave with them.

"Minus the happy ending, though," he said. "I knew she had one foot out the door. Out of town, I mean. She never made a secret of it. Soon as she graduated, she was gonna hit the road. But we were doing so well I thought . . ."

"You thought?"

"Maybe I could convince her to stay, you know?"

"No such luck?"

"Nope," he said. "She didn't even wait until graduation. One day she just packed up and left. Caught a bus to Fredericksburg, then a train to New York. I didn't even find out until after she was gone. My father broke the news to me. He'd heard from her parents. Guess Ruby had a bit of a row with them on her way out."

Considering she never came back, not even when they died, I thought "a bit of" was an understatement.

"It wasn't until three or four years later that I heard she was working at a circus. Somebody came back from a trip and said they saw her there. They said she had all these tattoos. I figured they made a mistake. Then they showed me a picture. Like the ones you had last night."

"That must have been rough," I said.

He shrugged. "Just kind of confusing, you know? It's hard to see how she got from here to there."

"Did you ever get a chance to ask her?"

"Nope."

Did that come out a little too quick? I was about to press him on it when the bell above the door gave a double chime and Sister Evelyn walked in. She waved to the white coat working in the back of the pharmacy. Then she looked down the row of booths and feigned a look of surprise.

She walked over.

"Joe," she said, smiling. "Fancy meeting you here."

"Hi, Evelyn."

She pointed her smile at me and turned down the wattage by half.

"Miss Parker, wasn't it?"

"Still is, actually."

She was joined by the white-coated pharmacist. He was a placid-looking man with an egg-shaped head and not quite enough hair to cover it. His coat did its best to hide black slacks and a white shirt that were so wash-worn they both leaned toward gray.

It wasn't until Joe said, "Hey, Bert," that I recognized him as Brother Carl's driver from the day before.

"Hiya, Joe," Bert said. "Didn't know you were here. I'd have come over to say hello earlier."

"No problem. Just having some lunch with our visitor." Joe's smile was believable enough, but the way his hand tightened around the root beer bottle let me know he wasn't thrilled at the drop-in.

Bert stuck out his hand.

"Bert Conroy," he said, with a smile suggesting he'd be

perfectly comfortable selling you a slightly used Chevy. "I'm Evelyn's husband."

"Bert's my cousin," Joe said.

"On his mother's side. God rest her soul," Bert added. "Joe and I were close as brothers, though. Did everything together when we were kids, didn't we, Joe? Got into a mess of trouble. Why I could tell you stories that—"

Evelyn, bless her, nudged her husband in the ribs.

"You wanted to tell Joe something, didn't you?"

"Right, I'm sorry. Joe—there was something I wanted to, you know, sort of make you aware of. In your capacity as law enforcement, I mean."

Bert looked at me uncertainly.

"It's all right, Bert," Joe said. "Whatever you tell me is gonna be all over town in half an hour so you might as well spill."

Bert didn't look entirely convinced, but he relented.

"Don Perkins heard from his nephew—not Lou, the other one—that there was a . . . well, a *burlesque* performance at the circus last night. That they had women showing . . . Well, it was burlesque. You can use your imagination."

Bert's face was flaming red from his cheeks all the way to his bald head. I resisted the urge to ask him what burlesque was and if he could describe it for me. I think if I did, he would have fainted.

"I'll talk to the chief about it," Joe said.

"Okay," Bert said, wiping sweat off his expanding brow. "Just thought you should know."

"Will we see you in church tomorrow?" Sister Evelyn asked Joe. Something in her tone suggested the question was a loaded one. "It's the first Sunday of the month, so Bert will be leading the service."

Joe shook his head. "I've got a twelve-hour shift. Maybe next week."

"You should tell Tommy Whiddle not to work you so hard,"

Bert said. "Don't know why you have to be on call all the time. Not like anything ever happens around here."

Bert shot an awkward look my way, running a hand through the memory of his hair.

"I mean . . . you know . . . usually. It was awful about Ruby. Just awful."

"Did you know Ruby Donner very well?" I'd learned from Ms. Pentecost never to pass up the chance for an interrogation.

"Oh, well enough, I guess," Bert said. "We were all church kids. All about the same age. So we played together. Though I can't say I ever got to know Ruby all that much. Evelyn and her were friends, though, weren't you, honey?"

His wife looked like she'd bit on something sour.

"As children," she clarified. "Not really when we got older. She . . . um . . . well, she just got interested in different things, didn't she?"

I could tell she wanted to enumerate those "different things." I imagined "books, movies, short skirts, and the general workings of the Devil" were on the list. But she gave a look Joe's way and held her tongue.

"Come on, Bert," she said, taking him by the hand. "Let's leave them be. I've got to get back to the flower shop."

"Oh, of course, dear," he said, as his wife slowly dragged him away. "Anyway, I just thought you should know about the . . . um . . . what Don's nephew said. See you later."

Evelyn went out the way she came while Bert headed back to his post doling out prescriptions.

"If this were a school dance, they'd have whipped out a ruler and checked our distance," I said.

Joe laughed. "Yeah, that wasn't real subtle, was it?"

"What's Bert's deal?" I asked. "He's a preacher, too?"

"Assistant pastor. He'll take over for my dad eventually."

I couldn't picture swapping John the Baptist for the placid pharmacist and told Joe as much.

"Better him than me," Joe said.

I gave him a look and he explained. "I was set to take over for my dad for a while."

"You? A preacher?"

"You don't think I have the chops?" he asked. "Shoot—I was set to go to school for theology and everything."

The disbelief must have shown through.

"Yeah, that was more Dad's idea than mine," Joe said. "He never went to college and he's always regretted it. Dropped out at thirteen to start cutting trees. Spent fifteen years felling hardwood in Maine before he got invited to a tent revival one night and . . . that was that."

"What happened to theology school?"

He put his left elbow on the table and shifted as if to do the same with his right. Quickly he realized what he was doing and sat back, embarrassed.

"I guess a lot of things happened. My dad would say I lost my faith."

"And you'd say?"

His eyes were on mine, but his focus was somewhere a thousand yards behind me. After a long moment, he shrugged.

"I guess I'd say I lost my faith, too."

I tried to shift gears.

"How'd you trade a Bible for a badge?" I asked. "Seems like a sharp turn."

He shook his head. "Chief Whiddle gave me this job when I got back. I think it was mostly out of pity."

It felt like our conversation had nosed up to a BRIDGE OUT sign and I didn't know how to jump it.

"Look—there's a lot of things I'd like to ask," I said. "But there's one question that's really eating at me."

"Go ahead and ask it."

"What's your opinion on milkshakes?"

———

Lion's Pharmacy might not have known a Reuben from a rat-trap, but they had their malteds in hand. I went with strawberry while Joe stuck to vanilla, which I tried not to hold against him.

We walked back to the police station. At the foot of the station steps I lobbed the question I had been putting off.

"So you didn't run into Ruby at the circus?" I asked. "Maybe an hour before she died?"

He stopped. His malted sloshed onto his hand. He struggled to pull a handkerchief out of his pocket while holding on to the cup. Eventually, I took out mine and wiped vanilla off his fingers.

"That's kind of specific. Why do you ask?"

"Somebody saw her chatting with a man that night. He fits your description."

Maeve said it was probably a man, so that was technically true.

"No."

"No?"

"No, I didn't go to the circus, and no, that wasn't me."

"Your old flame comes to town after pulling a Houdini and you don't look her up?" I mused. "That's some willpower."

"Who's this person you say saw me?" he asked. "That didn't come up in the interviews."

He was ticked and he wasn't bothering to hide it.

"I didn't say you, specifically. Just a man."

"But who said it?"

Silence.

"Right," he said. "Because you're a big-city detective. Can't trust the hick cops."

He tossed his cup at a trash can. It bounced off the rim before going in, splattering white malted everywhere.

"Dang it."

He walked to the station house steps, then stopped and turned.

"Look, I know the Russian is your friend. You want it to not be him. I understand that. But keeping information from us—from me and the chief—isn't going to help," he said. "This is personal for us, too. We want to get to the truth as much as you."

I could feel my cheeks growing red. I'd fumbled the interview on the one-yard line.

"I'm sorry. I didn't mean—"

"No, I'm sorry," he said. "I was just trying to be nice. I thought . . . I don't know what I thought. And I'm sorry all the evidence points to your friend. He fought with her. It was his knife. He doesn't deny it. Grill me all you want, but that's not going to change."

He whirled away, heading up the steps toward the station's double doors.

I called after him. "I wasn't trying to grill you. Not really."

"Sure you were," he said over his shoulder. "It's your job."

He had to twist to fling open the door left-handed, but he managed. He got the slamming part right, too.

CHAPTER 17

I went over our conversation on the drive back to the farmhouse, taking it apart and putting it back together again to see what I'd learned, what I still didn't know, and where I could have done better.

The answers were "not much," "a whole lot," and "that part where I called him a liar." In that order.

Oh, well, I thought as I pulled into the driveway. He might be a looker, but he was still the law. I didn't need him to like me. Especially since I had every intention of proving Kalishenko innocent and Joe's boss a southern-fried ass.

I was prepared to catch my boss up on the conversation, but she decided not to cooperate, being absent from the farmhouse when I arrived. Instead, I found Doc settled at the kitchen table, making a dent in his beer supply, a pile of postcards spread out in front of him.

"Your boss, she went over to the circus," he informed me. "Think she was gonna catch the two o'clock show in the big top."

Knowing her, she'd put two and two together, figure out the killer, and have him in cuffs by the final bow. But in the event she didn't, I thought I'd best keep busy.

"Are these the ones Ruby sent you?" I asked, gesturing at the postcards on the table.

"Yeah, I . . . uh . . . I dug 'em out of my footlocker," Doc said.

"I had to . . . had to move some of your things to get to it. Put 'em back, but . . . uh. . . . sorry if I uh . . ."

I wasn't clear on what he was sorry about and neither was he. I counted off the empty bottles that were lined up against the wall at his feet. Many more and I'd run out of fingers.

"Hey, Doc. It's been a long day, and we've got the wake tonight," I said. "How about you catch a few winks. I'll go upstairs and do the same."

He looked up, his eyes bleary and unfocused behind his spectacles.

"You think?" he said.

"I think."

I walked the old man into the drawing room. As I was getting him laid out on the settee, he grabbed my wrist.

"The theater. The Majestic," he said. "I gotta open the Majestic."

I pried his fingers off. "It's closed today," I reminded him. "You put a sign up."

His brain took a three-count then remembered. "Right," he said. "The funeral. I closed it for . . ."

And he was out.

I walked on cat's feet back to the kitchen. Scooping up the postcards, I made my way upstairs, cringing at every groan and creak in the old farmhouse steps. Halfway up I realized that it wasn't going to wake Doc. From the snores that were coming out of the drawing room, I didn't think Gabriel could have woken him if he'd pressed his horn to his ear.

I went into my borrowed bedroom and found what Doc had been trying to apologize for. He had indeed put my clothes back on top of the footlocker. If by "put" you mean "piled." I smoothed things out as best I could, then retrieved the laundry bag from under the bed. Luckily, Doc's searching had been limited to the footlocker. I don't think he'd have appreciated seeing his niece in the buff. And I definitely didn't want him fumbling

with what I'd stashed between the mattress and the box spring.
Drunk as he was, he could have shot his toe off.

I sat on the bed and started sorting, trying to put Doc's postcards from Ruby into a rough timeline with the ones we'd found
in Ruby's trailer. The earliest ones were mostly sent by Doc
with a few letters of reply from a teenage Ruby. From the look
of things, he'd bounced around a lot after the war: Baltimore,
New York, Boston, Portland, Maine. The cold must have gotten to him, because he eventually fled out west: Oakland, Los
Angeles, San Diego, and down into Mexico for a while before
finally ending up in Denver, where he spent a whole two years.

He described each new place as if it were the best of all possible destinations, talking about the buildings and people and
food. Trying to live up to the four-color pictures on the front of
each postcard.

I'm not calling Doc a liar. But omission makes fibbers of us
all. He was definitely sifting through his journeys and present-
ing only the most golden grains.

The jobs he described—working assembly lines, sweeping
floors, hauling scrap, fruit picking, dock work—none of them
paid a wage worth writing home about. They certainly didn't
pay enough to travel first class, or even steerage. I pictured a lot
of train hopping in Doc's past. But every one of the postcards
he sent to Ruby had its corners dulled. Every one was creased,
the ink faded where Ruby had held it, her thumbs wearing the
paper thin.

Of course her parents had asked him to stop writing. It was
all well and good when she was a child, hearing fairy tales of her
uncle's grand travels. But what about when she grew up? When
she became old enough to chafe against the narrow walls of
that little bedroom of hers? That little life of hers?

When Ruby ran away, her parents probably imagined
her riding the rails like her uncle. Sleeping on the sidewalks,
scrounging for jobs. Walking the Devil's path.

But the postcards Ruby sent Doc told a different story.

"Hope you're staying warm up in the Mile High City. Guess you heard I've skedaddled from Stoppard. As you can tell from the picture of the Empire State Building on the front, I ended up in New York City! I'm doing well. Sharing a place with a few other girls. They're showing me the ropes and I hope to have exciting news soon. Give my love to Mom and Pa. —Your favorite niece, Ruby."

And a few months later:

"Hey, Unc. Still biting my way through the Big Apple. I'm working as a seamstress. Good thing I had to hem all my own clothes as a kid. Most of the job is boring but sometimes I get to help stitch costumes for Broadway shows!

"Remember when you told that story about how your war buddies all got the same tattoo but you wouldn't because you don't like needles and they thought that was funny? Well, you were right about them hurting. That's right. I got a tattoo! Don't worry. It wasn't a dive like the place your friends went to. Maybe don't tell my folks if you write to them. Love, Ruby."

I did the math on the dates and figured by the time that postcard was sent she had more than one tattoo. Guess she wanted to ease her uncle into it.

Her next postcard was one showing the circus—a pair of tigers standing proudly in the foreground, the big top looming in the back.

That one began, "You'll never guess where I am, Uncle Pat!"

The cards that followed were a lot like the ones from her uncle—cheery missives from the road. Though she didn't pave over all the potholes.

"Men can be real idiots, no offense. They think they know best when they really know nothing at all."

A response to the breakup with Val? Maybe. It was a tail that could be pinned to a lot of donkeys.

"Me and some of the girls spent a night in the hoosegow

courtesy of the local sheriff. Turns out the county had some ordinances about how much skin you can show, and apparently ink doesn't count as clothes. Don't worry, Bob had us out the next morning."

Not long after that, a trio of telegrams from Doc to Ruby.

"Ruby—Parents in car accident. Both dead. Returning to Stoppard. Will telegraph soon. Very sorry."

"Ruby—C&A's car hit black ice. They did not suffer. Arrangements need making. Can send money for train."

"Ruby—Service next Sunday at Blood of the Lamb. Will delay if need to. Can wire money for ticket home. Love, Your Uncle."

After that, a telegram from Ruby to Doc. Just a few sentences.

"That's so awful about Mom and Pa. It's good they didn't suffer. I'm sorry I won't make the service. Will write again soon. Love, Ruby."

The next postcard didn't come for months. In it she talks about the towns she's visited, the movies she's seen. Nothing about her parents. No plans to come home to leave flowers at the grave. I wondered why.

Maybe she didn't want to show off her new skin in front of the good folks of Stoppard. The audiences at the Midnight Circus probably felt safer to her than the lunch crowd at Lion's. Another possibility was that she had a more pressing reason for leaving home in the first place. That there was more wrong with her home life than its narrow horizons. Did her folks subscribe to the old dictum of "spare the rod, spoil the child"? Or worse?

People think that secrets are hard to keep in a small town, with everybody knee-deep in everyone else's business. But that's not always the case. Especially in communities like Stoppard, where there are more people living out in the country than on Main Street.

I'd grown up like that. Far from the nearest stoplight, no neighbors in shouting distance. A lot of terrible things can happen in those houses on the outskirts. And if people suspect, they don't always talk about it. Small towns can be like life rafts; people in them are just trying to survive. You don't rock the boat if you don't have to.

There was no evidence anything like that happened to Ruby. But that's where my mind was on account of one other postcard I found in Doc's collection. Between the salutation and the so-long, Ruby wrote:

"We picked up a hitchhiker at our last gig. Says she's eighteen, but if she's a day over sixteen I'll eat Ray's stash of crickets. Dee told Bob we didn't have the space or the dough and we needed to drop her off at the next stop. I talked a couple of the girls into sharing their trailer and told Dee I'd donate my tips from the late show for her pay. I guess I have a soft spot for strays. Someone's been hurting her bad. The bruises on her back were something awful, Unc. I couldn't send her back to that."

I read and reread that paragraph until my eyes blurred. Ruby had gone to bat for me and I'd never even known. Without her, who knows where I'd be, above ground or below.

Ruby Donner had saved my life and I'd never gotten a chance to thank her. Catching her killer would have to do.

CHAPTER 18

So that's the long and short of it. If Ruby left a grudge behind in Stoppard, she didn't write home about it. But that doesn't mean much. It's not like she'd spill her dirt to her uncle. All in all, I didn't discover much. Other than that Lion's Pharmacy makes a pretty good strawberry milkshake."

Ms. Pentecost and I were making our way carefully along the path that cut through the line of trees separating Doc's house from the plot of land where the circus was set up.

I kept my eyes fixed on the ground ahead of us as I talked. It was nearing midnight and the trickle of moonlight coming through the branches wasn't quite up to the task of picking out the roots and gopher holes that threatened to swallow the shit-kicker boots I'd changed into.

I'd rotated the rest of my wardrobe as well. The men's undershirt was more gray than white and the denim overalls were worn thin around the joints, but they were some of the only articles I still had from my circus days and they still fit. Mostly.

I'd put on about ten pounds thanks to Mrs. Campbell's ruthless use of butter. Consequently, the overalls rode up in a way they hadn't done previously and I had to keep from reaching down and adjusting them all the time. Still, it seemed an appropriate costume for the wake.

"I disagree," Ms. P said, pushing aside an errant sticker bush with her cane. "I think the absences in her correspondences tell us much."

"Okay, I'll bite," I said. "What do they say?"

"The only person she wrote to regularly, or cared enough about to keep his cards, was her uncle. There were no letters from friends, none from other family. Her ties to Stoppard seem limited. Or at least relegated to the past."

"Doesn't mean she wasn't writing someone else," I argued. "Someone around here might have a whole stack of cards tucked away."

"Who do you imagine this person is?" my boss asked.

"A secret lover. An old friend. Take your pick."

"Someone who never wrote Ms. Donner back? Or at least meant so little that she discarded that person's letters?"

Later on I would remember a phrase Ms. P employed on occasion: "Absence of evidence is not evidence itself." If I'd remembered it at the time, I'd have recited it and felt pretty swell about myself.

As it stood, I let Ms. P take the lead while I set my mind to sorting. There was little chance of losing her in the dark. She practically glowed in her sleeveless, high-necked blouse over loose linen pants, both in Mira-Glo white.

She'd worn the same duds during her day at the circus and had managed to walk away without so much as a speck of dirt. Put me in that combo and five minutes later I'll have mud on my cuffs and coffee stains on my collar.

While I had been lunching with Officer Joe and sorting through postcards, she'd spent the afternoon and early evening playing the rube: wandering the circus, seeing the sights, the shows, striking up conversations with as many staff and performers as she could corner without making them nervous.

During normal times this would have been my gig: bouncing around, poking my nose into places, talking to whoever about whatever, and then hauling the essentials back to my boss. But these weren't normal times. We were untethered from the office, strangers in a strange land, and we had to put our usual routines on the shelf.

I think Ms. Pentecost actually relished stepping out from behind her desk to stretch her investigative limbs. As I was reminded again and again, she'd been doing this job long before I showed up, and her talents at getting people talking were top-notch.

She hadn't returned to the farmhouse from her circus jaunt until a little after dark. We'd still had a couple hours until the wake, so the two of us sat on the farmhouse porch and she gave me the lowdown.

"It's fascinating," she said. "The circus is both employer and home to those who work there. And to one another they are both coworkers and family to varying degrees. Rivalries, romances, the casual slights that accumulate from living in such close quarters—all of these are inexorably tangled together. And yet, the daily operation of the circus seems not to be impacted."

"Dysfunctionally functional. I could have told you that," I said. "Whatever you've got going on with the person next to you, the show must go on."

"But the passions still exist. And these are passionate peo-ple to begin with," my boss contended. "For example, in my short time there today I discovered that Ray and Paulie have a long-standing feud about space in Sideshow Alley, Mr. Pagliano being of the opinion that the House of Oddities deserves the prime spot that the reptile house currently holds."

"Old news. They've been going at that for years."

"The youngest of the Sabatini daughters was planning to leave the circus and move to New Orleans with a young man who crewed the big top. I use the past tense because her broth-ers had a conversation with the man and he left the circus alone the next day."

I wondered if the fellow had left with all his limbs intact.

"And more than a few members of the staff, including several performers, disapprove of the relationship between the contortionist and the tiger trainer."

"Frieda and Carlotta are an item?" I asked.

"For much of the past year."

That put a whole new light on their whip act.

"Let me guess. The problem isn't that they're women."

"Correct. I heard the word *miscegenation* used more than once."

It ignited a spark of shame in my gut. Even at the circus, with its vast array of people and predilections, love and understanding only went so far before it butted up against plain old human ignorance.

"My point," Ms. P continued, "is that the feud between Ms. Donner and Mr. Kalishenko was not unique. Its equivalent likely exists by the dozens, many of which are not common knowledge. It is very possible that someone, several someones, could wish Ms. Donner ill. Even to the point of murder."

It was at that point in the conversation that I noticed both hands on my watch creeping up on the twelve. We paused things and began our trek to the circus. I filled Ms. P in on the postcards, and that ended with us butting up against the evidence or absence thereof.

I was still mulling that over when we emerged into the open field between the trees and the circus. Most of the grounds were doused in darkness, except for the flickering orange of firelight coming from near the crew trailers. We aimed ourselves in that direction.

"You know," I said, "the circus doesn't have a patent on secret feuds. It's just as likely there was something simmering in town: somebody who hated her and didn't bother paying the postage to tell her as much. Seeing Ruby back could have set him off."

My boss nodded, shifting her good eye from the circus to the ruts and rocks in front of her and back again.

"That is certainly a possibility," she said. "If such a secret relationship exists, perhaps our gambit tomorrow will unearth it."

I opened my mouth to argue against this supposed "gambit" for the twentieth time, but quickly closed it. She had her mind fixed, and unfixing a Pentecost plan was more heavy lifting than it was worth.

When we got to the trailers, we discovered a ring of oil drums had been filled with scrap wood and set alight. A hundred shadowy silhouettes milled about, laughing, singing, reclining on folding chairs, playing music, and generally having as good a time as you can under the shadow of death.

The copious bottles being passed around didn't hurt.

"How do you want to divvy this up?" I asked.

"See if you can speak to Frieda alone. You know what to ask."

"And you?"

We entered the ring of firelight and caught sight of Big Bob having an animated conversation with Doc and Maeve. He was using the whiskey bottle in his hand as an exclamation point.

"I think I will have a drink," my boss said. "And keep an ear open."

She moved toward the trio and ten seconds later Bob had found a glass and was pouring her a snort.

I dug around in an ice-filled bucket of bottles until I located a soda, popped the top off, and went wandering.

I found Frieda lounging in the door of her trailer. Carlotta was sitting on the step above her and Frieda was reclining, her arms draped over the cat-wrangler's legs. She'd folded her blue bodysuit away for the night and changed into a white sundress that showed off all the best parts of her elastic limbs.

"Hey, Frieda, you got a minute?"

"Sure," she said uncertainly. "What about?"

"Just a few questions." I nodded to Carlotta. "I won't keep her away long."

"Take your time," Carlotta said. Then she grabbed Frieda around the waist and kissed her. I'm not saying tongues were involved, but I wouldn't rule it out.

Carlotta's point was clear: Chat all you want, but she's coming home to me.

Frieda and I walked away from the fire and the crowd into the moonlit midway of silent games and empty concession stands.

"You know what I'm going to ask," I said, referring to the packet found at the bottom of Ruby's laundry bag.

"I know," the Rubber Band Girl admitted. "I don't know what she was doing with it."

"Where was it hidden?" I asked.

"It wasn't. It was right on top of her trunk."

That didn't make any sense. I don't care if you've got a private trailer—you don't leave your heroin sitting in plain sight.

"What about a fix kit?" I asked, meaning the needle, spoon, lighter, and whatever else a junkie needs to shoot up.

Frieda shook her head. "Nothing like that. If we found it, it was in that bag I gave you."

"Are you sure?"

"Yeah, I'm sure," she said, stopping and turning on me. "Why give you the dope if I was going to hide anything else?"

It was a good question and I didn't have a good answer.

"Do you think she was using?"

"Hell, no."

"Is anyone at the circus using?"

She stopped in her tracks.

"Are you kidding? You know the score. Booze, some pot— sure. No junk."

"You can hide needle marks," I argued.

"But you can't hide being on the nod. Someone's using the hard stuff, everyone's gonna know fast."

She was right. Not only would heroin addiction have been noticed, it wouldn't have been tolerated. Being a boozehound was one thing. Kalishenko wasn't the only person at H&H with a bottle-a-day habit. But being on the nod from a needle was something else entirely. Not the least of which was that it would be hard to keep up that kind of habit while on the road.

The lack of needle marks on Ruby's body combined with Frieda's story about finding the packet in plain sight pointed to the heroin being a plant. But who planted it? And why? I switched gears.

"How about her home life? Ruby ever talk about that? People she thought about, kept in contact with?"

Frieda shook her head.

"What about plans to see old friends? Maybe an old flame?"

"Sorry," Frieda said. "If she said anything, it wasn't to me."

A dead end. I swerved.

"If you had to pick the person at H and H most likely to put a knife in Ruby's back, who would be at the top of the list?"

She stopped and turned to me.

"Are you serious? You're really asking me that?"

I held my hands up in front of me, ready to catch a slap if it came my way.

"Hey, it's my job, all right? That's why I'm here. It's nothing personal."

The fire in her eyes only flared brighter.

"It's *personal* to me," she growled. "This might be your job, but it's my family."

It wasn't a slap but a gut punch. *Your* job. *My* family. And never the two shall mix.

I'd been thinking of myself as still part of the H&H family. Maybe I had moved out of the house, but that didn't mean I couldn't come home for holidays.

But I wasn't. Of course I wasn't. Like Ms. P had said—the

circus was a world unto itself. And if you weren't part of it, you weren't part of it.

"I'm sorry," I said. "It was a stupid question and I'm sorry I asked."

After a long moment, Frieda nodded, accepting my apology.

A hot summer breeze ruffled my hair and a low groan vibrated out from the far end of the midway. We both turned our eyes up to the Ferris wheel, its skeletal hulk barely visible in the moonlight. Its carts swung slowly, creating a creaking chorus that turned the entire circus into a haunted house. The sound sent a shiver up my spine.

I started us walking again, turning in to the Loop. Because I wasn't sorry I asked the question. It needed asking. And maybe walking by the spot where Ruby was stabbed would agitate Frieda enough to answer.

Yeah, it was a nasty trick. I figured if I wasn't family I might as well start acting the detective. But when we got to the entrance to the side tent, we found the lights on and a figure standing in the middle of the playing space. It was the Amazing Annabelle, Mysterio's assistant.

She had a silk-draped table set up in front of her with an assortment of props spread across it.

"What's her story?" I side-mouthed.

The contortionist shrugged. "No idea," she said. "Been here a year, but hasn't placed a premium on making friends."

"Personality problems?"

"I mean, she's a bitch, but so are a lot of us," Frieda said. "Thing with her is she's all business, all the time. If she's not performing, she's practicing. If she's not practicing, she's got her nose in a book."

I watched as Annabelle ran through a series of quick card palms, which included a deck swap that looked flawless from a distance.

Frieda shuffled her feet beside me.

"If you're done with me, I'd like to get back to the party," she said.

"One last thing." I pulled her away from the tent entrance. Out of what I figured was earshot. "So . . . you and Carlotta?"

I saw her tense and wondered what question she was expecting.

"You two are serious, huh?"

She relaxed some and I saw her smile for the first time that night. "Serious enough for circus life."

"You catching any grief?"

Her smile grew barbs.

"Not to my face."

Something was itching at me—a question I wanted to ask but knew I shouldn't. I gave in and scratched.

"You think we could have been serious?" I asked. "If I'd stuck around?"

I saw the answer in her eyes before she spoke.

"I don't know, Will. We were good for some fun, but . . . I don't think we would have worked."

I could tell she wanted to say more, so I stayed quiet and gave her the chance. She bit her lip, hesitated, then let it fly.

"It was all the anger, you know."

I don't know what I was expecting, but it wasn't that.

"Anger? Look, I know I have a temper but I'd never . . ." I didn't even know how to finish that.

"I'm not talking temper," she said. "I mean, sure, you have one. That's nothing I can't handle. But you were always more likely to hurt yourself than me."

I didn't pick up what she was putting down, and it must have showed.

"Like the time Rita Sabatini said you'd probably piss yourself if you ever went out on a wire. You remember that?"

I nodded. I wasn't likely to forget. I hated heights. Somehow Rita found out and turned it into a taunt. So I started training on the wire the very next day. Did it for two weeks straight. It probably took five years off my life, but I could make it across by the end.

I made Rita eat her words.

"Every night you'd come back sweating and shivering and wanting to die," Frieda said. "You suffered every second, but you wouldn't stop."

"Come on," I said. "That was just me showing her up."

"You were angry at anyone who told you what you couldn't do. Or be. Or be with," she said. "You nursed it, too. Sharpened its teeth. How many times did we lie in my bunk, you talking about this or that so-and-so who said some stupid thing? I've known girls like that. I've loved girls like that. Ones who run on anger. I watched it chew 'em up. Until they caved in on themselves, or that thing inside them snapped its leash and . . ."

Frieda peered up into the star-specked sky, frowning. She stayed like that for a long time, thinking about what to say next. Or searching for a constellation that should have been there but wasn't.

"Anyway, I just didn't want to watch that again."

She tilted her eyes back to earth, back to me.

"Anytime we're in a town big enough to carry the *Times*, I pick one up and hunt for your boss's name," she said. "Reading about how you're helping catch these killers and firebugs and all that, it makes me happy. Lets me know you're still going. That it hasn't eaten you yet."

She leaned toward me and kissed me on the cheek. I caught a whiff of her. Frieda was never one for perfume. Just the familiar scent of skin and hair and breath.

"If it makes you feel better, I like this version of you," she said. "Being a detective suits you."

She turned her back and continued along the path toward the sound of singing.

CHAPTER *19*

I was still punch-drunk from Frieda's words when I looked back at the entrance to the side tent to find the magician-in-training staring at me.

I waved, wondering if she'd caught any of the conversation. Or, if not, what she'd thought of the dumb show.

"You need a volunteer from the audience?" I asked, looking for an excuse to think about something—anything—else.

She was silent for a moment, then gave me the nod to approach.

She was wearing the same outfit from the late show—spangly vest that served as a display case, skintight shorts, and black fishnets. She was barefoot for rehearsal. Remembering the jacked-up heels of her thigh-highs, I didn't blame her.

She held up a deck of cards. With a flick of her thumb, the queen of hearts popped out.

"The queen of hearts—beautiful and bold. Like nobody else around." She tapped the card back into the deck and gave it a shuffle. "When you see her, she's usually rubbing shoulders with all the beautiful people."

She fanned the cards out on the table in front of her. All of the face cards were clustered together, the queen of hearts smack-dab in the middle. She scooped and shuffled.

"Most of the time, though, she feels like she's utterly alone."

Another fan. This time the queen of hearts was in the dead center of the deck, all the other face cards shoved to the far ends of the spread.

Scoop. Shuffle.

Over the next couple of spreads, the queen bounced around the deck. Sometimes it was paired with its king, sometimes with another queen, sometimes pressed in a gang of jacks.

Sure, it was buffed-up three-card monte. But it was elegant.

"Eventually our girl gets tired of the game. She goes out to find one of her own."

One last fan of the cards. Not a single face card showing.

"And without her, the party's over."

I gave her an honest round of applause.

"Not bad," I said. "That's the end?"

"You don't think it's a good ending?" she said, wrinkling her crooked nose at me.

"You've only got two acts. Act one: Here it is. Act two: Now it's gone. When it comes to a disappearing trick, the crowd's always hungry for the reveal."

She extended her arm toward me, rotating her hand to show she wasn't palming anything, then reached into the pocket of my overalls and plucked out a card. She showed it to me.

"The queen of spades?"

"You look more like a spade girl. They used to be knives, after all."

So she wasn't ignorant of who I was, or my history at H&H.

She flicked her hand, and the card disappeared. I know it had to be tucked on the other side of her hand, held there by the barest backward grip of a finger. But I couldn't see it.

Just as quickly, the queen of spades reappeared in her hand, this time accompanied by the rest of the face cards. She put them on the table and began resetting the deck.

I know when I'm being toyed with and I usually don't mind,

especially when the toying comes from someone in fishnets. But I had the distinct impression that flirting wasn't in the cards.

Never one to avoid mixing business with just about anything, I asked, "Were you cleaning up with Mysterio Tuesday night when he saw Val walk by?"

She nodded, not looking up from her business.

"You see him, too?"

A headshake. "My back was to the entrance."

"Huh."

Her eyes flicked up, something sharp glittering in their centers.

"If he saw him, he saw him," she said. "There's no percentage in lying."

She'd given me the same look when we'd locked eyes at the Midnight Circus. Again, I wondered where the hostility was coming from.

"If you say so," I said, purposefully baiting her.

Apparently she saw the bait for what it was, and smothered whatever feelings she had.

"Yeah, well, I say so," she told me, voice as bland as Sunday supper.

"When you stumbled over the body, you didn't see anybody around?"

"Just her. And the knife sticking out of her back."

She gave the deck a quick shuffle.

"Now if you don't mind, you're eating into my ring time."

I knew when I wasn't wanted. I thanked her and headed to the exit. In the doorway, I felt a pang of something and turned back.

"You should come to the party," I said. "Like it or not, they're your people."

I might not have been family anymore, but I wasn't beyond giving a little sisterly advice. Annabelle wasn't feeling sisterly, though. Her lips curled into something that was more sneer than smile.

"You think those are my people? Clowns and spec girls whose only talent is their bust size?"

I nodded at her low-cut vest.

"Girls wearing glass corsets shouldn't throw stones."

She grabbed her chest and gave it a hike.

"This isn't the show, honey," she said. "If my tits get me in the door, fine. I'll take it. But it's *this* that keeps me there."

She turned her seemingly empty hand over and a waterfall of cards began to tumble to the floor. A whole deck's worth appearing out of nowhere, each card identical. Fifty-two red ladies fluttering down to land at the magician's fishnet feet.

CHAPTER 20

Back at the wake, I found Ms. Pentecost reclining in a beach chair, both hands cradling a glass. The liquid in it glowed golden in the firelight.

She was the apex of a half circle of chairs that included Big Bob; Maeve; Ray; Paulie; Vincente, the oldest of the Sabatinis; Doc, who was softly snoring; and Sam Lee, who had his head propped in his hands, eyes rapt, like a kid listening to ghost stories.

I settled into an empty chair between Ray and Paulie, who was nearing the end of a story about Gimlet Jerry.

I'd never met Jerry, but I'd heard all the tales. He'd been a clown who thought making people laugh was a man's highest calling.

Problem was, he had no talent for it. No balance, no rhythm, no sense of timing. Juggling clubs slipped out of his fingers; cartwheels were fumbled; punch lines landed so bad you could hear their legs snap.

Thing was, he was so bad he was good. If greatness could be weighed by the guffaws coming out of the crowd, Jerry was the greatest clown H&H ever had.

"People thought it was an act," Paulie was telling my boss. "They thought he meant to be that bad. So they figured him for brilliant and they laughed their asses off."

Ms. P sipped her whiskey and put on her pondering face.

"So the question becomes," Paulie continued, "was he a success? Even though his technique was a failure. And that is what Bob and I have been arguing about for going on twenty years. I fall on the side of if it works, it works."

Ms. P turned to the ringmaster, who was nestled in his folding chair, his legs tucked under him, vest undone, jet-black hair loose and falling into his face.

"What say you, Robert?" she asked.

"He wanted to do one thing well, and he couldn't hack it. I mean, sure, the audience didn't know that, but he knew. That's what mattered."

The dwarf kicked back a little of what was in his flask, then added, "Unlike those audiences, I know how he ended up. In a flophouse in Cleveland with a rope around his neck."

That hit the brakes on the chatter.

We listened to the music and the conversation coming from the other clumps of revelers, their shadows projected huge and dancing against the sides of the trailers. Being uncomfortable with silence at the best of times, I decided to lighten the mood.

"Hey, Ray," I said, giving the snake handler a prod with my elbow, "what's this I hear about you clocking a cop with a birdcage?"

I've never seen a man do a full-body blush, but Ray managed it.

"Oh, that was a terrible misunderstanding," he said. "The landlord said he'd wait until I found homes for all my animals. I didn't care about selling them. I just wanted them to be safe. Then there was this officer and he had a padlock and he said I had to leave right then and there. I tried to explain that there would be no one to feed the animals, that they would starve, but he wouldn't listen and . . . Well, I acted very rashly and . . . I paid the price for it."

The ache in his voice said more than the words did. State-

ville wouldn't have been a kind place. Not for someone as loving and compassionate as Ray.

"Never again," he said, as much to himself as me. "I'll never
let something like that happen again."

More silence. This time I let it stay for a while.

Doc snorted awake. After a shaky moment he remembered
where he was. He excused himself, thanked Bob again for setting everything up, and began stumbling in the direction of
home.

I kept an eye on him until he was lost to the darkness. I figured it wasn't the first time he'd been called on to find his way
home drunk.

At some point, Paulie and Vincente wandered over to the
musicians, adding their voices to the stream of barroom hymns.
Not long after, Sam Lee excused himself to bed.

"Gotta get up at dawn to muck out the pens," he said. "You
would not believe how much that little Jingles can push out. Or
maybe you would, Miss Parker, having slopped the stalls yourself. You all have a good night."

Eventually the conversation in our diminished group
started up again and quickly spiraled down the drain of one of
the favorite topics of performers everywhere: the good old days
and how these weren't them.

"Used to be we could put on a two-hour show and not
repeat a performer once, except for the clowns," Big Bob said.
"These days, everybody's got to do an encore or the crowds
think they got cheated."

I'd been too distracted by my own feelings at the funeral to
do a head count, but now that he mentioned it, I realized a lot of
faces had been missing from the mourners.

"What happened?" I asked.

"The usual," Bob said. "People joined bigger outfits. Places
that could pay better. Or they just got old. Bart retired to Ari-

zona to open a dude ranch. Dee fled to Florida. Pretty sure Vincente's looking to leave. He's getting up there."

I felt a twinge of guilt. I'd been one of the people who had fled for better pay. Sure, Big Bob had pushed me, but I hadn't put up much of a fight.

"We've been shedding crowds, too," the circus owner continued. "Ten years ago? Even up to right before the war, we'd have had twice as many people coming through the gates."

Maeve flapped a ring-covered hand at him.

"Honey, Stoppard's a two-horse burg. You can't come here expecting Chicago numbers," she said, her words slurring on the back end. "I think things are just crackers . . . crackerjack."

"You think that because you spend your day in your tent taking the punters one at a time," Bob argued. "Of course the crowds don't seem thinner to you. And don't talk to me about Chicago numbers. We haven't been anywhere near Chicago in years. Same with Cincinnati or Baltimore and now Richmond. Bigger outfits keep pushing us out. I'm shocked we held on to Pittsburgh this season."

He knocked out the last couple of drops from his flask.

"Places like Stoppard are our future," he said. "If we have one."

Ray unfolded himself from his chair with a groan and a sprinkling of popping joints.

"That's it for me," he said, smoothing out the wrinkles in his vest. "You start talking money woes, I have to leave."

"Ah, come on, Ray!" Maeve lamented. "The night's young."

"It's morning, Maeve. Well past my bedtime. My babies will wonder where I went."

Ray tottered off toward Sideshow Alley and his eight-legged and no-legged friends.

"I guess that's it for me, too," Maeve muttered. "Gotta be a . . . whatchacallit? Adult."

Big Bob leaped up and helped her out of her chair.

"Come on, honey. I'll see you to bed."

"Don't get fresh, Bobby," she said. Her eye shadow had dried out and was crumbling on her lids like old spackle. Maeve looked all her years and then some.

"You need anything from me?" Big Bob asked us before leaving. "I'd ask if you've had any luck, but I'm afraid of the answer."

My boss stayed put in her chair, leaning back, eyelids at three-quarters mast. She traced the edge of her nearly empty glass with an idle finger.

"I wouldn't call it luck," she said. "Though we have developed some interesting avenues of investigation."

That was our standard line when clients asked how we were faring. Though this time it wasn't a total dodge. As avenues went, heroin was certainly interesting.

"One question," she added. "You told me that many of the company have criminal records. Do any involve narcotics?"

Big Bob cocked an eyebrow.

"Narcotics? You mean cocaine?"

"Cocaine, opium, heroin—substances beyond alcohol or marijuana."

"If anyone has a rap like that, I don't know about it," he said. "Maeve, you know of anyone?"

Maeve swiveled around. She would have toppled if Bob hadn't been there to prop her up.

"Know any of who now?"

"Anyone with dope in their past?" he asked. "The hard stuff?"

She shook her head. It took a while to stop wobbling.

"Nah," she said. "Not to say no one here ever used it. I did enough toot in my youth to give Mabel Normand a run for her money. Why you asking?"

My boss managed a nonchalant shrug.

"I've found that drug use frequently coincides with violent behavior. As Will would say, I'm merely covering our bases."

It was a smooth dodge and I thought Maeve bought it, but I could tell Big Bob didn't. He gave me a look—curiosity and just a hint of resentment at being played.

"Yeah, okay," he said. "Well, I don't know of any. But I'll ask around. Come on, Maeve. Let's tuck you in. Good night, you two."

We said good night and watched as he led the old fortune-teller back to her trailer. Other clusters of partygoers began to drift away, including most of the musicians. Eventually, the only one left was the violinist, who played an old klezmer tune that I'd heard Hiram whistle on occasion while tending to his charges in the morgue.

Ms. Pentecost reached down to a whiskey bottle at her feet and poured another finger in her glass. I restrained myself from asking how she was faring. The only thing she hated more than the multiple sclerosis was me bugging her about it.

"You want to talk here or when we get back to the house? You look pretty comfortable."

She twisted her neck around to see who was still in ear-shot. There was no one in the vicinity. But we were surrounded by trailers, any of which could have somebody listening at the window.

"I suppose we should go back to the farmhouse," she said. "There's no reason to chance being overheard."

She downed her whiskey in a single gulp and nodded at me to help her out of the beach chair. She had half a foot and maybe thirty pounds on me, and there was a moment when we were both in danger of toppling, but eventually I got her upright.

We'd made it about fifty yards across the field when I heard the sound of smashing glass and something like a low, loud cough. I glanced back, expecting to see a drunk roustabout stumbling his way home.

Instead, I saw a flickering light from somewhere on the far corner of the circus grounds—an orange glow that was growing brighter by the second.

Ms. Pentecost saw it, too.

"Is that . . . ?"

"Yep."

I started running, circling around the outside of the canvas fencing, Ms. P following as quickly as she could.

I was halfway there when I heard my boss shout something unprintable. I looked back to see her lying in the dirt. She waved me on.

"Go, go!"

I did.

Cries of "Fire!" were echoing throughout the grounds and I saw people squeezing out of breaks in the fence and running toward the same place I was—a spot on the edge of the grounds where a wall of flames was starting to claw its way into the night sky.

Sideshow Alley was burning.

CHAPTER **21**

About twenty feet of the canvas fencing was on fire, as were the backs of the wooden booths behind it. A bucket brigade was already forming, carrying water from the big tank near the animal cages.

Hart & Halloway rehearsed for this as diligently as any performance. In a traveling city of canvas and wood, fire was a top-five fear. Clown, contortionist, or candy butcher—everybody slung water when they heard the alarm go up.

At the speed people were moving, they'd have the fire out in minutes. Figuring to add my hand to the effort, I went to fill in a gap and almost ran into Paulie, who was stock-still and staring up at the center of the flames.

"Ray!" he cried out. "Anybody got eyes on Ray?"

The reptile keeper was nowhere in sight. Then I realized what had Paulie panicked. The House of Venomous Things was dead smack in the center of the conflagration. While the main body of the converted train car hadn't caught, the whole backside of Ray's upper loft was in flames.

Before anyone could stop him, Paulie darted through a gap in the burning canvas and into Sideshow Alley.

And before anyone could stop me, I followed him.

Together, we ran around to the front of the old train car and inside the reptile house. Paulie grabbed a stool, placed it under the hatch to the loft, and climbed on it.

The glass cases were a flurry of scurries and slithers, their occupants sensing the danger.

"Ray! Ray, you up there!" the clown yelled.

He pushed against the hatch. It shifted some but he couldn't get it open.

"Ray's bed is a fold-up," he said. "I think it's on top of the goddamn hatch."

Which meant Ray was up there, in bed, and for some reason he wasn't answering.

We ran back out. While we'd been inside, the fire had crept up onto the roof of the loft and was making its way around the sides. Soon the whole thing would be engulfed.

The side of the loft we were facing—the one that had the tiny window set in it—was still mostly clear. The window was open, but I didn't see anything moving inside.

"We need buckets over here!" Paulie yelled.

Someone shouted a reply from the other side of the fence, but I didn't catch it. Paulie and I shared a look and I knew he was thinking the same thing. They weren't going to get here in time.

In desperation, he leaped up and got his fingers around the burning edge of the trailer roof. The old wood tore off in his hands and he landed rough.

He stumbled halfway to his feet, twin lines seared into his palms.

Seeing him in that position—crouched, hands out—gave me a terrible idea.

"The number three!" I yelled.

"What?"

"Give me the number three. Extra sauce!"

To Paulie's credit, he didn't dither. He immediately laced his fingers together and made a cradle for my foot.

Back when I was with the circus, I did a stint training with the clown crew. To poke at the aerialists, who had grand names for all their maneuvers, the clowns treated their tumbling routines like items off a Chinese restaurant menu.

The number three was usually pointed in the direction of one of the big-top nets. This time my target was a lot less forgiving.

I took half a dozen running steps, the last one sending my foot right into Paulie's waiting hands. He stood up, propelling me up and onto the trailer roof. I managed to hit the side of the loft with my shoulder rather than my head.

I scrambled to my knees and squirmed headfirst into the window.

Immediately I was blind, coughing, choking. The tiny loft was filled with smoke. I dropped to my belly and found six inches of breathable air.

There was the cot. I shimmied over and reached up, grabbing hold of the body lying on top of it. I dragged Ray off his bed and onto the floor. I pressed my head to his chest. After a second that lasted a year, I felt a shaky breath.

Ray was a boxers-only man at night, so finding a handhold wasn't easy. By the time I got him under the window, I couldn't tell if the darkness was from the smoke or if I was getting ready to pass out. I took a deep breath, inhaling a shaker of embers and ash along with the oxygen.

Tongues of flame were licking around the edges of the window frame. I crawled out first, then reached back, got a grip under Ray's armpits, and began to pull. I was dimly aware that one leg of my overalls was on fire and part of my brain occupied itself wondering how long it would take before the flames got through the fabric and started in on flesh.

The question was made moot when a bucket's worth of water hit me square in the back, washing away the flames and stripping the breath out of my lungs.

Another hit. Then another.

A pair of massive arms reached around one side of me and grabbed Ray. I turned to find Clover perched on top of a ladder. He pulled Ray the rest of the way out the window as easy as you would a rag doll.

He slung the reptile keeper over his shoulder and went carefully down the ladder. Once he was clear, I scooted down after him.

Paulie was there with a half-dozen others, throwing water up on the last of the flames. In the distance, I heard the wail of sirens.

Ray was stretched out on the ground. His eyes fluttered open and he immediately began coughing, then turned to his side and threw up that evening's dinner.

I took a deep breath, then immediately bent at the waist and began hacking up what felt like half a lung. Paulie came over and threw a boxer's arm around my neck.

"God damn, Parker. That was something else."

I tried to say, "Learned from the best," but all that came out was the other half a lung.

Once I caught my breath, I stumbled back through the scorched remains of the fence and looked around for Ms. Pentecost. Eventually I sighted her on the edge of the crowd, being propped up by Sam Lee.

"Are you all right?" I said, heading over.

"I saw her lying in the field back there. Think she maybe sprained her ankle," Sam Lee said, handing me her cane.

The detective shook her head. "It's merely twisted," she said, shrugging out of the young cirky's grip. She immediately started to topple, and Sam Lee swooped back in and caught her.

"Argue semantics all you want, I don't think you're whipping out your dance card anytime soon," I told her.

We watched as a fire engine made its bumpy way across the field. Not far behind it was a Stoppard Police car.

"Can you keep her upright?"

"Of course, Miss Parker. I've got her," Sam Lee said.

To my boss I asked, "Will you relent to being propped and not mess up that ankle any worse?"

The look she shot me suggested I should get out of striking range. I hurried toward the growing crowd.

The fire engine emptied its load of volunteer firefighters, who found that the flames had been doused and all that was left to do was stomp out the embers. The door of the cop car opened and Joe stepped out. He was wearing his uniform shirt over grease-stained dungarees, like he'd gotten dressed in the dark and hadn't cared about mixing and matching.

Big Bob caught sight of him, too. The ringmaster stormed over and began shaking what looked like the neck of a broken bottle at Joe, who was staring at it, confused and bleary-eyed. I walked quicker, afraid Joe might get gouged.

"Hang on—calm down, Mr. Halloway," he was saying. "You've got to keep calm."

"Keep calm? Keep calm!" the ringmaster yelled. "Someone tried to burn down my goddamn circus!"

Joe looked around at the organized chaos, like he was searching for a cue card. I had to remember he hadn't been wearing the badge all that long, and that things weren't usually so hectic in sleepy Stoppard.

I threw him a line.

"The wake had just wrapped when somebody decided to put a torch to the sideshow over there," I explained. "Almost took out Ray in the process."

The mention of someone nearly dying seemed to focus him.

"Were people drinking? Could it have been an accident?"

"Accident, my sweet fanny!" Big Bob shouted. "Smell this. Go on, smell it."

Joe took the bottleneck and gave it a tentative sniff. Whatever it was finished the job of waking him up.

"Smell that?" Big Bob said triumphantly. "We've got some strong stomachs around here, but nobody is sipping gasoline."

He pointed at the scrap of scorched rag that was still hanging from the neck of the bottle.

"What I think is, someone filled that sucker, stuffed a rag in for a wick, lit it and—"

Joe interrupted the flow. "A Molotov."

"A what?"

"A Molotov cocktail. Saw them used in the war," he explained. "Not sure if the Russians invented them, but they perfected them."

"There you go!" Big Bob declared.

I chimed in again.

"I think I might have heard it hit," I said. "Glass breaking followed by a sound that could have been the gas going up."

Joe looked at me like he was seeing me for the first time. He gave me the once-over and I wondered just what brand of mess I looked.

"Right," he said, placing the broken bottleneck gingerly on the hood of his car. "I'll hold on to this as evidence. And I'm gonna need to talk to whoever was around. Get statements. Maybe you should consider keeping the circus closed tomorrow. For safety's sake."

"Safety's sake. Safety's sake!" Big Bob shouted. "Whoever did this—us shutting down is exactly what they want. You think I'm gonna just bend over and give it to 'em?"

Joe managed to hold his ground better than most when faced with a tirade from the little man.

"We don't know if scaring you away was the intent," Joe said, in the kind of measured tone you'd use to talk down a jumper.

"Why else pull a stunt like this?" the ringmaster said, sweeping an arm toward the destroyed fence and the scorched reptile house behind it.

Why else indeed, I thought.

This section of the fence was decorated with the banners advertising the acts you'd find in Sideshow Alley. Several of them were now ash, but the tattered edges of the burned section remained. A bare leg, green scales, the word *skin*.

Discover the secrets etched onto her skin.

CHAPTER 22

After giving Joe the rundown of my version of events, I got Sam Lee to drive us back to the farmhouse. Once there, I woke Doc long enough for him to help get Ms. Pentecost settled into the downstairs bedroom formerly occupied by our murder victim. Her ankle was already starting to swell.

While I changed out of my scorched overalls, Doc dug up a first-aid kit. The metal box looked like he'd filched it from that ambulance in Verdun. But the pain-relief cream and gauze inside were fresh enough. I released him back to the drawing room to resume sleeping it off.

While I rubbed and wrapped my boss's ankle, we discussed the firebombing and how it might tie in to the murder.

"It can't be a coincidence—them aiming for the spot with Ruby's picture on it," I said.

"I do abhor a surfeit of coincidence," Ms. P said. "But what did this act accomplish? Other than . . . place the perpetrator at risk. Even if, as Robert suggested, it was . . . meant as an act of intimidation against the circus, it was a . . . halfhearted one at best. It has the . . . qualities of a desperate act, but it resulted in . . . little."

"Other than to almost kill Ray," I reminded her.

"True. Mr. . . . Nance was . . . fortunate you were . . . there."

That hitch in her voice meant she was nearing the end of her rope as far as stamina was concerned. It was caused by something the disease did to the muscles in her throat that controlled her volume knob. It came and went, and it drove her nuts. I wasn't a big fan of it, either. But I'd learned early on that the quickest way to start a fight was to play mother.

I ignored it and kept going.

"You think our killer is coming unglued?" I asked. "Or maybe his seams weren't all too secure to begin with?"

"I'm thinking . . . there are gaps in our knowledge that make any . . . hypothesis . . . too flimsy to bother erecting."

She winced as I massaged the pungent liniment into her ankle.

"Speaking of filling in gaps . . . what did you . . . learn tonight?"

I gave her a précis of my night, leaving out that last exchange with Frieda. I told myself it wasn't pertinent, but really I didn't want to look at it that closely.

"Do . . . you believe her?" she asked, referring to Frieda's story about finding the heroin in plain sight.

"She's a good performer," I said. "So there's always the chance she slipped in some fibs. But if she did, I don't know what they are. The only way it adds up is if someone planted that heroin in Ruby's trailer. A rickety frame, but still a frame. I just can't figure out who or why."

She let out a noncommittal "Hmmm."

"The other girl. The . . . magician. She . . . doesn't . . . seem to care for you."

"The way Frieda talked, Annabelle is prickly with everybody," I said. "The overactive work ethic makes sense, considering her sex and her job. I can count the big-name lady magicians on zero hands."

"Could she . . . become one?" Ms. P asked.

I thought about the question as I pulled out a long length of gauze bandage and tore it off.

"I have a pretty small sample size of her work to judge," I

said, swiftly wrapping the bandage around Ms. P's ankle, then over and under her foot. "But Mysterio's giving her a lot more rope than he usually does. When I assisted him, he taught me some moves, but they were always in service to making him look better. If Annabelle was another kind of girl I'd suspect she was trading favors, but she doesn't seem the type. So he must see something in her."

I pulled the bandage tight and examined my work.

"You're gonna have to use that sword cane a little more regularly the next few days."

She leaned back on her stack of pillows and let slip a few less-than-ladylike swears.

"Okay, your turn for show-and-tell," I said, situating myself at the foot of the bed. "What did you manage to squeeze out of the evening?"

My boss doesn't believe in abridging anything, so she gave me the lot. Not verbatim, but close to it. In the interest of time, space, and typewriter ink, I'll stick to the ledes.

Nothing new in regards to active grudges against Ruby, at least none that anybody would cop to. Not a surprise. It was a wake, after all. Even my boss couldn't expect to sweet-talk mourners into speaking ill of the dead.

However, Ms. P had managed to pinpoint when Ruby had gotten the ugly cover-up. It was late in her first year with Hart & Halloway. The circus was on winter break down in Florida. Ruby and a bunch of the girls had gone out one night to see off one of the spec girls. She was on the trigger end of a shotgun wedding, and they wanted to give her a last night to remember.

They passed a tattoo parlor and Ruby talked the girl into a more permanent reminder of her circus days. The bride-to-be got a mermaid where her husband was likely the only one who would ever see it. At the last minute, Ruby asked for the cover-up. Nobody knew the reason. And none of the girls she was with were still around.

Lastly, Maeve had confirmed that she had known about the reasons for Ruby and Kalishenko's fight. That Ruby had been meddling in Kalishenko's family affairs.

"She said she did . . . not want to air . . . others' dirty laundry."

"That's bull," I said. "Maeve will gossip with the best of them. She was protecting Val. She didn't trust us with the truth."

More pointedly, she didn't trust me with the truth. Another hatpin to the heart.

"Not exactly the mother lode," I noted when my boss was finished with her report.

"Perhaps." She began picking out the hundred and one bobby pins that keep her braids secured. "Though . . . better familiarizing myself . . . with . . . the personalities was useful."

"Now we've got another firebug in the mix," I said. "We're one for one on those so far."

She made a noise that could have been amusement or indigestion. She shook her hair loose, releasing the streak of gray from its braided auburn prison. Sliding off the bed, she slowly put weight on her ankle, then hobbled to her suitcase.

I'd have given her a hand, but I was too busy pondering. Mentioning Sendak got me thinking about what we'd shown the jury. That animal inside him. That led to thinking about what Frieda had told me. How cracked her whole view of me was.

"Is there anything else to report?" Ms. P asked.

"Hmmm? Such as?"

"Your . . . mind seems . . . preoccupied."

I never play poker with Lillian Pentecost because I don't like losing.

"Nothing that hasn't been said," I lied.

She gave me a look I couldn't decipher.

"Hey, I did just leap into a burning building. Give me a minute to contemplate the precarious nature of mortality," I said. "Speaking of which, I better give my hair a wash tonight. Otherwise it'll still be smelling like smoke tomorrow."

Ms. P nodded. She pulled her nightgown out of her suitcase, tossed it on the bed, and began undoing blouse buttons.

"Then . . . I suppose . . . we should retire," she said. "We . . . want to be fresh . . . for tomorrow's . . . assignment."

"Yes, ma'am."

I showed her my back and left.

Upstairs, I stood in the shower scrubbing until the rickety pipes stopped coughing up hot water. When I was finished, I still smelled like I'd fallen in a campfire, but you had to get within kissing distance to notice.

By the time I dried off, it was closing in on five in the morning. I collapsed into bed, exhausted. But I couldn't sleep. I lay there, twitching, thinking about what Frieda had said. How the thing really driving me was anger, and how that might do me in before bullets or blades or burning buildings.

Headshrinker nonsense, I told myself. I did what I did because I wanted to. Not because I was out to spite the whole goddamned world.

Because, like Frieda, I knew people like that, too. Men and women who felt the world had wronged them and wore it in every move they made. Who let that anger carve out a home for itself in their gut and live there rent free.

Frieda was right. People like that ended up dead or in jail or at the bottom of a bottle or the end of a needle or just living inside the collapsed shell of their lives.

I knew those people real well. And I wasn't like them. No, ma'am.

No.

What bothered me most was the part where she talked about seeing me pop up in the papers and how it let her know that the anger hadn't eaten me. She'd ended that sentence with the word *yet*. Like it was something that could only be put off, not avoided altogether.

I was certainly angry enough that night. I drifted off with my fists clenched around the sheets, pissed at Frieda for putting me out of sorts, at my brain for not letting me sleep, at the unknown murderer for bringing me and my boss down here and making me dig up all this history, all these feelings.

I was even angry at myself for being angry. Wrath is a sin, after all.

And in the morning we were going to church.

CHAPTER *23*

The Blood of the Lamb Church was a pretty popular place to be on Sunday mornings, with about a hundred or so congregants packed shoulder to shoulder in the pews.

The building itself was a picture-perfect example of a country church. The outside was freshly whitewashed, the peaked roof topped with a rough-hewn wooden cross. Most of the inside was devoted to the single, large meeting room. A dozen rows of long benches led to a foot-high platform just big enough for a pulpit built in the same rough style as the cross, a couple of chairs, and a beat-up piano that could have been pulled out of a frontier town saloon. Up in the dusty rafters, a trio of lazy ceiling fans pushed the hot air around.

Ms. Pentecost and I arrived early and scored second-row aisle seats. Consequently, we were sitting in the soup for a good twenty minutes before the service even started. I could feel the sweat sinking into the thin padding of the pew.

That morning, while sorting through the outfits I'd packed, I'd considered a short-sleeved blue number that stopped mid-knee in an awkward kind of way. It was perfectly drab and I would have fit right in. But a combination of vanity and pigheadedness made me shove the dress back in my suitcase.

Vanity because I had an ugly collection of bruises running from my right shoulder down my upper arm and I didn't feel like giving them billboard space. Pigheadedness because I refused to make an attempt to fit in at the Blood of the Lamb. They could take me as I was, and that included the tailored single-breaster in soft gray wool over a pale blue shirt and navy tie, both in Italian silk.

I'd added a leather clutch to the ensemble just big enough for a notebook and a pistol. Though Ms. Pentecost made me leave the gun under the bed.

Yeah, I was showing off for the Bible-beaters and doing a damn fine job of it. I was also in danger of dissolving into a giant puddle on the pew.

My boss, on the other hand, had dressed more accordingly. She'd traded in her usual tailored suit for a sand-colored jacket and skirt over a peach blouse. It was an ensemble that rarely made it out of the closet, since it dulled the edges of the great detective's usual severity.

Though no amount of fashion switch-ups could have blunted her expression. It's the same one I imagine a sniper must have when he's fixing his sights.

The service kicked off promptly at ten with a series of sing-along hymns. Sister Evelyn played the almost-in-tune piano while a beefy man with a farmer's tan strummed a beat-up guitar. After the singing Bert stepped forward and led a prayer that had me cracking my eyelids to glance at my watch. If this was the prayer, I dreaded what his sermon was going to be like.

I never found out. After the "Amen," Bert stepped back and Brother Carl came forward. He settled his hands on the pulpit, gripping it like he was afraid it or he were about to be swept away. Despite wearing three layers of black wool, he looked bone dry.

A real man of God, I thought, would have had the decency to sweat along with the rest of us.

"I want to start out this morning in Romans. Chapter 5,

verse 8: 'But God commendeth his love toward us, in that, while we were yet sinners, Christ died for us.'"

He used Romans as a jumping-off point to talk about human frailty and forgiveness and something about love thy neighbor. I'd braced for fire and brimstone. Instead we were treated to something that could have been lifted from Thornton Wilder. Homespun and straightforward and about twice as long as it needed to be.

He tied everything up at the end.

"God," he said, "does not ration his love for us. It is eternal. It does not run out."

I thought it veered into hokey, but the crowd seemed to appreciate it.

At no point during the hour-long sermon did he even come close to brushing up against the topic of Ruby's death, even though there were plenty of opportunities for segues.

After he finished, there were a couple more hymns, then Brother Carl asked, "Is there anyone here who would like to come up and testify? Anyone with a story of God's grace?"

Edna May Currant came up and thanked God and her neighbors for helping her through the grief of losing her son overseas.

Homer DeCambre gave thanks to Brothers Bert and Carl for delivering food and a new pair of shoes. He also gave a wave to God for curing his gout. The way he hobbled, I suspected the cure didn't quite take.

There were a few more, and eventually Brother Carl asked, "Is there anyone else?"

Ms. Pentecost raised her hand.

"May I address the congregation?" she asked.

"Of course—all are welcome here." I'll give him the benefit of the doubt and say he meant it.

My boss rose and limped her way to the podium, leaning

heavily on her cane and taking the steps with care. She spent a moment settling herself behind the pulpit.

"Good morning," she said. "My name is Lillian Pentecost. I believe most of you know why I'm here."

Being at the front, I had to rely on the sound of shifting bodies to cue me that, yes, they knew who she was and why she was in town. I resisted the urge to rubberneck.

"The last time I stood before an audience and testified it was in a courtroom in service to justice. This is a little bit different. For one, I assume most of you didn't need to be subpoenaed."

That won her a few laughs. She cocked her head, pretending to consider her words. She hadn't rehearsed in front of me, but I knew my boss well enough to know that everything she was about to say had been planned and plotted.

"I suppose it's not so different," she said. "Because I'm standing here today again in the service of justice."

She propped herself on her elbows and leaned forward, treating the pulpit like she would her great oak desk. Her voice wasn't failing her that morning. It carried in a way the other congregants' had not, rising up to the rafters before plunging back down, hitting the back row with crystal clarity.

"My father was a minister. Not so different from Mr. Engle. His congregation not so different from this one. People would come and go. Some would leave town, and sometimes never come back. But no matter how long they had been gone, my father always referred to them as his congregation. Even when they left because they no longer believed. Whenever anyone challenged him on this, he would say, 'You cannot walk away from God. There is no place in this world where his light does not touch. No matter what path you walk, you will find the light there because that light is in you.'

"So I come to you today about one of your congregation who has been taken from you. Ruby Donner grew up here. She learned and laughed and loved here. Maybe you grew up with her. Maybe she was your friend. It's true that she left. That she walked a different path. Had a very different life—one that must seem almost alien to you. But she still loved and laughed and was one of you. A prodigal daughter, who, not two days after she returned home, was cut down."

She aimed her sniper's stare across the congregation, and I imagined everyone in the pews tensing as they felt it land on them.

"The authorities have a suspect in custody. I have reason to believe they've acted in haste. I believe there is still a killer walking free, and I need your assistance in rooting that person out."

The nervous shuffling behind me grew louder. They hadn't been expecting to be deputized. I wondered if our fire-bomber was back there. If I'd been running the program, I'd have stopped everyone at the door and sniffed their fingers for gasoline.

"It will be easy, I imagine, to tell yourselves that this is none of your concern. That you have not seen Ruby in years. You have your own struggles, your own burdens. To this I would call back to something Mr. Engle said in his sermon. God does not ration. He does not ration love, he does not ration forgiveness, and he does not ration justice. And while we fall short all too often, we are tasked with striving for the same when it comes to our own charity, selflessness, and bravery."

That was a nice bit of improvisation, I thought. Now to drive it home.

"So it is our duty—not just mine but that of each and every one of you sitting here—to ensure justice for Ruby Donner. To do that, I wish to learn more about her. Was she still in contact with anyone here? Did anyone see her or speak to her in the short time between her return to Stoppard and her unfortunate demise? What were her worries when she lived here? What were her passions?"

She let the questions hang in the air for a moment.

"I am currently staying at Patrick Donner's house. I will be available for any and all visitors. If you are not comfortable coming in person, I will also be available by telephone. Thank you."

Thus ended the sermon.

CHAPTER 24

We lingered in the parking lot as the churchgoers did a round of handshakes and how-have-you-beens. Ms. Pentecost got a few friendly nods but they were vastly outweighed by the nervous side-eyes.

Eventually Brother Carl emerged from the phalanx of parishioners and made his way over to us. His smile came across sincere enough, but there was something moving underneath it. Some big emotion swirling the seemingly placid waters.

Or, I admitted to myself, I could be seeing fish that weren't there.

"Thank you so much for coming," he said, shaking our hands with those lumberjack paws.

"I took your invitation to heart," Ms. Pentecost said. "I wanted to see what must have been a substantial part of Ms. Donner's childhood."

The preacher nodded along. "I suppose we were," he said.

"I'm surprised you didn't mention her in your sermon," I said.

Ms. P had requested I be on my best behavior, but I couldn't resist throwing the jab.

Whether he was ready for it or not, the preacher slipped the punch with ease.

"Brother Bert was set to preach this morning. He was going to touch on it," he said, rubbing his chin bristle. "But I was concerned about exploiting her. Putting her on display. She endured enough of that in life. I prayed on it and was moved to write a new sermon."

I nodded along like I believed it.

"Do you really think our congregation can help you discover something the police have not?" he asked.

"It's an avenue worth exploring," Ms. P said.

"The way you spoke, it suggests that you think the reason for her murder has something to do with Stoppard."

I wanted to say, "You bet your bottom dollar." But my boss only gave him her patented noncommittal shrug.

"I think that a life worth avenging is a life worth understanding."

He raised his eyebrows at that. I don't think he expected philosophy from a gumshoe.

"Well, I wish you success," he said. He veered away to a group of churchgoers that included Sister Evelyn, who was eyeing us like we were a pair of strange dogs prowling her backyard.

Immune to the glare, my boss limped toward the truck, its carnival-bright banner standing out like a sore thumb among the plain pickups and sleepy sedans.

"Something's off with that guy," I said. "And before you bring it up, I know I have a thing against Bible-beaters and, no, I don't think it's that."

"I agree," she said. "But is it pertinent to the case, or just the usual side effect?"

She was referring to a phenomenon particular to our business. Very few people come face-to-face with a detective, badge-bearing or otherwise. Consequently, when they do, they start thinking about all their deepest, darkest and sweating bullets for no good reason. Or at least no reason we were getting paid to investigate.

Was the good preacher among that number?

I opened the passenger door and held Ms. P's cane while she hoisted herself into the truck.

"I'll guess pertinent," I said. "Just how much is anybody's guess."

I swung around to the driver's side and got behind the wheel. The engine coughed like a pack-a-day smoker, but eventually turned over. As I pulled out of the church parking lot, Ms. P turned to look back at the gossiping churchgoers.

"How many do you think will reach out?" she asked.

"I'd put my money on zero," I said.

I turned the truck onto the blacktop and pointed it in the direction of our home away from home. My boss leaned her head back on the cracked vinyl of the seat and closed her eyes.

"Ye of little faith," she said.

I dropped Saint Pentecost off at the farmhouse. Her plan was to spend the afternoon in bed, where she could keep her ankle up while sorting through what we had so far.

She was out like a light before I even closed the door.

I recognized that it had been a long week, and it was only getting longer. But I'd hoped she'd employ that big brain of hers to beating out an investigative path. Because I wasn't seeing any.

Or to put it better, I was seeing too many. Our last really complicated case was a locked-room affair. Motives abounded, and while the list of suspects wasn't short, it was limited.

It seemed to me that Ruby's murder was the opposite. Any of a thousand people had the opportunity to kill her. The question was, Who wanted to?

While my boss wandered dreamland, I took the truck back into town for a quick visit to the jail. I didn't want a day to go by without Val seeing a friendly face.

I walked into the police station only to find it vacant. Voices echoed up from the door to the cells and I headed down. When I got to the bottom of the concrete steps I was surprised to find Chief Whiddle sitting in one of the chairs outside Val's cell, deep in conversation with the prisoner.

Not good.

"Sorry to interrupt the interrogation," I said.

"Oh, it wasn't an interrogation," Whiddle said, standing. "Just a conversation."

He pressed his hands against the small of his back, setting off a series of cracks and pops. Whatever it was, it hadn't been short.

"I think maybe you should give that Richmond lawyer a call next time you want to chat," I suggested. "Just so you're following the letter *and* spirit of the law."

If having his own words thrown back in his face bothered him, he didn't show it.

"Also, maybe you could spend a minute figuring out who tried to burn down the circus last night," I added. "A friend of mine almost died."

"Don't worry, Miss Parker. We'll turn up the culprit," he said. "Whatever you think, there ain't a lot of people around here willing to chuck a firebomb."

I considered arguing that point but opted to pick my battles wisely for once.

"You need me, I'll be in my office," he said, then gave his pants a hitch and went upstairs.

Once he was well out of earshot, I took the still-warm seat, leaned in, and whispered, "What was that about? What did he want?"

"He asked me about what I did in San Francisco," Kalishenko hissed back. "He knew I worked for a . . . a businessman."

I let slip one of my favorite expletives. That wasn't good news. If this ever got to trial, it wouldn't do for a jury to learn Val had once been a leg-breaker.

"Also my daughter," he said.

"What?"

"He asked about my daughter. If I knew where she is staying in Charlotte."

"What did you tell him?"

"Nothing! I tell him nothing about anything," he said, a thread of panic weaving its way in. "Will—how does he know this? Did he ask you? Did he ask your boss?"

I assured him he hadn't. I didn't like that I had to.

"You really think we'd spill the beans?"

He blushed. "I'm sorry," he said. "I am not thinking clearly. Of course you would not have told."

"That's all right," I said, not entirely sure it was. "Trust is in short supply these days."

I told him about Maeve keeping mum about his fight with Ruby, and Frieda being shy to share details. I also told him about Frieda's whole speech about me and anger and keeping something caged inside me.

"It was like she was scared of me," I said. "Or more like *for* me. That if I kept running on anger, I'd—I don't know. Explode? Implode? Fall apart?"

I waited for Val to say something—something that would let me laugh it off. I kept waiting. Eventually, he leaned back in his bunk and sighed.

"Why do you think I train you?" he asked.

"Because I could throw a knife at your head and not hit you."

"More important is that you wanted to throw. You had reasons. Holding the blade in your hand—you liked it."

I thought back to that first training session. When I was missing the target by a mile.

Think of the person who deserves the knife, he'd said.

"Me?" Val went on. "I am angry at myself, so I drink. Not you. You are not angry at yourself, I don't think. This thing you

do now. Hunting killers. Frieda is right. It's good for you. It is
good to have a target. Otherwise . . ."

Otherwise what? I'd turn out like those other girls Frieda
mentioned? Hurting myself? Or someone who didn't deserve it?

"You're wrong. Both of you," I said. "I'm not angry. I mean,
not as a rule."

He didn't respond. He just looked at me with those dark
eyes, the skin beneath them sagging under the weight of five
decades of baggage.

That look, his silence—it was making my blood rise. I didn't
know why it bothered me so much, but it did.

Partly because it was true, and I knew it.

I remembered how I felt when I saw Ruby go into the
ground. That cold rage. Like a knife I could pull out and stab in
someone's gut.

I also remembered a time a few months previous when I'd
busted into a tenement room to break up a domestic disagree-
ment gone sideways. I knocked the husband flat on his back
and put a knife to his neck. He was down for the count, but as a
capper, I still busted out his front teeth.

I didn't like to think about that episode too much. Not
because I was ashamed of my actions, but because of how good
I had felt after.

I dragged myself back to the present, to Kalishenko in his
bare cell. I pulled out a smile and slid it on.

"It doesn't matter," I said. "This isn't about me. This is about
Ruby's murder. The important thing is we're getting answers.
We're going to get you out of here."

The confidence in my voice—I should have won an award.
I steered the conversation to trivia for ten minutes, then I told
him I'd see him the next day and to hang in tight.

Once I was upstairs, instead of heading for the exit I bee-
lined for Whiddle's office, tearing open the door and storming

inside. The wannabe Pat Garrett was hunched over a copy of the Sunday *Times*, pencil in hand, working on the crossword.

"So is the jail wired for sound or did you have Mrs. Gibson listening at the top of the steps when we were interviewing him?"

He calmly put the pencil down, a question creasing that slab of forehead.

"I'm afraid you're going to have to explain yourself, Miss Parker."

"San Francisco? His daughter? What kind of crooked deal are you running here?"

I swear I didn't go in there looking to pick a fight. Really, I didn't.

He gave one of his infuriatingly slow nods. Then he opened a drawer, reached inside, and pulled out a stack of letters and envelopes. He fanned them out across his desk like a spread of cards.

The letters were creased and edge-worn from years of handling. The envelopes were covered in stamps, the addresses printed in careful, hesitant block letters.

"We took these during our search of Mr. Kalishenko's trailer," Whiddle said. "As you can see, they're all in Cyrillic—that's the alphabet they use in Russia."

"I know what Cyrillic is," I snapped.

"Well, I didn't," he admitted. "Had to call up a professor at the college in Fredericksburg. She taught me the word. Also offered to translate them for us. She's still making her way through, but she's come up with some interesting details so far."

He leaned back in his chair, resting his hands on the shelf of his gut.

"I'm still sorting out what motive Mr. Kalishenko had to murder Ruby Donner. But his reaction to my questions, and the fact that his criminal history and his family matters were both topics of your and Ms. Pentecost's conversation with him, that makes me think I'm on the right track."

My heart sank somewhere south of my guts. Not only had I gone off half-cocked, I'd handed the hick fresh ammo.

"If you're really looking to get on the right track, has it occurred to you that her dying right after she comes back to her hometown is too big a coincidence to swallow?" I said.

He started into one of those five-second nods and I had to stop myself from leaping across the desk and throttling him.

"That's occurred to me," he said when his head returned level. "And if you showed me a suspect half as good as your friend downstairs, be assured I'd take a close look at him."

He paused, giving me the opportunity to hand him such a person. Problem was, my pockets were empty.

Seeing I had no suggestions, the police chief leaned forward, and began carefully restacking the letters.

"Either way, he won't be my problem too much longer. The county attorney is getting the paperwork together. Your friend should appear before Judge Berry this Tuesday. Then he'll head off to the county penitentiary until trial. Unless he's granted bail, which I sincerely doubt."

He slid the bundle of Kalishenko's correspondence back into his desk.

"Now if that's all, Miss Parker, the Sunday *Times* crossword is one of the few pleasures I allow myself," he said, taking up his pencil again. "But if you need anything else, don't you hesitate to ask."

In my head I scribbled in a twelve-letter word for Oedipus, turned on my heel, and left.

CHAPTER 25

Bogart leaned Bacall over backward for an almost-kiss. The two threatened to fall into the Mummy's tomb, which was shaking grave dust down on King Kong's head. The big ape beat biplanes away with one hand, and made a swipe for Lou Costello with the other.

Maybe there was wallpaper somewhere underneath all the posters and show cards pasted to the walls of the Majestic's lobby, but it would take an archaeologist to find it. The movie house had been in the picture business for twenty-odd years, and it looked like every single one of the films that had passed through its projector was represented in the wheat-paste strata.

I had a few minutes before the matinee. Doc had issued an open invitation, and I thought two hours in the dark might be a good cure for my mood.

The lobby was dim and narrow, with a ticket counter that doubled as a concessions stand. It offered fresh popcorn in paper sacks, licorice in a rainbow of flavors, and a case filled with room-temperature soda.

Doc was stationed behind it, munching popcorn, sipping a bottle of Coke, and staring through his wire-rimmed specs at the front door. Like a scarecrow in reverse, willing a flock of movie-lovers to appear and peck him clean.

Only three people were sitting in the theater: an elderly man who told Doc flat out he was there for the air-conditioning, and a pair of teenagers who'd walked in glued at the shoulders, and whose wandering hands suggested they were more interested in two hours of privacy than the cinematic revelations of *Cat People.*

"Sundays always this slow?" I asked.

"Sundays, Mondays. Any day ending in *y*, really," he said.

"Not a lot of cinema fans in Stoppard?"

"There are. But they mainly go to the big theater up in Fredericksburg. They always get first-runs. I have to wait a month or so before I can afford them."

He ran his fingers through his beard, dislodging a flurry of crumbs.

"Of course, I knew going in I wasn't going to make a mint."

"So why go in?" I asked.

"When I was bouncing around city to city there were a lot of times I didn't have a place to live. Movie houses were great places to get dry and warm, and if it wasn't crowded and the usher was the kind to look the other way, you could stay there all day. Besides, I loved the films. They made the world seem . . . safe, I guess. Sane."

I followed the course of his eyes as they tracked across the posters on the wall. I'm not sure *I Walked with a Zombie* was a prime example of "sane" but I could see what he was getting at.

"When I moved back here after Charlie and Abigail died, I kind of found myself at loose ends. Didn't know nobody. The ones I did were thirty-some years older than I remembered. So I started coming here. Felt like home."

He used a thumbnail to pick a kernel out from between his teeth.

"You know, after Pearl Harbor, I tried to enlist again. Funny, right? At least the recruiter thought so. Then I found out the owner of the Majestic was selling. I told him I'd like to buy it. He thought that was funny, too. But I needed to do something if I was going to stay in town."

I put a nickel on the counter and picked five black licorice sticks out of the jar.

"Why stay?" I asked. "Why not sell the farm and leave?"

"Not my farm," the old man said, dropping my nickel in the cashbox. "Ruby owns it. Owned it. I was just taking care of it for her."

"She wanted to keep it?" I asked, gnawing on a licorice.

"Didn't have a choice," Doc said. "It was in Charlie's will. She wasn't allowed to sell, not the house or the fifty acres it's on. Rest of the land's a different story. I've been selling that off piecemeal to buy this place and keep it running."

"Why put that in the will?" I asked. "Did her parents really expect her to move back and live there?"

"I think maybe they did. I think they were trying to force her to settle down."

"Didn't seem to work," I said.

"Nope. She never came back. Not even to bury them."

"Was it how she felt about the town or her parents that kept her away?"

He shook his head.

"I know my brother. He wasn't the easiest to get along with. But he and Abigail loved her. Didn't understand her, maybe, but they loved her. I can't . . . I can't imagine her not coming to the funeral was out of spite."

"She never said outright?"

I'd been through the postcards, but there were a lot of gaps, and I had a feeling neither Ruby nor her uncle had saved everything.

"She never did," Doc said. "I always figured it was because she'd spent so long slipping the lock on a cage and she didn't want to step back inside."

I thought about that. Having slipped my own childhood cage, I knew I wouldn't willingly step back in. Not in this lifetime.

I steered back to less emotionally rocky waters.

"What's the deal with the house now?" I asked. "Now that Ruby's dead is it still in a trust?"

I waited a five-count for an answer.

"Doc?"

"Hmmm? Oh, the house!" he said, snapping back. I wondered if he had mixed something stronger in with his soda. "Talked to the family lawyer. He said if she didn't have a will saying otherwise, it'll go to me. So I can go ahead and sell if I want."

He looked up at the clock on the wall. It read five minutes past noon. He slapped on a tissue-thin smile.

"Best get inside and get a seat," he said. As if they were in short supply.

He put out a jar with some loose change at the bottom. Anyone coming in late would be on the honor system. Then he went up to the projection booth and I walked into the theater.

I made my way past a hundred empty seats upholstered in various shades of tattered, the toes of my shoes catching on worn carpet. The older gent was snoring in a corner, the teens settled low in the very back row and already warming the engine.

I planted myself second-row center, where the old man's snores wouldn't reach and I was far enough from the lovebirds so they could round second in comfort.

Shortly after I sat, the lights dimmed and the projector whirred to life. The feature might have been a couple years old, but the newsreels were up to date.

The Big Four met in Paris to divvy up the world now that Hitler was worm food.

The United States set off an underwater atomic bomb in the Marshall Islands. Just to see what would happen.

The FBI graduated eighty-four fresh-faced acolytes of J. Edgar Hoover. At the ceremony, charismatic congressman

Daniel Ellis gave an impassioned speech about how the recruits "would be on the front lines of the fight against Communism and subversion of America's founding principles of—"

I stopped paying attention, letting the news skim off my consciousness like a skipping stone. My mind threatened to go back to what Val had said. About the anger.

There was an adjacent thought, too. One about my childhood and the things that are passed down by blood.

I shoved the lot aside and busied myself sorting through the case.

We had Ruby needing to see Big Bob about something, something important, and turning up dead before she got to his door.

We had a packet of heroin sitting in her trailer, probably not hers, and very possibly planted. Why and by who? No idea.

Then there was the man Ruby had words with not long before she died. Was it Joe? Maybe. But why would he lie? Even if it was, that didn't lead anywhere because the killer was right-handed and Joe most definitely wasn't.

Then I remembered how Brother Carl had reacted when I brought up Ruby's name. How he'd made a point of avoiding mention of her death during the service.

Could it have been Carl Engle who'd come to see Ruby at her booth? Did he have some built-up resentment about the way Ruby had walked out on his son?

That was weak and I knew it.

I tried to juice it up. I started imagining a scenario where Carl Engle had put the moves on his son's girl. If younger Ruby was anything like the woman I knew, she'd have bitten his fingers off.

That was an interesting thought. The look I saw flit across the preacher's face when we were talking to him in the parking lot: That could easily have been shame.

I recognized I was working with more fantasy than fact

and tried to rein myself in. Who actually benefited from Ruby's death?

The only person I knew of for sure was Ruby's uncle. Doc was now free to sell off the old homestead and use the proceeds however he wished.

I'd come across men and women like him before. Wandering, aimless, spiraling down the drain and no idea how to pull themselves out. The Majestic was a poor substitute for a life raft, and he was sinking fast. Desperate men were capable of desperate things.

I couldn't picture Doc as a killer, though. Unless, as Kalishenko was suspected of doing, he committed the crime in a booze-fueled blackout. But Doc seemed more like a sad drunk than an angry one. So unless there was a Hyde hiding behind his Jekyll, I wasn't buying it.

The newsreels sputtered out and the movie began. I was of half a mind to walk out. What was I doing in a movie house while Val was stuck in jail?

Then the other half of my mind decided to give it a chance. It wasn't like I had a hot clue to track down.

Halfway through the movie I came to the conclusion that it wasn't much of a thriller. Sure, you had a woman who thought she turned into a murderous feline whenever she got worked up. But I knew bars in New York where you could find three dames who fit that description and a handful of others who'd fake it for a fee.

Ruby loved this flick? I didn't see it. I certainly didn't see her in the anxious, haunted lead played by Simone Simon. If anything, I thought Ruby resembled the husband's coworker—the straight-shooting girl who shoulders her way into the role of the other woman.

Maybe she empathized with a girl trying to fit into a cookie-cutter life and failing. Or maybe she just liked the flick and thought her uncle would get a kick out of it. It was a pitfall of detective work, reading too much into the little things, imbuing the tiniest details with a weight they didn't deserve.

I left before the final reel. I could feel the tragic ending coming and I didn't have the stomach for it.

Real life was tragic enough.

CHAPTER 26

Walking up the aisle, I was surprised to see that the audience had grown by one. The latecomer pulled his cap low and sank down in his aisle seat. I slipped into the row behind him and leaned forward, whispering in his ear.

"Hey, Sam Lee, how's it going?"

"Oh, not too bad, Miss Parker," he said, going for casual and missing by a mile.

"Enjoying the movie?"

"Not so much. I like comedies, myself."

"I don't blame you. Why don't we hop on out to the lobby. I'll buy you a Coke."

We walked out into the vacant lobby. On the way, the teenagers paused their pawing to give us curious, somewhat hostile looks.

"So what's the deal?" I asked, once we were alone. "And don't say you're a movie buff. No way a circus diehard like you plays hooky from a weekend show."

He tucked his hands into the back pockets of his dungarees and shuffled his feet, but at least he had the nerve to maintain eye contact.

"Well, Miss Parker, Big Bob was talking about how someone has it in for the circus. Trying to burn it down, almost killing Mr. Ray. I got to thinking—it's got to be the same person who killed Miss Ruby, right? And here you and Miss Pentecost are going around and asking questions, and if they're willing to burn down whoever and whatever, then what would they be willing to do to you? So I suggested to Big Bob that maybe you could do with, you know . . . well, an escort. I stopped by where you're staying and Miss Pentecost, she told me that Ruby's uncle had invited you to see the show and . . . here I am."

It took a second for my ears to catch up with his mouth.

"An escort?"

"Yes, ma'am. Someone to keep an eye on your rear." I saw him realize the unintentional entendre. "I mean, not *on* your rear. But, you know, to the back of you. To watch your back."

"I gotcha."

I tried to conjure the best way to let him down gently.

"Well, I appreciate the thought. But I was about to head back to the farmhouse. Unless some clue leaps out and bites me on the way, that's probably where I'll stay. Not sure I need a tail gunner."

"Not going so well?" he asked.

"Not well enough."

"I'm sure you two will come up with something," he said, smiling. "I read all about that firebug case. If you can figure that out, I'm sure you can figure this."

The optimism of youth. If I could bottle it, I'd retire.

"To be honest, Sam Lee, we got lucky with the Sendak case," I admitted. "I'm not saying we wouldn't have gotten him. But if we hadn't crossed paths so early, another tenement or two might have been torched before it was all said and done."

His face fell, but not by much.

"But Miss Pentecost is a genius," he said. "And you're real sharp. That's what Big Bob and everyone says. I'll bet you and her have got all sorts of tricks to find clues or get people talking or whatever you need to do."

Oh, we had tricks, all right. But they were less sleight of hand and more like a shotgun. I explained as much to Sam Lee.

"For example, we had one case a while back where we needed to track someone down. We knew she was probably from a certain area of the state, but had been known under a different name. So I cold-called every librarian and town know-it-all in two hundred miles trying to find someone who fit her description. Two straight days of that, my dialing finger nearly fell off."

"But did it work?" he asked. "Did you find the woman?"

I nodded. "Eventually. But, again, it was luck."

His furrowed his brow. "Doesn't sound like luck. Sounds like you just asked the right people."

He wasn't wrong. I made a note to give credit where credit's due. Especially when it's due to me.

"Stoppard's got a library," Sam Lee said. "I mean, if you think that would be useful."

"I doubt it," I told him. "That only worked before because we were hunting a specific person. Can't really go into a library and ask . . ."

An errant idea derailed my train of thought.

"Ask what, Miss Parker?"

I had been going to say "ask who in Stoppard might be capable of putting a knife in Ruby Donner." A librarian was unlikely to find that particular title on the shelves. But there was someone who might.

"I've got an idea," I said. "But it means I have to fly solo."

He opened his mouth to argue, but I barreled through it.

"It's not that I don't appreciate the offer. I really do. If I find I have need of a bodyguard, I promise you're at the top of the list. Right now, the best place for you is back at the circus, keeping your eyes and ears open. Whoever threw that firebomb might try for a second bite at the apple."

He didn't quite buy it, but he realized he would have to take no for an answer. Outside the theater, I kept an eye on him long enough to make sure he was heading in the direction of the circus. Then I went back to the police station.

I found Whiddle blessedly absent and Joe manning the front desk, pecking away at a typewriter. He looked up from his work and smiled.

"Hey, if it isn't Wonder Woman."

He seemed ten times sharper than he had the night before. Jolly, even.

"Wonder Woman wouldn't be this sore the day after."

"Well, I'm typing up the report now," he said. "I used the word *impressive* twice. It's not spelled right either time, but it's there."

He rolled the page out of the typewriter with a speed and smoothness I couldn't manage two-handed.

"Here to see your friend?" he asked, looking up at the clock on the wall. "Visiting hours are almost over. I'd stretch it, but the chief's pretty strict on that."

"Actually, I was hoping to have a chat with Mrs. Gibson."

That surprised him. "Why do you want her?"

"I'm trying to get the lay of the land around here," I half lied. "She seemed like a good person to ask."

"Well, she's got Sundays off."

"Where's she lay her head?" I asked.

"She's on the western edge of town all the way at the end of Plymouth Avenue. It's right past where the old general store used to . . . Actually, let me draw you map."

He grabbed a fresh sheet of paper and started sketching directions.

"I heard you went to church this morning," he said. "Your boss made an impression."

"That was the point."

"Do you think it'll work?" he asked. "If anyone knows anything useful, I don't see why they'd tell your boss and not us."

I shrugged. "Sometimes it's easier to talk with a stranger than with someone you know."

He handed me the map and I thanked him and headed for the door.

"Hey, Will?"

I stopped and turned back. He had his one hand shoved in his back pocket and was biting nervously on the corner of that big bottom lip of his.

"You . . . um . . . you got plans for tonight?"

"Nope," I said. "You taking a poll, or do you have something in mind?"

"I don't know if you've heard, but there's a circus in town. I haven't been. Other than on official business."

More fraternizing with the law. I weighed the pros and cons. While the cons outweighed the pros, the pros had dimples.

"Swing by Doc's around seven?" I asked.

"Better make it eight. I button a shirt pretty slow these days."

I gave him a smile I hoped passed for coy as I headed to the door. "Shirt's optional, lawman. Wish me luck with Mrs. Gibson."

"Good luck!" he called after. "You're gonna need it!"

CHAPTER 27

After three rights, four lefts, and one U-turn that almost sent the truck's front wheels into a ditch, I arrived at my destination.

Ruth Gibson lived at the end of a dead-end residential street just outside town limits. I parked the truck a good two blocks away. I figured Mrs. Gibson wouldn't appreciate the eyesore or the publicity.

Also, I wanted to give her a heads-up that I was coming. Considering how many people were sitting on their porches trying to catch a breeze, I figured she'd get half a dozen calls warning of my arrival.

As I strolled up the weed-cracked sidewalk, I thought about how I was going to approach this. By the time I reached her mailbox, I had settled on my strategy.

Her house was a single-story number with white siding, a tiny screened-in porch, and a front yard that was more flower garden than grass. The garden was well tended and the flowers were in full bloom. The grass was cut, the siding was scrubbed, and I bet if I climbed a ladder I could run a finger across the gutters and have it come away clean.

Perfect.

I was halfway up the walk when the front door opened and the lady of the house stepped onto the porch. She cautiously pushed open the screen door, which swung out, oiled and

silent. She'd traded the brown pantsuit for a pair of denim overalls and a blue smock, both stained with dirt and sweat. But
her blue-tinged curls were as smooth and tight as during office
hours. The same scowl peered back at me from the other side
of cat-eye frames.

"Miss Parker? Are you . . . Can I help you?"

"Yes, Mrs. Gibson. I was hoping to speak with you. I have
some questions that I think you may be able to lend a hand
with."

"I'm afraid police department business has to be
conducted—"

I held up a hand.

"It's not really police business, ma'am. It's you specifically I
want to talk to. May I come in?"

I made a show of wiping the sweat off my forehead.

"Of course," she said, good Virginia manners overriding all
else.

She held the screen for me, and I walked across the porch
and through the front door, which opened directly into the living room.

"I just got in from pulling weeds. Would you like something to drink? Water? Iced tea?" she asked.

"Iced tea would be great."

Still looking a little confused, she disappeared into the
kitchen while I took in my surroundings.

The inside of the house was as neat and tidy as the outside.
I was planted in a cramped but orderly living room. Two wing-
back chairs and an overstuffed loveseat faced off across a coffee
table. One wall was taken up by a picture window displaying
the front lawn, another was given over to framed photographs.
Most of the snaps were dedicated to the stop-motion journey
of a pair of pudgy boys growing into lanky men. The few that
weren't featured a younger Mrs. Gibson paired with a tall drink
of water who would have fit right into a John Ford flick. In most

of those pictures he was sporting a cowboy hat and a wry gun-fighter's grin.

The pair were touching in nearly every shot—holding hands, locking elbows. And in every picture where they were together the missus was smiling, proving that the scowl wasn't permanent, or at least it hadn't always been.

Mrs. Gibson walked back in carrying two tall glasses of iced tea.

"Here you go. Hope it's not too sweet. I know they fix it different up north."

I took it, sipped, and smiled. "It's great. Thank you."

She took the smaller of the armchairs and nodded for me to take the loveseat. I sat down and immediately sank four inches into spongy cushions. I repositioned to a perch.

The second armchair would have made conversation easier, but I knew better than to switch seats.

In my house growing up, there was a particular kitchen chair that my mother always sat in. It had a seat cushion that she had sewn and stuffed herself. Red-and-white-checked. After she died, neither my father nor I ever sat in it again. We never discussed it. We just didn't. I knew a memorial masquerading as furniture when I saw one.

"I don't see how I can help you. Like I said, I can't talk about police business," Mrs. Gibson said. She was clutching her glass with both hands—a familiar prop in an unfamiliar scene where she wasn't sure of her lines.

"I understand, ma'am. And I'll try to stay away from the official side of things," I assured her.

"Then I simply don't see what we have to talk about, Miss Parker."

Growing up in a house where honesty could earn you a beating, followed by five years with the circus and nearly as long again in the detective game, I had developed a certain skill at finessing my way through a conversation.

Basically, I was a champion bullshitter and I had the trophies to prove it.

There were a dozen ways I could approach her and have a half-decent chance of getting the information I wanted. But another skill I'd learned was reading people, and the story I got from Ruth Gibson was that the best tool hanging from my belt was the straight truth.

"To be perfectly frank, Mrs. Gibson, I know your loyalty is to Chief Whiddle," I said. "He thinks he's got his man, and I'm not going to try and convince you he's wrong. But even he admits there are holes in the story he's telling. The biggest is the fact that she's gone for more than a decade and turns up dead half a minute after she gets home. That's a big coincidence."

I paused to give Mrs. Gibson the opportunity to protest, or to tell me to pack up and leave. She did neither, but her scowl hadn't softened.

"Then there's what happened last night. I'm assuming you've heard about the firebomb."

The word *firebomb* made her blink, but she nodded.

"Whether or not the hand that tossed it is the same one that put a knife in Ruby Donner's back is up in the air. But the fact is that they came close to killing a man last night. A friend of mine."

This time she took the cue.

"I heard about what you did," she said. "That was . . . Well, that was very brave of you."

I made a note to include the praise in my official report.

"Now, if this were New York City, I'd have a long list of usual suspects—people with the motive and the temperament. At the very least, I'd know the places to begin looking. But here I don't know where to start. Stoppard is a stranger to me. Joe told me that there was no one who knew the ins and outs of this town better than you. So my question to you is this: Who would you peg as capable of tossing a gasoline cocktail?"

"Nobody!" she exclaimed. "I'm sure I don't know a single soul who'd do such a thing."

She waved an arm toward the picture window, as if to encompass the neighborhood on the other side and the town and county beyond that.

"This is a good town; these are good people."

I nodded and took a sip of the heavily sugared tea, feeling the cavities already starting to form.

"No offense, ma'am, but that's crap."

"Excuse me!"

I held up a placating hand.

"I don't mean that this town isn't filled with good people. I'm sure ninety-nine out of a hundred have halos tucked under their pillow. But there are always those one or two who have a pitchfork stashed in their closet. You know that as well as anyone."

I glanced at the photos on the wall. She couldn't help but follow my eyes. Her cowboy and his smile stared down.

No reason I couldn't mix my honesty with some good ol' emotional manipulation.

"I know you don't have any reason to trust me," I said. "Your loyalties are to this town. But Ruby was my friend. My loyalty is to her. And to the truth. No matter what it is."

Maybe it was the memory of her lawman husband. Maybe it was the raw emotion that she heard in my voice. I only had to jack it up a little. Whichever it was, I watched the scowl melt like ice cream in August.

"Well . . . there are always bad apples."

I nodded vigorously and casually pulled my notebook out of my clutch.

She ran through some names—all regular visitors to the cells beneath the station. Most were alcoholics, wife-beaters, or ne'er-do-wells specializing in petty thievery. I didn't think the guy who'd gotten labeled the "Sheffield Valley Rooster Thief" was a good candidate for murder or attempted arson, but I jotted down his name along with the others.

"What about drugs?" I asked during a pause.

"Drugs?"

This was the one point where I had to finesse. I couldn't very well tell her about what had been found in Ruby's trailer. Not when we hadn't let Chief Whiddle in on it. So I took a page from my boss.

"I've found that one kind of criminal behavior usually leads to another, and drugs make a great starting point. If I were looking for people using things like marijuana or, let's say, heroin— things like that—where would I start looking?"

"We don't really get a lot of that around here," she said. I could see the conjunction coming a mile away. "But . . ."

"Yes?"

"There are the DeCambre boys."

"Boys? These are brothers?"

"Brothers, uncles, nephews—it's a whole family and we just end up calling them the DeCambre boys."

The name sounded familiar. Then I remembered the old man from church that morning. The one who'd praised God for his not-so-gone gout. I described him to Mrs. Gibson.

"That's Homer," she said. "He's the white sheep of the family. Maybe a gray sheep, if I'm being honest. He did a lot of bootlegging back in the day. He's got a son, Culpepper, and two grandsons, Luke and Leroy. Culpepper used to steal from Homer. At the moment, Culpepper's doing a stint in prison up near Baltimore. Armed robbery. So now Homer's grandsons steal from him. His pension check. Ration stamps. It's a real shame. Everyone knows it, but he won't turn 'em in. There's a whole bunch of cousins, too. All of them in some sort of trouble or other. That family tree is . . ."

She reached for the right word.

"Ingrown?" I offered.

She nodded. "That's about right. They run a bar out on Razor Strap Road. It's not much more than clapboard held together with hope and spit. It's outside the department's jurisdiction. And the county sheriff rarely gets out there."

"Are drugs a part of the DeCambres' repertoire?" I asked.

"They've never been arrested for it," she said. "But occasionally we'll hear about high school boys going out there. Coming back drunk or . . . more than drunk."

The scowl came back stronger than ever.

"One time, one of the boys brought his girlfriend along. While they were intoxicated, Leroy or Luke—I'd guess Leroy—he . . . Well, this girl wouldn't say, but I heard from her mother that she was assaulted."

She took a long swallow of sweet tea, like she was trying to wash the taste out.

"Chief Whiddle talked the state troopers into going out there. They didn't find anything. It was pretty obvious they'd cleaned the place up. And the girl wouldn't testify, so . . ."

So that left the DeCambre boys at large and maybe thinking they were invincible.

Now we were getting somewhere. Drugs were in the picture. And someone who was willing to rape a woman was a good candidate for killing one.

"Any connection between the DeCambres and Ruby Donner?" I asked.

"Oh, my, yes," Mrs. Gibson said, as if it had just occurred to her. "I hadn't thought about it before. It was so long ago. But Ruby went to school with Luke and Leroy. Leroy, mostly. I think Luke dropped out pretty early. Ruby and Leroy were only a year apart, I think. He chased Ruby a lot during their school years. She was pretty and Leroy was—well, some people think he has a certain charm."

"You don't?"

"He's handsome enough," she said. "He's got a line of sweet

talk for the girls. But it only works if they're intoxicated or . . . I'll be kind and say naïve. But anyone with a lick of sense can tell he's rotten. I mean, you seem like a sharp woman. Did he seem that way to you?"

"To me?" I asked. "What do you mean?"

"You were sitting there yesterday when Joe let him out of lockup."

The drunk-tank swimmer who'd flashed us the nervous glance on the way out the door. I tried to conjure up what he looked like but I mostly remembered the smell.

"That was Leroy DeCambre?"

"Yep. Got in a shouting match with some out-of-towner. Chief Whiddle kept him overnight to cool down."

"From the odor, I figured drunk and disorderly," I said.

She shook her head. "That boy always smells like that. From working at that bar of his."

I tried to remember the exact quality of his nervous look. Was it the casual distrust of strange faces? Or did he know exactly who we were?

"You said Leroy chased Ruby. Did he ever catch her?"

She shook her head.

"Oh, no," she said. "She was always very firm that she didn't have any interest. It was a . . . Well, it was kind of a running joke, really. How he was always after her and she was always saying no. Everyone knew about it, even the grown-ups. Then she got together with Joe and that was that."

Young men, especially young men with a mean streak, didn't like to be the butt of a joke. I was betting that Leroy hadn't enjoyed it. I wondered how long that resentment had lingered.

I leaned forward in my seat.

"Mrs. Gibson, where exactly can I find this fine establishment on Razor Strap Road?"

CHAPTER 28

Right on Red Toad Road, left on Old Route Five—not to be confused with New Route Five—go about a quarter of a mile, then at this big double-trunk oak, you bear right onto Razor Strap, then go three miles and you'll find the Hogshead Tavern. Though everyone just calls it the Pig's Hole. I can't imagine why."

I flipped my notebook closed and leaned back into the rocking chair.

"My kingdom for a grid system."

Leaning back in her own rocker, swollen foot propped on an empty apple crate, Ms. Pentecost declined to comment. Instead she sipped lemonade out of an old Mason jar and peered through the porch screen. The sun lapped the top of the cornfields, throwing an orange wash across the dusty driveway and up onto my boss's face.

She hadn't packed much in the way of lounging wear, so she'd borrowed a pair of my dungarees and a red flannel shirt that Doc had pulled out of a trunk in the basement. If she was going to be reclining the rest of the day, no sense in creasing one of her good suits.

Barefoot, sleeves rolled up, braids fallen into disrepair, she could have passed for an honest-to-God hillbilly spending the last hours of the Sabbath in relaxed contemplation. That is if it wasn't for the look in her eye, which was a good country mile from relaxed.

"We'll need to approach it carefully," she said. "Strangers would be noticed. This isn't New York City."

"You don't say."

"We should ask Mr. Halloway for assistance. He could provide us with agents who at least look like they would seek out a place called the Pig's Hole. Men who could inquire, very discreetly, whether they could buy heroin there."

"Clover would be up for it," I said. "Paulie, too, if you asked nice. They wouldn't even have to hide they're from the circus. They go in tomorrow night. Circus's night off. They're looking for a little fun, heard they could score there. It could work."

She thought about the plan for a minute, finally blessing it with a satisfied grunt. She rocked back in her chair, her good foot nudging against the ledgers stacked beside her. They represented five years' worth of H&H's financials, delivered by Big Bob earlier that day. Ms. P had been nose-deep in them when I'd returned.

"Looking to start your own circus? Or were you just bored?" I asked when I saw the books.

"I recognized that I know very little about how a circus functions," Ms. P explained. "I felt I owed it to the investigation to be better informed."

She flipped to a particular page.

"Did you know how much it costs to feed a full-grown tiger for a month?" she asked. "It's staggering."

"What do you think they do with all the kids who run away to join the circus?" I quipped. "I'd have been kitty chow, too, if it wasn't for my winning personality."

"You jest, but the cost of meat, even organ meat, has skyrocketed in recent years. Just one of the many financial pressures Mr. Halloway is under. If it were not for the largesse of this anonymous trust, he would likely have had to sell years ago."

While the price of organ meat might be interesting to some, I wasn't counted in their number. Once I'd gotten my own glass of lemonade and settled into the matching rocker, I got my boss's brain back on track by giving her the full report of the day.

That included my run-in with Chief Whiddle and his translation of Kalishenko's letters; my chat with Doc at the movie theater; and the *Reader's Digest* version of my conversation with Mrs. Gibson.

Unburdened of information and with at least the beginnings of a plan of approach for the Pig's Hole in the works, I decided it was time to reward myself with a meal. All I'd managed that day was licorice, soda, and sweet tea.

I got up to investigate the grocery situation when Ms. P spoke up.

"I received several phone calls while you were gone."

I retraced my steps and sat back down.

"Potential suitors or something relevant to the case?"

"They were in response to my plea at the church this morning."

Translation: *I told you so.*

"Anything useful?" I asked.

"There were four calls, all women," she said. "Two identified themselves as contemporaries of Ruby who grew up with her here in Stoppard. Another was much older and used to teach English literature at Stoppard High. She is not a member of Blood of the Lamb, but her sister is and knew she would be interested in my request. Ruby was a student of hers. All three women had received postcards and letters from Ruby following her departure."

"And their contents?" I prodded.

"Assurances from Ruby that she was well. Descriptions of her early activities in New York City. Only with her former teacher did she mention her tattoos, and then only getting the first one."

"That's interesting," I said. "You'd think she'd slip that to the girls her age."

"Because Ms. Lamplough—she now lives in Chapel Hill—is not a member of the church, Ruby might have felt safer confessing that particular detail to her," Ms. P explained. "Also, she seemed like a rather open-minded woman. She spoke freely and swore considerably."

"Sounds like my kind of dame."

"That first tattoo that Ruby mentioned in her letter was a bouquet of daisies," my boss added. "And before you ask, no, she did not mention their significance and Ms. Lamplough did not hazard a guess."

I wasn't too disappointed. I was growing more and more convinced that the cover-up could be chalked up to capricious whim rather than significant biographical detail.

"Anything else of note?" I asked.

"All three women agreed that Ruby's departure from Stoppard was sudden, but not unexpected. Ms. Lamplough was quite certain that Ruby would not stay in Stoppard. Though she was equally certain that she'd been determined to graduate high school before departing."

That story sounded familiar. My own flight from home had followed the same course. A whole lot of dreaming, then a split-second decision to run.

"I don't suppose any of them mentioned Leroy DeCambre."

"They did not," Ms. P said. "Though I did ask all three about Ruby's use of drugs and alcohol. In a surreptitious way, of course."

"Of course. And?"

"The younger women were convinced that Ruby abstained from both. Ms. Lamplough could not say one way or another. She saw nothing of that in Ms. Donner."

But would she? I thought. An English teacher would only

see Ruby an hour a day, if that. And it's not something she'd flaunt for the church folk. I knew for a fact she wasn't on the water wagon. She could tipple with the best of them.

"What else?" I asked.

"I inquired with all three about grudges, arguments, people who might wish Ruby harm. All three said they could think of no one."

"Yeah, but that's what people always say, isn't it? Nobody wants to think they're brushing shoulders with a killer."

"I probed the subject considerably, and none would budge. The two younger women admitted that it was possible something had happened in the few weeks leading to her departure from Stoppard. Ruby had grown distant from her friends, especially those who went to her church."

"Distant how?" I asked.

"Quiet, thoughtful."

"Worried?"

"They did not use that word."

That was interesting. Sure, Ruby might have always been planning to leave, but what if something fired the starter's pistol?

Something's preying on her mind. She leaves town. Comes back half a lifetime later. Something starts her worrying again, and not a day later she turns up dead. Cock your head a certain way, it looked like bookends.

I wondered if she'd been worried about the same thing. Or the same person. Like an old drug-using, rapist wannabe-boyfriend. I put the question to Ms. Pentecost.

"I agree that there's an echo in Ruby's behavior before she left home and after she came back," Ms. P said. "But it's just as likely that she became distant because she was making her plans to flee to New York. And equally likely that whatever was worrying her was circus business."

I gave her the point but suggested we call all three women back and ask about Leroy DeCambre. Just for a lark. My boss concurred.

"Is that the lot?" I asked.

"From those women, yes."

Then I remembered how Ms. P had started the conversation and did some quick math.

"Hang on—you said four calls, all women. Who was the fourth?"

Ms. P's lips curled up into the shadow of a smile.

"She didn't give her name. And she spoke in an obviously accentuated rural accent."

"And what did this mystery lady say?"

"She said, 'Ruby Donner was a Jezebel and she got what she deserved.'"

"Verbatim?"

"Verbatim."

"You gonna make me crack open a Bible?" I asked.

"Jezebel was a queen of Samaria who came into conflict with the prophet Elijah," Ms. P explained. "He prophesied her violent death and the consumption of her corpse by wild dogs—an event that eventually came to pass."

"Sounds like a back feature in *Uncensored Detective*."

"More pertinently, Jezebel's name is frequently used as a pejorative for women who value their appearance, who use makeup or wear revealing clothing. Though Jezebel's adornment of herself with makeup and fine clothing in the Book of Kings seems more a show of power and dignity rather than seduction, and perfectly keeping in line with her role as—"

I waved a hand to cut her off.

"I know you're a preacher's daughter, though I'm still skeptical on that. But I think we can save Bible study for later. The more important question is did you recognize the voice?"

Ms. P shook her head, but the half smile remained.

"The message was eleven words and the feigned accent was very strong."

"So why do you look like the cat who chowed down on the canary?"

"Consider it. She knew of my request for information. She used a biblical reference. And she felt she needed to disguise her voice."

To my credit, I only had to consider it for about five seconds.

"Huh," I grunted. "That *is* telling."

"It's certainly something we will have to follow up on."

I checked my watch. The hour hand had just passed the seven.

"I'm going to get something in my stomach, then start getting ready," I said.

Ms. P raised an eyebrow.

"I thought your date with Officer Engle was not for another hour."

I stood up and displayed the limp, sweat-stained remains of my going-to-church suit.

"I've got to dig up some new duds, shower, shave my legs, and see if I can undo the crime the humidity has perpetrated on my hair."

"You have my sympathy," Ms. P said with a straight face, looking perfectly comfortable in her borrowed clothes.

"Yeah, I know," I said, making for the kitchen door. "Being a Jezebel sure is hard work."

CHAPTER **29**

The sun might have taken a powder, but the heat had stayed in the fight. Add in the BTUs put out by the lights, rides, popcorn machines, and the body heat of a few hundred folks milling about the midway, and it was threatening to undo all my primping and powdering. I could feel my blush starting to sluice off and my hair retreat to its natural frizz.

But at least I wasn't sweating a liter a minute. I'd ditched the Sunday suit for a short-sleeved rose-print number that came in snug at the waist and had a hemline that kissed my knees. At the other end of my stems was a pair of red slingbacks. I'd had a cobbler replace the heels, shaving off an inch and widening them by half. I liked to know that, if called upon, I could sprint without snapping an ankle. Plus, they dangled in a pleasantly saucy way when I crossed my legs.

Joe had also cleaned up nice. Though his scouring probably took all of five minutes. He was wearing a pair of white linen trousers and a short-sleeved button-up with stripes in brown and yellow. He'd undone the top two buttons, giving me a peek at the scenic landscape underneath.

No makeup for him, though he did shave. He'd nicked himself on the right side, a tiny line of red cut across those pleasantly plump lips. The dangers of shaving with your off hand, I guess.

Not that I could talk. I had two good hands and had still

managed to nick my legs half a dozen times. As we strolled, I had a growing worry that I'd left a bloody dab of toilet paper on the back of my thigh and kept trying to sneak a hand down to investigate.

Bloody dabs or not, Joe had the good manners to compliment my outfit when I arrived. Sort of.

"Not bad," he said, giving me the once-over. "I didn't think you went much in for dresses. I'm honored."

"You think this outfit is about you?" I scoffed. "Nine times out of ten I'll pick something with pockets. But Virginia broke me. It's a thousand goddamn degrees. You'd wear this, too, if you had the option."

"I don't think I have the legs for it," he quipped.

"Neither do I, but you don't see that stopping me," I quipped back.

Not exactly Tracy and Hepburn, but you take what you can get.

Joe treated me to cotton candy and we strolled the midway, both of us spending more time watching the people than the attractions.

He suggested catching Mysterio's act, but I nixed it.

"Not a fan of magic?" he asked.

"Magic's not a fan of me," I said. I didn't want to tempt Annabelle into making me the "lucky volunteer" and end up with egg on my face. Possibly literally.

We walked by the entrance to Sideshow Alley for the third time, both of us silently agreeing that we'd take a pass. From up ahead, we heard a whoosh and a mechanical roar, followed by a chorus of squeals. The Roto-Rama.

"How's your stomach?" I asked, nodding at what was basically a human washing machine.

"Strong enough," he said with a smirk.

We waited for the ride to slow down and vomit out its dizzy occupants. I use the word *vomit* because the ride's nickname among the staff is the Barf-o-Rama. Every tenth spin someone proved why, forcing the unlucky attendant to go at the insides with a mop and bucket.

There was no mess this time and we were ushered on with the next bunch. Joe and I and a dozen others were placed around the edges of the drum. Picture a giant wooden cake pan with a motor through the center and straps to cling to.

"Hold on tight until we're up to speed!" the attendant shouted. Then he hopped off and set the Roto-Rama going.

The drum started spinning slow then got faster and faster, the centrifugal force pressing our backs against the edges. Once it was up to speed, giant levers in the ride's base rose up, tilting the drum at a forty-five-degree angle.

Gravity became an afterthought as all our innards shifted and we were given a hint of what it's like inside a dive-bombing Spitfire.

It sounds harrowing, but really it wasn't. Everyone was laughing and shouting, me and Joe included. The Roto-Rama did to my dress what that machine has a tendency to do and I caught Joe getting an eyeful of leg. Only fair, I figured, since I'd already ogled him with his shirt off.

It wasn't until we stepped off, both of us teetering side to side, that he leaned in and whispered.

"Do you have a gun?"

"Shoot, did I flash that?" I said. "The ad claimed these thigh holsters never slip. Guess they didn't factor in the Roto-Rama."

"You brought a gun to the circus?"

I shrugged. "It's only a little .25-caliber Baby Browning."

"Only?"

We stumbled toward the Masked Marksmen booth, where a cluster of twelve-year-old boys were knocking down tin gangsters with pellet-gun rifles.

"It's nothing personal," I assured him. "Last time I was on a real date I didn't have a piece with me and I ended up with this."

I pointed to the scar on my cheek.

"I hope the guy didn't get a second date," he said.

"She wasn't the one who gave it to me."

The words were out of my mouth before I could drag them back. I don't drop that kind of information early, especially not to men. You'll have to chalk it up to the Roto-Rama and being out of practice.

I pretended to absorb myself watching the boys shoot, laughing and clapping one another on the back when they made a good shot. Would Joe ignore the pronoun, think he'd just misheard, or make it into something?

After a solid three ticks of the second hand, he nodded at the kids.

"You think you can do better?" he asked with a grin.

So we were ignoring it.

"Better than the kids or better than you?" I asked.

"Better than me."

"I think it'd be competitive."

"Want to make it interesting?"

"I can't afford to make it too interesting," I said, patting my purse. "I'm packing heat, not a wad."

He put on a mock thoughtful look.

"How about this? Winner picks the next ride."

"Okay," I said. "But if I win, we're getting back on the Roto-Rama."

"And if I win, we take a spin on the Ferris wheel."

Translation: *We go up a hundred feet where we can get cozy in private.*

"It's a deal," I said.

The boys ran out of ammo and Joe approached the attendant—I didn't recognize him—and handed him a pair of dimes.

"The lady shooting, too?" the attendant asked.

"You better believe it," I said, taking up one of the rifles.

After giving the battered Daisy Red Ryder a once-over, I

leaned toward the attendant and whispered, "Look. We've got our own wager going, so you can keep your plushies no matter how many hits we make," referring to the stuffed animals dangling above the tin targets. "But we'd be obliged if you could tip us to how far the sights are off."

"Little lady, these sights are as level as they come. They were certified and tested by Blackheart Bart himself," the attendant declared. "Why, if you aim true, you could hit the wings off a fly. The pip off a playing card. The—"

I cut short his spiel.

"Bart wouldn't have touched these rifles with welding gloves and a ten-foot pole," I said.

I reached into my purse and palmed a buck. Out of sight of the pack of boys, who were watching us with interest, I slipped him the bill. He just as neatly tucked it away in the pocket of his vest.

The attendant leaned in and whispered, "The lady's gun bears down and left two inches. The gentleman's fires right about three." In a louder voice, "Best of luck to you both!"

I pressed the rifle's stock into my shoulder and aimed, bearing up and right to compensate. Beside me, Joe crouched down, using his stump to prop up the barrel.

"Ready?" I asked.

"Yep," he replied.

"Go."

Ping! Ping! Ping!

One tin gangster after another was slapped down only to pop back up again on rusty springs. Behind us, the boys cheered. So did a few grown-ups. I'd have turned to look, but I was too busy putting pellets between Al Capone's peepers.

We blew through our ten pellets in as many seconds. The final tally: nine for me, eight for Joe.

"Damn," he said, rubbing the end of his stump. "Flinched on that last one."

The gaggle of boys were still mightily impressed. I heard one of them whisper to another, "That dish can really shoot."

I gifted him a smile. I take my compliments where I can get them.

We handed the rifles to the boys, who were newly energized and raring to spend their dimes to meet or match us. As we walked away, I caught Joe glancing back, a look of profound sadness carved into his face.

"It was only a one-shot difference," I said. "I'll give you a rematch if you want."

He shook his head. "No, I'm all right," he said. "I was just thinking."

"I can probably scrounge up a penny if you want to share."

He nodded at the boys.

"I was wondering where their war's gonna be."

"What do you mean?" I asked.

"I mean . . . I don't know what I mean. Losing makes me sappy, I suppose."

He took my hand. "Come on," he said. "I owe you another whirl in that death trap."

"You know what? I've changed my mind," I said. "Let's hit the Ferris wheel."

"You sure?"

"Absolutely. It'll get us above the heat."

We weaved our way through the crowd and got in the line for the Ferris wheel, an electric bull's-eye burning in the night sky.

We took our seats in the car and the attendant locked the bar down over our laps. We started the slow ascent, rocking to a stop each time another car was filled. Once all of them were full, the attendant let it run, sending us on a relaxing clockwise course that took us high above the noise and the heat, then back down and up again.

I have certain fond memories of time spent on the Ferris

wheel. Like the back rows of movie theaters, it affords a certain amount of public private time, and if any bystanders catch
a glimpse of canoodling, Emily Post says they should feign
nearsightedness.

But Joe didn't seem to be in the mood for necking. His mind
was clearly still back on the boys and their rifles and the question of what their future held.

Doc Donner's war had been billed "The War to End All
Wars." Somebody should sue for false advertising.

No one was saying that about this latest one. Fool me once,
and so on.

Already there were rumblings about Russia and South
America and countries I couldn't point to on a globe. It was
a legitimate question: When those boys stepped out of high
school, were their diplomas going to come complete with rifles
and a ticket to some foreign battlefield?

Since pleasure seemed off the menu, I flipped the switch to
business.

"I'm gonna take a flier and assume you have opinions about
a choirboy by the name of Leroy DeCambre?"

The funk gave way to surprise.

"Leroy? Sure I do. I have to talk to him enough. What about
him?"

I decided on the same tack I took with Mrs. Gibson. Everything except the heroin. I might have been game for some light
petting, but I wasn't ready for him to get his hands on our key
clue. Not yet, anyway.

"You really think Leroy might have had something to do
with Ruby's death?" he asked when I finished.

"You're the one who grew up with him. You tell me."

The wheel began another slow spin up into the sky. The
lights from Stoppard—what there were of them—came into
view. A constellation of stores and streetlights surrounded by a

modest nebula of residential sprawl, and farther out the distant flickering of farmhouse satellites.

Joe peered out, like he was trying to find the far-off speck that marked the Pig's Hole. When he spoke his voice was a little halting, like he was digging the memory out of a back closet.

"He wasn't too bad in high school. Good-looking, smart. He didn't grow his mean streak until later. After he got out of school and started working at his father's bar."

"You don't think he'd be the type to nurse a grudge against the girl who got away?" I asked. "The girl who made him the butt of a joke?"

That made him pause.

"I asked Ruby about him once. Kind of kidding her. How I would have thought she'd be more into rebels like Leroy. I was pretty straitlaced back then."

"Really?" I said. "I can't imagine."

"You're very funny."

"I'm glad you recognize that. What did Ruby say?"

"She said I shouldn't sell myself short," Joe said. "Also, she said Leroy wasn't really interested in dating."

"He wasn't?"

"I don't remember how she put it, but basically he was interested in crossing home without bothering with bases one through three," Joe explained. "He was pretty blunt about it, too. It kind of shocked her, I think. Ruby wasn't naïve. But at the time she was a . . . I mean she hadn't . . ."

Color was creeping up his neck and onto his cheeks.

"You can say 'virgin,' Joe. I don't think there are any in earshot."

He let out an awkward chuckle.

"Anyway, once she made it clear sex was off the menu, Leroy lost interest," he said. "Eventually he started dating Betty Kent and . . ."

"She was willing to let him round the bases?" I asked.

"If locker room gossip can be believed."

I played out a scenario. Ruby gives Leroy the brush, says she's not up for going all the way. Then she gets together with Joe and changes her mind. At least that's what his use of "at the time" when talking about Ruby's virginity suggested. That same locker room gossip would have let Leroy know it, too.

"So there was never any friction between Leroy and Ruby? Not after you and she got together?" I asked.

"No," he said. "Not that she told me."

That last bit came out a little wobbly. Like he wasn't sure what she would and wouldn't have told him.

But even if Leroy had stayed away back then, what seed of resentment might still be festering in his heart? Maybe it had grown tall and strong over the years that Ruby was out traveling the country, giving a show to any rube with two bits, while Leroy was trapped in Stoppard having never even gotten a peek.

Then there was the drug angle, which made Leroy an even better candidate.

"This last run-in with him—the one that landed him in a cell for a day—what were the particulars?"

"It was the stupidest thing," Joe said, shaking his head. "This woman, some out-of-towner who got lost, rear-ended Leroy's car in the parking lot of the A&P. It was barely a ding and his car's a piece of shit anyway. But it'd knocked over a sack of groceries and spilled powdered milk all over the seat."

"If he was the wronged party, how'd he end up in the clink?" I asked.

"Because of what he screamed at the woman in the parking lot of the A&P at nine o'clock on a Thursday morning."

Joe gave me the direct quote.

"Wow," I said. "Bet she learned some new vocabulary words that day."

"So did a number of small children and a county councilman's wife. She's the one who called us. We locked Leroy up more for show than anything else."

"How about when it wasn't for show?" I asked. "What were the charges then?"

"Theft. Assault. Fencing stolen goods. Half a dozen more. All alleged. Never convicted."

"Fencing? Out here in the sticks?"

Joe laughed. It was the first time he'd smiled since our marksman adventure and it looked good on him.

"We've got everything the big city does, just in more modest quantities," he said.

"Does Leroy have children?"

"No. Why do you ask?"

"Oh, just being thorough," I lied.

The Ferris wheel slowed and began the stop-start operation of letting people off. When it was our turn, we hopped out. I checked my watch.

"The big-top show is in five minutes," I said reluctantly. "Guess we should grab our seats."

"Yeah. I guess," he said, with about as much enthusiasm.

We stood there for a few breaths, neither of us making a move toward the tent. Joe broke first.

"What do you think about skipping the show and taking a run by the Pig's Hole?"

"I thought you'd never ask," I said. "You drive."

CHAPTER 30

The circus jalopy would have been a tad conspicuous, and swinging by the Pig's Hole in a cop car was plain idiotic. Which is how we came to be wheeling Joe's motorcycle along the grass by the Donner farmhouse driveway.

We weren't sneaking, I told myself. We were simply avoiding an unnecessary and time-consuming argument about whether or not this particular excursion was half-cocked and reckless and foolhardy and other such vocabulary my boss had access to.

After which I'd go off and do it anyway. I was merely saving time.

Once we reached the road, Joe straddled the bike and dropped his foot down on the kick-starter. On the third try, the machine roared to life, its high-compression engine echoing for miles across the flat farm country.

So much for stealth.

There were a few hiccups in the engine, but it sounded smooth enough. Joe had rigged all the controls for left-handed use, and he seemed perfectly comfortable with his one-handed grip on the handlebars.

"Don't worry," he said. "All the parts are firmly attached."

"I'm not worried," I said. "I'm working out the best way to do this in a dress. I don't want the whole county to see my . . . holster."

I hopped on back and after a few judicious tucks I wrapped my arms around my date.

"Any tips on riding on the back of one of these?" I asked.

"Lean hard to the right. I'm light on that side." He looked back and grinned. "I'm kidding. Just settle in and relax."

Then we were off.

Immediately, we began to wobble, and I clamped down tight. But once we got up to speed, we evened out.

That late on a Sunday night, the two-lane highway was practically deserted. Joe gunned the machine and we left the circus and the speed limit far behind. Telephone poles and fence posts whipped by faster than I could count.

I adjusted so I could peer over Joe's shoulder. All I saw was darkness and a narrow stretch of unfamiliar highway, which the bike's tiny headlight picked out thirty feet at a time.

How good were his brakes? I wondered.

How much practice did he have on this thing, especially with only one arm? If something stepped into the road in front of us, he'd have half a second to respond. Not even that.

I felt Joe squirm under me, and I realized that I had been gripping him hard enough to bruise. I forced myself to relax and get my lungs back on a steady in-out. Then I managed to loosen my grip and sit up straighter. Doing that flipped a valve in my back and shoulders, releasing a hiss of tension I didn't realize had been building up.

I closed my eyes. Felt the wind cyclone through my curls.

I loosened my grip more.

After a moment, I let go entirely. I spread my arms out to the sides. I was flying.

I've never met a roller coaster I didn't want to conquer. But this was different. Better. Because there were no tracks. We could go anywhere. Take any turn. Any direction. Pure, exhilarating freedom.

The bike hit a divot in the road. The wobble was enough to snap me back. I clapped my arms around Joe.

As my boss would have reminded me: Freedom and recklessness frequently go hand in hand.

I occupied myself tallying the facts about Leroy DeCambre. He stole from his grandfather—from more folks than his grandfather, apparently. And he fenced stolen goods. I knew fences back in New York City. Some were more pleasant than others, but every one of them had the mindset that everything had its price, including people.

I thought about what kind of man would scream obscenities at a stranger in a grocery store parking lot. Somebody with an excess of temper and a dearth of self-control.

More than anything else, I thought about Leroy DeCambre's grocery list.

CHAPTER **31**

I had some preconceived notions of what to expect from the Pig's Hole, and it did not disappoint.

It had clearly started life as a cheaply made shotgun shack and had only gone downhill since. The years had stripped the boards down to the raw wood and stolen most of the shingles off the roof.

What had been the front yard was now a patch of dirt that served as a parking lot. It was half to capacity with a trio of pickups that looked like they had crawled out of the same scrapyard and a mid-1930s Dodge that had not weathered the last decade very well.

The place was surrounded by dense, scraggly trees—the kind where every branch is a claw, every knot an evil eye.

"If a witch walks out of there and asks if I want a peppermint, I'm running," I told Joe.

We were idling on the other side of the road, trying to get a look at who might be inside. Light was pouring out the front windows, but a rag hadn't been taken to them since Coolidge was president, so all we saw were dusty blurs.

"I'm surprised anyone's here at all," I added. "I thought this was a dry county on Sundays."

"There's work-arounds," Joe said. "People bring their own bottles, pay for a seat. Then when the bottle is kicked, if it was even full to begin with—"

"The friendly bartender lends them some from his personal stash," I finished. "Free of charge, but tips encouraged."

"Something like that."

"Same thing happens in New York in the off-license places."

We peered futilely for another minute, but no one came out and the windows remained opaque.

"We should probably go," I said.

"Yep."

"It'd be pretty stupid to just walk in there, right?"

"Absolutely."

Another half minute.

"Then again . . ." I began.

"It'd be nice to see Leroy's face if we ask him about Ruby," Joe finished.

We walked across the street and into the barrel of the shotgun shack.

I've been in some dives, but the Pig's Hole deserved an award. The floor was mostly sawdust and peanut shells, the few tables scavenged from ditches and junkyards, and the air was three parts cigarette smoke to one part oxygen.

There was also that familiar perfume of stale beer, sweat, and motor oil that seems to be the standard for every dive from Biloxi to the Bronx.

The light was provided by a half-dozen naked bulbs hanging from frayed wires that had been stapled to the ceiling. If five out of six blew, it would have done the bar a favor. The clientele, as well.

Faces turned in our direction. Every one had the dead eyes of serious alcoholics. What conversation there was stopped so quick it left skid marks. One or two may have thought about making trouble, but that would have meant a pause in their drinking, so I figured it was even odds as to whether we'd go unmolested.

Joe led me to the trigger end of the room, where a length of two-by-four and some cinder blocks did for a bar. Leroy DeCambre—looking a lot more polished than when I had seen him the day before at the jail—stood on the other side, deep in conversation with a curvy brunette in mechanic's coveralls, who was perched precariously on one of the two rickety barstools.

She was keeping her voice to a whisper, so I couldn't make out what she was saying, but it had the familiar whine of someone pleading for a shot on the house. The zipper on the front of her overalls was at half-mast and she was doing her best imitation of a nickel-drop peepshow.

Leroy must have liked the view, because Joe was two steps from the bar before he looked up. He did a blinking double take. I saw confusion sandwiched between two slices of panic before it was covered up with a Bible salesman's smile.

"Well, look who it is. What brings you out here, Officer?"

Joe smoothed any wrinkles out of his spine and slipped on his cop voice. It was basically his usual timbre minus any hint of humor.

"Hey, Leroy," he said. "We were passing by and I wanted to stop in. Had a couple questions for you."

I hadn't gotten much of a look at him at the police station, so I took the opportunity to give him the once-over. I could see some women falling for a specimen like Leroy. The casting notice would have called for Jimmy Stewart if you lopped off half a foot and injected him with a healthy dose of weasel. Big fish, small pond, all swagger.

The brunette quickly zipped up.

"Hey, Chief," she slurred.

"It's just 'Officer,' Martha," Joe said. "You keeping out of trouble?"

"Sure, sure. Leroy was just . . . We were . . ."

Leroy dived for the fumble. "We were talking about this clunker out back. Old Buick of my dad's? Martha's gonna take a look and see if she can get it running again."

"That's right," Martha said, remembering her lines. "Can't do on what Al pays me. Now that his boys are back from the navy and working at the shop again."

"Why don't you go around back and take a look at that Buick. Tell Luke I said it was okay."

"Right. Thanks, Leroy."

Martha the Mechanic turned, plotted a course, and started weaving toward the door. The process took a while and I couldn't imagine any Buicks were getting correctly diagnosed that night.

"So what can I do for you, Joe?" Leroy said. "Don't tell me that bitch decided to press charges. She's the one rear-ended me."

"No, it ain't about that."

"Well, I can't offer you a drink, as it's Sunday. And it doesn't look like you brought a bottle. Though you did bring a beauty. Hello, darling. I don't think we've met."

"Everyone's luck has to end sometimes."

While Leroy was deciphering that, Joe said, "It's about what happened to Ruby."

"Awful thing," Leroy said, shaking his head. "Sweet kid. Can't believe something like that would happen around here. I hope that Russky fries."

"I was just wondering what you and she talked about."

Leroy scowled. "What do you mean? When?"

"When you saw her."

Not bad. Joe was employing the same tactic I'd used on him. Leroy wasn't biting, though.

"You talking recent?" Leroy asked. "Because I ain't seen that girl in years. Not since she left town. Who told you otherwise?"

Joe shrugged. "Heard it around. That you'd run into her at the circus right before she died."

"That's bullshit," Leroy said. "Someone's feeding you a line. Besides, you got the guy. Shoot—I heard the sad bastard crying in his cell all Friday night. Pathetic."

If he was lying, he was good. But a career criminal would have scrubbed away his tells long ago.

Still, if he kept on about Kalishenko, I wasn't sure I could keep my face from flashing murder. I decided to get out of the way of Joe's program.

"Where might I find the ladies' room?"

Leroy chuckled. "We don't have a ladies' room, per se. We have an outhouse. You go outside around to the left and it's right there. Probably not up to your standards, though."

"That's all right," I said. "I'm no stranger to shitholes."

Outside, I located the outhouse. The stench was so thick, I could have found it blindfolded.

He was right. It wasn't up to my standards. If I really had needed to use the facilities I'd have opted for the woods and taken my chances with the witches.

I kept walking to the back of the building. There I found a cleared-off patch of dirt, at the far end of which sat a Buick. At least it used to be a Buick. The tires were rotted flat and I figured if I popped the hood I'd find a nest of something calling the engine block home.

"That doesn't need a mechanic," I muttered. "It needs a mortician."

The driver's door was open and Martha was sitting behind the wheel, her head tilted back on the seat, her body slack and unmoving.

During my years with Ms. Pentecost, I've had the occasion to stumble on more than one body in situ. It's never a pleasant experience, and I was worried that was what I was looking at.

Seeing nobody else in the vicinity, I approached the open door. I leaned my head in just as Martha gave a deep, shuddering breath.

"Shit!" I yelled.

Her lids popped open and she looked around, dazed and blank-eyed.

Then I saw her right arm. The sleeve of her coveralls was pushed up and a needle was dangling from the crook of her elbow.

"Hey," she said, her voice coming from somewhere deep underwater. "This is my spot. You gotta wait your turn."

I was still fumbling for how to respond when I heard shuffling steps behind me.

"What are you doing back here?"

I whirled around to find myself arm's length from a gorilla. At least he was proportioned that way—all arms and chest on top of stubby legs, the bulk of him testing the manufacturer's limits on a pair of ratty jeans and a button-up that might have been white once upon a time.

His face was obscured by shaggy hair and two weeks' worth of beard, but I caught the resemblance to Leroy. If you'd subtracted the weasel and replaced it with bulldog.

"You must be Luke," I said as nonchalantly as possible, hoping he wasn't seeing my inner flywheels spinning.

"Yeah, who are you?"

My brain tossed out an idea. I would have disposed of it but I was short on ideas and beggars can't be choosers.

"Leroy said it was okay," I told him. "He said to get the stuff from you."

I tried to will myself into a flop sweat, which wasn't hard, considering.

"I'm hurting bad," I told him. "I really need some, okay?"

Luke tilted his head, looking even more like a junkyard mutt.

"Nah," he said. "I don't think so."

"No?"

He shook his head.

"Then I guess I'll have to take my business elsewhere."

I moved to get around him and he reached out with one massive arm and barred my way.

"I don't think so," he repeated.

Behind me, Martha scrambled out of the car and hurried off down the side of the building.

"I'm not looking for trouble," I said.

His lips curled back, showing off a mouth of chipped yellow teeth.

"Sorry, girlie. You found it."

My chest tightened. I flashed back to that roadhouse parking lot where Kalishenko had saved my life. Back then I'd been young and dumb and next to helpless. But I'd learned a few tricks in the interim.

I looked over the brute's shoulder and said, "Hey, Leroy. Tell your brother I'm on the level."

I guess I sold it because he turned his head to look. As soon as his eyes were off me, I drove my knee as hard as I could between his legs.

He managed to shift his hips so it wasn't a direct hit, but he still grunted and doubled over. I dodged past him, but only got two steps before he stretched out, extending his whole body and catching my ankle.

I went sprawling hard in the dirt.

I rolled onto my back and began kicking as he tried to crawl up me. One of my slingbacks caught his forehead so hard the heel snapped off. He just grunted and kept coming, wedging himself between my legs, trying to get up high enough so he could pin me to the ground.

He pulled his right fist back, telegraphing the punch he planned to send to my face. When his arm shot forward, I bumped my hips and threw my head to the side. His fist plowed into the dirt. Then I wrapped both my arms around his one and brought my left leg up and around, shoving my calf under his chin.

In the best of circumstances, I could break his arm from that position. But these weren't the best of circumstances. He had a hundred pounds on me and my grip was slipping. I had maybe two seconds before he'd break free.

Recognizing the cause for lost, I gave him his arm back. It sent him off balance, but he still managed to take the opportunity to wrap a set of fingers around my throat. He was bringing his left hand around so he could strangle me proper when I very calmly placed the Browning under his chin and thumbed the safety off.

He let go of my throat immediately. He was smarter than he looked.

"I don't particularly want to kill you, but I'll make an exception," I said. "Now you back up nice and slow."

Continuing his streak of good decision-making, he did. He got to his feet and I followed suit, keeping the gun trained on a spot right above the bridge of his nose.

"Back up," I said.

He did.

"Sit in the car."

He looked confused.

"Having you on your feet makes me nervous. You don't want me nervous. I'm likely to give you a third nostril."

He bent down and squeezed his bulk into the now-vacant front seat.

"So, tell me, Luke. How long have you and your brother been in the heroin business?"

"What heroin?"

Luke told lies like he threw punches—slow and obvious.

"The stuff you gave Martha," I said. "I'm thinking it wasn't insulin. And that you cut it with powdered milk. Am I right?"

"Who told you that?"

"A little birdie," I said. "Another little birdie told me you gave some to Ruby Donner."

"Who?"

"Ruby Donner. Had herself an accident a few days ago. Fell backward on a knife. You went to school with her."

It was a slow count of five before "Oh, her."

My inner lie detector failed me. I couldn't tell if the delayed response was because Luke was a slow thinker, he was innocent and confused, or he was the type to stab a woman and forget her name.

I was preparing a follow-up when something over my shoulder caught his eye.

"Leroy, run!" he yelled. "She's got a gun!"

I swung around, expecting to see his brother. Instead, I heard a crash from the car and turned back in time to see Luke scrambling out of the passenger door and tearing like a wounded bear into the woods.

"Son of a bitch," I said. "He stole my trick."

I fired a shot into the air, hoping that would give him pause. But the trees provided good cover, and he knew it. A few seconds more and he was out of sight entirely.

I heard the bar's front door slam open, then the sound of footsteps. A moment later, Joe ran around the back. He stopped dead, his eyes focusing first on the gun then the rest of me.

I looked down at myself. My dress was ripped, one heel was broken off, the other shoe gone who knows where, and I looked like I'd been rolling around in dirt. Which I had.

"Are you all right?" he asked.

"I'm fine. But Luke's gone cross-country," I said, nodding toward the woods. "He and his brother have been dealing heroin out of here."

Dumbstruck wasn't an attractive look on Joe, but I forgave him.

I was about to suggest we go have a more nuanced discussion with Leroy when there was the sound of an engine growling to life. We got to the parking lot just in time to see the taillights of the Dodge disappear in a cloud of dust.

Leroy had hit the road.

I turned to Joe.

"You know," I said, sliding the .25 back into its holster. "As dates go, this really wasn't so bad."

CHAPTER 32

I stifled a shriek as a torrent of icy water poured over my head and down my back.

"Where is this stuff getting pumped from?" I gasped. "The North Pole?"

Joe gave the old pump handle another go and I sluiced the last of the dirt out of my hair. The drive back to the Donner farm had blown off most of the dust from my legs, but had only pushed the grime farther into my curls.

The lights in the house were out and I didn't want to wake up Doc or Ms. Pentecost with a late-night bath. Plenty of time in the morning to give my boss the lowdown.

So Joe and I had stashed the motorcycle back in the barn and found the old well, hand pump included, around back.

We opted not to call the county sheriff, who technically had jurisdiction over the Pig's Hole. For one, we had no evidence. For two, Joe was convinced Leroy and Luke's first hiding spot would be their grandfather's house, which was smack in the Stoppard Police Department's radius. He wanted first crack.

I told him I'd go to the station tomorrow morning and fill out a report on Luke for assault. It'd be a weak charge, but enough to get folks hunting.

I trusted Whiddle about as far as I could throw him. But if he nabbed the DeCambre brothers, that meant a stay in the

Stoppard jail and good odds that my boss and I could get a few
words with them.

My lie detector was good, but Ms. Pentecost's was world-
class. If either of them was Ruby's killer, she'd catch him out.

Joe pointed out that Leroy seemed to have answered honestly when we'd asked about him seeing Ruby. I pointed out
that he might have spent some time memorizing his lines.

I still hadn't mentioned the heroin in Ruby's trailer, which
would have tipped the scales in favor of Luke and Leroy having
a hand in her death. If we were going to make that part of the
official record, I wanted to run it by Ms. P first.

I stuck my bare feet under the pump to catch the last trickle.
I'd managed to find the one shoe, but the one with the broken
heel was a lost cause. I gave myself a once-over. My dress was
ruined; I was sore, soaked, and a little windburned from the
bike ride, and my knees looked like I'd slid bare-legged into first
base.

I felt great.

"Follow me," Joe said. "I've got some towels."

Inside the barn, Joe lit one of the hurricane lamps and went
rummaging. He came back with what could be called a towel
if you didn't have *rag* in your vocabulary. I used it to dry off as
best I could.

"I know Leroy went blank when you pressed him about
Ruby," I said. "But I can't think it's a coincidence. Everyone
keeps saying this is a small town. Things like this don't happen here. So you've got a woman killed and a guy who used to
be obsessed with her dealing drugs. There's something there.
Maybe it wasn't him. Maybe it was his brother. Luke obviously
has no problems with violence. And he's just stupid enough to
head into strange territory and stick a knife in someone. Either
way, I'm real interested in chatting with him again. In more
contained circumstances, of course."

I didn't know if it was the freezing water or lingering adrenaline or because we finally had a suspect in the crosshairs, but my heart was racing to beat the band. I gave my curls a last run-through with the towel and tossed it to Joe.

"Maybe we should call Whiddle at home," I went on. "I know this isn't an emergency, but we could get a head start on chasing them down. No, scratch that. You don't want to go knocking on doors until first light. Too easy for them to get the jump on you. Somebody could get shot. What time does the chief get into work in the morning?"

I took the needle off the record long enough to catch's Joe's smile.

"What? It's my hair, isn't it? If I don't brush it out before it dries, I get a real Bride of Frankenstein look going."

He stepped toward me, reaching up to brush down some errant strand. Even though the barn was an oven, I could still feel the heat coming off him. He smelled like talcum and Club-man aftershave and something I couldn't pin down.

"What are you waiting for?" I asked. "An engraved invitation?"

I grabbed his shirt collar, gave it a yank, and kissed him. He got the idea quick.

There were a few minutes of that. After we came up for air, we agreed we both wanted to change venues, but neither of us had the patience for long-distance travel.

There was a quick discussion about supply requisition and Joe hurried to a duffel in the corner and came out with a tin like the one we'd found in Ruby's things, only this one was newer and had PROPERTY OF U.S. ARMY stamped on it.

"Gotta love the army," I said. "Always be prepared."

"That's the Boy Scouts."

I wasn't in the mood for being copyedited and I let him know it. Two of his shirt buttons flew off into a dark corner of the barn and were never heard from again.

He grabbed the lamp and led me up the ladder into the hayloft, which was blessedly free of hay. I was a country girl and knew that, while hay in bulk might be soft, the individual stems tended to poke.

Instead of hay, there were dry, clean boards and a pile of blankets.

"Sometimes I sleep here," Joe explained. "When it gets too late and I don't want to head home."

"It'll do."

Not wanting any accidents, I took a moment to unbuckle the thigh holster. I let Joe handle the rest. He only got a little hung up on the bra clasp, but he was working one-handed so I graded on a curve. Eventually I just tore the thing off myself.

As for what followed . . .

You know in movies where a couple are getting hot and heavy and then the screen fades to black and the next thing you see they're tucked under the sheets and the guy's lighting them both cigarettes and the woman's got those heavy-lidded eyes and you're left with your imagination to fill in the blanks?

Yeah. Like that.

Fade to black.

We were side by side, me on my stomach, him on his back, both of us sweat-soaked and pleasantly sore. Joe didn't have any cigarettes and I might have been doing the heavy-lidded thing. I can't be sure. Also, there were no sheets in the loft to tuck ourselves under.

Some time had passed. I don't know how much. My watch kept getting caught in his chest hair, so I'd ditched it. I was mostly content to let myself drift, suspended between the stifling summer air and the cool hardwood boards of the loft, a corner of my consciousness already pondering a second round.

However, the rest of my brain was doing its best to short-circuit the afterglow.

A cop? While on a case? It broke three professional rules and two personal ones. What was I thinking?

I hadn't been, or at least not with any part of me concerned with rules. My thoughts—the few that there were—had gone along the lines of: I could have been killed tonight, but I wasn't. I'm still alive. Now let's jump in the sack and prove it!

A perfectly reasonable response.

Or was it? Was it normal to find violence to be an aphrodisiac?

I was stuck on that particular merry-go-round of over-thinking when Joe began to massage his stump. During our calisthenics, I hadn't paid too much attention to the limb. Now I caught myself staring. So did he.

"Hey, lady. Peep show's a quarter."

I patted my sides. "I seem to have left my pockets at home."

He smiled.

"Does it hurt?" I asked.

He had to think about it.

"Yeah," he said. "Sometimes. A lot of time it's not the stump that hurts, it's the arm. Isn't that funny? It's not there, but it still hurts. There's a name for it, but I can't remember."

He rubbed vigorously at the stump, like he was trying to summon the truant limb back into existence.

"It'll go away eventually," he said. "That's what the doctors tell me."

I reached out and touched the stump, then moved my fingers down to his side, which was peppered with a constellation of scars.

"Shrapnel?" I asked.

"Most of it," he said. "Some of it was splinters. Their artillery was hitting the trees."

He looked like his mind was drifting back to the Belgian forests. I pulled him into the present.

"Splinters? Who hasn't gotten splinters?" I pointed at a thin scar across my ribs. "Stiletto."

"Stiletto?"

"Luckily, the guy didn't know how to handle it."

He held out his hand, palm up.

"A tank did this," he said, displaying a rough stripe cutting across his lifeline.

"Must have been a pretty small tank."

"I was climbing onboard and the .50 cal. was still hot. Didn't make that mistake twice."

I bent my left leg around so he could see my calf.

"That little circle there? That's Rosco."

"Rosco?"

"Neighbor's mutt," I said. "Got along with everybody else, but couldn't stand me."

He reached over and ran his fingers across the small of my back.

"What about these?" he asked, tracing the pale, raised lines of flesh that I always forget are there. I shivered.

"Belt," I said.

I could see him searching for the right words. I saved him the trouble, pressing my mouth against his before moving his hand to where it could do some good.

So much for rules.

One more fade to black.

CHAPTER 33

I woke in the dark, hot and confused. It was a long, disorienting moment before I remembered where I was. I looked over and could barely pick out Joe's sleeping form.

Sometime after I'd drifted off, Joe must have turned off the lamp. The only light in the loft came from the stray bands of moonlight slipping through gaps in the roof. I didn't know what time it was and my watch was somewhere in a pile of clothes. It felt very late or very early.

Then I heard it. Footsteps, slow and cautious. Someone moving in the barn below.

My first thought was that it was Doc or Ms. Pentecost come to see where we were. I nixed that quick. Doc slept the sleep of the drunk and Ms. P had enough sense to figure what we were up to without confirmation.

Besides, either of them would stand at the door and call out. Not creep across the barn in the dark.

Other noises followed. More creaks. The faint scrape of metal on metal.

I belly-crawled to the ladder and peered down. Someone was crouched beside Joe's motorcycle. It was too dark to make out who it was, but they were holding a flashlight, its narrow beam picking out the bike's innards. I saw a gloved hand holding some kind of tool.

Unarmed and stark naked was no way to confront an

intruder. As quietly as I could, I eased back from the edge and felt around for my holster. Eventually I located it far off to the side, hidden under Joe's shirt. That solved the first problem. I slipped the shirt on, which solved the second.

As I did, I felt something tumble out of the shirt's breast pocket. In the quiet of the barn, the quarter hitting the loft floor sounded like a line drive at Ebbets Field. To add insult, it promptly slipped through a crack in the boards and fell to the barn floor below.

Dang.

"Move and I'll shoot!" I yelled.

The flashlight beam darted around, then landed square on my eyes. I held up my free hand to block it, but the intruder was already running out the door.

"Whuz going on?" Joe asked groggily.

"Someone in the barn!" I yelled as I monkeyed down the ladder. "I'm going after him."

"Will, wait!" he called. I was already gone.

It was marginally less dark outside than in. Only a sliver of moon was visible, and it was disappearing behind some clouds. I lost a few seconds frantically looking around for our intruder. I finally caught sight of the flashlight beam bouncing across the field opposite the farmhouse from the circus.

Gun in hand, I ran.

As soon as I was off the grass and into the played-out corn-field, I regretted not having shoes. Stones and old stalks tore into my soles.

I kept going.

Fifty yards ahead there was another cornfield. This one was planted, its stalks high as an elephant's eye and ready to harvest. I knew if he made it there, I could lose him. But even without shoes I was gaining.

The flashlight's beam took a sudden sharp turn. I instinctively changed course to follow before I realized the beam wasn't turning, it was falling. He'd tossed the flashlight.

I canceled the quick turn, foot digging into the ground. My right heel came down on something sharp. I stumbled and went sprawling. I managed to hold on to my gun, but came up spitting dirt for the second time that night.

Ahead of me I heard the rustle of cornstalks being shoved aside as the intruder ran into the field. I pushed myself up out of the dirt and began staggering after him, trying not to put weight on my heel.

I paused for half a second at the edge of the corn. I'd like to say I took the time to weigh the pros and cons and logically concluded he probably wasn't armed—otherwise he'd have already taken a shot at me.

Really I was just dirty, sore, and pissed. I dove into the stalks.

Ten lurching steps in, I stopped, listening.

Silence. One breath. Two. Then the sound of rustling from somewhere to my right.

I started moving, slower now, trying to keep up but not wanting to close the distance too quickly.

I brought my gun up, finger loose on the trigger. I thought about firing a shot into the air. But that might spur him faster and would deafen me in the process.

The pain in my heel had faded. In fact, I wasn't feeling much of anything from that foot. Not a good sign.

I stopped again. I couldn't hear the rustling anymore. That could mean he'd gotten far ahead of me. Or that he was opting for stealth and was circling back to ambush me.

I slipped through the next row of stalks and emerged into a cleared row about a tractor wide that ran from one end of the field to the other. Both ends were lost in darkness.

I held my breath and waited.

Suddenly there were footsteps and frantic rustling in the direction I'd come from.

I swung the .25 around and squeezed the trigger. At the last second, I managed to jerk the gun up and the shot went high, carving a path through the stalks right above Joe's head.

"Jesus Christ!"

"Sorry," I said. "Thought you were someone else."

He'd managed to find his pants and shoes.

"Where did he go?" he asked.

I shook my head.

"I don't know," I whispered. "Where does this path lead?"

"To the road, probably."

I turned in that direction, took a step, and hissed in pain. I stumbled and Joe caught me, lowering me to the ground.

He pulled a lighter out of his pocket and sparked a flame, holding it by my foot. The left sole was scraped and dirty, but the right was covered in blood. An inch-long gash was carved into the tender flesh of my heel.

I sighed. Another scar to add to the collection.

CHAPTER 34

Joe scooped me up and carried me out of the field and back to the house. Both Doc and Ms. Pentecost were waiting in the yard. Thankfully I'd taken a minute to button Joe's shirt, which was long enough that it covered everything that needed covering.

Apparently my boss had been in bed but not quite asleep and had been alerted by the shouts and the gunshot. Lurching toward us sans cane, she looked like a runaway from a gothic novel, nightdress glowing white in the moonlight. She'd managed slippers, but not her glass eye, and her socket was empty and dark.

"We had a midnight visitor," I said, as Joe set me down. "Someone messing with Joe's bike."

"And you gave chase over broken glass?" Ms. P asked, examining my foot.

"Probably a rock," I said. "I'd have put on shoes but I broke the heel off on a guy's face earlier."

She gave me a look, but bookmarked further questions for later.

Joe helped me inside, Ms. P leading the way, while Doc went to fetch the first-aid kit again.

"You should go check on the bike," I told Joe. "See what mischief this guy got up to."

Just as Joe left, Doc appeared with his well-stocked kit and some wet towels.

"Perhaps you should accompany Officer Engle," Ms. P told Doc, taking the kit out of his hands. "The perpetrator might still be close. I believe I can attend her injuries."

"Are you sure?" he asked. "It's been a while, but I can still stitch a straight line."

Ms. P gave him the least impatient look she could muster.

"I have doctored wounds before," she said. Then she grabbed one of the towels and began cleaning the blood off my foot.

He got the picture. "All right. You need anything, just yell."

Once he was gone, I gave the shortest version of the evening's events I could manage. I skipped the part in the middle, but considering all I was wearing was a man's shirt, I figured she could do the math.

The only time I paused was when she pulled out a needle and a spool of nylon thread.

"Have you really done this before?" I asked.

"I've watched Mrs. Campbell do it a number of times," she said, threading the needle. "The technique is simple and my hands seem relatively steady this evening. Now continue with your report. And try not to move."

I managed to get through it with only the occasional four-letter punctuation. By the time I was finished, Ms. P had dropped in seven tightly spaced stitches. If you squinted, you could have mistaken them for professional.

"Not bad," I said. "Dr. Kildare would be proud."

I hobbled upstairs to my bedroom and grabbed a pair of slacks and a blouse, figuring Joe might want his shirt back eventually. By the time I limped back down, he and Doc had returned.

"It was the front brakes," Joe told us. "The line was half sawed through."

"Only half sawed?" Ms. P asked.

"It would probably handle light use, but anything heavy and it would have snapped."

"Like when you hit one of those backwoods curves going fifty miles an hour?" I suggested.

Joe nodded.

"Do you think the man you saw was Leroy?" he asked.

"Could have been," I said. "Could have been a woman, for that matter. I really didn't get a good look. Definitely wasn't Luke, though. Whoever it was, they weren't that big."

"We'll have to report this to Chief Whiddle along with your adventures at the Pig's Hole," Ms. P said.

Joe, who was halfway through buttoning his shirt, looked down and shuffled his feet.

"If you . . . um . . . don't mind . . ."

Again—my boss ain't dumb.

"While I don't think we can subtract Miss Parker's presence from the narrative, her exact location can be adjusted."

"I was sitting on the porch," I said. "I couldn't sleep and was getting some air. Saw someone coming out of the barn. Gave chase. Et cetera."

Joe nodded gratefully.

Behind him, Doc's eyes widened as he caught up with the group. "Oh, you two were . . . Oh."

If I hadn't been blushing already, I certainly was now.

Joe looked over at the clock on the mantelpiece. A few ticks past four. "Chief Whiddle's an early riser. I'll go into the station and give him a call, then get the paperwork started. Once that's done, we can go out to the DeCambre place and see if Leroy or Luke have shown."

"I'll see you back at the station," I said. "Remember—*Willowjean* is one word. *Parker* spelled how you say it."

Joe left. Through the window I watched his sedan head down the drive and toward town.

"Might as well start the coffee," Doc said, heading into the kitchen. "Not like any of us are getting back to sleep."

Ms. P and I retired to her bedroom, both of us limping. She took one side of the bed, I took the other, and both of us propped up our sore feet.

"Do we need to exchange words about me going off to the Pig's Hole on my own?"

She shook her head. "You were armed. You were accompanied by a police officer. And you walked away with only a broken shoe and some very interesting information. The altercation with Luke DeCambre was unfortunate, but unavoidable."

Had it been, though? Or had part of me gone in looking for a fight?

Ms. Pentecost picked up on my pause.

"Should we exchange words?" she asked.

"I don't know," I said. "Frieda said some stuff. Then today I went and saw Val and he got me thinking."

"May I ask what exactly was said?"

"They both kind of agreed that underneath it all, I'm angry. That a lot of the things I do are driven by anger. And Frieda— she figures that eventually it might do me in, you know? That it'll eat me up or something."

I tugged at a knot in my hair.

"Maybe they're not wrong," I said. "I think about all the times I've hurt someone, or wanted to hurt someone. The number of times I've pulled a gun on someone, or a knife, and didn't think twice. How good it felt. Normal people aren't like that, right?"

"Are you really worried about being normal?" Ms. P asked.

"Hardly," I said.

"Then what are you really afraid of?"

It took a while for me to answer. It wasn't that I didn't know the answer. It just took an effort to yank it out of my gut and get it past my lips.

"That in some way . . . I'm like my father," I finally said. "He was angry. He was angry all the time. About everything. He liked to use his fists, too. And he wasn't always like that, at least I don't think so. He turned that way. What if I . . . I don't know . . . I inherited that from him? Whatever was inside him that drove him to be that way. It ate him up. He let it loose on me and my mother, but I can see how it ate him up, too."

Ms. P took a long time to respond. Eventually she rolled to her side, her good eye meeting mine.

"You are many things, Will. Your father is not one of them," she said. "Though I have no doubt he imprinted himself on you in irrevocable ways, you have something he did not. You have compassion. And understanding. And a purpose that goes beyond your own inner desires. For that reason alone, I do not think you will let your anger corrode you. Now that you've identified it, now that you know it, you can make doubly sure it will not."

She paused, slender fingers picking at the hem of her nightgown. Her next words were so quiet, I almost didn't catch them.

"I am angry, too."

My response was delivered just as softly.

"Because of the disease?"

She let out a short, sad bark of laughter.

"Oh, yes!" she said. "But so much more. As ugly as it might be, I find anger very useful at times. To drive me forward when it would be so much easier to stop. This ugly engine at the heart of what I do."

She took a deep, shuddering breath. Like a swimmer coming up after a long dive.

"And it's not always a bad thing to let the anger show," she said. "Sometimes it's useful for people to be afraid of you. As long as it's the right people."

We gave that conversational capper the moment of silence it deserved, then got to work.

"So—busy evening, lots to unpack," I said, propping myself up against the headboard. "Someone tried to kill me. Twice. Not a record I want to beat. Also, do you mind putting in your eye?"

"There is indeed lots to unpack," she said, taking the glass eye from the folded handkerchief on the nightstand. "Though I would argue with your math."

She set the eye against the empty socket, placed her thumb on it, and pushed. The sound it made was a cross between a pop and a slurp and never failed to elicit a full-body shiver.

"What math?" I asked.

"That there were two attempts on your life. There was one, by Luke DeCambre. And then a second person tampered with the brakes on Officer Engle's motorcycle."

"Right," I said. Then . . . "Oh. *Right.*"

Joe's motorcycle. Joe's brakes. An attempt on *Joe's* life.

"Sorry," I said. "It's been an eventful evening. My brain is still racing to catch up with the rest of me."

I thought about the implications.

"It had to have been Leroy," I said. "Joe must have spooked him."

"Spooked him how?"

"Asking about Ruby. Then finding out about the heroin. Leroy decided to get him out of the way."

She shook her head. "The removal of Officer Engle would not stop an investigation. If anything, it would draw even more unwanted attention."

She was right. Leroy didn't need telling that Chief Whiddle would take the murder of one of his officers personally.

"Maybe that's why he tried to make it look like an accident," I suggested. "So nothing would come back on him?"

"Even so, it's an irrational, useless gesture."

"Prisons are full of irrational and useless people," I said.

Ms. P tilted her head side to side. Maybe, maybe not.

"It's the inconsistencies that concern me," she said.

I waited a polite three-count then took the bait.

"Which inconsistencies are we referring to?"

She held up a finger.

"Someone kills Ruby Donner. Stabs her in the back. They do it quickly and brutally and in a place where they could be discovered at any moment."

Another finger.

"Someone firebombs the circus. In the middle of the night with little chance of discovery and minimal effectiveness. Had they ventured farther in and chosen a more opportune spot, they could have done significantly more damage. They chose not to. Or were afraid to."

A third finger.

"Someone tampers with the brakes on Officer Engle's motorcycle. Assuming they were unaware of your presence in the loft, then they were again minimizing their chance of getting caught."

I saw what she was getting at.

"They're deescalating," I said. "Going from murder to attempted arson to . . . I don't know. Attempted murder. In a half-assed sort of way."

We lay there for a minute, both quietly thinking. I broke the silence first.

"Two people?" I suggested. "Maybe two brothers. One who's quick to violence, the other who's more careful."

"Motive?"

"Leroy runs into Ruby. Maybe seeks her out. See if she's more willing than she was as a teenager. Coaxes her with the drugs. She's not interested, tells him off. Threatens to squeal. Leroy tells Luke. Luke takes matters into his own hands. Everything after is Leroy trying to clean up the mess."

"And the reason she was planning to go to Mr. Halloway about the situation?"

"He's her boss. She trusts him. He also runs the show, so he could make sure Leroy was kept out."

Ms. Pentecost made a grunt that could have been agreement. Then again, it could have been gas.

"Yeah, I know," I said. "There are a lot of links in this particular chain of events and most of them I'm hammering out of thin air."

Another grunt.

"Feel free to throw in your two cents," I said. "Your name is on the business cards, after all."

I glanced over. Her eyes were closed, breathing steady. The only clue she hadn't fallen asleep were her fingers still playing with the hem of her nightgown. After a minute of that, she spoke.

"Did you pack our address book?"

"Of course. Who do we want to send a postcard to?"

"I would like to place a call to Agent Faraday. Do we still have his home number?"

"We do. Home, office, and mistress's home. Unless she's moved again."

Ms. Pentecost and I had crossed paths with the FBI before. Agent Faraday of the Bureau's New York field office was our liaison, for want of a better word. That better word might be *wrangler* or *man who drew the short straw*. The feds didn't think much of local police. Private operators ranked even lower. However, he owed us favors.

"What do we need the boys in matching suits for?" I asked.

"Heroin," she said. "I want to ask him about heroin. Namely its distribution in this part of the country. At the very least it will give us a clearer picture of the world we're dealing with."

"Not bad," I said. "It could help us locate the DeCambre brothers if they don't turn up at their grandfather's house."

"It could."

"So," I said, "figuring Agent Faraday won't be up and about for a few hours, what do we do in the meantime?"

"I go back to sleep." She folded her hands across her chest and closed her eyes. "Just because I am in a farmhouse, does not mean I have to keep farmers' hours."

"And me?"

"You think about your statement to the police. I will leave it to your discretion as to just how much to reveal about our investigation," she said. "Also, you might consider bathing."

"Are you saying I stink?"

"I wouldn't go that far," she said. "But I imagine Chief Whiddle would be curious as to why you and Office Engle wear the same brand of aftershave."

My boss ain't dumb. She ain't subtle, either.

"I'll hose off and start in on the coffee. You get your beauty rest."

CHAPTER *35*

To say that Chief Whiddle was irritated would be underselling things. Most of his ire wasn't directed at me, though.

"What the hell were you doing out at the Pig's Hole? You were off-duty, you got no jurisdiction, and you know that place is nothing but trouble."

I imagine Joe had been yelled at by professionals in the army, and he took it without flinching.

I raised my hand. We were all squeezed into Whiddle's office. I'd washed away the last of the dirt and blood and changed into my summer best: white linen slacks and matching jacket over a blouse in robin's-egg blue. I'd swapped the thigh holster for my shoulder rig and the .25 for my .45.

It might have been pushing Whiddle's hospitality, but after the night I'd had I was going armed and wanted the world to know it.

The chief finally noticed the student in the back row.

"Yes, Miss Parker?"

"Visiting the Pig's Hole was my idea," I said. "I'd heard about Ruby's history with Leroy and wanted to get a look in person."

Whiddle sucked air through his teeth and let it out in a whoosh.

"Oh, I have no doubt it was your idea, Miss Parker," he said.

"As my officer is not a complete idiot. However, he can apparently be swayed by a pretty face."

Both Joe and I opened our mouths to protest but Whiddle cut us off.

"I don't want to hear it!"

He did his bellows imitation again. On the exhale, I slipped in a few more words.

"It might not have been the smartest move, but it poked a hornet's nest you didn't know existed."

Whiddle was about to argue, but this time I cut him off.

"And whether or not you approve, you need to follow up on it. We've got to track down Leroy and Luke DeCambre before they dig in too deep."

He rolled his thick neck, letting loose a chorus of pops and cracks.

"Of course we need to find them," he said. "They assaulted you. They're selling narcotics. They very possibly tried to get Joe here killed. So, yes, Miss Parker. If they're in my jurisdiction, I will dig 'em out. And if they're not, I will work with the county sheriff or the Virginia State Police to dig 'em out. Because that is my job."

He leaned forward in his seat, pinning me with those piggish eyes.

"Your job, as I understand it, is to get your friend downstairs off the hook for Ruby Donner's murder. So what am I missing? Why did you head out to that place?"

Joe fielded the question.

"Leroy had a history of bothering Ruby. Since then he's chalked up a long record of—"

"I know his record, son. I wrote most of it," Whiddle said. "What I want to know from Miss Parker is why she really went hunting him."

He turned back to me.

"A high school crush? I'm not buying it. I want to know why

you went out to Mrs. Gibson's house to pick her brain. And why you specifically asked her about drugs."

Joe looked at me, the same question on his face as well.

"We've found that drug use can be a good indicator of other criminal—"

"I know what you told Ruth. Did you think she wouldn't give me a blow-by-blow? And, again, I don't buy it. It's flinging darts and Lillian Pentecost does not fling darts."

Shoot.

Ms. Pentecost had said I was to use my best judgment as to what I let slip, and my judgment said it was time.

"There was heroin found in Ruby's trailer," I said. "About one needle's worth."

Whiddle and Joe looked at each other, then back to me.

"Not when we searched it, there wasn't," Whiddle said.

"Some of her coworkers cleaned it out before you got there. They thought they were protecting her reputation."

The police chief spat out a series of words I'd never heard strung together before. I looked over at Joe. *Stunned* was a word to describe his expression. *Betrayed* was probably a better one.

Whiddle followed my eyes.

"You didn't know this?" he asked his officer.

"No, sir, I did not."

Back to me.

"And you kept this information to yourself because . . ."

"Because I wanted to protect her reputation, too."

"That's bull!" he snapped. "The girl didn't have a reputation worth protecting."

"And, to be honest," I added through gritted teeth, "you didn't seem all that interested in alternative theories."

He ran a hand through his shellacked silver mane.

"I am perfectly willing to consider any reasonable theory put before me," he said. "But that requires me having all—and I mean *all*—of the evidence. Which I'm not even sure I can right-

fully consider evidence because it passed through who knows
how many hands already. It's goddamn useless in court."

I wanted to argue, but I couldn't. He was right. Keeping
what was found in Ruby's trailer to ourselves had been for our
sake, not the law's.

"I can get you the names of who took it out of her trailer."

"You better believe you will," he said. "You are gonna sit
right here and write out everything in detail. Who found it,
how you came into possession of it, and any other details you
and your boss saw fit to keep to yourselves. And if I'm satisfied,
just maybe I won't charge you with obstruction."

His face was beet red and I'm pretty sure mine was flushed
as well. The only person in the room who wasn't red was Joe,
who was looking pale and sick. I couldn't blame him. Caught
between his boss and his . . . one-night stand, I guess. A second
stand certainly wasn't on the calendar.

"In the meantime, Joe, you tell Mrs. Gibson to go down the
list of reserves and start ringing people up. I'm gonna go over
to Al's Auto and talk to Martha. Find out how long she's been
buying from Leroy. Then we'll head up to Homer's place and
see if his grandsons are hiding out there. Also, give Lieutenant
Connolly a call and tell him to send some staties out to the Pig's
Hole to take a look around. Better ring Sheriff Bowser, too. Not
that he'll do anything. Man can't take a piss without putting it
up for a vote."

"What are the chances you can find the DeCambre brothers?" I asked.

"Leroy's smarter than the average criminal," Whiddle said.
"But he's never lived more than five miles from this very spot.
People run to the familiar."

The chief stood and retrieved his hat from a rack in the
corner.

"But you don't have to worry about that, Miss Parker," he
said. "You just need to worry about writing out a complete and

completely truthful statement. Then you need to go back to the Donner place and tell your boss that your welcome in Stoppard has run out. Now, if you'll excuse us, we have a posse to organize."

With that parting threat, he walked out. Joe followed, but not before passing me a look. He opened his mouth to say something, thought better of it, and left.

I took a notebook from the chief's desk and began writing out my statement, laying out the who and when and how of what had been found in Ruby's trailer. Frieda would be pissed, but she'd get over it. Like she said herself, I was a detective now.

Halfway through I realized I was alternating between English and shorthand. I asked Mrs. Gibson if I could borrow her typewriter and she relented. She even offered me a cup of coffee.

"You really think Leroy DeCambre had something to do with Ruby's murder?" she asked me when she delivered the mug of cop-shop brew.

"Like you told me, it's a small town," I said. "Not a lot of criminal goings-on. Kind of hard to believe Ruby's murder and Leroy's sideline aren't connected. Especially with their past."

She didn't agree or disagree, just nodded thoughtfully. Which is about the best I could hope for under the circumstances.

Once I was done, I read it over, made a few handwritten corrections, and signed the statement. Then I went downstairs to check on Val.

He looked much like he had the day before, which is to say not great. I gave him the rundown on the previous twenty-four hours.

"You think this man or his brother—they kill Ruby?" he asked.

I was getting asked that question a lot. I gave him what was becoming the standard line about not liking the coincidence.

"I hope they catch him," Val said. "I hope they catch him and put him back down in here with me. I'll find out if he did it."

The look in his eyes said it wasn't an empty threat. There was the knife-flinger I remembered.

CHAPTER **36**

It was past noon by the time I made it back to the farmhouse. Doc was away at the Majestic doing some general upkeep, or so said the note tacked to the door. My boss was awake but still in bed, propped up by a mountain of pillows, her head framed in a corona of auburn and silver.

I gave her the update.

She agreed with my decision to cut Whiddle in on everything we found. As for his threat to ride us out of town on a rail, she took it in stride. I did not.

"This isn't the Old West and Whiddle's not Wild Bill. He doesn't decide whether we stay or go."

"No, he doesn't," Ms. P said. "But he does decide whether to charge us with obstruction of justice, interfering with a murder investigation, or whatever appropriate statute happens to be on the books in the Commonwealth of Virginia."

I gave her the point.

"Probably not doable to solve a murder from a prison cell."

"Not impossible," she said. "But needlessly difficult if we can avoid it."

"The way Whiddle talked, it sounded like we have until he gets back from hunting down the DeCambre brothers. So the end of the day. Tomorrow morning, at the latest."

"Which gives us between eight and sixteen hours to solve this case," Ms. P mused.

"Oh, sure," I said, waving a hand. "Just solve the case. Like we haven't been trying."

She leaned back on her pillow and aimed her good eye out the window at the empty field, the trees, and the circus beyond.

I took the opportunity to examine her. The bags under her eyes were strained to bursting while the rest of her face looked too thin. But she was an adult who could take care of herself and I'd learned that fretting about her wasn't going to do either of us any good.

I leaned against the dresser and attended to my cuticles. I was through six of ten fingers when she spoke.

"We haven't," she said.

"Haven't what?" I asked.

"Been trying. We've been picking at threads."

"In our defense, there are a lot of threads to pick," I said. "And we've been here all of three days."

"Too long. And the delay put your life in danger. If I hadn't been coming off the Sendak trial . . ." She waved away the thought. "But excuses are beneath us. There's still time to turn in an adequate performance."

I didn't know what she was talking about. Some of our thorniest cases went on for weeks. Months, even. But I kept my lips stitched except for the obvious question.

"Do we have a script for this adequate performance?"

"First, please visit Mr. Halloway and find out the name of the lawyer representing the trust he mentioned. The one set up by the anonymous benefactor."

"Are you thinking Big Bob is crooked?" I asked. Needless to say, I was skeptical.

"I think I would like the name of the lawyer."

"And in the next scene?"

"The next scene is I dress and do something with my hair," she said, easing out of bed and testing out her ankle. "Just

because most of our business this afternoon will be telephonic
is no excuse to conduct it looking like a Dickens character."

Scene one went easily enough. Big Bob wasn't in his trailer
so I had to go hunting. Monday was the circus's day off, but
there was plenty of activity. Rides were being oiled, animals
fed, and performers were grabbing half-hour slots in the tents
to practice their acts.

I ran into Ray, who was pushing a wheelbarrow filled with
scorched timber out of the mouth of Sideshow Alley. He was
looking spry enough, but the fire had relieved him of half an eyebrow, making it seem like he was asking a perpetual question.

"Good to see you up and about," I said.

"Thanks to you. If you hadn't gone up there and got me, I
would have . . . I don't like to think about it. I don't know how I
can ever repay you for that."

I gave him my most modest shrug.

"Don't worry about it," I said. "How goes the cleanup?"

"My little room is pretty well gone," he said. "The fire didn't
get to the trailer proper, but the water they threw on it leaked
down. Some of the pinktoes drowned."

"I'm sorry about that."

He forged a smile. "We're managing. I'll have the House
back open by tomorrow. Wednesday at the latest."

I told him that sounded super and asked where I might find
Big Bob. He pointed me toward the chow tent, then went off to
dump his wheelbarrow.

I found the circus owner perched on a bench at a corner pic-
nic table, a half-dozen scribbled-on calendars arranged in front
of him. He was in civvies—a pair of jeans tailored to fit and a
grease-stained shirt with the name TONY stitched on the breast
pocket. A raven wing had escaped his ponytail and dangled
over one eye.

"Who's Tony?"

He looked up, startled out of his scheduling fugue.

"Who?"

"Never mind," I said. "My boss is looking for the name of the lawyer handling that trust. The one that saved H and H's bacon? It wasn't in the financials you gave her."

"It's a firm. Alcorn, something and something. Their address is in the black notebook, top of the bureau in my trailer."

To my surprise, he didn't follow it up with asking why she wanted to know. Just turned his nose back to the calendars.

"Scheduling problems?"

"Sure, but the wrong kind," he said, tucking the errant lock of hair behind his ear. "Had two more regular gigs drop out for next season. One of 'em was Pittsburgh, so . . ."

Pittsburgh was one of Hart & Halloway's biggest stops. That left a serious hole in the schedule and in the circus's pocketbook.

"Now I get to try and squeeze in three more tin-horse towns to halfway make up for it. Maybe catch a last-minute southern stop late in the season. One of those Florida burgs."

The way he said it, I wasn't placing bets in favor.

"So black notebook. Top of bureau. I need a key to the trailer?" I asked.

He shook his head, sending the hair down into his eye again. He didn't bother tucking it back.

"It's not locked."

He took my silence as a question, looked up, and shrugged.

"We trust each other around here."

I found the notebook right where he said. It was Alcorn, Avis, and Patch and gave a Chicago address. No phone number. I jotted it down in my own notebook and headed back to the house.

There I found a freshly scrubbed Ms. Pentecost. She'd done her hair up in its usual braids and had tucked herself into a loose sage-green two-piece over a white shirt with brass buttons. She'd removed the wrapping around her ankle so she could squeeze her feet into a pair of soft leather ankle boots.

Was anyone likely to see this ensemble? No. Did she look fabulous? Absolutely.

The phone was mounted to the wall in a nook just off the kitchen. I moved one of the kitchen chairs over next to it and planted my boss in it. It wasn't the usual plush leather she made calls from at the office, but it would have to do.

"The fed first?" I asked.

"No, I think our first call should be to Sidney. Our conversation with Agent Faraday could take a while."

Calling Sid was a new addition to the show, but not an unexpected one. A former mob moneyman, Sid owed us a favor he could never repay. He was our go-to guy on financial questions.

I knew his number by heart and dialed. I was rewarded with a nasally "Whatdyawant?" direct from his basement apartment in Queens.

I handed the receiver to my employer.

"Hello, Sidney," she said. "Yes. . . . Yes. . . . You're welcome. . . . Certainly. I'll ask Mrs. Campbell to mail along the recipe. Now, Sidney, I have a quick assignment for you . . . No. . . . No, it really should be brief. . . . Uh-huh. . . . Hmmm . . ."

She furrowed her brow, then held her hand over the receiver.

"Apparently Slim Whitkins is crossing sticks with Jimmy 'The Thumb' Acevedo this evening. Sid has two large riding on The Thumb and wants to be there to make sure there's no double-tapping."

"Billiards and betting," I explained. "Knowing Sid, there's probably some broad in the mix. Tell him he should be done in time for opening break."

She put the receiver back to her ear.

"Sidney, I can assure you that . . . Oh, you heard her? . . .

Good. . . . Oh. . . . Really? . . . Mmm-hmmm? . . . Well, she sounds lovely. Sidney, I want you to inquire about a law firm based in Chicago—Alcorn, Avis, and Patch . . . Nothing specific, just the usual, though a client list would be helpful. Please call me back as soon as you discover anything."

She gave him the address attached to the law firm and the number of the farmhouse, then signed off.

"He says there is indeed a broad. Her name is Camilla. According to Sidney, she has a number of fetishisms that dovetail nicely with his own."

"I shiver at the thought," I said. "Shall I dial our friend at the FBI?"

She gave me the nod and I started spinning numbers.

That is where our program stuttered to a halt. A secretary with a distractingly adenoidal voice told me that Faraday was out on assignment and she didn't know when he'd return. This meant nothing, as the feds, even their secretaries, lie as easy as breathing.

I tried his home, where there was no answer. Then I tried his mistress, where there was an answer but not a helpful one. I took a flyer and tried a handful of bars I knew him to frequent. No joy.

Eventually I looped back around to his office and asked the adenoidal secretary to pass on a message to him, and ask him to please get back to us at his earliest convenience. I left the farmhouse number, but not our real names. Faraday wouldn't appreciate it getting around that he was taking calls from Lillian Pentecost.

Subtly inserted in the message was the insinuation that he owed us and we would take it personally if he didn't come through. I also mentioned I'd tried him at his home and elsewhere.

Knowing Faraday, he'd put two and two together and come up with a threat that, if crossed, we'd squeal about his mistress. Which, to be clear, we would never do. It was dirty pool. Besides, I'd met his mistress and I liked her more than I did him.

But people tend to expect others to live up to the level of nastiness they themselves are capable of. And Agent Faraday was capable of some truly unpleasant tricks.

The curtain came down on the first act of our script.

CHAPTER 37

Left with nothing to do but wait, I rummaged in the recently restocked fridge. I put together a pair of roast beef sandwiches and some potato salad that didn't seem too offensive. It wasn't up to Mrs. Campbell's standards, but it did the job.

We sat at the kitchen table and ate our late lunch and talked through the facts of the case. For the purposes of the exercise, we considered any testimony corroborated by two or more people to be fact. It was lowering our usual bar, but it was necessary, considering the dearth of information.

As usual, we didn't start with the murderer but with the victim.

Fact one: Ruby Donner left home at the age of seventeen. The only people who were surprised were her English teacher and her boyfriend, who likely had a blind spot. Also, I was beginning to wonder just how sharp a knife Joe really was.

Fact two: She joined the circus less than two years later, already well on her way to becoming the Amazing Tattooed Woman. Her first tattoo was a bouquet of daisies that she would later cover up, seemingly on impulse.

Relevant? To Ruby, sure. To her murder, it was looking less and less likely.

Fact three: Eight days ago she returned to Stoppard for the first time since her abrupt departure. She arrived already upset at the death of Bertha, the boa constrictor.

On Monday, she helped set up Sideshow Alley, came over to Doc's for dinner, then went back.

Fact four: She and Val had a dustup Tuesday morning due to her meddling in his family life. But according to him, she was too distracted to participate. Something was eating at her, something bigger than a dead boa.

Fact five: An unknown man visited her at her booth in Sideshow Alley on Tuesday not long before she was killed. This was actually only according to Maeve, but we decided to err on the side of veracity. As I put it to my boss: "If Maeve was lying, she would have fed us more details."

Fact six: Ruby blew off helping set up for the late show because she had something she wanted to talk over with Big Bob—likely the thing that had been preying on her mind all day—and she took the long way around the Loop to do it. On her way there, she was stabbed in the back.

Fact seven: Kalishenko was seen in the vicinity immediately prior to the deed.

Fact eight: That night, heroin was found in Ruby's trailer.

Fact nine: No needle marks were visible on her body. Certainly no evidence of regular use.

Fact ten: Someone firebombed the circus, obliterating Ruby's banner and nearly killing Ray in the process.

Fact eleven: A less-than-reputable character who'd pestered Ruby for sex in high school was discovered selling heroin out of his bar.

Fact twelve: Shortly following that discovery, someone tried to sabotage the brakes on Joe's bike.

There was plenty more, a gross of assorted details that filled in the cracks. But I'm saving on typewriter ribbons. You'll have to take my word that none of what I've omitted caused a lightning strike for either Ms. P or me.

Actually, we both had the feeling that we were missing something—a domino somewhere in the middle of the chain.

"This does not feel like something long plotted," Ms. P mused. "There is the sense of cause and effect. Something sparked Ms. Donner's murder. She saw something. Or said something."

"Any sense of what that something is?" I asked, reaching across the table with a napkin to erase some mustard from her chin.

She shook her head. "A sense, yes. Specifically what, no," she said. "There are pieces missing, one piece in particular."

"Where does that piece fit?"

"Monday night, I think. Or very early Tuesday morning."

"Why there?" I asked.

"Her uncle said that she seemed pleasant and engaged at dinner Monday night. By the following morning when Mr. Kalishenko confronted her about the letter to his daughter she was too distracted to engage with him," Ms. P explained. "Something happened during the interim. Something changed. Something that meant, for someone, that Ruby Donner had to die."

We spent an hour chopping apart the story and fitting it back together in what Ms. P referred to as our "constant search for clarity."

We failed. Things were as blurry as when we started.

Around four, Doc arrived back at the house but not to stay.

"Spent the day stitching up the seats that needed stitching. Then I thought, why am I doing this? Got a hundred and a half chairs and never more than two dozen butts for them at a time," he said. "So I'm going over to the circus and invite Bob and anyone who wants to come see the evening show for free. I don't care about money. I just want people, gosh darn it!"

I thought that was a swell idea and told him so. An excuse to get off the lot? And free? I predicted a full house.

He went off to make his pitch to the circus crew and Ms. P and I continued moving puzzle pieces.

I was rummaging through my memory, seeing if I could shake anything loose when something fell out. I picked it up and looked it over.

"We included Val being seen in the vicinity in our list of facts, but we've only got Mysterio's word for it," I reminded her. "And we haven't had a face-to-face with him yet. Just his assistant."

"I inquired about speaking with him the night of the wake," Ms. P said. "I was told by Mr. Halloway that he was feeling ill and would make himself available later."

That was news to me. The Nedley Johnson I knew wouldn't miss a party, even if he had double pneumonia. Any opportunity to get handsy with the girls.

I wondered why he was avoiding us. The only time I'd even put eyes on him was at the funeral. And for that quick second when Big Bob was giving us the tour and he pretended he didn't even . . .

"Son of a bitch."

"You've had an idea," Ms. P said. A statement, not a question. By that point in our relationship she could decipher the subtext of my expletives.

"I have, but I need to run over to the circus to confirm it. Will you be okay here if one of our calls comes in?"

"Let me see." She craned her neck to look over at the phone. "The part farthest from the cord goes by my ear, correct?"

My response was not dignified.

I went out the door wondering if I was rubbing off on her and whether that was a good thing.

CHAPTER 38

I knocked on trailers asking for Annabelle until someone pointed me toward a smallish, battered job far down the line. I gave its door a quick rap. It was opened by the magician's assistant. She was out of uniform and wearing a faded chiffon robe, belted tight at the waist. It was a purely practical number, not one of the gauzy silk things a lot of the spec girls favored.

"What do you want?" she asked, crossing her arms and cocking a barefoot leg.

"A quick chat."

"About what?"

"About what you said happened the night Ruby was murdered."

Her eyes flared death. "What about what I said? I found the body. I called for help. I never touched her. End of story."

"Not your story. Mysterio's."

I leaned into the doorway and whispered low enough to foil eavesdroppers.

"He's going blind, isn't he?"

I wouldn't want to play poker with her.

"Get in," she finally said.

I did.

Her trailer was nipped and tucked with military precision.

There wasn't an ounce of wasted space. She had even managed to fit in a bookcase. I scanned the titles. Each one dealt with the history and mechanics of magic.

I took the cot while she unfolded a trick stool. She locked its legs so it wouldn't collapse and perched, legs crossed, leaning forward like a bird of prey.

The only decoration in the place was a handbill carefully taped to the wall at the foot of the cot. It showed a curvy brunette in nothing but a frilled skirt and some strategically placed hands.

In screaming red font it declared, SINFUL SALLY APPEARING NIGHTLY AT THE PALM! The date below put the handbill at twenty years old. I'd have pegged Annabelle as having a thing for busty burlesque dancers if I hadn't noticed that Sally was sporting Annabelle's eyes and a grin that fell just on the sweet side of mean.

"Your mother?" I asked.

All I got was the poker face. But it made sense. Someone who'd spent a childhood seeing the ups and downs and downs and downs of show business would grow up to be particularly mercenary.

"What was the tell?" she asked.

Right to business.

"A couple things," I said. "There was you, for one. The Mysterio I knew liked his assistants meek and mild. Willing to keep their hands off his tricks while he kept his hands on theirs. You're different."

I nodded at the collection of books.

"You've got ambition," I noted. "And it looks like Nedley is willing to train you. What's he getting in return? Because, and I mean this in only the best way, I think if he snuck a hand on you he'd come away a finger short."

Her raptor grin told me I was right.

"Then there was that first day when Big Bob was giving us the tour and I locked eyes with him. Ten yards away and if he knew me he didn't show it. At first I thought it was Mysterio being his usual prickly self. Then it hit me. He didn't recognize me because he didn't see me. And if he couldn't see me at ten yards in broad daylight, how is he recognizing Kalishenko moving fast by a tent flap with only a few light bulbs to go by?"

Annabelle shifted her hips on the stool. It wasn't quite a squirm but it was close.

"He can see well enough," she said. "He recognizes people at a distance. The shape of them. Especially if he's familiar with them."

"He didn't know me."

"He hadn't seen you in five years."

"Did he tell you beforehand that he'd seen Kalishenko?" I asked. "Or was it only when the police asked?"

"He's not lying."

"Maybe not on purpose. But if the cops ask, 'Hey, did you see the Russian around?' and he remembers seeing a blurry somebody pass by, he could fool himself into remembering it was Val."

She looked down at her feet, curling her toes into the threadbare rug.

"Let me put it this way," I said. "Are you saying he'd be able to swear under oath that the person he saw was Kalishenko? Literally swear in front of a jury? Because that's what he'll have to do. And you better believe the defense attorney's gonna give him an eye exam."

She was caught and she knew it. If it got out that Mysterio was losing his vision, his days were numbered. He might draw a crowd, but half of them would be waiting for flubs and the other half would be on the lookout for how his lovely assistant was shouldering the load.

"I'll talk to him," she said. "But he really does think it was Kalishenko."

"Just ask him how sure," I said. "Maybe use the phrase 'reasonable doubt.' Then have him give the police chief a call."

She nodded. She knew the practical thing to do.

"So what's the deal?" I asked. "Mysterio passes on his tricks and you take his place here when he can't cut the cards anymore?"

She laughed. It was a harsh sound. Like there was grit in the works.

"Don't be stupid," she said. "If Hart and Halloway lasts two more years, it'll be a miracle."

She plucked a deck of cards off the top of the bookshelf and idly shuffled, her fingers moving with a mind of their own.

"Nedley still has contacts," she said. "New York, Vegas, Atlantic City. Some places overseas where a female magician would have fewer hurdles. He's already made introductions. I made certain of that up front. I've got half a dozen gigs waiting for me. Little things, but they're a start."

I caught the palmed ace of diamonds, but only because she let me.

"Nedley has me through the end of the season. After that, I take three months off to smooth out my act, then start touring on my own. Probably under a new name."

"Sinful Sally?" I suggested.

She gave a smile, but not a mean one.

"I've heard worse," she said, showing the palmed ace again. She twisted her wrist and it became a queen. Another twist and it was a jack.

"What about Mysterio?" I asked. "What happens to him? If there's a Home for Old Magicians, I haven't heard of it."

She shrugged.

"He'll have to do what everybody in this business does," she said.

"What's that?"

A last twist of her wrist and she flicked the king of hearts onto the bed. The suicide king, plunging his own sword into his head.

"Look out for himself," she said.

CHAPTER **39**

When I got back to the farmhouse I found Ms. P putting the phone back on the hook.

"Who was that?" I asked. "Sid or our friend with the collection of bad ties?"

"Neither," she replied. "It was Mrs. Campbell. We have neglected checking in with her."

Uh-oh. That was my fault. I'd meant to call her the night before, but what with all the fighting and sex and gunplay, it had slipped my mind.

"You tell her we're safe and sound?"

"I did."

"Did you happen to mention our respective injuries?"

If Mrs. Campbell heard that both of us were hobbling around, she'd catch the next train down and we'd be stuck with a Scottish nursemaid for the duration.

"I thought to save those details until our return," she said. "So as not to worry her."

Or inconvenience us.

"I approve," I said.

I gave her the lowdown on my conversation with Annabelle. She seemed pleased, but not entirely surprised.

"Did you see this little twist coming?" I asked.

"It was an inconsistency," she said. "One that cost Mr. Kali-

shenko his liberty. Without an eyewitness, it's unlikely that
Chief Whiddle would have arrested him, and just as unlikely
that the case will hold up in court. Though juries can be unpre-
dictable, especially when faced with people outside of their
experience."

In short: They might decide to hang the Russky, eyewitness
or not.

So we were back to waiting. We brainstormed what we
could accomplish while within earshot of the phone.

"There's your caller from yesterday," I suggested. "The one
who had very definite opinions about our victim."

Ms. P thought about it.

"It could be irrelevant," she said. "The rehashing of a childhood squabble."

"Hey, you're the one who always says that when it comes
to murder, everything is relevant. And as much as I'd like to be
in on the call to Agent Faraday, you don't need me to answer
the phone for you. Besides, what the hell else am I going to do?
Might as well kill some time."

She gave me the nod, so I went and did.

The errand killed exactly twenty-three minutes.

Five minutes in the circus jalopy got me into Stoppard
proper, one minute wedged me into a parking space on the
town square, one minute of strolling got me through the door
of the Bountiful Blossom flower shop.

Sister Evelyn was behind the counter arranging a collection
of flowers for an octogenarian. I caught her eye over the woman's shoulder: confusion, then panic, then anger, all quickly
papered over.

Yeah, I was in the right place.

One minute of flower arranging and another two of the

woman boasting about her granddaughter who was fresh out of the box and cute as a button. Then the woman was tottering out to deliver her bouquet to the maternity ward.

I walked up to the counter. Instead of her usual basic blue, Evelyn was in a sleeveless flower-print number. It still hung to her ankles but it gave her a pop of color. Unfortunately that color didn't extend to her still-pale skin, or the limp, mousy hair, or the look in her eyes.

I was struck that this woman was the same age as Ruby. When I first met her, I'd have tacked on an additional five, even ten, years. Clean living, it seemed, guaranteed nothing.

She slapped on a smile.

"Miss Parker, what a pleasant surprise," she lied. "How can I help you?"

"Well, I have a question I hope you can answer," I said.

"I'll do my best."

"How do you personally define Jezebel?"

Her smile cracked like dropped china. I kept going.

"I was unfamiliar with the term until my boss set me straight. It seems to have a pretty broad array of uses. Like all the best slurs, you can shape it to fit any face. So, tell me, was Ruby a bona fide whore or did she just wear too much lipstick?"

There were probably better ways to go about it, but I'd used up my supply of tact and hadn't bothered to pack extra.

Evelyn picked up the pieces of her smile and glued them back together into something crooked and sickly.

"I'm afraid I don't know what you're talking about," she said. "Now, if you'll excuse me, the storeroom needs . . ."

"Organizing?" I suggested.

"Yes," she snapped. "Exactly."

She had just enough time to turn around and take a step before I asked, "What did she do to you?"

She froze.

"She never did anything to me," she said, still facing away. "We barely knew each other."

"Really?" I asked the back of her head. "Because you said you used to be friends. I even saw a picture—a bunch of kids running around, playing. Ruby was there. I bet I could find your face, too. And, yeah, people grow apart. I got plenty of friends I ain't friends with anymore. But I don't get on the phone and bad-mouth them the day after they go in the ground. So I'll ask again. Why did Ruby deserve what she got?"

She turned back. Her smile was gone, her face sculpted into something far more genuine.

"She broke his heart."

"You mean Joe?"

"Yes." She had to push the word out. Like it was something that had been caught in her throat. "When she left, she broke his heart and she broke his faith in God. She was never going to stay. Everyone knew it. She was just toying with him. He deserved better. He deserved a lot better."

Before I could toss the obvious follow-up, she turned and walked as fast as she could into the storeroom. I thought about chasing her, but I doubted she'd be willing to continue the conversation.

I left. Out on the sidewalk I checked my watch. The exchange with Evelyn had lasted two minutes, start to finish.

On the way back to the truck, I was bothered by the nagging feeling that I'd missed something. Was it something Evelyn had said? Something she'd done?

I tried to nail it down, but it was no good. Experience had taught me that the best way to coax a reluctant thought out into the open was to aim my mind at something else.

I was in luck. I looked across the town square and saw one of the police department's black sedans pull up in front of the station. Whiddle got out of the driver's side, Joe out of the passenger's.

Nobody got out of the backseat.

I cut across the square and caught Joe before he went in the door.

"No luck at the DeCambre house?"

The look on his face when he saw it was me was not flattering.

"No," he said. "Homer said he hasn't seen them in days."

"They're his grandsons," I said. "He might be fibbing."

"Yeah, we're pretty sure he's lying. He never even bothered to ask what we were hunting them for. We left one of the reserve officers there to watch the driveway. See if they show."

"So it's a waiting game," I said, pretending I didn't see the sour, guarded look on his face.

He nodded, looking up the steps at the door, anxious to get inside.

"Family has a hunting cabin at the south end of the county. Used to use it for bootlegging. The chief and I are gonna head out that way."

Another look up the steps.

"Look, I should . . ."

"You should go."

Without even a goodbye, he did.

Another minute spent.

I pulled back into the driveway exactly twenty-three minutes after I'd left. On the way in, I ran into Doc coming out.

"Bob thought it was a great idea," he said. "He's gonna get a whole caravan of folks together to head into town for the movie. Wouldn't let me do it for free, though. Said they were gonna be paying customers and he was picking up the tab."

He was smiling. It looked good on him, even under that bird's nest he called a beard.

"Gotta go start making popcorn!" he yelped, then jumped in his pickup and tore dirt up the driveway.

I found myself smiling, too. Apparently it was contagious.

Inside my boss was where I'd left her, sitting at the kitchen table. The only additions were a half-eaten slice of apple pie and a Mason jar of iced tea.

"Any suitors call?"

"None," she said. "Any luck with Sister Evelyn?"

Since it was such a short one, I gave her the conversation verbatim, but not before cutting my own slice of pie.

"How would you decipher that exchange?" she asked. It wasn't that she was in the dark; she was just giving my powers of deduction a quick workout. I obliged.

"Little Miss Evelyn had the hots for Joe growing up. I'm going to guess unrequited. Ruby leads the preacher's son into temptation. Then she disappears, leaving him stranded off God's path. Evelyn blames Ruby for that. If it wasn't for that painted hussy, Joe would be clutching a Bible with one hand and Evelyn with the other."

"Do you think that's reason enough to kill her?" my boss asked.

"If it was just the church angle, I'd say no," I told her. "It's hard to rev up to murder when the motive is so . . . I'm gonna go with *esoteric*."

Ms. Pentecost nodded approvingly at the choice of vocabulary.

"However, when you add in the fact that she loved him and Ruby stole him away, that's a whole different kettle."

I took a bite of pie, chewed, and thought.

"The way she talked about how he deserved better. It sounded like she wasn't just referring to Joe. She deserved better, too. If it wasn't for Ruby she would have had it. That makes it personal."

Another bite.

"That's enough to warrant a knife in the back," I said, spitting crumbs.

Ms. P passed me a napkin.

"She's not a dainty woman," I continued. "That look she had at the end there? That was some grade-A hate."

My boss thought about it.

"It's not impossible," she concluded, "that the murder stemmed from old hates and old traumas, and that the rest is merely a confluence of events."

Translation: *What's a red herring and what isn't?*

We didn't know. All fish look the same when you're in the dark.

CHAPTER 40

The first glimmer of light came an hour later when the phone rang. I'd put my money on Sid getting back to us first, and I was a winner.

Ms. P sat in the chair next to the mounted phone while I leaned over her shoulder, my head pressed to hers. I was dearly missing our office, with its two lines.

"What were you able to discover, Sidney?" my boss asked.

"Okay, so first thing is Alcorn, Avis, and Patch is a real-life law firm, which I wasn't expecting."

"Why is that?"

I didn't catch his answer and apparently neither did my boss.

"Sidney, are you talking with your mouth full?"

There was an audible gulp.

"Pastrami and pickle from Gino's," he explained. "I ain't eaten all day and I gotta keep my energy up for Camilla."

"Well, if you don't mind waiting to finish your meal until after you've reported, I would greatly appreciate it."

"Sure, sure. Sorry about that. My manners ain't never been nothing much."

There was the sound of paper rustling as Sid wrapped up his sandwich, though I'm pretty sure he snuck in a few bites later in the call. Here's the blow-by-blow, with the pastrami-gnawing omitted:

LILLIAN PENTECOST: *You were saying you thought this company might be fraudulent?*

SID: At first, yeah. I figured this Alcorn place to be a cut-out job. A fake name to funnel things through. I figured that because the address is a fake. Or the address exists but there's no office there. It's an apartment building. But the room number? The one these lawyers have as their address? It don't exist.

LP: *And what does that signify?*

S: It probably means that the mail gets dropped off there. There's probably even a box for that apartment number. Then someone comes along daily or weekly and picks up the mail and forwards it along.

LP: *But you said this firm is legitimate.*

S: I said it was real. Legitimate's another matter.

See, I got to thinking. The name Alcorn. It rang a bell. Not a loud one, just a little dainty chime. I couldn't remember exactly where from, but I thought it had something to do with my former associates' Windy City pen pals. Capiche?

LP: *Could you elaborate?*

S: Okay, so back when I worked for . . . uh . . . that particular organization, they had semi-regular communications with . . . uh. . . . franchises. In other cities. If you know what I mean?

LP: *I do.*

S: It was mostly for making sure they didn't step on each other's toes. But sometimes they'd partner up on things. Import, export opportunities. That kind of thing. And when they did that, they hardly ever talked direct. A lot of the times, they had their pet shysters do the chatting.

LP: *And this firm was one of them?*

S: Pretty sure, though I don't have the paperwork no more. And back then it was just Alcorn and Avis. Don't know when Patch got added.

Anyway, I made some calls to Chicago. The firm's on the books there. Registered, pay their taxes and everything. But no office or phone number. Not that I could find.

LP: Is it still in use by your employer's former pen pals?

S: Not sure. The calls that I'd have to make to find that out would trip some alarms that I don't want tripped, considering I'm supposed to be out of the game. Not to mention, half of those folks are probably in stir. The Chicago franchise ain't what it used to be.

I'll tell you this, though. Firms like these, they usually diversified their business. Had to if they wanted to provide that—how do I put it—veneer of respectability. So they'd do routine business along with the shady stuff.

LP: Such as manage a trust?

S: Sure. That kind of thing would be perfect. No face time with the client, 'cause they're dead. But you get to put billable hours on your books and it's all legit.

LP: How difficult would it be to create a fictional trust?

S: You mean a trust for someone that ain't ever existed?

LP: Yes.

S: Shoot—it's easy as pie. Forge a birth certificate, a death certificate. Cobble up a will. Then put your firm down as the executor of the estate. As long as nobody goes digging too deep into your fake dead guy, it'd hold. Even then, there are dodges. What's this fictional corpse's name? I can dig around if you want.

LP: The trust is from an anonymous benefactor.

S: There you go. Anonymous is another wall you gotta scale.

LP: Indeed.

S: Anyway, that's all I got for ya. You mind if I skedaddle? Camilla don't like to be kept waiting.

That was all Ms. P had, and she told him as much. We all exchanged pleasantries and hung up.

Once the receiver was back on its hook, my boss and I shared a look.

When the hell did the mob get involved in this thing?

CHAPTER 41

We talked that over for a while, but it got us nowhere. I bent over backward trying to link the DeCambre brothers with the Chicago mob, but all I did was give myself a cramp.

The Outfit was big business. Luke and Leroy were the criminal equivalent of a lemonade stand.

I did congratulate my boss on confirming her belief about gift horses and dental exams. She shrugged it off.

"An anonymous source of funds at the exact moment the circus needed it? It would have been ridiculous not to be suspicious. Robert should have been as well."

I was guessing Big Bob had suspicions aplenty. But if you're drowning, you don't refuse a rope just because the guy throwing it might be cousins to Capone.

"The problem is, we still don't know where the money is coming from," I remind her. "Sid said some of the work these firms do is on the level."

She raised an eyebrow.

"Yeah, okay. Naïve is not a good color on me."

I added mob lawyers and mysterious cash to our list of facts. It helped fill in the picture, but there was still a big gap there. On one side of the canyon you had money funneling into the circus, maybe courtesy of the Chicago mob. On the other you had Stoppard and Ruby and a bunch of heroin-dealing yahoos who'd probably never gotten within a hundred miles of the Windy City.

The puzzle was incomplete. But I didn't like the picture it was forming.

We waited.

I called Agent Faraday's office two more times, being told each time that he had not yet returned and that my message would be passed on and could I please stop clogging up the federal wire.

The sun was tipping toward the horizon when I heard a chorus of motors revving up in the distance. I walked out on the porch to see a caravan of trucks and trailers heading into town.

I didn't think *Cat People* would be that much of a hit, but circus folk know how to turn any time into a good one.

I was heading back inside when the phone rang. I ran to pick it up.

"Parker? Is that you?"

Agent Faraday's voice was its usual blend of irritation and suspicion. I didn't take it personally. He was irritated with the world in general. Also, he was constantly afraid of being recorded. Considering who his boss was, he probably should have been.

"It's me, Agent Faraday. A pleasure to hear your dulcet tones. Please hold for Ms. Pentecost."

She was making her way to the phone as quickly as two legs and a cane would carry her.

"Is this a secure line?" he asked.

I tugged on the cord.

"As secure as it gets," I said. "You at a pay phone?"

"Of course I am. Can't call from the office. Ears everywhere."

"How is J. Edgar, by the by?" I asked while my boss got settled in her chair.

"Busy making lists of naughty little boys and girls. I'm betting your boss's name is on there somewhere."

"Well, give him a kiss from me next time you see him. Speaking of bosses, here's mine."

I passed the phone and pressed my ear to hers.

"Hello, Agent Faraday."

"Pentecost."

He injected so much venom into those three syllables it's a wonder my boss didn't fall over dead.

"Thank you for returning my call," she said, sweet as can be.

"Thank you for not leaving your real name," he snapped. "You're not on anybody's Christmas card list around here. What's this about?"

"What do you know about the distribution and sale of heroin in the United States?"

A pause. "Heroin? Really, Pentecost? What have you gotten yourself involved in now?"

She gave him the general idea but blurred the specifics.

"My question is: What does the FBI know about the drug trade in this area of the country?"

The useful thing about Faraday is his paranoia, a by-product of which is that he keeps abreast of everything going on at the Bureau on the off chance it involves something that will eventually fall on his head.

"The Bureau's focus isn't on drugs these days," he said. "We're gearing up to take on the Commies. When we do step into narcotics, it's usually cracking down in Negro neighborhoods in the cities. New York, Baltimore, Chicago—places like that."

The mention of Chicago perked my ear.

"Nothing in rural communities?" Ms. P asked.

"Well . . . I don't want to say nothing. That's just not where our focus is," he clarified. "We've gotten reports."

A three-count, then . . .

"Reports?" my boss prompted.

"Mostly from confidential sources. Less so from sheriffs or state police. Local law doesn't reach out to us unless they have a gun to their head."

"And what were the contents of these reports?" Ms. P asked.

A five-count this time. I stuck my mouth to the receiver.

"Come on, Faraday. We've shared with you when you needed us to."

A brittle laugh.

"Yeah, Parker. You two are real generous."

Apparently the dice tipped up in our favor. He continued. "We've heard rumors of dope cropping up in out-of-the-way places. Not a lot. Nothing compared to what you see in the city. There's been talk of dealing in Ohio, Kentucky, West Virginia. Small towns, midsize cities. It's even cropping up around military bases."

"How long has this been going on?" Ms. P asked.

"First rumors started arriving a few years ago. Been coming in faster since the war ended," he said.

"And the source of these drugs?"

"Same as always," Faraday said. "The war pretty much froze the opium supply. Now the ice is breaking up and the mob is taking advantage. They bring the dope into the ports, then get it to the cities. Then they finesse it out to the suburbs and the sticks."

"How is this finessing accomplished?" she asked.

"Couldn't say. Like I told you, the Bureau has bigger fish to fry."

"Surely your confidential informants have given you some idea."

"Yeah, yeah. Fine," he said. "We think the mob is using independent contractors. Sometimes they're low-level members of smaller organizations, but mostly they're on their own. A guy who knows a guy, you know? The distribution routes don't seem set, either. It's looser. Catch-as-catch-can. Twenty years ago, these chumps would have been bootleggers. Now they're doing this."

That sounded a lot like the DeCambre brothers. Maybe that old bootlegging cabin of theirs had been repurposed. The DeCambres couldn't make heroin from scratch like they could moonshine, but a remote cabin would be a good place to store it.

Faraday was still going.

"That's one of the reasons the FBI hasn't taken a hand in it," he said. "Compared to what we see in the cities, it's penny ante stuff. And with a loose network like this, there's not much chance of following the trail back to the big bosses."

Translation: *Unless they were Negroes or Commies, the FBI was interested in Capone-size criminals only.*

"Is there anything you haven't mentioned that you think I should know?" my boss asked.

Faraday thought about it.

"I think you should retire, take up knitting, and not call me again."

Ms. P opened her mouth to reply but was greeted by a click and dead air.

"He's a real peach," I said.

Ms. P stood, leaning heavily on her cane to do so.

"I have quite a bit of sympathy for Agent Faraday," she said, stretching and popping half a dozen joints in her back. "Fundamentally, he's a good man. It makes his job difficult."

I thought about that, but couldn't agree with the premise that he was a good man. Though I had to admit that some of the NYPD's feelings about the Bureau might have rubbed off on me.

We went to the kitchen table, where I got my notebook and began jotting down the new "facts." I was transcribing some of the crumbs Agent Faraday had let fall from the Bureau's table when my boss leaned back in her chair and started talking. Not so much to me, as to the room in general.

"I knew a man," she began, "who had also been diagnosed with multiple sclerosis."

She took a breath here, which gave me time to put my pencil down and give her my full attention.

"By the time I knew him, he had been living with the disease for years," she continued. "The physical effects were constant and unpleasant, for him and for the people around him. Despite this, he was surprisingly functional. While he had some cognitive troubles, they did not interfere with his day-to-day life."

She eased herself out of the chair and limped to the half-empty bottle of whiskey by the sink. She poured three fingers into a glass and leaned back against the counter.

"He also regularly used opium." She took a sip. Then another. "Enough that he had amounts delivered twice weekly. Though very few people, even his closest friends and family, were aware of it."

She limped back to the chair and sat.

"He rarely became intoxicated to the extent that he could not function," she said. "As he explained it to me, he used it so that he could function better. While the drug did not do away with his symptoms, they made living with those symptoms easier. He was, he said, increasingly a slave to his malfunctioning body and the opium allowed him to forget that for a time."

She leaned back again and sipped. After a respectful interim I spoke.

"What happened to him?"

"He killed himself," she said.

She downed the rest of her glass in a single swallow.

I was scrambling for what to say. I knew she'd made friends with other people who shared her diagnosis. I also knew a lot of them were dead and a few had gotten impatient for the reaper.

Was she looking at this guy as a role model? She was doing good, I thought. Her symptoms hadn't progressed much in our time together. A little, sure. But that was to be expected. She had years left. Double digits, even.

I must have let the panic show. She reached out and grasped my wrist.

"It's all right, Will," she said. "I have no present plans to end my life."

I breathed a sigh of relief. Though I made a note of the word *present*.

"I bring up that story because of the man's friends and family. How they did not know about his drug use. It went on for years and they never suspected."

She let go of my wrist and pointed to a line in my notebook. One of the details from the Faraday interview.

And I saw it.

The missing domino. I slid it into our timeline. It fit perfectly.

I was about to confirm it with my boss when there was a pounding at the kitchen door. I jumped, hand reaching instinctively for my .45 before realizing that it and its holster were hanging on a coat hook ten feet away.

There was a silhouette in the window. A man backlit by the bloodred wash of the setting sun.

Another pound.

"Ms. Pentecost?" Carl Engle called out from porch. "We need to talk."

CHAPTER 42

Wedged into one of the overstuffed wingbacks in the drawing room, shoulders hunched, hands folded atop his knees, Carl Engle resembled an oversize child called inside by disapproving parents to account for his rascality. But whatever was on his mind, it went beyond pilfering the cookie jar. His clothes looked like they'd been slept in. His eyes were bloodshot from booze, tears, exhaustion, or all three.

"I've been praying," he said, his voice cracking. "I've been praying a lot."

I wanted to ask how this was news but restrained myself. The preacher continued.

"I kept telling myself that it had nothing to do with her death. That it was long in the past. That I . . . that I didn't have to speak up," he said. "Then I realized that it didn't matter whether or not it had to do with her murder. I needed to come forward. It was a secret and a sin and it has been festering in my heart for many years."

I had taken a moment to slip my holster on, keeping it politely hidden under my jacket, before joining Ms. Pentecost on the settee. But Carl seemed more frightened of us than vice versa.

"What is this secret sin that you're referring to?" Ms. P asked.

He wiped a layer of sweat off the back of his neck, went to

rub his hand on the arm of the chair, then stopped and switched to his pant leg. He reclasped his hands in his lap.

"I didn't approve of Joe dating Ruby. I told him so as soon as I knew it was going on. She came from good parents but I thought she was a bad influence. I thought she would . . . distract him."

"Distract him?" I asked.

"From God's plan for him."

"Yeah, I could see Ruby being more appealing than life behind a pulpit," I said. "But it's a low bar to hurdle."

My boss gave me the gentlest of nudges with her elbow.

"You were saying, Mr. Engle?"

"I should have let it be," Carl said. "If his mother had still been alive, she would have found the right words."

Carl's eyes tracked up to the mantel and the framed photographs of the Donner family sitting there.

"I even passed a quiet word with her parents. That didn't do any good. If anything, it drove Joe and Ruby closer together," he said.

He twisted his hips, causing the chair to groan in protest.

"One day, Ruby came to see me at my office. She and Joe had been seeing each other nine, maybe ten months. She said she had something she wanted to talk to me about."

All of a sudden the nagging feeling I'd had after my confrontation with Evelyn came back in force. This time it dragged the thing I'd missed along with it: the old woman and her flowers.

"She was pregnant," I blurted out.

Carl and Ms. Pentecost gave me identical looks of surprise.

"It was the daisies," I explained. "My mother had a flower garden. She'd put together little bouquets as presents for people on special occasions. She told me all about how different flowers meant different things. Peonies for weddings. Lilies for funerals. And daisies for births. That was what her tattoo meant. A baby."

Ms. P looked at Carl for confirmation.

"You're right about her being pregnant," he said. "She hadn't told anyone else. Not her parents. Not even Joe. She wanted me to be the first to know."

He said it in a tone of confusion. But I understood.

Ruby knew the score. She'd been planning to leave Stoppard. She didn't see a life for herself there. Now here was a possible alternative. A future where she stayed.

Carl Engle was her boyfriend's father and her parents' pastor. Before she let the secret slip, she wanted to know if he was on board with Ruby becoming part of the family.

Considering the outcome, I was pretty sure I knew the answer.

"I did not respond with grace," he admitted. "All I could think was how Joe wanted to go to college. And what would my parishioners think?"

"Was there not precedent?" Ms. Pentecost asked.

"Of course," he said. "We've had some . . . unexpected weddings. But Joe wasn't just anyone. Would they accept him behind the pulpit afterward? I didn't know."

Through the window behind him I saw headlights pull into the driveway. I could just make out the driver in the last light of day. I thought about saying something. Then I thought different.

I have a nasty streak, I guess.

"How did you respond?" Ms. P asked.

Nothing.

"Mr. Engle?"

He came back blinking, confused.

"What?"

"What did you tell her? When Ms. Donner said she was carrying your grandchild."

He flinched, doing that stiff-backed swivel at the waist. Like he was trying to throw off a set of invisible reins.

"I told her . . . I told her there were a lot of good Christian families who would love to adopt a baby. Who couldn't have a child of their own. And then . . ."

The rest of the story got caught in his throat.

"What then, Mr. Engle?" my boss asked. "Did you offer to direct her to one of those good Christian families?"

It was a needle and my boss wasn't ashamed about driving it into his side.

"No," he said.

"Then how did that conversation with Ruby Donner end?"

"I gave her some money. To help with things."

There it was. He'd been clawing at the dirt, but he'd finally reached the root of the thing.

"To help with things?" I didn't even try to keep the sneer off my face. "Was abortion not in your vocabulary?"

"I never suggested that. Never!"

"The truth, Mr. Engle." My boss's words had half the decibels but stopped his cold. "A sin and a secret. That's what you called it."

Another flinch from Carl.

"You might not have said the words, but you made it clear," Ms. P went on. "Her having the baby in Stoppard wasn't something you would support. Which meant her parents wouldn't support it, and perhaps not even your son. She had no family elsewhere. Only her uncle, who was in no position to help. So when you gave her the money, you knew the likely outcome."

He focused at a point on the floor between his feet.

"Yes, I knew," he said.

If you didn't know Ms. Pentecost, you might have mistaken her face for placid. But that extra crease in her brow? It might as well have been an arrow pointed right at Carl Engle's throat.

"How long after this encounter did Ms. Donner leave Stoppard?" she asked.

"Not two days later," he said.

I thought about Ruby. A teenage runaway. Pregnant. Probably had two changes of clothes and whatever Carl Engle figured an abortion cost in 1933. Enough clarity to know that her future in her hometown—if she ever thought she had one— would be a rough hoe.

I wondered for a moment whether she'd actually had the child. Maybe that's what the daisies meant. That she'd had a baby and given it up.

But I couldn't make the timing work out. Those tattooists on Coney Island would have been sketching on a pregnant belly, and it was clear that hadn't happened.

Also, I recalled how Ruby was the go-to woman on the crew when one of the girls found herself in need. How she knew how to find a doctor, how much it would cost, how long the girl would be laid up after.

No. She'd gotten rid of it, then gotten the tattoo as a reminder. Of exactly what, we might never know. Only that she eventually decided she didn't want to be reminded anymore.

"I . . . um . . . I'm stepping down," Carl said. "From the church. I'm going to make a clean breast of it. Leave someone more worthy to minister. I already called Bert and told him I needed to see him. That I was going to bring something to light that would probably hurt the church. But I told him I needed to talk to you first."

I'd kind of been hoping this confession would end with "And then I killed her," but it didn't look like that was in the cards.

"I'm just so sorry," he said.

A figure stepped in from the kitchen.

"You son of a bitch," Joe said. "You sorry son of a bitch."

It had been a couple minutes since I'd seen him pull into the driveway, so I guessed he'd caught most of his father's confession.

Carl looked how you'd expect—a man cornered.

"Son, I'm so sorry. I never meant to—" But Joe was already walking away.

Told you I had a nasty streak.

CHAPTER 43

I caught up with him halfway to the barn.

"Hey, hold up a minute!"

Joe stopped and turned.

"That bastard," he said.

"I know."

"That bastard!"

"No arguments from me."

"You know what he said when Ruby left? When I thought maybe it was something I'd done? Or hadn't done? He said it was God's will. He said that with a straight face. Lied right to me."

I reached out a hand and put it on his shoulder.

"Yeah, I know," I said. "People do that when they're ashamed."

Maybe it was something in my eyes that tipped him off, but I think he saw what was coming and braced for it.

"It was your heroin, wasn't it? The packet we found in Ruby's trailer. She got it off you."

He didn't answer, but he didn't need to. Turns out Joe was a better liar than I thought he was, but not that good. His face was answer enough.

A few years ago—that's when Faraday said the mob started sending out their little small-town feelers. Right in the middle of the war, when the wounded were coming home in droves.

Wounded and in pain, given morphine at the hospital and then sent home.

But it was his mention of the military bases—that's the bit my boss pointed to in my notebook. Why set up a market if there weren't buyers?

That had led us to the domino that bridged the gap. The event that happened between her arrival in town and her death that upset Ruby so much.

"I'm guessing she saw you when she came over to visit her uncle the night before she died," I said. "Probably the same way I did. Noticed the light in the barn. Went on in. Maybe your stash was sitting out. Maybe she caught you shooting up."

He couldn't help but look back at the barn, eyes tilting up to the loft.

"One thing I don't know is if she just took it. Or if you gave it to her."

When he still didn't say anything, I let some of my anger show.

"Hey! When Whiddle slammed me for not telling him about the heroin, you let me take that little guilt trip alone. When you knew longer than anyone. It's time to come clean."

It took some effort, but he managed to look me in the eye.

"I gave it to her," he said. "I don't use it often. I told her that. Only when the pain gets bad. My doctor says to use aspirin but he doesn't know what—"

A whine was creeping into his voice and he had the good grace to snap it off at the root.

"She made me promise to stop. I said I would. I gave her what I had on me. Then she left."

He bit into his lip. A tiny pain to distract from the bigger one.

"She looked so disappointed. And angry. Really angry," he said.

I didn't want to ask the next question. I didn't think I'd like the answer. But all my business cards say "detective" and I didn't want to splurge to get new ones made.

"Did you?" I asked. "Stop?"

"Yes."

His face might as well have been the window at Macy's, the lie front and center in the display. He saw me catch it, too.

"I mean . . . When I found out she was dead, that was . . . that was a bad time . . . It's not like I . . . I don't use it a lot," he repeated. "Just when things hurt."

"Hey, Joe," I said. "Were you high on our date?"

"No!" he exclaimed. "Of course not."

There was no "of course" anymore. Everything was up for grabs. I tried to remember that night. He'd seemed sharp. You couldn't be high and hit eight out of ten tin targets. Could you?

I don't know why the question bothered me. It wasn't like it was love. Just garden-variety lust. Two lonely people fumbling in the dark. But the question still sat there like a little poison pill under my tongue. I spat it out. I didn't have time for it.

"What I don't get is the whole performance with Leroy," I said, getting back to business. "You can't tell me you didn't put the pieces together. Ruby grabs some heroin off you. She turns up dead. Your dealer has a history with her. I get not squealing. You didn't want him telling Whiddle about your habit. But then you take me out to the Pig's Hole and stick me in the same room with Leroy. Why do that? Why chance it? Or was that your ass-backward way of making sure he got in the frame?"

"I didn't know Leroy was selling drugs."

He saw the disbelief on my face.

"I didn't. I swear!" he pleaded. "I'd never buy anything from that skunk."

"Then where did you get yours from?"

"I got mine legally," he said. "I mean, mostly."

I was about to ask if "mostly legal" is like "kind of a virgin" when I heard the screen door on the porch creak open. Ms. Pentecost's voice called out.

"Willowjean! Willowjean, could you come here, dear?"

My boss was standing in the doorway of the porch, cane in one hand, the other waving me over.

If I hadn't been mid-interrogation, I would have caught the signals, I swear.

Willowjean? Dear? Ms. Pentecost might as well have been waving a red flag and screaming to the heavens. But instead of doing anything sensible like running or drawing my gun, I took half a dozen steps toward her.

"What's going on?" I asked. "I've got a rhythm going here."

Ms. P stumbled down the porch steps before planting her cane and catching herself. Carl followed behind her.

At first I thought he'd done the shoving. Then he helped my boss regain her footing before raising his hands in the air.

I finally clued in and reached for my .45.

"Don't move!" a voice yelled from the porch. "Get your hand away from that gun or I'll shoot her—I swear I will."

I saw the pistol first. Then the arm and the shoulder and Brother Bert Conroy's pudgy, placid face aiming down the sights at the back of my boss's head.

CHAPTER 44

Bert, what the hell are you doing?" Joe demanded, taking a step toward his cousin.

Carl raised a hand in warning. "Don't, son. Something's wrong. Something's very wrong with him. I don't think he's right in his mind."

"Just get the heck over there," Bert snapped. "And you—throw your gun away. Real slow."

I did as he instructed while Ms. P and the pastor came over to join us. I didn't like giving up my only weapon, but I liked that gun aimed at my boss even less. Something was indeed very wrong with Bert. His hand was shaking, and he was sweating a lot more than the summer night called for. From his other hand dangled a heavy canvas bag that clinked when he moved.

"All right. Good. Where's your gun, Joe?"

Beside me, I felt Joe tense.

"Don't even think of making a move," Bert snapped. "Now, where's your gun?"

"In the car."

I glanced at Joe's face, hoping to see another lie. I didn't.

"You find Leroy?" Bert asked.

"Found evidence they'd been at the cabin, but they were gone."

Bert nodded. "Good. That's good."

I leaned my head toward Joe and whispered, "I think I can guess who you got your heroin from."

The black eye of the gun turned to me.

"You keep quiet!"

Fear reached out and grabbed hold of me. Not all of me, just a part. I'd had guns pointed at me before. While you never quite get used to it, it gets easier with repetition. Easier in the sense that you're able to think about things other than dying.

For example, I managed to pinpoint exactly what was wrong with Bert. He was out of his element. A milquetoast who'd been miscast as the gun-toting heavy. The costume didn't fit him, and he was chafing.

That didn't make him any less likely to pull the trigger. If anything, he was more likely to—by accident, if not by design.

"Bert, for God's sake, what are you doing?" This was from Carl, who looked more confused than afraid. "This isn't you, son."

Bert sneered.

"Don't call me son," he spat. "I know you know."

"I don't understand."

Ms. P obviously did.

"Mr. Conroy is under the impression that you know that he's been distributing heroin. Possibly other narcotics as well. I imagine he believes that's why you called him and said you needed to talk," she explained.

She might have been sitting comfortably behind her desk. If she was scared, she wasn't showing it.

"I assume much of the actual distribution came while Mr. Conroy was delivering food around the county. For example, Mr. DeCambre—the elder one—was a regular stop on his journeys. He mentioned as much during the Sunday morning service. That, I imagine, is how Leroy DeCambre received the heroin he would eventually sell to customers at the Pig's Hole."

I decided that if my boss was unafraid, or acting it, I should play along.

"So the DeCambres are purely retail?" I asked Ms. P.

"I suspected that from the start," she said. "From all accounts, neither brother has ventured far from their hometown. It would have been difficult for them to develop connections in Chicago."

"Okay, I follow, but how's Bert here hooked up with the Outfit? These are hard guys. And Bert's about as soft as—"

"Shut up! Both of you shut up!"

If the goal had been to piss off the man with the gun, we'd succeeded.

Carl, who had been closely following the conversation, was still clearly behind.

"I don't . . . I . . . I don't understand," he said. "You've got a good job at Lion's. The church pays you a stipend."

Bert laughed. "Ten bucks a month? Jesus Christ, Carl."

Joe took a step forward and the dark eye jumped to him.

"You said you got it through your pharmacy supplier. That it was a special order."

Carl turned to Joe.

"You knew?"

Another laugh from the man with the gun.

"Knew?" Bert barked. "He was shaping up to be my best customer."

The preacher went from dumbstruck to stricken.

"That's right, Carl," Bert jeered. "This is who you wanted to take over for you. A crippled dope fiend."

His amusement whiplashed to anger. He jerked the gun toward the barn.

"Get over in the barn. All of you. And go slow. No funny business."

Even his dialogue was from a Cagney movie, but we did as he said, shuffling over to the open barn doors. The canvas bag in Bert's other hand swung as he walked. More clinking—glass on glass. I caught the faintest whiff of gasoline.

Ms. P stopped just outside the doors and turned.

"Get inside," he snapped.

If she was worried about catching a bullet, my boss didn't show it.

She nodded at the bag. "The makings of another Molotov cocktail?"

"I said get in!"

Did the barn have a back door? I couldn't remember. There were windows up in the loft, but they were narrow and boarded up. If he got us inside, we were done for. Bert could padlock the doors then take his time mixing up another firebomb.

I figured he'd thrown the first one in an attempt to run the circus off. To stop all the questions. This next one would be a lot more effective. The dry wood, the air inside dusty with old hay. The barn would go up in seconds.

"It won't work," my boss said, taking a stumbling step to her right. "This feint of yours. You will be found out. If not from the evidence, then when the DeCambre brothers are captured."

His worm-red lips twisted into a grin.

"They aren't gonna find Leroy. If he knows what's good for him, he's in Canada by now. And if they do find him . . ."

He trailed off, but it wasn't too hard to complete the thought, so I did it for him.

"If worse comes to worst, you can peg the whole thing on Leroy—the heroin, Ruby's death, firebombing the circus, Joe's motorcycle. Up to and including two detectives, a cop, and a minister turned to bacon in a barn."

Joe looked surprised.

"My motorcycle?"

"I'm guessing Leroy called Bert here after he ran out of the

Pig's Hole," I said. "Couldn't have you asking too many questions. You were one of the few people who could put Bert and heroin in the same sentence. With us gone, it's Leroy's word against Bert's. And who's gonna believe a two-bit, hick crook like Leroy DeCambre?"

My boss shook her head.

"I think Chief Whiddle will believe him," she told Bert. She stumbled again. Again, it was forward and to the right. He turned slightly to keep the pistol on her.

"The chief is not a stupid man," she continued. "Recent events have placed him on guard. And I believe if he takes a close look at your finances, he will hit upon the truth."

Ms. P was choosing her words carefully, and this time I noticed.

I took a step, a little forward and to the left. Then another. Bert swiveled toward me.

"Stop!"

I did, raising my hands higher while taking another shuffle-step. Over his shoulder I saw my boss begin to close the distance.

"It's not about the money, is it?" I said. "I mean, sure the money's good, but there are safer ways to scrape together dough. This is about pride. About being your own man, isn't it?"

He didn't answer the question, but I had his attention.

"Or you tell yourself it's about pride, at least," I said. "But it's really about being angry. Angry at everyone, I bet. I mean, look at you. Hand-me-downs your whole life. Secondhand suits, secondhand car. Even a secondhand gig as pastor-in-training when Joe decided he didn't want the job."

As I talked, I eased another step, then another. Bert had to pivot to keep the gun trained on me. And in doing so, he gave my boss his back.

She took another step toward him. If he noticed, he didn't

seem to care. I was the danger, after all. Not the half-crippled woman with the cane.

"You even got a secondhand wife," I said.

Something shifted under his pale, milquetoast face. Something long-simmering. Something with teeth.

Behind him, I saw Ms. Pentecost take her cane in both hands. She made a twisting motion and I saw a gleam of metal in the moonlight.

"I talked to Evelyn. She told me all about how she had the hots for Joe back in the day. She's still nursing a thing for him, you know," I said, adding just a little venom to my voice. "How's that feel? Knowing you were the consolation prize?"

The thing under his face snarled.

"Shut up! One more word and—"

Ms. P lunged forward and a foot of honed Spanish steel burst out of Bert's right shoulder. He screamed and twisted, ripping the handle of the sword cane out of Ms. Pentecost's hand. She stumbled and fell under her bad ankle.

Bert's arm went limp, but he still managed to pull the trigger before the gun tumbled to the ground at his feet. Carl fell back against the wall of the barn, hand clutching his side.

"Dad!" Joe yelled.

I dove and scooped up Bert's pistol. Prone on the ground, I fired off a shot, but it went wide. By the time I got to my feet, Bert was running off in the direction of the circus, my boss's blade still lodged in his back.

I turned to see Joe crouched by his father, blood covering his hand. Ms. Pentecost was pushing herself to her feet using the empty sheath.

"Call an ambulance!" I yelled. "I've got Bert."

I was off running.

Behind me, I heard my boss yell. I couldn't quite make it out. Something something, then "okay!" I didn't stop for clarification.

It was my second time chasing Bert through a dark field. But this time there was no eye-high corn to hide in. His white shirt glowed in the moonlight.

Also, he was injured and unarmed and I was wearing shoes. Sure, the cut on my heel burned something fierce, but I was running on adrenaline and rage.

Here was Ruby's killer. Almost in my sights.

Just before he made the woods, he twisted and nearly stumbled but stayed on his feet. I caught a glimpse of the sword cane flying off into the dark. Then he was on the path through the trees. I figured he must have stashed his car somewhere over there and then walked over to Doc's.

I had the presence of mind not to plunge in after him this time. You don't go running into a room without clearing the corners.

I stopped, caught my breath, and listened. When I could finally hear something apart from the working of my lungs, it was footsteps and crackling branches getting farther away.

I plunged.

On the other side of the trees I caught sight of him again. He was running full-tilt toward the circus, which sat dark and empty, everyone having gone to town for the movie.

No. Not everyone.

As Bert got to the scorched opening in the fence—the one he'd made with his firebomb—someone stepped out holding a length of two-by-four.

"What's going on?" the person yelled. "I heard a gunshot." Bert skidded to a stop.

"She's got a gun," he gasped. "She's gonna kill me."

I caught up, pistol trained on Bert's egg-shaped head.

"He did it," I said. "He's the one who did it. He killed Ruby. Get me some rope. Or handcuffs. I think Frieda's got handcuffs. Probably in her trailer."

"Oh, my," the third party said. "Of course. I'll go . . . I'll go look."

They took a step past me toward the fence. I kept my eyes nailed to Bert. His were almost twitching in their sockets. I thought he was looking for an opening. But I misread it.

I didn't catch the glimmer of victory until it was too late.

Behind me, Ruby's killer brought the board down on my head. I was unconscious before I hit the ground.

CHAPTER 45

The pain came first. A sharp throbbing at the base of my skull. Who the hell had put a rock under my pillow?

I reached up to move it and whacked my knuckles on something hard.

My eyes flickered open. Or maybe they didn't. Everything was pitch-black.

Was I still asleep? Was I dreaming?

I reached my hand out again and found flat, hard wood two inches from my nose. I pushed. Nothing. I slid my hands across until I came to the edges. A splinter pierced the pad of my left palm.

More pain. Not a dream.

I tried to move my legs. My knees hit the same wooden barrier. I kicked my heel down. Same thing.

I smelled something sharp, acidic.

Formaldehyde. And pine.

A pine box. I was in a coffin.

"Help! Let me out!"

I'd been buried alive. They'd dragged me to the graveyard. They'd dug up Ruby, tossed her body out, and thrown mine in.

I pounded on the roof of the coffin.

"Let me out! Let me out of here!"

My heart was pounding, breath coming short and shallow. I could feel myself starting to pass out again.

Air. Have to conserve air, I thought. I have to give Ms. Pentecost time to find me, to dig me up.

I forced myself to take a deep breath. The exhale came out as a choking sob. I took another.

I pictured my boss opening the lid of the coffin and finding me, eyes wide, skin blue, fingers bloody from clawing at the wooden lid.

I started to hyperventilate again.

"Stop," I gasped. "Just stop it. Stop it."

I clenched my hands into fists, pushing the splinter deeper into my palm. With the burst of pain came a narrow window where I was able to think. I used it to take another deep breath. This one stuck.

"Breathe," I whispered to myself. "Just breathe. Breathe deep and let it go. Breathe deep and let it go."

I whispered the mantra over and over.

Slowly, the wave of panic receded. In its place, it left a ration of clarity and calm. Sure, I was trapped in a box, probably concussed, possibly running out of air. But at least I could think again, and that was the important thing.

First on the docket, explore my surroundings. I felt along the edges of my narrow wooden prison and found nothing except hard wood and tight seams. No loose nails. No cracks.

I pushed against the lid. Nothing. No movement. No glimmer of light. I pounded again.

"Hello!" I cried out, far less terror in my voice this time. "Is anybody there?"

No answer.

Which made sense if I was six feet underground. But I was starting to suspect I wasn't. Knocking someone unconscious isn't like in the movies. For one thing, they don't shake it off so quick. Thus the crippling throb in my skull.

Secondly, it doesn't last long. Either someone goes out for

a minute or two or you put them in a coma. It's hard to finesse that middle ground.

Which meant there hadn't been time for Bert and his friend to get me back to the Donner family plot, dig up the coffin, exchange me for Ruby, then bury it again. For that matter, they'd have had to do so within sight of the farmhouse and Ms. P and Joe and hopefully an ambulance and assorted cavalry.

So I wasn't buried alive. Probably.

The last scraps of panic fluttered loose and blew away.

I figured since I was trapped and not going anywhere, I might as well solve the murder.

I thought about what Ms. Pentecost had yelled at me as I ran off. I realized I misheard her. She hadn't yelled, "Okay!" If I'd deciphered it right, it meant she'd managed to figure it out. And she didn't have the benefit of being clubbed in the head by the killer.

Of course she's a genius. Also, she didn't have the handicap of refusing to believe that anyone at the circus could put a knife in Ruby's back.

But that's what had happened.

The signs had been there from the start; I just didn't want to believe it.

Monday night, Ruby found her ex-boyfriend, father of her never-to-be baby, with a needle in his arm. She confiscated his stash, took it back with her, put it in her trailer. Tuesday, she simmered. When the last load of circus-goers was ushered out, she went to tell Big Bob.

Which meant it was a circus problem. Something Big Bob would need to know about.

But how was Joe's drug use a circus problem? And how did Ruby know that?

Because I was betting that hadn't been the first time Ruby had come across heroin recently.

Sure, Bert was playing delivery boy to nickel-and-dime dealers like Leroy and probably half a hundred or so wounded vets and other casual addicts. But he had to get his supply somewhere and no way was he getting it direct from Chicago. I hadn't just been needling him. Bert really was too soft to play with the Outfit boys. Meaning there had to be another link in the chain.

Like a traveling circus. Moving from town to town, city to city. Selling wholesale to some version of Bert at every stop— greedy little men willing to make a buck off people's suffering.

If Ms. Pentecost had gotten that far, then she could narrow it down even further. Ruby wasn't just heading to see Big Bob. She was taking the back way. Which meant she didn't want to go through Sideshow Alley.

She was afraid of who she might run into. Probably the same person she'd had a tense conversation with not an hour earlier. The person Maeve had almost seen.

The practicalities of secretly moving even moderate quantities of heroin narrowed it down to about two. Mysterio thinking he'd seen Kalishenko—tall, bald, white shirt, black vest, holding a knife—whittled it to one.

That's when I realized where I was. Not a coffin. And the smell wasn't formaldehyde. It was the same vinegary smell as from that paper packet we'd found in Ruby's things.

I felt something. Vibrations coming up through the box. Footsteps. The murmur of voices. Something heavy being lifted off the top of the box.

I tensed. I figured I had one shot at this.

Go for the eyes, I thought.

The lid of the box creaked, shifted. Suddenly light was streaming in, blinding me.

I lunged up, leading with my nails.

My fingers got caught in a tangle of braids.

"It's all right, Will. You're safe." My boss extricated my fingers from her hair. "Chief Whiddle, could you please assist Miss Parker? I would, but I've misplaced my cane."

The chief grabbed my arm and helped me up and out and to the ground. I teetered on my feet, the pain in the back of my head returning with a vengeance.

"Watch yourself, Miss Parker."

I felt the back of my head and found a knot the size of an aggie. My fingers came away smeared with blood.

From down the aisle there was a shushing sound, like the wind pushing dry leaves. The tarantulas were stirring in their cage.

Ms. P put an arm around my shoulders to steady me.

"You took long enough," I said. "I was getting bored in there."

"My apologies. There were delays."

As she led me out the door and down the steps of the House of Venomous Things, I saw what she meant.

There were people everywhere. Over to one side a handful of men with rifles stood around a prone Bert. His hands were cuffed behind him and he was squirming and squealing and covered in blood. Over to the other side, a few more of the gun-toting locals were clustered around the Alligator Boy's booth.

"All my reserve officers were still at the station shooting the shit when Joe called," Whiddle explained, following us out of the trailer. "Good thing, too. We had enough bodies that we were able to surround this place. Made sure nobody slipped through."

Some of the circus folk were there. Paulie was hovering around the second group. So were Frieda and Maeve, who were huddled together and whispering. Big Bob stood far off to the side, leaning against the wall of the House of Oddities, face like a funeral dirge.

"Not that we needed to do too much wrangling," Whiddle added. "Bert wasn't fit to fight. The other guy was tougher.

Fought tooth and nail until he saw there was no getting loose. Then he just gave up. Told us he'd show us where they stashed you. But somehow your boss already knew."

"Don't you read the papers?" I asked. "She's a genius."

"We should get you to a hospital," Ms. P said. "Your head will need to be X-rayed. Again."

I let that little jab go. Then I asked her to give me a minute. She relented.

I walked over to Big Bob just as he lit up the end of one of his cigars.

Puff, puff. Blow.

If the night breeze hadn't diverted it, the cloud of noxious smoke would have cut between Frieda and Maeve, through a gap in the rifle-toting posse, and eventually settled on Ray, who sat slumped on the stool usually reserved for the Alligator Boy. His chin was tucked, spectacles pointed down at his splayed size-twelves.

Bob looked up at me, clocked the blood on my hands, the sweat, the dirt, whatever the heck was going on with my hair.

"You look like shit, Parker."

"Looks aren't always deceiving. How was the movie?"

He shrugged. "Who the hell knows? The final reel broke. We were waiting for it to get taped when we heard the sirens."

Puff, puff.

"They're saying Ray stuck the knife in Ruby," he said. "I called bullshit, but he ain't denying it. They put the cuffs on and he just folded. Now they're telling me nothing. Like I'm nobody."

He turned to me, smoke drifting up out of his mouth and into his eyes.

"Am I nobody, Parker? Or can you do me the courtesy?"

I nodded. "I can. But it won't be easy."

Big Bob shrugged. "Is anything ever?"

I took a second to sort it in my head then started laying out the pieces.

"The circus is going bankrupt, right? Everybody knows it. Even before I left, people were saying it didn't have long. That about right?"

Big Bob frowned but nodded.

"Well, Ray couldn't have that. The circus is his home. What would happen to his babies? It would be like the pet store all over again."

Ms. P came and joined us. Someone had found her a cane—a gaudy, gold-painted number with a rubber clown nose for a knob. Each step was accompanied by a tiny honk.

"Speaking of the pet store, I'm guessing it was his stint in Stateville where he made the connections," I said, looking to my boss for confirmation.

"Almost certainly," Ms. P said. "This was during a time when a number of leaders of the Chicago criminal organizations were in jail. Mr. Nance would have made some interesting acquaintances. People he could reach out to later, when the circus required an infusion of cash."

I took the baton.

"Lucky for Ray—if you want to call it luck—around the same time he gets in touch with these friends, they're looking to set up a network for selling heroin out in the sticks. Ray was perfect."

"Dope?" Bob said. "Out of my circus?"

"Also," Ms. P said, "these friends would have been useful when he needed to manufacture a way to get those funds to the circus without drawing suspicion."

I saw the penny drop. The look on Bob's face broke my heart.

"The trust. That was him?"

I nodded.

"He did this for H and H? For me?"

"I'm sure that's what he told himself," Ms. P said. "Though self-interest—the loss of his livelihood, his home, his pets—is likely the stronger motivator."

I mulled that over a bit, then picked up the thread.

"Anyway, the Chicago mob, or parts of it anyway, were kind enough to set Ray up as a heroin distribution line. He takes the dope the long distance, then delivers it to men like Bert, who get it into the hands of local users and dealers. There are probably Berts all over, everywhere you had a show. Ray could fit an awful lot of heroin in those crates he used to prop up his critter cages."

That was too much for Bob.

"He had it right there, right in the reptile house the whole time?"

"Not a bad hiding place," I said. "Circus gets stopped on the road. Things get searched. What state trooper is gonna volunteer to rummage through a bunch of spiders?"

He threw his cigar into the dirt and stomped it out.

"I still don't see how Ruby sorted into this."

Ms. P joined Big Bob to lean against the House of Oddities. She slid down to the ground, bad ankle kicked out in front of her, heedless about the dirt on her suit.

"Excuse me," she said. "It's been a long evening."

Really, I think she wanted to put herself closer to eye level for this next bit.

"While this will need to be confirmed with Mr. Nance, I believe Ms. Donner's involvement came with the death of her beloved boa. Likely a storage mishap led to an accidental overdose. An exhumation of the snake's body and a few simple tests will confirm that. Though I don't believe it's strictly necessary. Regardless, something happened that made her aware of Mr. Nance's activities. If I understand Ms. Donner's character, she would not have been pleased."

I nodded. "Yeah, he probably put her off by saying he was helping save the circus. That if she blew the whistle, she'd cost everyone their jobs. Besides, it wasn't hurting anyone. Victimless crime. Who cares if some people she never met want to inject their sorrows away?"

"So what happened?" Big Bob asked.

"It got personal," I said, keeping it vague. I didn't want to air Joe's dirty laundry. "Tuesday she tells Ray she's coming to you with it. Probably gives him a deadline. You spill or I will. He found her at her booth later and tried to talk her out of it. No dice."

Bob had the look of a guy watching his house burn down and all his buckets are empty.

"So he just killed her? His friend? How could he do that?"

I didn't have the answer to that question, but I damn sure wanted it.

I shouldered my way through the milling crowd. Someone must have told the rifle-toters that I was a VIP, because they made a gap and let me walk right up to Ray, still sitting on the stool, head facing the ground.

"Hey, Ray."

He looked up. His watery blues were red-rimmed and a mile deep. Soon as he saw who was talking, he started in on the apologies.

"I'm so sorry, Will. I . . . I panicked. Bert said we needed to get rid of you. He wanted to kill you, but I wouldn't let him. I wouldn't let him do that. I said we could put you in the—"

I waved a hand, signaling for the brakes.

"That's all blood under the bridge," I said. "Though why you bashed me and not him, I don't know. He tried to kill you—you know that, don't you? To cover things up. That firebomb wasn't meant to scare the circus off. It was meant for you."

Ray blinked. His scorched eyebrow added to his look of confusion. Apparently he hadn't put those particular pieces together. I mean, I hadn't, either. Not until that moment. But I was playing catch-up. What was Ray's excuse?

That Ruby's banner had gotten burned up in the process? Sometimes a coincidence really is just that.

"I've only got one question, Ray," I said. "When you followed Ruby that night, were you planning to kill her?"

"No!" he cried. "I just wanted to talk. But she wouldn't stop. She just kept walking and . . . and I don't know what happened."

"Where'd the knife come from?" I asked.

"It was . . . I don't know. Val left them all over."

"Was it lying on the ground?"

A blank stare.

"Did he leave it in the reptile house?" I asked.

"Probably." He gave a quick, pecking nod. "Yes, that must be where I got it."

My body language must have shifted, because while Ray remained blank-eyed, the cops around me took a step closer. Like they were worried about their prisoner's health.

Maybe they should have been. I leaned into him.

"You took the knife with you. When you went after Ruby. To *talk* with her."

I watched as that sank in. He tried to make words but all he managed were shapes. His tongue lay at the bottom of his mouth. Like something he'd feed to his snakes.

"You took the knife, Ray."

There it was. A glimmer on the other side of his eyes. The guilt.

He took a breath and got his mouth under control. I didn't want to hear what came out of it. I turned and walked away.

Big Bob was helping my boss to her feet.

"We should go," I told her. "Apparently I need to have my head examined."

So we did, slowly, both limping, one making barely audible honks with each step. Despite everything, that made me smile.

"So how long have you suspected Ray?" I asked. "Was it the Chicago mob? Knowing he was in Stateville? Did he just look like a murderer? What?"

She shook her head. "From the start I was interested in the other sideshow performers. The fact that Ms. Donner used the back way, the fact that the killer could be immediately on hand to intercept her."

"Yeah, yeah—I did some catching up while I was buried alive," I said. "But when did you latch on to Ray? That's what you yelled at me, right? Watch out for Ray?"

"I first suspected when I heard about the birdcage."

"The one he hit the cop with that got him sent to Stateville?"

A nod.

"Everyone seemed amused by it. But he received a five-year sentence. Which means it was not a light blow," she said. "Someone threatened his livelihood, his world. And he picked up the nearest object and viciously struck out, not thinking of the consequences. I wondered if there could be a pattern there."

I thought about what Ray had said at the wake. How he would never let anything like that happen again. I thought he was referring to going to jail. But it was the shuttering of his home, his life. That was what he'd never let happen again. Ruby had threatened it. He'd kept his promise.

"Everything's relevant," I said.

"Yes," she answered. "When it comes to understanding people, it really is."

When we hobbled under the opening archway of the Hart & Halloway Traveling Circus and Sideshow, I didn't know it would be for the last time.

But it wouldn't have surprised me.

CHAPTER **46**

What did surprise me. A short, but not complete, list:

There was the fact that my skull wasn't fractured. By the time we got back to the farmhouse and recruited Doc to drive us to the hospital in Fredericksburg, the pain in my head had gone from a moderate clubbing to a sharp, sustained chisel.

The doctor at the hospital assured me that everything was intact, save for a small cut that required three tiny stitches. That put the total number accumulated on this adventure to a nice round ten.

The pain, he said, was exacerbated by stress and lack of sleep and would fade with rest. He did suggest that I try to go more than eight months without getting clobbered. My boss doubled down on that.

"Mrs. Campbell will be very displeased," she said, with a not-insubstantial amount of dread.

It was also a surprise when I ran into Joe on the way out of the hospital. He was there checking on his father, who at that moment was getting a collection of his own stitches. The bullet had been an express line—no stops at major organs or arteries and straight through to the other side.

"I don't know what Ruby told Ray about you," I said. "Maybe he knows, maybe he doesn't. But Whiddle's not stupid. He'll see the same missing pieces we did."

Joe sighed. It sounded more like relief than regret.

"I'll tell him. I don't think this job was a good fit for me anyway," he said. "It was too much, too quick."

I nodded. I couldn't disagree.

And that was it for us. I wished him well, he wished me well, and we parted ways. I wasn't angry. Not at him.

That surprised me, too.

By the time we walked out of the hospital, the sun was rising. In the parking lot, Ms. P instructed Doc to take us back to the farmhouse.

"Miss Parker will be going to bed. She desperately needs rest."

I didn't argue. Which probably surprised my boss.

In my borrowed bedroom, I stripped out of my favorite summer outfit. The white linen was stained gray where it wasn't torn, the shoes scuffed beyond repair, and the robin's-egg blouse not even fit for the rag bin. I added it to the pile of irrecoverable clothing I'd accumulated during this case.

I drew a bath and washed out the blood and dirt and the lingering vinegar reek. Some time later, I jerked awake. I'd fallen asleep in the tub.

I managed to wrap myself in a towel and stagger to the bedroom before I collapsed on my borrowed bed. I fell asleep to the smell of mothballs and whiskey.

When I woke, the pounding in my head had eased and the light coming through the window was notably different. I grabbed my watch from the nightstand. Nearly four o'clock.

Downstairs I found Ms. Pentecost and Doc deep in a conversation about French cinema. I asked them to put a pin in it.

"We need to get to the jail," I said. "We need to make sure Val's getting sprung."

"I'm confident Chief Whiddle is seeing to it," Ms. P assured me.

My own confidence was lacking, so we headed to town, Doc again playing chauffeur. We parked just off the square and walked to the station.

We were half a block away when we caught sight of Val and Chief Whiddle standing at the bottom of the steps. Val was in conversation with a woman in a bright flower-print smock and high-waisted shorts. The ensemble looked brand new. Like someone who was fresh to the States and hungry for new duds.

She had long black hair and even from a distance I could see the resemblance between the two. She was in tears and so was the old knife-thrower.

Whiddle saw us and strolled over.

"Mr. Kalishenko's daughter, I presume?" Ms. P asked.

The cop nodded.

"Ruth's idea," he said. "She tracked her down at a hotel in Charlotte, then got the staties to go down and fetch her this morning."

I raised an eyebrow high enough so he couldn't miss it.

"Lot of folks remember her husband," he added. "She called in a favor."

"You don't approve," Ms. Pentecost said.

"I think that if we'd kept working through his correspondence we'd have found evidence of something or other," Whiddle declared. "I know a man who's got rats in his woodpile when I see one."

At the foot of the steps, the woman wrapped her arms around her father. I heard him sobbing from half a block away.

"We all have things lurking in our past, Chief Whiddle," my boss said. "Luckily for you, Mr. Kalishenko's do not reside in your jurisdiction."

He didn't seem entirely convinced.

"Besides, if Mr. Kalishenko were to remain in your town,

then so would we. And as it was pointed out to me not long ago, I do have a tendency to attract headlines."

Translation: *Keep after the Russian and risk an above-the-fold story about how you've been out-detected and outclassed by a couple of carpetbaggers.*

He hitched up his belt. His gut hitched it back down.

"Well, he's out of my hands now. I've got a lot of paperwork to do. I expect you'll be getting subpoenas when the trials come up."

Ms. P handed him her card.

"We will make ourselves available."

I predicted the card would last two minutes before going in the nearest waste bin. The subpoenas would come from the district attorney. Chief Whiddle, I was betting, was done with us.

He looked up and off to the west at a line of dark gray that was cresting the horizon.

"Looks like we're finally gonna have a little rain," he said. "Farmers'll be happy."

He tipped his hat.

"Have a safe trip back."

With that he walked back to the station. In front, father and daughter were still locked in an embrace that didn't look like it was going to end anytime soon.

We left them that way.

CHAPTER 47

We stayed one more night.

The chief had predicted true. By seven that evening a steady downpour had begun, which promised relief, if not flash floods.

Over a dinner of roast chicken we'd picked up at Henry's Eats, Doc let us know that Joe had given him a call. He'd be getting his gear out of the barn. The motorcycle was a new brake line away from complete. And removing his hideaway in the loft might help him kick his habit.

"He told me about his problem," Doc said. "He also let Chief Whiddle know, so I guess it'll get around town."

He tore off a hunk of bird. His hands shook when he did it.

"I told him I'm giving up drinking," he said. "Didn't realize how bad it had gotten until this last week. Told him if he wanted to talk about the war or anything, I'd be around."

I told Doc I thought that was a good idea.

The next morning, it was still drizzling and the world outside was gray and muddy. Bags packed, I took one last walk across the field and through the trees to the edge of the circus grounds.

There was a flurry of activity. Crates were being packed, animals wrangled, banners rolled up. Trailers were being pulled out of ruts that had become mudholes overnight. The smaller tent had already been taken down and the big one was halfway there.

I found Maeve standing at the tree line, wrapped in a bright blue shawl. Like she'd stolen a scrap of the sky before the clouds covered it. I walked over and stood next to her.

"I thought you were here through the weekend," I said.

"Bob called it. Figures we've worn out our welcome," she said with grim resignation. "The folks down in Charlotte said we can set up early."

We watched as a crew of men with winches lowered the frame of the Ferris wheel onto its side.

"He ain't saying yet, but I'm figuring this is our last season," Maeve said. "Bob's in town sending telegrams, seeing if the offer from Baxter and Brass is still on the table."

"He's selling it?" I asked. I was surprised, but I shouldn't have been.

Maeve nodded. "He's already hinting to the regulars. Talking about a long winter break. Saying we might want to find work in the interim. But I figure that interim ain't gonna end, so . . ."

I thought about my friends, old and new.

Sam Lee might find work at another circus. There were always opportunities for young men willing to do anything for next to nothing. But I thought I might be able to find him something better. I promised myself that I would make some calls when I got back to New York.

As for the performers, some would end up with Baxter and Brass, while others might find work at one of the few other traveling shows that were still running. Annabelle would do all right. She had her landing all planned out.

Kalishenko might last, but it wouldn't be a terrible time to retire. He was good, but getting old. And now he had new family to think about.

Frieda was probably done, as were most of the denizens of Sideshow Alley. There were few sideshows running anymore. Maybe she could play assistant to Carlotta and her tigers.

Wherever they landed, I hoped it was somewhere they could stay together. Where they could hold each other beside a bonfire and not be afraid.

You don't have to tell me the world isn't like that. I know.

But a girl can hope.

I looked over at Maeve. There was a question I wanted to ask her. It went something like: Did you really not see who Ruby was talking to at her booth that night? Did you really not recognize Ray's voice? You, with the keenest ears and sharpest eyes in this circus or any other?

Or did you figure that the damage was already done? Ruby was dead and nothing was going to bring her back, so why throw another friend to the wolves, even if he was a killer? And that me and Ms. Pentecost were sure to get Val off the hook, and if we failed, then maybe you'd rethink things.

If she answered yes, I'd have told her I understood. Even if I didn't agree. Maybe I wasn't family anymore, but I understood.

Instead, I asked, "How about you? You gonna hitch a ride with another tent show?"

The old fortune-teller shook her head.

"I'm getting a little too long in the tooth for the road," she said. "I think I'll head back to New York. Coney Island, maybe. Somewhere I can set up shop permanent."

She flashed me a sad smile.

"Never a shortage of people wanting to be told a good story."

We stood silently in the rain, watching the last of the big tent come down. I said goodbye, but her eyes never left the billowing canvas, now brought to earth. I don't even think she heard me.

———

Ms. P and I caught a two o'clock train back to the city, this one an express line with only a few stops. We'd be back in our office in time for dinner.

We called ahead to let Mrs. Campbell know. She had half a dozen messages for us, all from reporters. Word had gotten out that Lillian Pentecost had uncovered a drug ring in farm country and they were clamoring for details.

The train built up speed. We watched as Virginia dissolved into a green-and-gray blur in the window. My boss placed a hand on my knee.

"How are you feeling?" she asked.

"Not too bad. The headache's almost gone." I reached back to feel the stitches just below my hairline.

"But how are you *feeling*," she repeated, the look in her eye suggesting she wasn't taking "No comment" for an answer.

I thought about it.

The circus was gone, or it would be soon enough.

The girl who'd stumbled through its gates at fifteen was gone, too.

Now this new woman was sitting here, wearing her face. This woman who jumped into burning buildings and chased killers through the dark. Who leapt into the detective life four years ago and had been scrambling to prove her worth ever since.

Was it anger that drove me? Anger at why that fifteen-year-old had been forced to run away in the first place? Or anger over knowing that, if I hadn't gotten extraordinarily lucky, if I hadn't met women like Ruby Donner and Lillian Pentecost, the world wouldn't care a lick about what happened to me?

Maybe it still didn't.

I was certainly angry that, of all those messages Mrs. Campbell relayed, not a single one mentioned Ruby.

DOWN SOUTH DRUG RING LINKED TO CHICAGO MOB, the papers would scream. The death of the Tattooed Woman? A footnote somewhere below the fold. Who cared about her?

I did. My boss did. We cared about Ruby and everyone like her.

I looked at my employer, the deep lines running down her cheeks and across her brow, one eye replaced by cold glass, the other holding a history she only hinted at. For the hundredth time, I wondered what had carved her face into that shape.

"I'm okay," I told her. "Really."

She took that as fact and patted my leg. Then she pulled out her file folder and began to read, placing each page on the seat next to her as she finished.

That was the final surprise. The last flick of the wrist.

Because it was true. I was okay.

So what if it was anger that fueled me? That kept me leaping into burning buildings and chasing killers through the dark.

As long as it kept me going, I didn't care. Considering the way of the world, my tank wasn't likely to get low anytime soon. There would always be rage to spare, and no shortage of targets to aim it at.

I reached over and took the stack of papers my boss had finished with and began to read. Ms. Pentecost glanced at me, but made no comment. She didn't need to.

There was work to be done.

WILLOWJEAN PARKER
LEAD INVESTIGATOR
PENTECOST AND PARKER INVESTIGATIONS
NEW YORK CITY

ACKNOWLEDGMENTS

Much of this book was drafted during the first months of a global pandemic. While it might have been written in isolation, getting it into your hands was the work of many.

Special thanks are due to:

My agent Darley Anderson and the wonderful team who held my hand through my first year as a published author. Those include: Mary Darby, Georgia Fuller, Kristina Egan, Rosanna Bellingham, Rebeka Finch, and all the other folks at the agency that I hope to meet non-virtually one day.

My editors Bill Thomas and Margo Shickmanter and the fantastic crew at Doubleday who have worked tirelessly to make this book worthy of its readers. That includes, but is not limited to: Elena Hershey, Jillian Briglia, Peggy Samedi, Erin Merlo, Maria Massey, Maria Carella, Amy Edelman, and Michael Windsor. And if you're reading the U.S. edition, that beautiful cover is courtesy of Rui Ricardo.

Matthew Pauli, who provided guidance on clowns, motorcycles, and the nut and bolts of life with a traveling circus. You might have seen Matt online clowning for the patients at Johns Hopkins Children's Center. Pauli Pagliano is very loosely based on him. And, yes, he really is that delightful. All circus-related errors and inconsistencies are wholly my own.

Jillian Kroos, who provided me with a funeral director's point of view on how one might accommodate a home burial sans embalming. Considering the subject matter of these books, I expect I'll have more questions for her in the future.

Liaa Walter, who has spent the last decade inking her art on my own skin. I'm looking forward to another ten years under the needle.

Melissa and Jill, who helped keep us connected, entertained, and relatively sane through lockdown. By the time this is published I hope to be seeing you both in person.

Jessica—my first and favorite reader—who will give me the note until I get it right. Will's world, and my own, wouldn't be nearly as rich without you.

To everyone who picked up this book, as well as *Fortune Favors the Dead*. I hope you enjoy walking around in Will's and Lillian's shoes as much as I do. I'm looking forward to a long journey ahead.

And finally to the Rubber Band Woman who bent herself into impossible angles for the delight of a young boy at his first sideshow. I don't remember your name or the name of the traveling circus. But I remember the wonder.

Thank you all.

About the Author

Stephen Spotswood is an award-winning playwright, journalist, and educator. As a journalist, he has spent much of the last two decades writing about the aftermath of the wars in Iraq and Afghanistan and the struggles of wounded veterans. His dramatic work has been widely produced across the United States. He makes his home in Washington, D.C., with his wife, young-adult author Jessica Spotswood.